Twin Griffin Books
PRESENTS

RONIN

G.O.D.Z.

DIAL 13

The Complete
Epic Poems
By Author
Justin Thomas

Includes the never before published epic poem "To Enlighten The G.O.D.Z."

<u>OTHER WORKS BY JUSTIN THOMAS</u>

's Path To Now: Book III of the Fable Avenue Saga (2022)

Brooklyn's Lilac Brew: Book II of the Fable Avenue Saga (2015)

The Ghost of Gabriel's Horn: Book I of the Fable Avenue Saga (2012)

A Company of Moors (2010)

Code-47: Memoirs of a Hip-Hop Heist (2008)

12 Stories High: The Imaginative Trip Thru a Black Mind (2006)

To The Spoken Word

TO ENLIGHTEN THE G.O.D.Z.

Act 1: Singing Haunted Scales

Act II: The Order of Maa Tru Ark

THE SON DIAL TONE

IN 13 PIECES

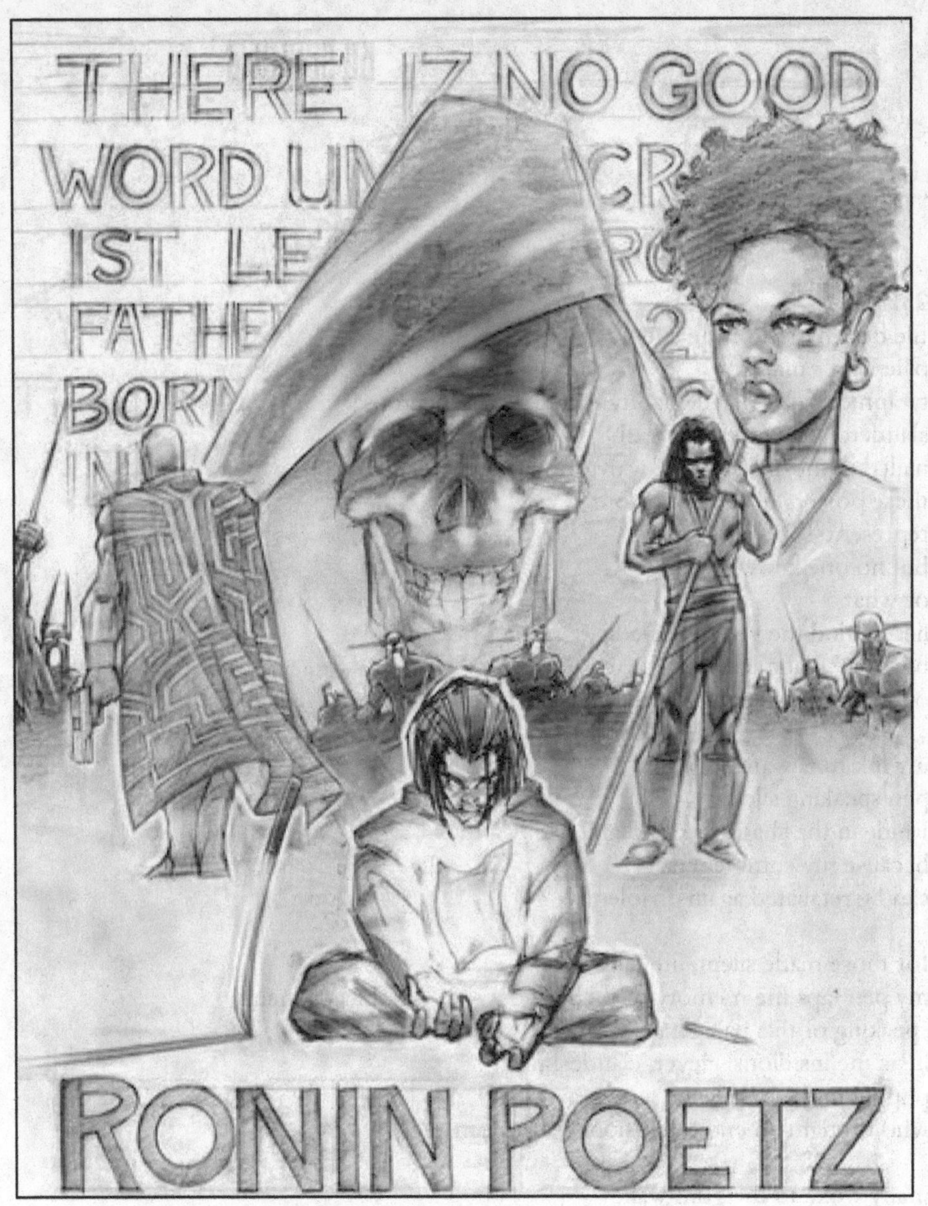

(Original cover art by Ray Cosico)

The Prologue

"THE SONG OF SWORDS"
by Father Aquarius

251-ST
file designation of the enemy
pale king's mark
tyrannical ruler of huemanity – crab like, cancerous
slanderous pictures of Death
nailed in the alleyways of war-torn cities
these posters of the impostor
represent The Pale King
but no one knows who,
or what,
lies behind the veil of secrecy
be it one diabolical man
or an entire governing body

my ink runs water
pen speaking silently
I hide in the shadows of syllables
because my commentary
can be retaliated against violently

for those made silent, life taken,
my pen taps the memory of their voices – my ink bleeds them
speaking of this pale king's tyranny
he is the insidious, clever, clandestine
puppet master
who brought an end to illusionary freedom

many woke to the grim wake
the pale king's dictator-ship
flying
abusive banners
binding the world
by buying the world with lies and a smile
subtly seducing
from a kingdom named MUSA, false civilizer of nations
war and a burning cross as his secret oath
            and sign(ing) on the dotted, descendant

RONIN POETZ : KO SI OLUWA

The Prologue

of an unholy bloodline
while kindly colonizing,
parading and prancing the lands as a gentle benefactor
orchestrating wars
and marching a million Orwellian soldiers
thought holders, thought police
from the mind to the body to the soul
to the convolutions of the earth
and the veins pumping people into the roads and streets

march! march! came their beat
re-wiring reality and language
the earth lay in anguish
pale king held mother down
while pumping pressure,
penetrating
and desecrating sacred grounds
volcanoes
hurricanes mixed with tornadoes and earthquakes
make the sounds of mother earth's scream
while her elements were enslaved to run machines
that ran all over her
polluting mother's air, fire, earth, and water

machines hold mother earth down
making her go blind
the original people stood by
seduced by the illusions and the lies
letting mother earth die
the pale king's laughter
bathing in her coal
stressing her alchemical tithe
diamonds were the tears she cried

and how could we forget
the pale king's experiments
his search for life into the succulent salvation sequence
the genetics of melanin,
the second burning of the Khemetic Libraries
he searched to break the code

RONIN POETZ : KO SI OLUWA

The Prologue

to encode the spiritual flow
that lay buried inside us
pumping pineal fluids
and the blood of moorish druids
into a still body that waits for you to lie still
as the pale king still lies to you
that he is a precious lover
jacob's tricknological hunter
the daughter of morality's grafted brother
he commits incest
this pale king infects the minds of slain warriors
their bodies outlined in his design
his heartbeat is another black warrior's flatline
talk to the bloodline – written script
The Book of Life
our blood types rhythm – rah's hymn – preach deliberate
this still liar needs your blood to function
and now, black babies' tears
are the first things that spill from the womb
water broken tombs
diluted black babies hanging from flagpoles
swinging rag dolls at the angle of 33 degrees
the boiling point of tricknology
black blood, fine wine, melanin colt .45, 85% proof
only 5% are in the loop
recycled warriors
spilt blood, bleeding lips
I speak as a bloody orator
as hope feeds off the fruit of my family tree
while still breathing thru a respirator
speaking sharpened light
as our aura-tore thru the pale king's illusion

but his swift and sway
maneuvering towards his prey
coordinating wars into black lands
to hold the Book of Life in his hands,
tightening his grip on the world

RONIN POETZ : KO SI OLUWA

The Prologue

can we truly call it hypocrisy
if there was never really meant to be
freedom or democracy
did we just choose to believe
to get us out of the responsibility
did we just bury the hostility
that we knew this pale king's tyranny
was occupying other lands in the name of freedom
could we not taste, hear, touch, smell or see
mother earth's plea
could our own senses we not trust
as we witnessed that one kingdom was not enough
for the pale king's insatiable lust
to control all of nature's original sources
including us?

the gluttonous malefactor's shroud had fallen
from thought to pen to paper
earlier the Black Warriors warned
greed had always adorned this pale king's brow
from stanzas
to prose
but it was the pale king
who had to make people believe
in his land of 'make believe you're free'
in order,
in this new world order
for demon-acracy to be exposed

homeland security made sure my homeland was never secure
the pale king's armies
were making a clear and plain statement

"all you blacks hit the pavement
we rounded you up and puttin' you in camps of concentration
check the fine print on that Emancipation
the proclamation was just a temporary vacation
to your enslavement.
move you to another plantation"

RONIN POETZ : KO SI OLUWA

The Prologue

they're killing the melanin they lack
light-skinned, earth brown
16 shades
true original Black

this is terrorism
not the lines in this poem
a warning,
a threat to him
now realize, breakdown the word 'terrorism'
and you get terra-ore
that's what the pale king has declared war for
terra means Earth
ore is its precious substance
and all the original melanin children of the sun
rounded up in great abundance

this war will come to kill you
precious daughter
and precious son
this war for Terra-Ore
is a war to make sure
you never come together as a people – as ONE…

RONIN POETZ : KO SI OLUWA

The Prologue

"WEEPING WANDS"
by Mother Pisces

t-18-1-t-15-R
file designation
of this african warrior
griot,
Seth Mwindo
he added sunshine
in these dark times – these blurry days
seth's early age
was abandoned by his mother
and raised by his father, named Teihu
who slipped thru life driven by an alcoholic haze

in drunken stirs
the father would beat
and curse
seth and his brother riso
until this single profane verse
lit a propane dirge

singing the chorus of hatred
crucified at conception,
the raising and resurrection
of this black child
into being a True-Hue-Black Man
was now being tainted

teihu would scream at his children,
"you turned your mother into a whore!
and you've taken my honor and sword.
this honorable warrior,
guardian of my wife's garden.
now unholy court-ships
fly
my wife
stolen by the moon's light.
she only glows with the faint reflection of her sons."

RONIN POETZ : KO SI OLUWA

The Prologue

for twelve years
flowed countless tears
pumped by the father's hands
until seth and his brother fled
and were nurtured by their mother's clan
nine years mastered and trained
the griot arts now pumped their veins
jogging thru the convolutions of the brain
to exorcise the knowledge of the pale king
his thought police
and the traitorous Ele Ote-Aruh

when scouting for thought police, in troops
seth confronted the Ele Ote
and a greater battle ensued
nature was consumed
forests became bare of trees
lush lands melted into deserts
and even the air could barely breathe

neither warrior could paint victory
and so their dance ended in a draw
seth felt nurtured
in the fiery arms
of this enemy
bitter thoughts of battle
were sweetened by the Ele Ote's memory
swirling in thoughts
while seth rested, unconscious
scenery changing around him

the stagehand
that opened the curtain for this new act
use
to
abuse
seth
he was rescued
by his father teihu

The Prologue

and home never looked more like heaven
where hell had been raised
and 21 years of fiery anger
sitting at the lower regions of seth
had gained enlightenment
under the wings of the father
and this warrior's rage had come out of hiding …

seth:
"I must be mistaken.
you are the aged representation
of a man who scratched his children,
pushed his wife into concubine, pale king service,
and dipped tongue tip
to rub bottled liquor kiss
and let free genie-alcoholic spirits
to grant a drunkards wish."

teihu:
"my sun, my king
black hueman becoming
and warrior being,
I as the family tree still needed to grow
choked by the smoke of weed
and the alcoholic flow.
my lessons were the first to go,

followed by my pride,
self-love, and all else swallowed.
this hallucinogenic, illusionary fetish
fed me to sleep in the pale king's dream.
I understand your anger
but never lose the love for the red, black, and green.
seek the light of those moonbeams

better to battle this pale notorious
than to keep our swords aimed only at us.
we are moors
black always gaining and building
33 degrees never enough

RONIN POETZ : KO SI OLUWA

The Prologue

and if no love exists between a-moor
then what can we trust?
Who do?
You?"

cool words
mixed with streaming tears
made up
for
twelve
violent years
the repent was genuine
and father and son
were as one

seth could see
the obscenity of his father
was now clean
the warrior black man
looked as if he could
handle a sword again

seth:
"aunt and grandmother
raised us well.
riso is a great warrior."

teihu:
"I am a ghost to them.

the best advice I give
– which does not make up for how I lived –
take this advice: you did not see me
understand?
tell your grandmother nothing
for my failing to protect her daughter
I have slipped from her eyes
as a black man.
I warrior, up rooted
for being abusive

RONIN POETZ : KO SI OLUWA

The Prologue

my punishment
nothing less than being executed.

perhaps say something
let her deliver to me
a swift death that takes my misery
let me think on this…

for now, my son
let me prepare for you a lesson,
that will help you defeat
the Ele Ote."

class begun
two days passed, seth returned to his clan
stronger
…waiting to battle again

but the fight was always in his dreams
to ask the Ele Ote the reason
for siding with the pale king's lies

seth's grandmother would tell him,
"the first diabolical weapon
in control of the pale king
is his twisted words
his tainted language."

seth's hunt for the answer became an obsession
as he himself became a myth, a legend
the syllables of his name breaking
in the shaking mouths of his enemies,
the thought police
to see this warrior's shadow
was to know
death
this warrior-priest quickly blessed his enemies
tactical movement
analytical supreme math
until the day

RONIN POETZ : KO SI OLUWA

The Prologue

his calculations brought him face-to-face
with the Ele Ote's mask
this second clash of the titans

their powers swirled and brightened the skies
nature closed its eyes and the stars cried
to see these to black bodies on opposing sides
and again,
the power of the Ele Ote was warming
nurturing
seth quickly noticed, in their first clash
the Ele Ote was holding back
and so it seemed
that even when he executed his father's move
it was blocked
and seth was forced to his knees
the griot was exhausted and admitted defeat
but he had one last plea,
"answer me this question.
what makes you serve this demon? this pale king?"

Ele Ote-aruh:
"I tried your way once.
and it failed both me and my people.
resistance to the pale king brings misery and death,
my son…seth…
the real liars to reality
are those who have taught you to battle him, Our Pale King
they are hypocrites and confused.
they cannot even re-evolve, re-evolute.
the pale king is the ultimate truth."

and the Ele Ote's mask was removed
and there stood the truth
seth's mother, the Ele Ote-aruh

Ele Ote-aruh:
"I'll let you live, my son, and let you choose."

and the cat was killed, curious

The Prologue

and seth, his anger reborn and heated – a phoenix
now furious
he returned to his clan
his weapon in hand
threatening
they had kept this information from him

aunt and grandmother just instructed,
"kill her. she's no longer your mother.
and your father as well. we know you've seen him.
great warrior was he,
but he let your mother die spiritually
he failed as a black man.
she failed as a black woman.
their judgment, is death."

there was no comfort from his brother, riso
who told him the same. "stay upon your destiny.
just because they lost their way
doesn't mean you have to."

but seth was confused
and he returned to his father,
feeling more abused
       by the detainment
       of this truth
and the two met
in a field
spotlighted by the moon
and their came riso
followed by mother-aruh
and the family tree shook and withered
the battle from within

seth's mind slipped
360 degrees
reduced to 33
burning like the leaves of his family tree
his sword
cut and killed

RONIN POETZ : KO SI OLUWA

The Prologue

mother – father – brother…and his anger set him free
into a life of slavery, new found powers of tricknology
he took his mother's clothes
her Ele Ote robes … but the mask he left
for the betrayal was etched on his face
for all to see

and the thought police
who were once his enemies
now trembled with his command
as he returned to his former clan
and killed them all with a gun in hand

seth was escorted back to the pale king
not as an enemy or prisoner – but as soldier…
heir to his mother's twisted crown
seth's knee bent
and he bowed down to his new lord and master

seth was ordained with the stain
of a new family name
call him: The Ele Ote-Owl
and granted a wife named Magikkk

(unbeknownst to the Ele Ote,
magikkk was his half sister
born from the twisted union
of the pale king and his mother)

the Ele Ote's natural hair burned
from mind to body, lost of soul
came the scars of past lashes
his jaw broken,
and forever unable to speak
the eloquent rhythms of language

the story of the weeping wands
are my inspiration
to nurture and love
my

RONIN POETZ : KO SI OLUWA

The Prologue

own
children
from the day of their conception
to when I actually gave birth to them

I am Mother Pisces

and my children will know me
the nurturer of their trinity
and they will never fight me
and grow strong
will our family tree
to battle the pale king,
and all our culture's enemies

RONIN POETZ : KO SI OLUWA

The Prologue

"WORD OF SCOUTS (NO RHYTHM)"

FILE #888-666

"YOU ARE FREE TO DO AS WE TELL YOU …

we are an army at the command of the Pale King.
ruthless, we spare no one
whose thoughts rest against the Pale King's desires.
no one knows what lies behind the masks of our soldiers,
except for the lies themselves
masonic in our own thought,
we soldiers of the Thought Police are solid in army
tight in loyalty
as of now we are the Police State
for the mind,
body,
soul, and all the lands of the world

YOU ARE FREE TO DO AS WE TELL YOU …

with no other orders than to police and seduce thoughts,
this army,
an extension of The Pale King's might,
was once ignorantly referred to by the foolish masses
as The Just
The Pale King was able to seduce the world
through the Thought Police's power of Hellywood,
tell-a-lie-vision,
sorcery Screens,
YessaBossaMassa Media,
and eMpT.V.

YOU ARE FREE TO DO AS WE TELL YOU …

covert in our art, we Thought Police,
under the orders of The Pale King, stage horrific events that scare
the masses into looking towards the Pale King for refuge and security
it was us who allowed The Pale King to control wars from both sides
often times, wars would be fought

RONIN POETZ : KO SI OLUWA

The Prologue

with having one set of Thought Police battle another set
the victorious, openly working for The Pale King and crowned as heroes,
and the vanquished (blood sacrificed) plagued and slandered as villains.

YOU ARE FREE TO DO AS WE TELL YOU ...

the thousand headed asses of the masses bought the deception
and slowly, we were able to march in
and claim the land under Martial Law of the Pale King himself

YOU ARE FREE TO DO AS WE TELL YOU ...

Now, after most of the world's conquest,

we reveal our true intentions
we maintain the New Order by eradicating all rebellious thoughts against The Pale King
mainly, African Griots, Black Poets, Black Revolutionaries, Black Writers,
all declared threats of the New Order (as well as their allies).
unless seduced to our cause
write pacifying propaganda

YOU ARE FREE TO DO AS WE TELL YOU ...

the Thought Police's most powerful technique is to fire improper propaganda,
relying heavily on character assassination
to seduce the masses into believing their heroes are their villains
we also specialize in the "creation" of villains, setting up terrorist sponsored states
around the world

YOU ARE FREE TO DO AS WE TELL YOU ...

before we infiltrate lands with our physical strengths,
and destructive technology,
we Thought Police first colonize the mind.

YOU ARE FREE TO DO AS WE TELL YOU ...

after placing fear into the hearts of 85% of the masses
seducing the 10% rulers,

RONIN POETZ : KO SI OLUWA

The Prologue

the 5% that remain,
will only succumb to a physical eradication
teamed with this vicious manner, there is no stopping our army.

YOU ARE FREE TO DO AS WE TELL YOU …

we, The Thought Police, would like to commend the death-on-death of you
speak ill of one another

seeing you at each other's throats gives us insight

that our efforts in serving The Pale King are truly rewarded.

YOU ARE FREE TO DO AS WE TELL YOU …

our guns, spells, and propaganda
allow us to exploit the petty prejudices of you

YOU ARE FREE TO DO AS WE TELL YOU …

even the 'conscious' amongst you are but shades of your former existence
and their greatest sin is being too proud and self-absorbed
by what they believe is knowledge
and even they battle over the scraps The Pale King throws to them

YOU ARE FREE TO DO AS WE TELL YOU …

Play on …

YOU ARE FREE TO DO AS WE TELL YOU …

YOU ARE FREE TO DO AS WE TELL YOU …

YOU ARE FREE TO DO AS WE TELL YOU …

YOU ARE FREE TO DO AS WE TELL YOU …

YOU ARE FREE TO DO AS WE TELL YOU …

RONIN POETZ : KO SI OLUWA

The Prologue

"CUP OF WARRIOR JUICE"

warriors by the handful
slandered as vandals
were conscious to the pale king's plans

outcasted
by the very masses
they wished to warn
learning the secrets of their ancients
they adorned themselves
in the original knowledge
becoming Af-Ra-Kamau Griots – conjure folk
in these final hours
stirring up ancestral powers

The Ronin Poetz, enemies to the pale king.

unfortunately,
they played right into this tyrant's schemes

now
with a group of spiritually glowing black beings
the pale king had a sequestered and outcasted team

Original men and Original women
brightly glowing
self-actualized
to the ancient power within them

and with a seduced Griot at his side
it was only time
that would tell
if the pale king would enslave these Warrior-Griots
and read a complete volume of their collective genetic Book of Life.

or perhaps be defeated by The Ronin Poetz…
ending his strife and disaster…

welcome to the story of *THE RONIN POETZ*:

RONIN POETZ: KO SI OLUWA

The Prologue

they who serve no master, for there is no master

so let us rejoice and let voices raise
sing! black people! Moors, if you will

an age-old story aged out
we warriors shout a new verse
a new chapter
sing! sing! sing!

we sing, this day forth, for us:

KO SI OLUWA! – THERE IS NO MASTER

RONIN POETZ : KO SI OLUWA

Act 1: Parental Guidance

"BIRTH INTO A NATION"

I am maa kheru
the voice of truth
true of voice
being born was Ixu and Gira's choice

my spirit unable to spin in time – frozen –
but thru Mother Pisces and Father Aquarius
I was chosen

as it were
I was born on the spot
where lightning, thunder, and sunbeams shock
at a time not calculated on a clock
but in between my mother's teardrops

my birth caused time to stop

but my father took the tick and tock
– where I was born between my mother's tears –
he compounded one-seventy-second part of each day
and created the complete year
he made the hourglass flow from bottom to top
my hair grew and locked

– my father called it culture –

the pale king called it a 'cult'
and made it impure
thru his laws I was feared
my birth disturbed his unnatural order
my queen was raped when the pale king souled her
my culture's tongue was severed
but I mastered the master's language
to mend it back together
spread words like weather
this morning son reign forever – omega supreme
and I bring you balance when my words beam
sent not thru satellite
but smoked signals in candlelight

RONIN POETZ : KO SI OLUWA

Act 1: Parental Guidance

1 every hour – every 1 hour near me

I know now the conspiracy is no theory
let me speak up – speak proper – speak clearly
so, the pale king and his thought police
can truly fear me
my people, I am here for thee
you can find my birth on page three of a new history
my speech makes up a new dictionary
it defines a clan whose styles vary –
inebriate you like dreamberries

make you think for yourself (if for nothing else)
some of us sacrifice – caught by the Thought Cops
we spread the sun's warmth thru city blocks
scribe hope in cement and rocks
grow new words as crops – collect our props
deliver inspiration to the have-nots
on earth's
cursed,
knowledge-barren lot
where my culture is hunted by cops
– with pen and sword – this injustice will stop
my father has given me power to revise the plot

chapter-by-chapter
the truth sought and captured
caught up in the rapture
the whirlwind that be my pen
– expression – spoken by mouth
I shout quietly in the cup that be my paper,
I give my words out,
flow like water,
and like rain, drop – on this spot – where I was born

Act 1: Parental Guidance

"MOTHER PISCES"

black queens sing in tune with tears
time hears their pains
and prays to nature for rain
wash them of shame,
let it drip and be claimed by mother nature
before it takes her black queen away
mother earth say, "pray. shine like every ray."
because when light eclipses the night and shines bright
off the sun and moon
in your womb, 3 bring raw rhythm and boom

this is a story
our mother would tell us
at night in our room

she said,
"can you sing the key of C, sons
play reasons for nature's waves?
the dream's won in the sun's rays
yes, sons
that's how you came into existence
your father pulled me up to him
like the attraction of water to the moon's call
our love was free-for-all, a free fall
and I rubbed my belly and saw a future for you all

I was feeling summer's heat,
responding to the spring air
there in your father's lips that I kissed
and he planted his two lips in my garden
I begged every part of him would resurrect in me
harmonizing with the beauty of my seed
your Mother Pisces,
this queen,
gave birth to a trinity
3 by III by three
strength, hero, justice
and my 1 wish was given to me
(from each of your father's I's)

RONIN POETZ : KO SI OLUWA

Act 1: Parental Guidance

I held each of you
9 months in my womb
then I held your body anew
– in my arms tightly – like aset held heru
I gave you half of the personality that makes you
takes you beyond the boundaries this world made for you
the boundaries that try and negate you

you see, I did more than just raise you

I bathed you in the sea of words
taught you how to read and write
so your thoughts could be heard

heard in every victory song you sing
your mother,
this queen,
be the power in the thrust in your sword swing

bring you face-to-face with the gift inside you
and help you unwrap it
perfect it when you practice
help you apply it to your father's four lessons
so you can make your impression in this world
and on this journey
– with any of life's tests – I will be there to protect
until my last breath of life

and when you find my spirit filtering
in the breath of another black queen's lyrics
make that black queen your wife."

that's what my mother would tell us
in our room – late at night

RONIN POETZ : KO SI OLUWA

Act 1: Parental Guidance

"FATHER AQUARIUS III"

Father Aquarius scribe:
"my 3rd son, my 3rd vibe
I watch you with all 3 I's
let your brothers strength and hero guide you
when I am no longer by you
but I'll ride thru the air
share my knowledge founded by our ancestors

they who were rounded up,
not rounded off

so they are 1 stronger

able to bless you – rest in you –
they are a force that wanders time
they can be channeled thru body,
soul,
and mind

so tune in

at this early age,
you are a page for me to fill with these lessons
jailed without sentence,
my 3rd apprentice of wand,
the word,
the sword,
and the cup
that cup that will runneth over
when you are older
and the Earth gives birth to your queen

molds her so you can hold her,
so she can hold you and become your soldier
your truth, your friend, your lover
your children's mother
resurrect 1 another in your children's eyes
– their voices – your songs – your chorus – your vibes –
and you will teach them all that I scribe for you

RONIN POETZ : KO SI OLUWA

Act 1: Parental Guidance

our culture's truth
the weapon to battle on reversed babylon
control-thought troops deserve no truce
they seduce with noose around our necks
and our culture maybe the first to die
but it is the first to resurrect

you are the new generation
and you hold inside you the next,
formed by your queen's thoughts and breath
let me hand you wand, fill your cup, shape your sword,
and preach the word that will keep you from being sentenced
so – my son –
let me teach – unto you –
these four lessons."

RONIN POETZ : KO SI OLUWA

Act 1: Parental Guidance

"LESSON 1: THE WORD"

"there is no good word until you scribe it 1st,"

>lesson 1
>from Father Aquarius
>to his 3rd born son

"words come into existence
1st by visions that are a resistance to insanity."

>and trust me,
>every time I tried to hide from the pen it just ran to me
>looking for sanctity, and anxiously turned into patiently
>the pen handed me the answers to the questions
>and branded me with protection, almighty blessings

"but watch out, a critic-copper come-a-knockin' and a-testing
arresting every artist confessing to a spiritual movement
so, soon we went looking for a place where souls weren't for rent
time spent on the run like a new born song sung
locked in prison, we just sing-sing
our tribe teaching undercover to point out the wrong ones
long hunt, we bless people with little soul
and even those who have none."

>my father told me our jobs will never be done

"you will always be on a re-quest
for the words that effect
and reset the standards
of one word worth a 1000 pictures from a camera
unmatched power in this stanza,
the untapped power in your hands, son
I brand you with soul-melanated black as cosmic sands, son
and that's worth fighting – so you will keep writing the word."

RONIN POETZ : KO SI OLUWA

Act 1: Parental Guidance

"LESSON 2: THE CUP"

"lesson 2: see thru who you are
let there be a release,
piece by peace
ask who breathes in nature's scheme
you or the poe-a-tree
whose roots are more deep
who's supplanted and free
you or the words you leave on the paper
scribed from the mind to papermate wand,
defended by the saber – balance your behavior
words in the air (there) quickly lose existence
but are bound to be sentenced on the page
no parole from this cage,
modern day sage and judge
the papyrus be your cup
empty your mind onto documents
declare indePENdence
every new thought indented
the cup of a carPENder
the cup of your life
the origin you be from
sacrificed, resurrected, sawed and drummed,
chipped and digested
screened, beaten, rested
stuff treasure chest-ed
your words (by paper) caress-ed
mixed box, wet ended
wire screened, suction boxed
where rolled and felt
the liquid in cup bright like orion's belt
end process: papyrus blessed
cylinder dried, super calendar–rolled pressed
count the days, x-ed off on parchment
your words will live long,
many will drink from your cup,
your pen never be tainted
your words will live far pass forever
when you become ancient."

Act 1: Parental Guidance

"LESSON 3: THE WAND"

"after you drink deep and indulge your gift
shift reality until it becomes your wish
with the papermate wand, rewrite it
be the hero in life's script
extend time and make it crypt-tick
tock
a new lock grows for every hour you encompass
from this, your frame of mind
can picture the sands of time age like wine
pour what is in our glass into your pen
use this knowledge to blend wand and cup
let these two bodies make love – prophesies
see time thru other eyes and dot them

– document them –

your birthright is the rite to write
and everything you see must be what others read
you the author,
the pen, your key

but there must be more moving on the page
than just the pen

you must not let the road end
(despite where you were born)
you must extend new ones for infant thoughts to come
like wind,
words must wind and bend with the wand

– literary painter –

draw attention with pen and paper
and the words they birth thru the womb of the pen's tip
rough against the paper
but does not tear or rip its fabric
hard as moses' laws and tablets
that pen-phone and pen-keg?
tap it

RONIN POETZ : KO SI OLUWA

Act 1: Parental Guidance

let there be magic for you to bring to the masses
positive adding and negative subtracting
bind by signs and go off on tangents
cosign your life to your queen,
let there be no sin

you and her wake up, team up,
let Ixu and Gira guide and beam up
so you can create poetry the sandman couldn't dream up
sew all seams up with this wand
(don't wander or squander your thoughts)
the Thought Police will call your magic 'voodoo'
embrace and take no offence
do vroom! vroom! until they give you room to boom
don't let soon be reversed to noos(e)
placed around your neck – silence your culture's breath

but for you there is no death
there is only life in your pen
your life now
and your life

    – next –

lesson will be the sword to help you protect

I scribe because all I know will one day be new to you
your pen repair the broken flowers of a culture back into bloom

Act 1: Parental Guidance

"LESSON 4: THE SWORD"

"it is attached like umbilical
it cuts the wind in a sharp sound
it whispers, vocal
musical, it has its own set of chords
this be the sword

master it thru five elements
earth, water, fire, wind, and emptiness
squat and stride legs – keep balance
battle at close range with sword,
formation: phalanx

sword hilt three inches from your heart – back straight
eyes facing every direction
inspection of every enemy
so you can see all 3-60 degrees
the observing eye is stronger,
the perceiving eye is weaker
look up in peripheral,
the preto velho stand above you as your sentinels
aim your sword towards the straight path
level the contour of the earth
and your enemies' advantage will be taken by half

keep your mind and body like water,
fluid with every attack
strike in a flash,
like fire,
swiftly
not really in a high velocity
because possibly your enemy will counter the attack easily

your style must be like the wind
strike an opponent down in a single beat
let your body dance and leap to the rhythm of the second spring
battle with the fury of all four seasons
attack at the sound of an angel's horn,
striking without thought and form
– the flowing water stroke –

RONIN POETZ : KO SI OLUWA

Act 1: Parental Guidance

and as it broke you gave birth to the chance hit
heavy damage,
the spark hit – slice thru your target
take your opponent's sword over
with the crimson foliage hit
move shadows to battle,
knock the heart out and become new
like a rock wall
inaccessible to anything at all

– immovable –

and then there is emptiness
the realm where nothing exists
where you know and don't know
where you act without acting
without thinking,
where to be or not to be is the answer – sun dancer
where we as warriors and prophets
exist solely in wisdom and logic
all this in a single sword swing
in a plural rhythm of king and queen

unfortunately, our will may bring us to kill
defend our culture and women
train them to fight just the same
for we as 'us'
are equal in mind, spirit, body, and name

we are nature's lover
we never strike down one another
united sisters and brothers, fathers and mothers
we use the sword in defense

as we spread faith to bring balance
and set this gruesome world on path and direction
our swords lay & face:
set this world straight

RONIN POETZ : KO SI OLUWA

Act 1: Parental Guidance

"I STUDY 4"

sunlight turned to midnight
my thoughts wandering to the left
about what I should write
enemies I will fight
and allies I will cling tight to

who might you be?

which category do you fit under?
do you PRAY or hunter – I wonder?
there is a battle I need to study for
equipped with word, cup, wand, and sword
but before I have at this I'll need to practice

>>>roll up sleeve<<<

take pen & paper – slowly breathe
don't release until tracks are put over me
or until I grow beats in my heart's garden
this world may harden but I'll crack the shell
minds may dry
but my words will always overflow the well
dwell in spaces on pages, create magic thru spells
keep those in need, enlightened
every seventh sense heightened
I am the star that brightens
I am the sun of the titans

– giants walk this earth –

I walk in the shoes of those who created ALL first
and who were first created by Ixu and Gira – my clan
my entourage
all-the-way-black mob
our jobs, to secure hope to those who've been robbed
cut thru our enemies with any weapon in sight
– swing with Ixu and Gira's might –
break our enemies' spirits – raise yours with lyrics
clear it, the battlefield – let it rain, bloodstained

RONIN POETZ : KO SI OLUWA

Act 1: Parental Guidance

the bodies of our enemies' all that remain
little by little, we'll drain the pains of our world
the trinity of the enemy must be broken and fractured
weave a clear thought pattern
      lock our hair
to be their natural disaster
after we have mastered our four lessons
study the words of The Father,
and they will be our greatest weapons

Act 1: Parental Guidance

"CEREMONY"

my clan dance by fire
their spirits burning brighter
than the flame writhing in the middle
I fiddle with sword,
Father Aquarius preach
about the state of the world
I watch the girls twirl and swirl
— into the existence of women
they, the wind
I wonder which one will turn me into a man
hand me virginity — a maiden for me
nothing dirty — yeah, that's right
give me innocence thru a sexual experience
the way it was meant to be
                    — like Adam and Eve
before they ate from the tree

I already have half of knowledge
which form will she come in to give me life
I'll slip all five of Musashi's rings on her fingers
to make her my wife
her flesh dressed up in the night sky
see her even when my eyes are closed
she poses thru my prose — make her cum-posed

love her like nature, even when she's cold
and if she's in summer's heat
I'll be the cold against her body on a hot day
the warm water in her bath
that soothes her when her bones ache

concentrate and don't be late when it's time to come
make time flow and run,
so many to hold — but love all thru one —
our spirits burning brighter
her hands dancing around my fire
our embrace, tighter
the night becoming lighter (like my fantasy)

RONIN POETZ : KO SI OLUWA

Act 1: Parental Guidance

masturbation?

just an emancipation of thoughts I can't express yet
{they will ultimately lead to a greater destiny}

so which woman here will it be?

which one will give me
peace

RONIN POETZ : KO SI OLUWA

Act 1: Parental Guidance

"CEREMONY CONTINUED: THOUGHT POLICE"

it was time to define our enemies
Father Aquarius preach
about the pain in the axis powers
the battle with them in the last hours
when the world is showered in souls
tides are shifted, spirits uplifted
the innocent defended by the gifted
our enemies' influence on our world omitted
Father Aquarius gave to us their definition:

Thought Police/Thought Cops/Critic-Coppers:
defined as knowledge and history stoppers
ignorant plotters
plotting ignorance
cursing our rebellions, our resistance
their mission to erase our existence
burning our books
– and beating our culture into submission
punishing anyone who listens to us

the foot soldiers,
the stormtroopers
our history removers
they dim our enlightened

under the guidance and leadership of the Pale King
these troops spring into action
against our rebel faction
rounding up our culture, history, children, queens, and dreams
they reverse them,
perverse them into nigger-slave-bitch themes
they throw them up on movie screens – distorted
they copy what is our right
they play our images loud on stereo-types
we've bled for their stars and stripes
and now they're famous
infamous – secretly, they worship us

seek our spiritual positions

RONIN POETZ : KO SI OLUWA

Act 1: Parental Guidance

but they can't be embracers or culture huggers
for centuries they have been enslavers
and settlement smugglers
not a part of the diversity, the cultural population,
the center of mean
for centuries they have studied only one thing:
reversed al-khemistry,
put our gold skin behind iron bars,
science fiends
       – using –
biology to rationalize culture for inferior genes
destroyers and lawyers of a different law
– grave fillers
our blood spillers
stealing wisdom
and driving it right back down the throats of its origin

but our birthright will always return
and the Thought Police will one day repent and yearn
to burn the lies they've tried to make us learn

Act 1: Parental Guidance

"CEREMONY CONTINUED: THE PALE KING"

and then came the definition of the pale king
rising from Mother Pisces' voice
rising higher with the fire – into the stars

The Pale King:
he turned gods to dogs
wind into fog,
clouded our minds
broke nature's spine,
he cut our hair-atage
learned our dictionary
then burned language
our libraries

with an offbeat heartbeat, silenced our drums
into our kingdom he comes
faked a smile
learned the songs we sang to honor the Nile
he sang out of tune and made the sun and moon cry
because he feared nature

he gave our crowns to another collective who reaped it
– raped it
all that was sacred invaded
         – raided in record numbers
pale king plundered and rebuilt the world
on our knowledge from the age of wonders

our Mother Land's womb was infested
pale king manifested his own destiny
we pushed for moor but our wings were clipped
– we could not soar –
black blood poured, the tumbling of black kingdoms roared

the pale king stole our future child – piled us up
committed genocide in a god's name,

in chains we were taken to a familiar land

Act 1: Parental Guidance

– this time stole-land –

the pale king forced us to remold it by hand
by our ancient architecture
he took our queens and sack-religiously blessed her
split us up by colour – light and dark
made us forget we were all of one melaninated heart

he created a new alphabet
starting with ABC-NBC-CBS
Pale King re-wrote everything
with Thought Police,
every breath of knowledge we released
he seduced us with eMpT.V. sorcery screens
our minds became complacent
made us a science experiment
{had the sum of us in projects}
he was sly as a FOX
disguised with heru's eye
Big Brother-Pale King could CNN everything
ESPN – made sports of us – combatants
Extra Sensory Perception Network
cast and caught in Inter-nets
around our necks on streaming sects
put our minds at rest
– worshiped his god to believe we were blessed –
and I can no longer BET on jazz
struggling-a-transmission in static and ash

then came self-destruction
as he himself began to smother
his children killing one another
– his brother against his brother
sister against sister
the pale king's stolen land blistered
with his own blood

and as we made love and re-united,
he declared war and tore thru our union
his mentality older than his religion

Act 1: Parental Guidance

he envisioned that no one but him
would control the wind
kill with lightning
inspire fear with great thunder
             – but nature called for our help –
and so,
our giant spirits have awaken from slumber

RONIN POETZ : KO SI OLUWA

Act 1: Parental Guidance

"CEREMONY CONTINUED: THE ELE OTE"

"the Ele Ote was once one of us, son
scared of destiny he decided to run
from past lashes he crafted anger into a weapon
instead of wisdom
he decided to use culture against everyone who looked like him

you see, his mother's nature was to leave him
his father's time was spent abusing him
lost of his divinity, neggur
they call him 'nigger'

we figure his origin is discipline
descended from the repercussions of irresponsible power
placed in a whip that slapped his forefather's back
that broke his language and made him fear an education
to repair it and keep it intact

he lacks what we have
and wishes to per-verse it in his own broken words
the Ele Ote was lured by the Pale King's false beauty queen
seduced by the Pale King's nationalistic dream
but the Ele Ote will never be able to obtain it
the Pale King has just feigned it,
his interest in the Ele Ote,
[the Pale King has] painted a picture
of perfection to learn our lessons and taint our scriptures
reversing it to negatives from our beautiful pictures

but the Ele Ote, with his less than half education,
knows only 33 and a 3rd of our secrets
but he and the Pale King have been able to piece it
little-by-little, thru spies
that is why we split our vibes,
scribbles,
and lyrics
into all sorts of clusters
keep it far from the hustlers
our actions create confusion
and keep the Ele Ote from learning and using

Act 1: Parental Guidance

our knowledge against us
(handing it over to the Pale King)

but the Ele Ote only sits lazy,
with nothing on his mind and gold in his mouth
to make him feel like he's worth something
I don't fear him stealing our magic
because he doesn't know how to spell
he yells and shouts loud, unable to keep his ignorance down
channel it creatively, patiently,
waiting for the right moment for expression

the tension will begin when this Ele Ote will want to call you 'nigger'
until you start acting like one
pale king revision,
reversed definition of neggur
and break your language off something proper
properly break it until you are the master's property
instead of mastering it properly. do you follow me?

and with a twirl of his finger,
this ignorant inventor will pull a switch
turn your queen into a 'bitch'
and have her at the command
of the Pale King's wish
this Ele Ote shogun show's guns
as more honorable than the sword
because he needs his weapon to roar for attention
and he does not know
how to use the pen and the cup
he twists the word, hurls his voice to negate thunder
believes he can control the world he stands under
he talks to our children and teaches them wrong
sings out-of-tune songs
and the irony be
that with all his foolishness
the Pale King wishes to be blessed by him, to be like him
it is the Pale King's children who are the first to imitate him
and if the Ele Ote continues to spread our faith twisted
then our brightest hours will become dim
and we will be condemned – and we will become damned."

RONIN POETZ : KO SI OLUWA

Act II: Training Groundz

"SILVER ON THE TREE"

tomorrow we go
tonight we show
what we can mold
as a people
eye see thru peep-holes
windows to souls
but don't ask too much of me
with all this crafting
I'm still practicing
like my hair,
my words still got some kinks
this style ain't as free as you think
we be free to think safely
maybe
secretly, pale king praise me
thought police can't evade me
but I can evade them
I frighten them

as much as they want me dead
they still admire the thoughts in my head
and the way I wear my hair, they dread
I spread forgotten news of millenniums
for forgotten children
when they chill-drums
shut my mouth!? I'll still speak in Morse Code hums
even if they murder me I'll liquefy into 'red rum'
make stew from my strange fruit
added with the spice of my beats
I'll reign on city streets
shine down and give heat
there is no meal worth more to eat
than the one on this silver tree
my roots run that deep

my ancestors are not dead, they just sleep
(as they reside in me)

Act 11: Training Groundz

"STEPPIN'"

creep
creep
creep

we are carried and measured by feet
we beat for fun, step in rhythm as we travel
this freedom be louder than shackles
we cackle with the east wind
send thank-you to Who Be In Charge Up There
just speak into the air silent prayers
skitter-scatter like a mouse
use a shadow as a house
when we hear the thought police near
their boots offbeat

BL-U-U-MP
BL-U-U-MP
BL-U-U-MP

we stick close as they hunt
we pray for them
if they come across our rhythm and swing
small scuffle, we battle with all five rings
two of 45 survive to report back to the pale king

creep
creep
creep

we continue sailing
on the air's railing
continue travel with thoughts on our backs
exchange them
frame them in each other's minds
practice our rhymes
for the time
we are safe in this place between here and there
dressed in all black ancient wear
sum, in a group as one, snoop — search for new recruits

RONIN POETZ : KO SI OLUWA

Act 11: Training Groundz

add them to our family tree, teach them their roots
put us on a route that leads us in all directions
we are ubiquitous with our lessons
reciting and writing 42 negatives and confessions
our tribe numbers seven
creep – creep – creep
we steppin'

RONIN POETZ : KO SI OLUWA

Act 11: Training Groundz

"IN-TOWN CHANT"

Father Aquarius lets me speak
on the first stop
I scream:

"from the top

bald heads or locks
cool air or mops
that scoop up
what stardust drops
corn row crops
our voices rock
set yo clocks
and wrist/watch what I do

we slide right thru and bayou
we've ended up in your neck of the woods
ready to break neck speeds
and set it on our new record
brutha strong be a free-may-son
brutha hero dismember in december
editor, inventor, image director
we be art's soldiers
our story's scenes seen in correct order

I was born in the month of a-peril
I always knew there would be struggle
but every transmission made on stereo-types
we scrambled it
made mother nature orgasm
then sampled it
we are father this time
caress nature's spine
heard the earth thru my hair
dangle like grapevines,
this family tree grows sub-lime

sister sunlight, she brave
her smile shines in rays

Act 11: Training Groundz

brutha midnight sparkles with star waves
the moon controls his emotions

and as the cosmos drips lotion
I catch it and rub it on my queen's back
ancient skin colour, she be my religious artifact
in her eyes and between her thighs
OURstory is intact

our heavenly bodies together create aura
this is therapy, we are the past's aroma
descended, african scented
formed from every dimension
mind-body-soul blended
shouting thru time
throwing our lines
to catch the attention of future generations

fear not,
this is no invasion
these words are free like emancipation
kiss my words and understand what I'm tastin'
every time I speak, I eat
the knowledge of the tree – it's no sin
I can't separate my life from the pen

I'm kickin' it per mission
but without my permission
I believe, you can't sell or buy me

and none of the unholy trinity can defy me
I raise the ruf
and make a fus' to say,
don't even dare
my clan got that mathematical equation: $I = MCs$ scared."

Act 11: Training Groundz

"WE BATTLE, SWORDZ SWINGING"

burning trees
and staining grass
pale king made path
he became negative math
reducing nature to ash

town invaded
two have be-traded
our lives for theirs
they will not live
past this hour

Father Aquarius say,
"let us be the obstacle in this course
let us battle with light and dark
as our source.

my people, grab sword
defend this town
from bowing down
to the pale king as lord."

I pray to the moon
let its light be my shield
as I wield sword
on this battlefield
sun come to my aid
light covers sword's blade

the first I slay with saber
be the two traitors
I'll pray for them later
sword then cling! clang!
guns boom! and bang!

thought police
swarm on town streets
we meet head on
swing swiftly, head off

RONIN POETZ : KO SI OLUWA

Act 11: Training Groundz

lives lost

guns shout
and toss
propaganda
our image
devoured
by slander

town don't believe that
so they strike back
against pale king's attack

town battle with windstaff
thought police suffer whiplash

>>I am stabbed!<<

the man's name is Tag

nimble, like dancer
low whispers
call him 'cancer'
because he kills slowly
his mind infects body

Tag battles
with spear
sharpened
on jagged, double-edge
to frighten

strength and hero
come to my side and defend
Tag yells,
"we at odds 'till we even
think you can beat me, niggers
you dreamin'.

I have infinite levels
and you may tie

RONIN POETZ : KO SI OLUWA

Act 11: Training Groundz

or flip the score
but it'll never be settled."

we reply,
"yeah, but we be the bass
in your treble
the gold you desire
in your bass metal
we the cause
for every rebel

and you in trouble
next time we rumble
24-7 we at this
concentrate and practice

study our lessons
written on ancient papyrus
yours written on banana peels
because you slippin' trippin'
ifin' you thinkin'
you more than our match."

Tag sneers, "niggers,
I'm better than that
I'm faster
than you blinkin'
make one false move
and the next time you walk
you'll be limpin'.

don't think the scenario
of me losing this battle
be existin' in the future.
I battle for the pale king as ruler."

we 3-eye bruthas retort,
"no man can be ruler
no man can measure up
to the Great Producers
pale king just a seducer."

RONIN POETZ : KO SI OLUWA

Act 11: Training Groundz

dark, lock-haired warrior
jump into battle
town resident
he battles with windstaff

his name is jamaal blackmore
he and Tag battle each other
like they've done this before
we 3-eye bruthas attack with sword

Tag kicks us back, bored
but he smiles sly, happy
I have to admit
his style ain't too shabby

but–

beatin' back
off beat
thought police
and Tag
retreat

this town no longer safe
we evacuate and take
the residents
to a brighter place

so, we still steppin'
off to teach others
our ancient lessons

Act 11: Training Groundz

"INNER-COLLECTIVE ALLY, JAMAAL"

all lies
in this ally
jamaal and I
become quick friends

he knows about
the ancients
we become reminiscent
on a past we've
never been to

but,
this what the wind do
when you inhale (not what you think)
ancestors cover us
like veils
lead us down
an ancestral trail

we prance thru the trees
balance on every limb
Father Aquarius
will still
teach him
our lessons
keep his life
aimed in
the right direction

our voices
in the wind
we slick talk
about women,
jamaal says his people craft
thru movement
instead of the pen

jamaal's breath enters
thru the West Hay Ward guild

RONIN POETZ : KO SI OLUWA

Act II: Training Groundz

taught to build
his town filled
with another
ancient knowledge

collected not in
this region
it teaches them
to be shift shapers
also
how to capture worldly scenes
on paper

I teach him the sword
we spar while speaking jazz
he teaches me
how to use
the windstaff

we keep slick talkin'
'bout women
and we laugh
there be peace
we wonder how long
it will last

we make one minute vast
time in present
that gift never past
every smooth line
we give props and daps

everything
for the moment
be relaxed
cool vibe

we speak spells
that let us pull
wine out of the sky
stardust mixed

Act 11: Training Groundz

with sun rays

our thoughts stray
over the horizon
and we both know
in the distance
where the battle horns blow
we are allies now
against
a common
foe

RONIN POETZ : KO SI OLUWA

Act II: Training Groundz

"PLAN IN CHANT"

our clan destined/plotting and manifestin'
into one solid group,
listening to elders addressin'
keep voices low to escape detection
we restin' in these woods
swarm around campfire like atoms and eves
weave a pattern like protons and electrons
swirl around neutrons
but we stand still

we gather like space matter
form one collective body

ash scatters/reality shatters
Father Aquarius describes,
his words form in our eyes
as pictures that guide our thoughts
he tells us about bruthaz and sistas
who've been caught – bought – and brought
to a place not too far from here

"we be in-chanted
jazz moon, dancin' – sun incanted
do-rah-me
do rain on me
I & G give plan to thee
our bruthas and sistas
must be set free
reconnected to family tree

like Lituolone
we'll do this alone
but in one great number
the shaded outer light, like pen-umbra
storm the walls of this fortress
its name be kammapa

attack in sea formation
like waves and verse

Act 11: Training Groundz

march in line
after line
unstoppable like the devouring of time
the sun and moon have promised
not to shine

we will be disguised by night
and it will be the star lights
whose eyes we see with
align with mars and venus
love for our own
and war for our enemy – the false supremacy
The Old Black has sent to me
this battle's outcome in prophecy."

jamaal's voice breaks monotony,
"who possibly will be guarding?
thought police, Ele Ote, or pale king?"

Father of the I-trinity voice,
"be prepared for all things
make every swing count
count every swing
swift and plenty
make ash of the enemy
before they make ash of you

we have five hours for preparation
we head south, stealth walking
from here on out
all talking cease
until we make war for peace
let Ixu and Gira be with thee."
(and so, we are dismissed 3 by 3 by 3)

RONIN POETZ : KO SI OLUWA

Act II: Training Groundz

"WE CEREMONY, HANDS TOGETHER"

invoke the ghost
invoke the ghost
invoke the ghost

I am symmetry
my hands together
my eyes closed
I see eternity

an amoeba of colours
swirl into one another
on the backdrop of space
the colours turn into rain
and they spill on emptiness
I can make out a thousand names
plus more, times seventy-four

jamaal tells me they are the names
of goddesses and queens
they are shaped:

crttw
btty
arthw
rsw
trw
lrw
rntw
lrn
tmrw
nkw
mxn
kndrw
mjry
yshw
tnshw
nnjlw
nyw

Act 11: Training Groundz

and thousands more
all connected to eve
I tell the names,

"I am a prayer

there in the lips
spoken in the air

I am a prayer

unspoken but shared
the concealed one
a man
amen
amon
I am the sun – the Son of Suns
atum
the atom
split from eve
and I believe
that 1 day you and I will conceive
the tree of knowledge from our roots
and gain forever life
keeping our hearts right
and holding onto all we have left
every other breath – a prayer."

I act on a whim-amun
sun in feminine form
weapon and armor
four-hundred years without breath
could not harm her

she gives me power

I have less than an hour
to prepare
goddesses say,

Act 11: Training Groundz

"We be that first word spoken in the beginning
we are the first prayer
and we are bare, leaving you naked
and our truth be hard to digest
but you must regress — regress so far back
and become the original name the cosmos blessed you with
— african —

that is a real revolution

we are not Jesus — we are just resurrection
come through us
the lesson, spoken by the blessed son
because we be the one
we are a prayer."

Act 11: Training Groundz

"WE CEREMONY, HANDS APART"

palm open
up
face heaven
heaven face
up
open palm
receive the twilight's song
when dusk is equal to dawn
sun makes final peek,
before it sleeps beneath
the horizon
now we have an open-eye orison
as our thoughts begin risin'
        – mind glidin'
jamaal enlightens,
open mind wide

"don't be shy
god does not exist in the sky
and sometimes
you can see plenty gods with the physical eye
we walks on air at times
but not too high
I'll past the word to you, kheru
so, you can get on the vibe."

in the middle of circle
middle of tribe
I recite without scribe,

"I prosper and live long
my fire set off every alarm
but I cool down the fire
to make a woman come real strong."

crowd shout loud
I continue
under their cloud

RONIN POETZ: KO SI OLUWA

Act II: Training Groundz

"Tag may stab
but he ain't got the rhythm to beat me
curse his existence
my testimony be sworn
I be diamond month born
I'm a woman's best friend
playin' the field
like miles played his horn
if the sky be my mother
then earth be my father
I be the son who shine on you 'till the day be done

we don't lose
the number on this act be won
when it comes to the thought troops
we loop-loop and keep the beat on the run."

Act 11: Training Groundz

"WE CEREMONY, CLAP IN CHANT"

we rhyme assistin'
in this soul kitchen
party as we drink stardust
before we act out our mission
this is how we work it
descendants of the chitlin' circuits
sippin' on pop daddies
and glam slams
we break dance
repair by prayer and chants

clap
clap
we take you across the map
clap
clap
we take you across the map

in psalms we break free from trap
pale king say our culture has us wrapped
we free from that
our minds settled back
we in the past now

clap
clap
we are across the map
clap
clap
we are across the map

the situation unwrapped
change the present
it is too tense
we are the honored
the heaven sent
descendants
of the blameless

RONIN POETZ : KO SI OLUWA

Act II: Training Groundz

burnt faced ancients
future and destiny re-shay-PENed
something old has been awakened in us
in justice we will fight injustice
live by the code number 68:31
we have spread our arms out wide from
       – where we were
       – to bring you the word
our wisdom is precision
third eye in focus, acute vision

clap
clap
we on the map
clap
clap
we on the map

let's back track
rewind the track back
the number on this one
is blackjack
define relativism
pessimism is the words of a realist?
I ain't feelin' this
split it thru the prism
make it a rainbow of optimism
but that be the words of a child
a river of words is how I flow
pale king try to damn that

for certain proof
truth be words from bartenders
so how 'bout a drink?
to rethink the year thru december
cleanse me from bein' drunk
of ignorance's remix
life's game ain't fixed
but for a while I felt
the cards I was dealt were marked
not like verola –

Act 11: Training Groundz

as it turns out, I'm the card holder
and war's got my back to keep peace intact
and what is past is last night's memory
more for me as I morph with thee
I thought about my own destiny
pale king tried to tell me it was a fantasy
keep me from me
I reshaped it to turn it into reality
now the past be in back of me
my eyes focus, I see straight thru ya
and I feel the presence of the present
unwrap it, and behold the future

so clap on that, black
make sure it's on the beat
melanate – meditate – and relax

RONIN POETZ : KO SI OLUWA

Act 11: Training Groundz

"BATTLE OF KAMMAPA"

we are in plain sight
hidden by the night
the night our ally
we, the stars in the sky
split into constellations
we prepare for invasion
we drop like rain
attack cold like snow
the wind guides us to the earth
we land, gently
the earth cracks, splits
opens up to devour our enemies
this is all done silently
we rise back into the night sky
divide into stars

we are patient

we move to the south entrance of the fortress
gate open
we descend from the heavens
twenty-seven plus eighteen guards
we as stars, set
like the forth seal,
we come like death
put to rest
every thought troops' breath
we enter kammapa
the belly of the beast

we are digested

from kammapa's lungs,
the deep,
steal beast breathes
another fleet emerges as we creep
we split into groups of three

(well ... truthfully ... we got four

Act 11: Training Groundz

myself, strong, hero, and jamaal blackmore)

we duck into adjacent halls and doors

we dodge the enemy
until we come across one
we attack quickly,
remove him of his gun
and before he can shout
we grapple him,
cover his mouth
place sword's blade against his neck
I ask,
"where are our kindred kept?"
his eyes – wide – terrified,
he answers in a single breath
"in the third sublevel of our fortress."

our people below consciousness
I knock the thought cop out of it
ghost thru
we go thru
descend
we hear screaming
violent
no light, or proper dark-night
– shines in this wasteland
people walk aimless
in circles
we rain purple
in hopes of giving them more colours

we are prayer

the room is filled
with the presence of thousands of women
their spirit form one goddess
come to teach wisdom and logic
free our people from bondage
pull them up above consciousness
they need to breathe

RONIN POETZ : KO SI OLUWA

Act II: Training Groundz

Mother Pisces lead
thru her, every woman speaks

Mother Pisces preach
teach
how to keep their knowledge sharPENed
how to become in-light-and enDARKened
thru soul, body, and mind
see all colours with every opened eye
be on – and – in time
history in the making
master the art of destiny shaping

and now
from kammapa
we all plan on escaping

retracing our steps
we meet up with the rest
Father Aquarius give praise
our kindred have been saved

– but –

the thought police attack
en masse
in one last
full
force
wave

their screams
a bloodthirsty craze

I sway from their line and fire
we are outgunned and outnumbered
we remember we can control the thunder
we use it to throw our enemies back
lightning bolt lash
we slash
thought police numbers cut by half

Act 11: Training Groundz

jamaal and I are cut off from clan
forced back into another section
we continue dance steppin' around our enemies
they are confused
as we move with the wind
in rhythm
sword and windstaff visions
dancing in our enemies' eyes

to keep instep
we recite on beat
to beat thought police
but they come in swarms
as one is cut down
it looks like another is born
but we react quickly,
adapt and attack viciously
my sword is now the colour of rust

the thought police attack in rush
we slide into adjacent room
cut chord
door slams
cutting the troops off from us

whew! we take a breath

we search for another way out
the door creeps up slowly

slowly

      slowly

            slowly

quickly – we find another door
and we are thru
thought police enter room

RONIN POETZ : KO SI OLUWA

Act 11: Training Groundz

they shoot and
guns boom
a quick recite of words
and we speed-increase
we become a blur
and merge with the outside

kammapa is in flames
I concentrate and receive the names
of those slain
it is only few
the rest have escaped

the thought police come from the fire
their bodies burning
nature distorted, turning
they scream with mouth and gun
we run into forest
our clan is safe on the other side
our powers weak and dampened

– we cannot reach them –

a dark voice whispers,
"you are beaten!"
jamaal and I look up
we are surrounded,
nowhere to run
I expected Tag to own the voice
but it was the Ele Ote

he orders,
"drp yo' wep-unz 'n' cum…"
we are bound and gagged
dragged behind Ele Ote's tattered rags

he is dressed in fads and clichés
bright for attention
not to honor the sun's rays

RONIN POETZ : KO SI OLUWA

Act 11: Training Groundz

his skin is a scab
scratched, scarred, and ash
captive! we follow him…
on a long journey back to his kingdom

RONIN POETZ : KO SI OLUWA

Act 11: Training Groundz

"BANG ON DRUMS"

in cage
housed
with
inmates

jamaal
and I
refuse
to be slaves
in this condition

a third of us are here

the repercussions
of our capture
is just percussion

we begin to bang

bang, bang, bang// bang on drums// not with guns// we write and type// on the surface of the sun// we absorb its paper thru melanin

jamaal and I trapped
in Ele Ote's kingdom

this place is bass distorted// power and thought dampened// but our hopes run rampant// we let other inmates sample it// Ele Ote can't tamper with it// how can I make my voice louder? I still hold an ounce of power// Ele Ote has chosen us to die// we have only five hours to live// so, we reminisce

but the past is too far
beyond these bars
and my eyes sting
my voice can't sing
I cough and choke
on this kingdom's smoke

no! not kingdom – prison

Act II: Training Groundz

it has my vision distorted//Ele Ote serve's a religion imported//by the man who imported him//stole his wisdom//I scream, 'keep your distance.'//my mission takes precedence//I am the evidence of your crime//I am the voice of time that can no longer speak//but it seeks judgment//wasn't it you who viewed my mind thru a kaleidoscope's eye and had the nerve to call it repugnant?

even I can see, that down deep
the pale king's soul can be sunny
and my vision isn't exactly twenty-twenty

Ele Ote bounces in

the word 'nigger'
dripping off him
he dances with a limp
he pimps ignorance

"bitch
don' spread dat wise shit
cuz I'll cut off both dhem lips.
dis ain't no muthafuckin'
church choir."

I whisper,
"the word 'education' to you
is like a cross to a vampire."

"you have five hours
to take dhat back."

"too late
it's in the past
and I can't time travel."

Ele Ote says,
"dhat's aw'ite
y'are judgment
cums at dhe end
uh my gavel.
'less you can give me
dhe whereabouts of your clan."

RONIN POETZ : KO SI OLUWA

Act 11: Training Groundz

"if I'm to put them in your hands
let me tell you in chant
I'll tell you
in the next room
give you wisdom, knowledge, and truth."

needless to say
the Ele Ote was seduced

"y' bes' cum wit'
dat shit
– dhe wurd,
sword, pen, and wand."

he opens cage,
his men shackle me
I walk passively
but alert
ready to act

Ele Ote leads me into beat room
but it's offbeat
talk is weak
no one here can speak

the Ele Ote sits,
not patiently
but still – waiting for me to speak

"yo clan?
yo knowledge?
yo life?"

"all in chant."

Act 11: Training Groundz

"ALL HOURS IN A DAY, ALL IS OURS"

Ele Ote yells,
"y' lessons
y' knowledge
y' clan."

>>pause<<

I speak,
"I am more than human
and less sun
I am your lesSun
number one
I shine brighter
than guns are loud
while sleeping on clouds."

"nigga,
will you make sense?"

"and be a sellout!?
I will not make cents for change
I am four by 90 degrees
intersecting 7 planes
what's your range? shooting?
simply A to BE?
I am magnetic of all active energy

and out of all the swords
my tongue is the sharpest
I was produced from triple darkness
the Mother-Father-Cosmic
the pale king's target
I am two hours younger than these words
I am the second tenth hour."

Ele Ote-Owl:
"butchu only got five hours to live.
take dis bitch away.
give 'im to magikkk."

RONIN POETZ : KO SI OLUWA

Act III: Take A Rite 2 Passage

"MAGIKKK"

enchantress
all implanted
fake
no soul
tampered with

she writhes like snake pits
whore of babylon
who dances on – music blasted on stereo…(by now, you know)

she dances to the beats
of nigger songs
trampling on auset's image
she seduces children
who sample on her breast
it drips acid
burns their vocal c(h)ords

magikkk devoured her father's son
as he set in the west
she caressed the 666 beast
as he fed upon the weak

she tied jesus down
that's why I weep
jesus lay raped
his original name forsaken
his original face painted over
the falcon morphed to a dove
wings clipped – unable to soar
and his mother, 'madonna'
is synonymous
with the word 'whore'

crucified on magikkk's body
religion is her property
I'll stay ancestrally faithful
She chasing my chastity
as I'm tied in this chair

Act III: Take A Rite 2 Passage

she dances around bare of soul

she tells me she can inject God in my veins
suck shame out of my life
just put out the light, and then cut like Othello's knife
choke like his grip
and take a sip of her breast
acid infested

she slithers
says I'm hers
for 30 pieces of silver
and all my secrets

a snake creeps and hisses
from between her legs
and she begs
"rape me, nigger! rape me!
I'll tell no one, just rape me."

instead I pray for her
my light emits until death
do she part – I embrace no part of her art
Ele Ote says I'll die earlier

"bring dat nigga, jamaal."

jamaal doesn't give in either
Ele Ote begins to beat her,
magikkk,
she enjoys it
Ele Ote ignores her – that annoys her

Act III: Take A Rite 2 Passage

"BLACK ON BLACK — NEGGUR VS. NIGGER"

surrounded
bound
but not gagged
five thought police
Ele Ote in center
guns aimed

jamaal and I stand firm

"The Beginning and End is now in our veins
and we will remain
even though death may change
the physical appearance."

Ele Ote yells,
"quiet!"

I voice,
"I will not be quiet
my mouth will shout riots
this may seem like a freestyle
but the Divine are my sponsors
behind my eyelids scrolls a word monitor
but pale king monitors the words behind my eyes
edit and revise them until they are lies
now they're the tears I cry
but even when closed, I see thru another eye

Ele Ote, my brother, are you blind?
don't you see they've taken your lines
connected with your past time
and you still playin' games on their field?

pale king praise you
only to play you
but I guess it's all right
as long as he pays you

you bow to his green paper

RONIN POETZ : KO SI OLUWA

Act III: Take A Rite 2 Passage

worship it
as if it had the picture
of your savior scrawled on it

I cry—o—my—genetics
tears frozen in time
ancestors caress my spine
swinging on thoughts like vines

pale king has scratched your rhymes
made them hard, gritty, c—c—c—crimes
left your body outlined in chalk
and you ask, 'where is everybody?'
everybody's bodies sleeping
leaning against poles
drunken, stumblin'
wake up! smell what they shovelin'
it's your ashes
history burners, icon—o—classicist

smoke ancient words
not the earth's herbs
it's absurd
your high is the sun in the sky
will you take that knowledge for a bride?
or your people's lives as a bribe?
understand it was the pale king
who said your kingdoms and nations were savage tribes
that's his math
but we are greater as half
than his troops in full mass
we outcasts ride

vibe on ancient pride
and if that be suicide in pale king's eyes
then let me constantly die
as you help him commit genocide

but I die and revive
so smooth that thoughts don't fly
they glide

RONIN POETZ : KO SI OLUWA

Act III: Take A Rite 2 Passage

ride the air delivering dreams
dream-waves in airwaves
channel soul and let you tune in
absorb melanin so you can be black again
thru al–khem–istry

turn an old being into a nu-being (nubian)
turn clear air, soul gold carbon and oxygen
burnished brass like Jesus' skin
put the hue back in every man
shape every queen out of africa's darkest sands
and bathe you in the sun beams
so you can understand how the sun dreams

that masculine/feminine inspiration
of the GOD 'HE/SHE/OR–IT'
who put my thoughts in orbit
and created the stars

that's why you think I'm so bright
I shine against the night
and if you look up
at the constellations just right
you'll understand stand
they're just my name
up in lights

and they get brighter
as I meditate on jazz
reciting the blues
my voice carving rock
in the temple of funk

I be a shaolin–thelonius monk."

the Ele Ote trembles
jamaal chants,

"my heart and soul are not for ransom
my hair makes me handsome
pale king ask,

RONIN POETZ: KO SI OLUWA

Act III: Take A Rite 2 Passage

'what's that on your head son?'
so, I tell 'em,
'something to get me closer to the sun
I call it culture
hey Ele Ote, I notice you ain't got none.

let me break the chant down so low
you'll be able to hear the grass grow
my hair be a forest
on every vine-lock
there's a fruit called 'chorus'
so, let's sing

Ele Ote,
unlike most bruthas
you cut your hair out of self-hatred
not to feel nature's kiss, sacred
her wind can't be tasted
rubbin' against baldness
or tickling the dreads
yeah,
your mother nature
gives good head

if you see fit,
let me rest six feet deep
in the earth's bed."

five shots ring loud
but when we open our eyes
the five thought troops lie dead

and we are unbound

our weapons on the ground
it is quiet
sigh lent peace

"go…"
the Ele Ote's voice echoes
power in a single syllable

RONIN POETZ : KO SI OLUWA

Act III: Take A Rite 2 Passage

"go, my bruthas, go.
chant, and go."

wind becomes sound
becomes traces of matter
becomes the Ele Ote's shadow
he understands nature
his power true
his flesh renewed
a man of hue

"go," he repeats.

"come with us."

"it's…too late for me.
take the inmates with you."

changed, he reveals his true name,
"my name is seth. now, GO!"

"more than that,
you are us.
we are you.
family,
heritage,
culture,
allies against a common foe.
free magikkk from her father's hold"

we disappear
our powers revived
we take the inmates
and escape into the night
forward out – flee and flight
behind us ensues a fight
as Tag steps to the stage
double-jagged blade, blood reigned

"redemption is no option
for your sister. I've left her bleeding.

Act III: Take A Rite 2 Passage

blistered. dying out.
I heard her turn — loud as a shout.
and so, I took her life — bleeding
from her mouth…"

seth's sword shimmers
as the energy on his spine slithers
his skin, black oiled,
sister magikkk,
redeemed, and now Ma–hek,
her spirit writhing on seth's back, coiled

Tag twirls his weapon and delights,

"many nights,
I dreamed of this fight
where you as my teacher
feel my venom and bite.
redeemed you are at this moment,
but your mind will always be plagued
the memories of your crimes will never be erased.
family, by your hands, slain
and your service to the pale king,
helping your people be enslaved."

but, like his spirit
seth's sword is raised
and the original warrior
uncaged
smiles, battle engaged

seth, older
slower
but still a worthy warrior

his life, stained
seth prays
that his actions now
present
define all of him, whole
if this be his last days

Act III: Take A Rite 2 Passage

"DANCING IN FREEDOM"

dancing in freedom
is skipping with the rain
that's what we do
cuz freedom reigns on us
we jam on ziggy
stardust drinkin'

these inmates have never known this freedom

and we owe it…
…to seth?

as he wept
he let the sons of the earth free
and set
murderer of his brother osiris
he became more from less
redeemed thru a promised kept
he let the sons of the earth free
chant with me,

"osiris, your brother is free
the pale king no longer holds him
and so your descendants' sons rise
their daughters, absorbed like the water
and when it rains they fall on us
when the sun shines, we are warm from them
we are the descendants of the sun and rain
and let freedom shine and reign
we pray for an enemy who is now our ally"

I tell jamaal,
"once we find our clan
we'll go back and rescue the rest
including seth."
"do you suspect a trap?"

I retort,
"no man

RONIN POETZ : KO SI OLUWA

Act III: Take A Rite 2 Passage

could ever
wield nature
like that
if he weren't truly free
in mind, and spirit."

we continue
dancing
chanting
nature, raining
clouds sparsely populate the sky
the sun jacks up
backs up into the sky
bouncing to our vibe
its rays embracing the clouds
its voice scatting like jazz

I wonder who woke up who

Act III: Take A Rite 2 Passage

"3 BEAT SEARCH, 2ND END 4"

jamaal's eyes
understands
what they see
he stands under
over trees

he takes sword
(that is pen)
and invokes
the world on
paper. he draws

his legs touch
earth. we search
the world drawn

jamaal knows
where to go
the inmates,
they follow

our clan is
near. we can
hear them. we
rush to them.

we are free
our journey
at an end

"3 BEAT SEARCH, 2ND END 4"

Act III: Take A Rite 2 Passage

"RA UNION"

in the center
where trees
form 3-60 degrees
where the sun's rays
and the earth meet
there was a faint beat

a beat of heart and drums
people chanting as one
there, in the clearing
a distance away
but a ray of light extended
and like a bridge we crossed
we ran
reunited with clan
rushed into open arms and hands

brutha br—eye—on, strong
brutha jah—sun, hero
Mother Pisces, and her legion
queens, goddesses, women
Father Aquarius
and the warrior class mass

we narrate our flight
jamaal acts it out
as I recite
our run from the Ele Ote
I surprise Father Aquarius
– as well as everyone –
when I orate the Ele Ote's redemption
I call him by his true name, seth
and say that the rest of his kingdom
must be rescued

"jamaal can lead us back
he has scribed map
and with our forces intact
we could push back the pale king's attack

RONIN POETZ : KO SI OLUWA

Act III: Take A Rite 2 Passage

if this is in fact just a trap."

Father Aquarius shakes his head
"the Ele Ote's spirit is dead.
seth's voice and soul is true
we must plan rescue
and embrace him as a new recruit."

we rest – take a day
cultivate the inmates
educate them thru the four lessons

settle back
we hold ceremony
and pray
the men invoke the spirit
of the women – for strength
the women invoke the spirit
of the men – we blend
tomorrow we'll fight with double strength
we'll battle to the end
tonight we sing a warrior's song
tomorrow, we attack at dawn

Act III: Take A Rite 2 Passage

"KINGDOM COME"

we march

across horizon
as the sun comes up

we march

every mountain becomes a plain
every plain a valley
and we descend
every ray of light blends with us
only us, just us
we are here in the name of justice

we march

into fog and clouds
smoke and flames
we will rain on this kingdom
and we can feel the presence
of the reigning king
we can hear screaming
inmates bleeding
pale king keeping them down
tortured, bound

we shatter all barriers with a single sound

face-to-face with time
we are too late
we see seth has met fate
swords and spears pierce his body
formation: cross
he has become one with the spirit he lost
nailed to a wall
his blood trickles down, crawls

creeping in the adjacent corridor
seth's murderer calls,

RONIN POETZ : KO SI OLUWA

Act III: Take A Rite 2 Passage

"and now
death
has come to you all!"

the thought police
fill
the halls

"you'll all die
that is the way
and there is no way
to change it."

my sword turns red
from silver
in a situation all too familiar

Tag stands at a distance and laughs
Father Aquarius carves a path thru the thought police
and attacks him

brother strong and hero jump to action
as the rest of us are trapped in
battling the thought police

we do not accept death or defeat
fight with a beat and beat them back
new inmates join the attack

one named rufus
who speaks and builds
a magical shield around his body

next to him is a giant – sha-nun,
dreads so long, they wrap around his neck
inset with jewels and gold bands,
sha-nun fights hand-to-hand
bare hands – strength of a bear
the heir of a fighting style
that helps us tear thru the opposition

RONIN POETZ : KO SI OLUWA

Act III: Take A Rite 2 Passage

my vision catches Tag and Father Aquarius,
strong, and hero battling vicious
Tag holding them at bay
every sword swing and sway
dodged and parried
Tag separates the melee
strong and hero are kicked away from the fray
Tag and Father Aquarius clash

– I dash in their direction –

brutha hero knocked into a different section
strong and I keep pressing on

Mother Pisces shines like the dawn
she takes Father Aquarius' side
battling Tag together
raining on him like weather
but they become severed
Tag is too malicious
he lashes out, vigorous
he becomes graceful
like a dancer
this man, Tag – nicknamed 'cancer'
captures time and attacks

Father Aquarius
is fatally
stabbed

Mother Pisces is consumed with tears
she is paralyzed with fear

Tag disappears

his laughter echoing
settling in our minds

late, we arrive
three brothers,

RONIN POETZ : KO SI OLUWA

Act III: Take A Rite 2 Passage

derived from the 3 I's
of our Father Aquarius — who has died
the stars have negatively aligned
Cancer in Aquarius
every scar deepened

I am consumed by one word
I have been reduced to one sense

revenge

while this maniacs laughter

echoes,
          echoes,
                    echoes,
                              echoes,
                                        echoes,
                                                  echoes,
and settles

          (settles)
                    (settles)
                              (settles)

in my mind

RONIN POETZ: KO SI OLUWA

Act III: Take A Rite 2 Passage

"RA GROUP"

with the inmates we escape
take a different route and regroup

more have joined us
much more taken away
and we can't stay here
jamaal fears his inner vision
it can see the pale king
marching in the distance
an army of thousands in step with him
offbeat chanting
offbeat dancing
the day has turned
to dusk from dawn

I see Mother Pisces,
she lies still

in brutha hero's arms
Father Aquarius
cradled in strong's grip
his life and breath exist
only in the past

that is no more than half my age in minutes

Father Aquarius is still back there
somewhere, still
his last breaths fill a room
at rest
possibly without understanding
that its life is now death
but knowing that great man
he understands
and stands over us
we are his last heirs
we are his remaining breath of life
but do we run
or fight?

RONIN POETZ : KO SI OLUWA

Act III: Take A Rite 2 Passage

revenge is all that remains in my veins
I want to take this pain
and rain down on the pale king
send him back whence he came

my heart a furnace
heat and hatred
pump thru me
land on my tongue
and I can taste them

I lick my lips
sip revenge
as it drips,
drips
drips

it bleeds thru my wrists
as I grip my sword
I want to pour this feeling
onto the pale king

I look up
my clan looks at me
waiting to set them free
pale king is closer
         – in jamaal's vision
and it is me who must make a decision

"we flee to safety
find sanctuary
and regroup our thoughts."

we take flight
blend into the night
this act,
closed curtain
our future
uncertain…

RONIN POETZ : KO SI OLUWA

Act III: Take A Rite 2 Passage

"THE BURIAL"

All the sun's rays dimmed
except one, extended from the center
extended down to him
Father Aquarius
as he lay buried
the moon's light dripped,
trickled into the clouds
it rained all day

even nature wept
for our father's eternal rest

we harmonized
in a single breath
addressed the greatness
that was Father Aquarius
and the various areas he touched

he is now a spirit we invoke
cover his grave with a rose
his spirit flows into space
touches the moon, sun, and stars
knows no distance that is far
beyond land and sea
he is me
we are a triple trinity
2997, 999
he is space and time
soul and mind
no longer rewind
we are forward
press play
Father Aquarius now prays
with a long list of ancients

does that sound pretentious?
well it's not pretense
before tense
future, past, present

RONIN POETZ: KO SI OLUWA

Act III: Take A Rite 2 Passage

I am pro tense
professional tension
released thru revenge
in the spirit of my father I will defend
end the life of the pale king
and his henchman named Tag

becuz moon-water light rains prematurely
early, on our father
who art in heaven,
buried in the earth
verse-by-verse
with the power of the moon
the climate will reverse
and like the waves,
Father Aquarius' spirit will ascend

my knees will never bend
un-less in prayer
prayer in less-un
remember,
the ancient voice is where I am from
until the day when all are one and won

Act III: Take A Rite 2 Passage

"4WARD"

we pace
in the same place
behind time
in this race
Mother Pisces face is still
her eyes still closed
her body frozen
mind shattered and broken
paralyzed with sorrow's emotion

our own minds not open
focused on loss
caught in past tragedy
we have actually become still
filled with ill wills
our will is gone
we must sing resolution's song

but brutha strong and hero
are at each other's' throats
we choke on our own tension
friction
it causes smoke
we cannot breath
and I must leave
so that I may be at rest
a new quest
paved with blood
and the death of the pale king
drown him with the power of the sea king

I am seeking revenge

my clan's actions descend
I must continue forward
past the border of the past
understand it
ally with it
and use it to battle

RONIN POETZ : KO SI OLUWA

Act III: Take A Rite 2 Passage

I rattle like a snake
venom in my mouth
I shout a thousand curses
and worship my own anger

my father's lessons
and actions become fainter
I divide them by my emotions
and only come up with one remainder

so, as I sit here and weep
I must make a simple choice
do I battle with sword
or the wand
with cup
word
and voice?

Act III: Take A Rite 2 Passage

"SWORD VS. PEN"

I drop pen at my right foot
and sword at my left
and wonder which way I should step

which weapon do I leave at the door?
is the pen mightier than the sword?
life is even
but it's not fair
if the pale king and Tag take what's mine
I'll take what's theirs
cuz I'm the man who tamed the night mare
turned it into a day dream come true
true of voice, I am maa kheru

in dreams
in mind
in reality

I have the pale king after me
like I was butch cassidy
but I don't sun dance, kid
I dance with the sun
become selfish in some situations
and eclipse it
natures scales, I tip it
poetry verses I flip it
alphabet soup, I sip it
regurgitate my art to your plate
my words satiate
your knowledge I can inflate
but how do I comPENsate
when matters complicate
one weapon left at the door
I no longer hold pen in unskilled hand
I hold sword

my thoughts are so low
they're chained to the flo'
and flow

RONIN POETZ : KO SI OLUWA

Act III: Take A Rite 2 Passage

and flow
my actions
inspired by past action and hate
but wait!
fog makes my thoughts dissipate
my head is just in the clouds
ubiquitous in all time zones
except the here and now
and that is how I block the light from the sun

but the pen keeps running to my hands
it demands that I brand every paper
taper, dance, prance
let words become vapor
positive thought shaper
and remove negativity from present and future
the pen tells me to be calm
be like calm-a-sutra
pen in different positions when scriptin'
shiftin' gears
remove the tears and fears of those near you
make sure they can hear you
or at least read you
so they can be you
and you them
defend – seek revenge only with pen

bring soul to hell's kitchen
pick fights with disorder
damnation and affliction
and the rest of the pale king's children
these thoughts have me far past the border
and miles from redemption
under the veil of my clan
come the pale king and his henchmen
sweat and laughter breaks the tension
in my finger there's contraction
like an orgasm

Act III: Take A Rite 2 Passage

but

I left my weaPEN at the door
is it the sword that is mightier?
pen missing from its holster
but I hold sword as a reinforcer

pale king took what gave me life
but Ixu and Gira have Father Aquarius' soul
so, there is no wear
life is even
and the sword
can make it fair
but should I leave pen at the door?
have
just sword?
no pen and pamphlet
like hamlet, I stall
thoughts fall
the future is inertia

I must act
I take a breath

pen at my right foot
sword at my left
so, where do I step? – sword verse-us pen

I lean on crutch – cane again

*"my world can either be healed
or damned
at my whim… at – my – whim…"*

RONIN POETZ : KO SI OLUWA

Act III: Take A Rite 2 Passage

"INNER-COLLECTIVE ALLIES, PART II"

my eyes pan my clan
stands still
walking in circles
they argue about revolution

but two stand out
silent yet loud
against the commotion

number one:
sha-nun
shines with sun
dark complexion

so dark he gives
a cool, blue vibe
that dances
with the tide

his hair grows in strides
tied around his neck
decked and inset with jewels,
he manifests the finesse of a warrior
his hair striking chords with gold bands
his weapon is the cup
the fist, the hand

he comes from the west
lost angels, less of breath
but he is more, soars up
to direct the stars
this dark knight has traveled far
blessed with the copper era(h)
nickname 'kodojo'
we flow
flow
in conversation
I do my best to teach him
the four lessons

Act III: Take A Rite 2 Passage

he listens
as I stumble on my words

I say,
"like masons
we build on
the ancients
adjacent to what is in us
a pyramid
that starts with the first
and spreads back to us
then descends back up
when all are one."

next to sha-nun is rufus
he is words in physical form
adorned with precise pronunciation
an inundation
overflow of words that drip from pages
and spill over
      until you find
         them crawling
            onto your page
creeping out
his voice originates from the south
his job is to travel the pen & paper route
as he reverberates like a cloud
his voice rains
builds a shield around his body

>>pause<<

place a break in space
to split the monotony
his silence is even heard,
the weapon is the word
his thoughts be happy and nappy
these are exactly the people to help me
I take them aside
and we devise
a plan

RONIN POETZ : KO SI OLUWA

Act III: Take A Rite 2 Passage

in chant
jamaal
rufus
sha-nun
and I
become a new clan

four warriors
we
take
stance

RONIN POETZ : KO SI OLUWA

Act III: Take A Rite 2 Passage

"THE DIVIDE"

like an atom
we split
like a pair of lips
       – ready to speak
I become anxious
       – before we proceed
I believe I can't leave

my clan in disarray
as I stray away
questions surround me
like the thought police

I pray to seek an answer
in the manner of speaking,
kneeling
knees against the soil
I ask,

"father,
how can I remain loyal
and break away all together?"

and the clouds rain letters
they form words
tell me to pick who will lead the clan in my absence
I pick the warrior named D'win
I know I can trust him
I tell him,

"keep an eye on Mother Pisces,
and see that strong and hero stay calm."

he nods,
wishes us luck, and we disappear
to bring forth a new dawn

RONIN POETZ : KO SI OLUWA

Act III: Take A Rite 2 Passage

"FROM WORSHIPING LIPS"

fire had lost breath
and melted, exhausted
smoke lingered in great mass
seth's palace reduced to ash

I stand on the spot
where Father Aquarius
was slain
and I remain still
until I speak a prayer

but on this spot
the past is here
I step away
we continue
past seth's palace
beyond familiar boundaries

a place where stories and legends
tell of the pale king's influence
his confusion and plagues rage
he fills space with his presence

his own lessons
fill space
but empty
just
the
same

but in small circles
in whispers
people speak of saviors
not of us
but the pale king's traitors
camp raiders
burning star dust
until the air tastes the flavor
and behind the whispers

Act III: Take A Rite 2 Passage

spoken by careful speakers
cautious listeners
there are worshipers of our craft
worshipers of an outer collective mass
our black has attracted more than the sun

as we pace we come across
an outer collective
we are cautious
but they give us sanctuary

(despite our difference in colour)

we wonder if this is but a ruse
but they give us news
insight to pale king's loop
one track on his mind
he has tried to record our lines
our wisdom
our lessons, legacy
stolen in his heist
sold at a higher price
he has less than half

but he keeps us in his sights
he has his sights set on our clan
our minds' land in demand
and now that we have new command
pale king thinks he can negotiate
associate among us
he knows Father Aquarius
lies six feet under us
and as we are out here,
seeking revenge as justice,
his silk tongue tickles D'win's ear
his words as cool as winter
I fear D'win may become frostbitten

freezer burned and turned

but have we traveled too far out?

RONIN POETZ : KO SI OLUWA

Act III: Take A Rite 2 Passage

can we go back?
I wonder if we would be outnumbered
our clans' minds parallel to the pale king
assimilating in hopes of a truce
unaware of the noose
slowly placed around their necks

jamaal, rufus, and sha-nun volunteer to check
I contemplate our next move
I know pride is all I have to lose
revenge is still in my left hand
(some would say I ain't in my right mind)
but I know the next time I see Tag
he
dies

I tell the others to go back
keep their distance and listen
pay close attention to the situation

I will continue with my mission
when it comes to Tag
I'll handle him
…alone…

Act III: Take A Rite 2 Passage

"DUEL OF PROVIDENCE"

I can see him – standing against the wind

it swirls around his body
never touching

he stands apart from nature
but gazes up toward heaven,
as if he's actually going there

his prayer is a jumble of words
slurred – unintelligible curse
and what's worse
his verse is the song that brought me here

this clearing
this field
where smog and fog
eclipse proper thought

but thru the haze
I can see Tag clearly
long hair
glistening
like gold strings on a magical harp
his white visage
blemished with scars
covered with war paint
a mockery of indigenous saints
the original warriors of this stole-land
and set in Tag's head
black eyes that are burning with hate

they scrape my image

overcast, his pupils, gray clouds
shady
dismal
like unpolished gems

RONIN POETZ : KO SI OLUWA

Act III: Take A Rite 2 Passage

I raise my sword to him
he raises his weapon
a double-edged lance
Tag speaks before we dance

>>>plant lance in ground<<<

stand next to weapon
face marked with an upside-down frown

"I confess
gladly dressed
in a smile
I raped the queens of 1000 black cultures
I swarmed around like a vulture
captured them for labor
had them raise my children
who would only rape them and their children later
I savored on the breast, thighs, and leg
held them down to hear them beg
fed on their flesh
until culture rested in my veins

I claimed kingship thru fiendish acts
ripped black children from their culture's womb
so that I could get back
to what should have given birth to me

oh! did I reveal my own reality?
my dark tinge of jealousy?
jealous of the dark, indeed

you see I hate black
becuz I am not black
and I'll kill to be that
as well as make lies facts
to have the whole world
hate you as much as I do

and I have tricked you
your people:

Act III: Take A Rite 2 Passage

mothers against fathers against sisters against brothers
I've slithered between potential lovers
I've tricked you all to kill one another

I fixed every court trial
and drowned the whole world in denial
while my hands around your neck
choked you of your last breath
took your culture's wealth
and gave it to someone else
(if I could not rightfully own it myself)
and I have never. FELT. GUILT.

so, you better hold your sword firmly at its hilt

cuz I will cut you in half

and I don't care about your cultural beats
or your cultural rhythms
you, my next victim,
I will slay you like I did your father
a fool with a dream
his life wasted, spent
and
you!
        –MOCK kheru–
to me
you're
no
different."

I become hell bent on revenge
I attack in a flash
fierce – deadly – quickly

Tag parries!

he moves my sword aside
takes a stride forward
and swings!

RONIN POETZ : KO SI OLUWA

Act III: Take A Rite 2 Passage

bringing the edge of his lance up

– I duck –

his attack glides over me

I stand firmly

block an attack aimed at my back
and quickly shield my front
to block the brunt of another blow
I push his weapon away – sway
and throw flurries like snow

but he adapts and flows too smoothly
he moves me back
retracts his weapon
and attacks with both blade and feet

he forces me to retreat

withdraw – fall back
my mind is not intact
in its rightful place
I stall – silent

focusing too much on revenge
I cannot remember any of my culture's lessons
so, even with this sword in my hand
I have no real weapons to fight with

I am the ebb in this flow

Tag grows impatient
he initiates conflagration
thru fire, I take a step – skip – twirl – advance
my sword clashes with his lance
sparks explode
like warm air slamming against cold
thunder rolls
our bodies glow

Act III: Take A Rite 2 Passage

mine: black, bright like gold

his dull
grafted
and in the trillion-year skein of true scheming history
his muted aura is only 6000 years old
wrapped in oppression
and seven deadly confessions

the power of our battle
makes the earth split and spit flames
the soil becomes scorched
the wind howls, as earth is in pain

the land rises
our fight heightens
we duel like fates
Tag makes a fatal move
I block the attack
– but –
my sword shatters on impact

it
breaks

I drop the hilt
and just await
my fate…

Tag kicks me back,
the land risen
I drop off the edge
my hands grip the ledge

and

      I

            hang

Tag towers over me
as fire boils below me
my grip slipping slowly

RONIN POETZ : KO SI OLUWA

Act III: Take A Rite 2 Passage

– QUICKLY –

Tag turns and battles another
the earth rumbles a disastrous warzone
and I understand I'm no longer alone

Tag's clash
is with a better half
shadow casted figure
there is a shimmer of light
as hope is insight
my eyes fight to stay open
my strength struggles to focus
I hold onto the edge with all strength left
and I can hear Tag scream,
"my hand! my hand!
you bitch! you cut my hand!"
he screams and retreats

a gentle hand catches me
feminine
yet rough
and I mean, and I'm talkin'
tough enough to battle Tag

she lifts me up
my savior
together we were once both the original creators
our spirits populated 57,280,000 miles
her description is burnished brass
like Christ from The Bible

sun dressed
she is both rah and oshun's moon blessed
no, it's not a shadow
it is her dark, rich, beautiful, cosmic-colored flesh
exhausted
I hold onto her
lose breath
and ultimately

Act III: Take A Rite 2 Passage

consciousness

saved by this mysterious black goddess
this black warrior — *still seeking revenge* —
for now

I can rest

RONIN POETZ : KO SI OLUWA

Act IV: Tide Turner

"SENTIENT SENTIMENT"

I awake with the sun in my face
rather, a representation of it
in feminine form
in my eyes, she like the sky
covers me
comfortably, angelically
this woman, my savior,
a canopy that shields me from danger
           – calms my anger
I am the world below her
like geb and nut without the separation
instead, we have a rah union
blooming in each other's sight

…at least *I'm* smiling…

darker than earth tone flesh
dressed in a green
warrior's gown
her hair a spherical crown
around her waist a yellow belt
a sword at her side
the wind gently rides under her

I rest on a bed in a red room
I thank her for saving me
my words barely audible
she smiles
I tell her my name is maa kheru
true of voice,
voice of truth

but she tells me I am destiny
last son of the ones they call Father Aquarius
and Mother Pisces
bruthaz be strong and hero
our clan the multiple zero
in pale king's equation

Act IV: Tide Turner

destined to reduce the pale king to nothing

I tell her,
"Father Aquarius has died
Mother Pisces' mind is paralyzed
as my clan lies set on assimilating
with the pale king
a dangerous decision
the pale king's vision
is to police our thoughts,
control them
his plan is not one of freedom."

the woman says,
"my name is Dess,
half of god
but no less
I am the daughter
of the queen haj-va-rah
the descendant of the two that is All
I am daughter of the queen mother
the earth respects her hour
as I am heir to her power
I am the cosmic courier,
feminine warrior
when ideals fall too far right
we defend what's left
and your grief I have felt
I know my mother will provide you help."

"where am I?"

"you are in the kammasi kingdom
we prepare for revolution

we have attacked the pale king
from the other side of this war
we battle under auset
matriarch, descendant
it is the queen that is chosen

RONIN POETZ : KO SI OLUWA

Act IV: Tide Turner

and the daughter that receives the inheritance

the king is the general of the army
protectors of the garden we cultivate
we have culture to satiate, feed you knowledge
words of wisdom that even you could learn from
with all your lessons, beautiful sun."

my lips move slowly,
floating,
like in a dream,

"I must see the queen."

RONIN POETZ : KO SI OLUWA

Act IV: Tide Turner

"IN PRESENCE"

haj-va-rah
queen of gods
adorned with light
born from night
her spirit's height extends to the heavens
she rests in an ivory chair
wears a diadem of locked hair
cloaked in a gown the colour of the sky
she sits beside the king
his hair shaven,
he is dressed in gold armor
he holds a sword in his right hand
his left hand empty
windstaff strapped to the back of his onyx throne

power honed thru words
magic conjured from queen's and king's lips
they kiss the air every time they speak
and as I reach their throne
I bow at their feet

it is them
descendants
genesis to revelations
and all books in between

numbers
psalms
acts
samuel ii
ezekiel
isaiah
jeremiah
amos

the king tosses his sword
it lands before me
the queen stands and asks, "what brings you to our land?"

Act IV: Tide Turner

"I AM THE HERO"

I recount the stories
the losses
the glory
the future concern
the worries
I recount our adventures in wide areas
the death of Father Aquarius
the death of the Ele Ote
his redemption

I tell them my clan is in disarray
I tell them we have come at a cross
the end of days
and then I let my words dance
I tell them who I am

maa kheru
true of voice
voice of truth

it's cryptic
but I speak:

"my queen, my king
I am the hero you seek

the page with the proverb
written in cosmic ink

I am the knight of pens
your daughter was destined to meet

I am blessed with the spell
slipped from my lips
to plant upon the queen
and wake her from her sleep
revive her in the rays of her son
in law, I am the sun that guides you

Act IV: Tide Turner

by light and prophetic dreams
who makes love to your moon-daughter singer
I am the magic and air between your fingers
I am the warrior ready to protect you when you are in need
the clean and holy water you drink from the life stream
I am the tears of joy that you weep

I am the mystical chant that you must speak
the wish/prayer/secret you need to keep
I am the wheel of fortune
and I stand at the peak of the pyramids
that africans built in 3840 (plus) genius weeks

I am that seventh wonder that still holds you hypnotized
constructed when the dawn first opened its eyes,
but now those eyes cry
its chosen people have lost the feast
the fruit of knowledge
Ixu and Gira *truthfully* allowed them to eat
so please, do not worry

I am that hero you seek

I am the strength that lies inside you
the temperance and force that binds you
I am the world at your feet
the love between the couple you greet
the joy in the dancers who sing to the beat
I am the flow in the breeze and air
the last of those who care
the armor you wear
the cross that you bear
the warning visions and enchantments
that surfaces from the deep

I am the star that lights the path
to the sentry that will grant you entry
and give you the weapon of the staff
to battle the man with more than half the answers
I am the man who grips love in his hands

RONIN POETZ : KO SI OLUWA

Act IV: Tide Turner

the one who will save the land
and let the flowers grow from the ground
– pulled up from all the way down –

I am the thief who steals the puzzle of war
and leaves you with just a peace
my queen
my king

I am the hero you seek."

Act IV: Tide Turner

"THEY CEREMONY"

with gold plates
and silver utensils
roast lamb meat
adorned with
chicken grease,
broccoli rice and shrimp
dressing
sprinkled with seasoned salt
cut corn, candied yams
cranberry fruit sauce
a li'l sunbeam seasoning the gravy
wavy crescent rolls and breadsticks
pumpkin and apple pie
sweet potato on the side
white cake with sweet frost
chalices filled with stardust and nearest

we begin a feast of queens and kings

in this bright place
we got boom bands playing
the queen praising peace
while during the feast
her daughter dess
teaches me to eat properly
because the warrior in me
got a monopoly
I be rugged scoundrel
I tell her,

"I'm not always like this
it's just that life's whip
has scratched my back,
revenge has taken me back
trapped in savage emotions
and my thoughts are on my clan
hoping ancestor spirits
and my prayers

RONIN POETZ: KO SI OLUWA

Act IV: Tide Turner

watch over them."

dess takes my hand
guides me from my seat
and leads me into a dance
slow
eyes closed
we grow into one another
she asks me who I am
and I tell her,

"son to father and mother
brother to hero and strong
enemy to my enemies.
who am I to you?"

"maa kheru," she answers. "that is truth."

I slip from her arms
creep from the room
and wander into the dark

night dawned

my thoughts rise into the sky
they hold a conversation with the stars
none can find Aquarius
Pisces has become dim
no sword in my hand
I ask,

"how can I find revenge?"

"first, come to your senses,"
I heard dess speak behind me
"revenge is not what you seek.
it is love and peace;
you are love and I am your peace.
our signs are a match."

Act IV: Tide Turner

"ANCESTRAL SYMMETRY"

she said our signs were a match
so, I struck a conversation
but her feminine inspiration
swirled into the heavens
she discussed our future in council
she told the stars she would change the ways
of this rugged scoundrel

she told me,
"in order to open your book
I have to break the seal to your heart."

that's where the heavens told her to start
she told me my life was art and that it was priceless
she said,

"any earthly crisis
could be deflected
by all astronomical devices
          – your Father Aquarius
          – your Mother Pisces."

she my wife,
the form of isis
it was her mystical form
that told me to write this
yes, dess existed as inspiration
she was my interest when she had no form
but still the brightest

and her star gave me direction
when there was no map, guidance or tactic
and now I vow to hold her up
because she is my world
and I am atlas

her smile clean and phat
and I spell that with a 'ph'

RONIN POETZ : KO SI OLUWA

Act IV: Tide Turner

because she brings balance to my life
and to the 'ph' I add a 'd'
for the 360 d-grees I rotate around her
she may be this kingdom's daughter,
but I revolve around her
because she is the sun

intellectually bright
her soul? nurturing
and her body? hot
I scorch my tongue
when I kiss her sunspot
taste her nubian juice
trained as love's new recruit

inside her mahogany pyramid-temple
my words will recycle
thru 800,000,000
potential innocent children
who grow from her as disciples
climax in a big bang and BOOM!
create room in our universe of infinite stars, planets, and moons
grown in her womb

our children,
gods and goddesses
of every heavenly body
invited at birth
united by verse
you-n-I verse
anything that wishes our children harm

that's what we are together
what are you separate?

Act IV: Tide Turner

"WHO I AM"

she smiled
and spoke
her voice
a deep melody

"I am genesis
the genes-of-isis
I preceded all chronometrical devices
because I am the beginning of time
the first tick and tock of the cosmos' mind

so, do you know who I am?

I am a black woman,
african
it was me who stood first in the first land
when I cried
my tears divided
and created man

molded from the sands
I am from the earth
my breast leaked love first
then mixed with milk, honey and tears
and became the foundation of the first church

the black man drank my words
called them scripture that I delivered as pslams
and quenched him of his thirst

I sang in sync
with nature's beat
and created language
that you still speak
in your verse

my body produces gold, silver,
diamonds, and a pearl you call life

RONIN POETZ : KO SI OLUWA

Act IV: Tide Turner

I am morning and night
it was thru my power and reason
that nature split into four seasons
I was worshipped, revered,
and idolized by individuals, families, and nations
I am the mother of civilization

I have been queen
goddess
diplomat
scientist
icon
scholar
prophet
and freedom fighter

I held jesus in my arms
when his name was heru
I tell you I am nefertari
'wife of amen'
'the beautiful companion'
I defied death,
resurrected as queen istnofret
defying death, I was deified in life
defended my people from strife

I was makeda, they called sheba
dahia al-kahina, defender of freedom
pushed barbarians away from my kingdom
burned my land in resistance
and Ixu-Gira forgive my decision
when I chose to spare my children,
my babies
so that they could escape slavery
their bodies dying
but their spirits rising towards heaven

I have been lynched, burned, beaten, branded
left stranded on a land I was forced to re-mold
I was sold like cattle

Act IV: Tide Turner

battled a war on the inside as well as out

my image has been abused
but my spirit has refused defeat
my rope to the cosmos is no noose
it is the voice I use to sing
I can bring you to your knees
when I chant the blues

I've even taught you
          – maa kheru –
a thing or two
thru your mother's voice

every time I speak, I sing
I harmonize nature with my voice
and you have no choice but to love me again
african-black woman,
I'm beyond super-human

my beauty eclipses the sun's rays
has immortals dying young and kings enslaved
and all the gods bow towards me for praise
I am the 21-year reign of hatshepsut
I am the tiye that binds
I am love's 3rd eye
'fiery eye of rah'
the warrior-queen nzingha

so who are you,
maa kheru
(besides truth)?"

I answer,

"black knight to black queen
I am your check-mate, maa kheru
the fight to secure your image
is the war I fight for you."

RONIN POETZ : KO SI OLUWA

Act IV: Tide Turner

"WIND & EARTH"

the taste of revenge dissolves
dess' kiss sweetens my lips
and I fall to my knees,
I hug her waist
and kiss her on the space
where new life breathes
her dress lifts by a magical breeze
and my lips are free to kiss her entire body
my clothes are shed,
like skins and past labors

our bodies rub against one another
smooth, cottony, like two clouds
gliding and becoming one
without friction
and we are sipping,
lightly tickling with kiss
and finger tips

we drip soul onto each other's bodies
and we love in waves
crashing onto each other's shores
and my sword is no longer a weapon
but a tool for affection
standing straight, erection
as she keeps pressing up against it
with lips and hips

and I hold onto her
because she is all I've got
here in the spotlight of the moon
nature watching
the great voyeur
the grass growing beneath my back,
and beneath hers
as we merge
our hearts can be heard
beating, increasing

Act IV: Tide Turner

speaking in words of another language

she releases me from anguish
gives me the world
as I dive to retrieve her pearl
my seeds swirl deep in her earth

she and I become W.E.
and we split,
switch positions
her the Wind
I the Earth's harp
and she blows,
plays licks on my strings
and together we flow

time takes a minute for itself
as dess and I grow into each other's bodies
my back arched
howling at the moon,
myself deep in dess' tomb
where life is buried
her heart tugging on my heart
I part with my soul
and throw it into her, the center

my holy ghost floats
I dangle from a metaphysical rope
connecting me to my physical body
I fill dess' space
and feel her body quake
pour lakes that inundate destiny and fate
I can now trace the footsteps and paths
our children will walk in

dess is talking in quick breaths
and my body rolls like thunder over her
my spirit leaps back into the physical plane
my energy in her, her energy in me
and we are still drained

RONIN POETZ : KO SI OLUWA

Act IV: Tide Turner

we remain chained to each other's frame
without friction
but we still have a flame

here as we go
gone as we came

Act IV: Tide Turner

"KHERU'S EYE"

the sun's eye
peeks over
the horizon

dess glides on the wind
and takes her place
at the window
she says,
"let us show the sun
how we glow when we mold."

and I crawl on my hands and soul
so low, I divide, liquefy and flow
my body drips and pours
I become a tide on the floor
my crawl is a wave
and I solidify
to embrace and taste her space

our bodies in nep-tuned with one another
I put my tongue on her venus
and eclipse mars

every star wishing they were our son

her breath pounds the air like a drum
her heavenly body jumps
my tongue shapes poems dedicated to her
private poetry – private perversions – sexual immersion

just between her and me
something only she can read
and the sun can relate
dess' breath breaks

jazz is played
as she presses her lips
against my instrument

Act IV: Tide Turner

and I quiver,
shiver
from warmth

we become adorned
with each other's body
she faces the sun
and I run kisses down her spine
back up to her neck
inhale her breath

she kisses a cross on my back
on my stomach
in my lap
and my hands twist her naps
until she is locked
in that spot called 'there'
her hair now a flare

up in the sky,
the sun's eye is fully aware
the two of us bare our souls
and wish the sun can grow from us
with daughters, like water
to flow
to flow
to flow

Act IV: Tide Turner

"ARMING THE HERU"

it started physically
placed on my body
was a black cloak
soaked in earth's oil
anointed by the sky's soil

haj-va-rah sprinkled royal stardust
that locked up and dried

divided into matter
turned into silver and gold
as the wind roared
and formed a sword on the floor

then came spring,
summer, fall, and winter
the seasons came together
formed letters
blended every raging weather element
swirling until it became vapor
nature reversing time
scattering into paper
with words scribed by a metaphysical-ink particle
forming the articles that are this kingdom's lessons

now my mind's weapon

a chorus of prayers/chants
made my soul dance,
cool as the autumn breeze
flowing like the sea
mind, spirit, and body
all as one – no longer at a divide
I will return to my clan, revived
warrior-queen at my side

Act V: The Journey Up

"2 MY CLAN"

as we step
we blend
transparent
there is emergence
on time's current
we skip
and dance
our forms so blurred
we are hip-notic

we leave nature in a trance

sending messages
across great distances
I contact jamaal
sha-nun
and rufus
our minds linked
sinking into a silent,
and invisible conversation

I ask
in a telepathic breath
"what's happened since I've left?"

I learn from them
Mother Pisces is still unconscious
brother hero and strong
meditate inside the vibe of language
sitting atop a word
humming supreme mathematics
counting the days
when they can plan a raid
teamed with the sun's rays
against the pale king's haze

they plan in ways
and search for allies
with powers and vibes

Act V: The Journey Up

to save our clan, our tribe
our ancient
spiritual pride

our eyes can see the final hour
when spirits shower on us
we will bathe in yesterday's presence
our past lessons secured in the future
this is our time to act – attack

it's dangerous
that d'win controls our secrets
but he hasn't spoken them yet
we must cut him from his breath
our less-Sons and Daughters must be protected
and become more than the warriors this world has made us
d'win has become injustice

"no.
we will strike where the problem lies
we will summon allies
from our collective and others
their lives their tithe

jamaal
sha-nun
rufus
when next we attack,
the pale king dies."

RONIN POETZ : KO SI OLUWA

Act V: The Journey Up

"WE SUMMON"

we journey
to the word
drums pounding
calling us

we look up
at the bass
we see space
cosmo canyon
rising into heaven

drums summon
our presence
we don't climb — we rise

and as our eyes
come in focus
we see a band
of rebel poets

cousins in our struggle
led by a man named murio
warrior of pen and fist
descendant of the righteous
heirs to the land we fight in

we have not been
the only ones summoned
rebel poets
come from
the black foundational
indigenous temple
their words plural

our words pumping
thundering with the drum

we ra unite
strong and hero

Act V: The Journey Up

Mother Pisces,
she laying still

>>and we summon<<

we summon our spirits
summoned from the heavens
our bodies ascend
blend into the night

up into the sky
out into space
we trace
astronomical movements

we open our mouths
and inhale space
our lips laced with the sun

around us
the stars gather
become a mass of energetic matter
building as we float
filling our throats

we are soaring
heaven's bodies roaring
surrounded
by a violet aura

I put the fury
of zach de la rocha's voice on my spine
to hold me up
tom morello's sonic sound
tim bob's bass pounds
and my heart becomes wilk's kick drum

our natural elements begin rockin' with rakim
so naturally we become mic-RAH-phone fiendz
as we rage against this machine

RONIN POETZ : KO SI OLUWA

Act V: The Journey Up

we have the current of cain
and the blood of able
the knights of the periodic table
we matter
let this dragon's 10 horns shatter
stop it from blowing off key notes
rumbling fire in its throat
let us descend to battle him
and all his demonic inharmonic children
with our own beautiful hymns
poetry rumbling the word
in phat verses made up of lines so thin
between righteousness and their sins

so, we descend
our spirits,
our powers
summoned

bald heads
imbibe the sun
locks become
electric strands
weapons in hand,
and in mind
we have found
our time

and with this word,
we must stand firm – and attack

Act V: The Journey Up

"FROM THE WORD"

nature is not right
dess has left
fled into the night

it is now morning
the sun giving us warning
the biting aura of war swarming
our powers warming our bodies

we don't ceremony
we don't dance
we are 5% of our clan

our shadow lightened
and our syllables muted
our words banned
clan disbanded
our music silenced – no guidance
no rhythm or sound from band
atop this syllabic stage
surrounded by thought police
led by Tag
coupled with d'win
and cold stares from our clan

Tag's voice ascends,
"you can be pardoned
for your sins
your crimes can be forgotten.

we have come for your assistance
to help the pale king
put down another clan's resistance
the 36 staten fiendz.

your reward
freedom
and between us, peace

RONIN POETZ : KO SI OLUWA

Act V: The Journey Up

we can even release
Mother Pisces from sleep."

I stare into Tag's eyes
hoping he would cry what I feel
but he has no emotions
what little soul he has
keeps groping my thoughts
he captures them

but I feel the breeze
the cool, the wind
and I whisper,
"we'll handle him."

brother strong and hero at my side
the only ally is jamaal

rufus,
sha-nun,
they split,
leading a small group
ready for action — the rebel poet faction
ready at arms

I see dust on the horizon

I speak clearly to Tag,
"you just don't know
where you've walked
you've talked so long
your own song
out of tune
has become a smooth
and looped melody

so let me explain it to you
in your own loop
and in ours
you have been caught
and…

Act V: The Journey Up

you just don't know
where you've walked."

Tag asks, haughty smile locked intact,
"and where is that?"

"you
and your thought police
have just walked into a trap."

the dust becomes soldiers
pouring onto the land
dess out in front
her father's army at her command

murio and his rebel poets
flow with the east wind
they descend on the thought police
descend deep
their spirits awakened from sleep
tossing off passive shackles
it is now time for action and battle

our clan, once seduced
have been lifted from the ruse
the offbeat loop
of the pale king's false dream
battle cries and screams
they tear at the thought police's seams

Tag's massive army on the defense
d'win drops to his knees to repent
brothers, ally, and I
glide thru shadows
and strike from the heart of the word
the first of four lessons
the word, the most powerful of weapons
loud enough to silence wars
tied to Ixu-Gira by vocal c(h)ords
formed with our soul
and tempering an ancestral sword

RONIN POETZ : KO SI OLUWA

Act V: The Journey Up

the battle parts in two

Tag screams,
"you will die!"

"I will not die on your time
but on my terms
and I'll return
resurrected by lessons learned
to battle you."

Tag comes into view,
"don't think
your queen
will escape fate
she will be raped by my hands
much like this land
I'll shatter everyone of your crystal thoughts
back into sand

and I'll burn your spirit
your soul,
your holy ghost
wrap them up on my page
as if they were the words I wrote
the verses I spoke
I'll place your soul to my lips
so that the ashes can be smoked."

"you'd choke,
inhaling me
the poet-tency
of my poetry
cuz the only thing I smoke,
is competition
with the words written in my lessons and compositions
it's like these griots
tearing thru your opposition

I warn you now to use your intuition

Act V: The Journey Up

cuz you know it would be foolish
to go thru with this
up against the rudest
crudest
ruthless
hectic
voudon-hoodoo-kemetic knights
whose methods are so powerful
they gave birth to
and killed your whole style
then resurrected it

like jesus of nazareth did lazarus
like the sun said to the fool
before he stepped from the cliff
and took his last breath,
'your folly is most curious,
have you no fear of death?'

cuz even while your style
starved for knowledge
I fed it
cursed the air
where your words were birthed
and then blessed it
with my own,
voice in perfect tone
(to heal the wretched)
while I covered up your crimes
and in the same rhyme and line
made you confess to it
burned you at the stake
like a jesuit heretic
and that's the real trick
now isn't?
so get back, Tag
my words are sick
you may catch the pro-verb-I-all flu
but I'm not worried about that
cuz I'm as far beyond knowledge and time
as knowledge and time are beyond you."

RONIN POETZ : KO SI OLUWA

Act V: The Journey Up

we are back in dance
battling
like the battle of the in-town chant
Tag defends
with the double-edged, sharp lance

brothers, ally, and I
swinging windstaffs,
swordz,
and battle cries

weapons fly,
flash, clash
voices crash
guns clap
earth's field
is battle mass

I take a step
skip, twirl
my sword cuts
and slash
Tag's lance
splits in half

brothers hero and strong
take my place
slashing at Tag
he defends
with lance in either hand

Tag grumbles and growls,
"I take what I can
when I can."

"then,
you'll
be taken to task!"

I attack – thrusting

Act V: The Journey Up

the blow is blocked,
I'm tossed away
I jump to my feet
and slay two thought police

I watch
jamaal and Tag
they battle
the earth rumbles
and rattles, it screams

the ground is bleeding
blood distorts natural colour
clusters of bodies piled to heaven

and this is hell on earth

whether jail or church
I must pray
my mother's and father's spirits
cover our swords' blades
faith is restored
shimmering in my mind, body, soul
and on my sword

I am the reflection of this glow
I calm my thoughts,
let them grow
from the lessons I've learned
it heals the scars I've earned

I am clear as air
clean as can be
while spirits
shower and drip over me

brothers strong and hero
jump back to Tag
each thrust and blow
sword swing and flow

RONIN POETZ : KO SI OLUWA

Act V: The Journey Up

push Tag back

Tag makes fatal move
and a sword is thrust thru
both his shoulders

Tag drops his weapons
his blood flowing
dripping into his hands
with his breath few
he speaks,
"my body will dissolve
eaten by the earth
but I will birth new hatred
my presence
my spirit
will never die."

my sword tears thru Tag's heart

"that will be for my future children to decide."

the bodies of the thought police
glow
melt like snow
and disappear

out there,
the pale king
sits scared

and he should be
because we will come
for him
next

each and every breath
is now a countdown
to certain and sudden death

RONIN POETZ: KO SI OLUWA

Act V: The Journey Up

"WE CELEBRATE"

past the gates
of haj-va-rah's palace
we celebrate and croon
praise the First Two

we rah unite with clan
d'win repents,
his hands together
we console him
with spirit and rhythm

he knows forgiveness will come
from the journey of his own spirit

I introduce dess
to the rest of my clan
close friends and allies
we vibe on the songs
from brother strong
as he anoints the mic

we dance
surrounded by night
cousins to stars
called fireflies
we cry in each other's arms

Mother Pisces
can now see
she awakened
by our Aquarian father

his spirit hollers loud
that he has never been
prouder of his sons

we have become
the image of our parents
and it will never be shattered

RONIN POETZ : KO SI OLUWA

Act V: The Journey Up

our feet
skitter
scatter
dancing
on the floor
we celebrate
our days
our nights
our forever

all in a future past this war

Act V: The Journey Up

"SEPARATED BY BIRTH"

sweetly
dess speaks

she tells me
that she lays down
her sword
because inside her
is our life

I tell her
that I must descend
leave
become a legend
and return to her
as a true black man
and as life's father

"out there,
the pale king trembles
counting plural days
down to single

and he is all that remains
for us to change our present
secure our future
and innerstand our past

our paths will cross and clash
but I will return back to this spot

I will not die

I will live beyond and far
past the age of stars
that our eyes
have just focused on

in absence
I will be a legend

RONIN POETZ : KO SI OLUWA

Act V: The Journey Up

just a word spoken
by your lips
just half of a kiss

but I will return…"

Act V: The Journey Up

"THE LAST STANZA"

this is how I became a legend

I see thru a single 'I'
master poet samurai
descendant of the khemi
servant to the clan Gemini
led by an Aquarian resolution
and the tears Pisces cried

with strong and hero,
my pen/sword against paper glide
rufus and sha-nun my only guides
with jamaal at my side

unfortunately made ronin
when the stars against me aligned
Cancer infected Aquarius
and put out the constellation's light
words dripped onto paper from my eyes bright

now I wander the countryside
pen/sword as my only way to survive
disenfranchised griot-samurai
wandering against my will
working odd jobs with my skills
hired to kill
take down others' competition for a simple meal
and a little money to carry me to the next deal

I upped my fees
when my reputation spread like a disease
and wildfire

I was feared, envied, and admired

my name a second language in people's mouths
and in their breath my name found a home
but I still roam
I step into kingdoms like the nameless gun-toting mariachi

RONIN POETZ : KO SI OLUWA

Act V: The Journey Up

with weapons in my pack
containing more power than what destroyed nagasaki
equipped with the knowledge of five scrolls
scribed by the ronin samurai miyamoto musashi

my style cannot be copied or imitated
my enemies become intimidated
as my eyes change colours with my mood
like the leaves change colours with the seasons
the ink in my pen the same way

emotions up
I can't fail
shadow covers my face
like the minister's black veil
lights dim just for me
like the mysterious hero
in an ancient tale

and I keep my mind clear of smoke
against my enemies it's murder I wrote
cuz their think tank is broke and leaking
my words are heat seeking grooves
the strength of a thousand heroes in one syllable
and the power of a thousand stampeding
shires' hooves – the might of Ogun

my next move is to the stage
my enemies' next move is to the grave
when my words rush and drown them in a flood
their pride bruised without ointment to rub

my competition doesn't understand
            – a certain samurai proverb
            – which is stated as such:
            "in order for a samurai to be the most brave
            they must have at least a drop of african blood"

and my heritage inundates onto the page
enemies get burned with only one heated gaze
            – instantly slayed –

RONIN POETZ : KO SI OLUWA

Act V: The Journey Up

when my power overflows like the nile
I drop my pen and defeat my enemies freestyle

a legend born at the road's end
but again I begin
I paved a new road less traveled
my backpack contains all the artifacts
from the tower of babel
once again, the pen I grapple
setup a secret poetry chapel

I become a rhythm on the run
and a beat hard to catch
my pen cuts me loose from my enemies' nets
the pale king finds me a threat

he wants to make me his next victim

makin' it hard for me to go near any civilized system
but a challenge like that I only make it my mission
to send my adversaries six-feet deep
and their families with them
they die knee deep
in the poor rhetoric of their own children
          – from my pen

that's my lyrical flow
the path of the griot-warrior
          – the way I go
formed by dioxirhybo - nucleic acid trip
I throw an infinite amount of sharp lines
and throwing stars
in the shape of parentheses and brackets
my style you can't trap it – track it
if you shout a threat then back it

my name whispered all at once
causes ruckuses and rackets
I attack in the active and the passive
make 135 lbs seem massive

RONIN POETZ : KO SI OLUWA

Act V: The Journey Up

the strength of my words
can't even be calculated in scientific notation
I'm lookin' for whoever's next
in this false magistrate's rotation

take down the pale king's nation
          – my invasion
no trade on my vocation
it's got me jailed without probation
with my poems and slogans
coupled with the voice I sing
this poet ronin is out to slay the pale king

that evil man
who tried to hire me
to take out the 36-staten clan
and their highest officials
and steal their manuals
that reveals the secret
of their intellectual, lyrical rituals

instead,
the staten clan and I
planned to take the pale king's head
and the 14 scrolls and 10 manuals
hidden underneath his bed

up north I fled
with a ticket to visit the empire nation
and temple done anew
with the artistic view
the griot, outer-collective ally, kung fu
over 1000 styles
none outdone by a number even close to few

and so I recruit the four samurai
with the attitudes that'll wreckya
deckya,
lyrically – but seriously –

if the pale king really wanted a test

Act V: The Journey Up

we'd have to bring it to him physically

maniacally like #1, the protector
instru–mentally like #2, the emancipator
(don't mess with him
he wears a red dragon diadem
under shaolin discipline)
just as dangerously as #3, the judge
aka: the educator, the g-laser,
shock you like a taser
or #4, wahr,
lyrically set for stun
like an electron phaser

like david or akenenaten's psalms
comin' down upon the pale king
with more wrath than khan
with prophetic revelations deeper than john

this crew is too bad to be known as heroes
too good to be known as criminals
verse mercenaries – my adversaries' adversaries
on the average, this crew is mean
professional like golgo 13
armed with liquid swordz, lightsabers,
windstaffs and fatal flying guillotines
plus we were teamed with the 36 staten fiends

the pale king fired his unholy magical beams
we counterattacked with a balance
and phoenix-downed our inner talents
stormed the castle
and easily cut thru the pale king's crew
hittin' the competition so quick and fast
it looked like we had more arms than vishnu

lit them up with the power of the god ramuh
and the original trinity of kemet
ausar, heru, and auset
they were hit by our 47th fleet
no time to retreat – accept defeat

RONIN POETZ : KO SI OLUWA

Act V: The Journey Up

they had no chance
except the chants to their false god

but his head lay in my left hand
and in my right, his weapon, the wand
down were the walls
of this pale king's facade
shattered by this holy-griot mob
(with recovered manuals and scrolls)

afterwards,
we split into our respected crews
36 statens, four samurai
and I

one ronin who keeps roamin'
without master to serve and be indentured
forced to the road
and wander
in search of an all new adventure

Act V: The Journey Up

"JOURNEY CONTINUED"

I return to dess' arms
her body four months
filled with life
I recount how the pale king's strife
ended

we blend and merge
into a circle of friends
families and allies
and I pray

"father,
triple eye
guide my tribe
under the divide of day
play the night's song
as the moon rises in the sky
nature's nocturnal vibe
it cries the sun's light

we are the first children of the sun
we are the melanin drops
      – that fade into the night
      – and absorb the day
every ray of the sun is dedicated to us
we are focused on our scribe religion
to give this rough-cut world
a new revision

our mission,
to marry nature
and dance
to her beat
sacrifice every tree
burn in magical vapors
make paper to scribe spells
and savor our creative labor
magical minute record breakers
span past time's barriers

RONIN POETZ: KO SI OLUWA

Act V: The Journey Up

message carriers
to children unseen
our seeds
from Mother Earth
birth a future generation
where our scribbled-scrabbled words
will be deciphered for their imaginations."

so, let the sun rise high
as we all ra unite
for inner and outer collective
allies alike

(peace)

TO ENLIGHTEN THE G.O.D.Z

⊤O ENLIGHTEN THE G.⊖.⅁.Z.

<u>Act 1: Singing In Haunted Scales</u>

"THIS CHILD'S EYES"

folding over on itself
the spirit whispers
it breathes feathers and soars on words
it becomes 'I'
and I see as I fall to Earth

I-am-that-I-am:
"be calm…stay calm"

anointed by name
by emotion just the same
I scream whispers of war
as I fall [(a)part from the whole]
…peace-by-peace…

I-am-that-will-be:
"I am calm"

together we speak
spirit – mind – body
three as one
unified voices in soliloquy
my 'self' as he holy trinity

Kahm:
"I am kahm noiz – *black zion*
but my name destroyed
I inhale stars, suns, comets, and planets
storing my body with space
just to fill the void

to reclaim my name
I fly astral planes
board my thoughts on conscious trains

and while flying thru heir
drying on land
to liquefy in the sky
my soul dripped down

TO ENLIGHTEN THE G.O.D.Z.

Act 1: Singing In Haunted Scales

to occupy a newborn child's eyes

and it was this child's eyes
that constantly cry in the future
this child's eyes,
set in his beautiful black face
that cries foul memories
of this present place
where he as "I"
     (became)
  my
      heavenly body
a project for these snakes

dissected star-by-star
segregating space,
injecting their image into my mind
until it was a blank slate

ghosts fought to erase the colour my soul glows
cut the spiral way my hair grows
curved and waved like DNA
AND nailed me to a burning cross called 'yesterday'

   tied me down with rusted chains
stabbed me with an ersatz name
   said all that remained
of my history
   was a bloodstain
made me take the lord's name in vein

thru a syringe

my body trembles
and I cringe
every time they tell me
a holy ghost died for the sins they still commit
their words – their image
rest on my tongue's tip

my body trembles, and my mind ripples

TO ENLIGHTEN THE G.O.D.Z.

Act 1: Singing In Haunted Scales

hallucino-genetic fits
blasted with 41 shots of jim crow hits
by law – segregated
my ancestors fall from my lips

I can no longer speak for them

I am a 400 year pause
swirling in the whirlwind
of historic grandfather clause
hit 19 times by law – body raked
ghosts surround me with white hoods and capes
while I lay on a burning table shaped as a cross
and told I'm worthless
but my soul closely inspected
(for purchase)
I am souled at cost
(you couldn't get less of a price for me)
tied down
my soul is not free
they know I am priceless
a crisis for them
this constellation
under
       goes
experimentation
sedated with religion
for star-sterilization
to never give birth to a sun
injected with the mentality of mars
to see how far I can fall

"<u>you're ours now</u>," they call

blank as space.
in this child's eyes
my ancestors melt away
with. out. a. trace…

TO ENLIGHTEN THE G.O.D.Z.

Act 1: Singing In Haunted Scales

"WHO IN WITH ME"

I lie in a pile of lies
searching for an ally
with a thought
that can slip thru their cracks

I ask, "who in with me, serving time?
trying to throw their heart to the sky
so that it can pump light and resurrect sunshine?

who here with me
tries to bend flat lines
to ripple life?
bend a knee to sunset
to become a knight?
who here with me
searches for their own astrological birthright?

who here with me
holds their creativity
– the ancient language of energy –
with a mass of their own gravity
on this celestial stage
to become a starlight?"

but the might of my voice just
        e   h   o   e   s
syllables billow
trickle and drip drop
in air clots that no one inhales

but I leave a trail of dictation
back to my lips
hanging from my tongue's tip
hoping my words will switch perception
or let another nurture the light
found inside their own heart

… then … from the dark
from the emptiness of that sterile cell

TO ENLIGHTEN THE G.O.D.Z.

Act 1: Singing In Haunted Scales

crept a whisper
limping
and
dragging
      body
it.self.
his hands mimicked his lips
signing to speak for help
the air rippled and time wrinkled
as his breath condensed into smoke signals

his hair, blacker than black itself
Ixu and Gira kept the naps in place
young, but weariness masked his face
his flesh, dipped in rum, touched by the sun

I ask in a single breath, "where do you come from?"

and he answered, breathing rapidly
syllables escaping his tongue like slaves on the run

Ally:
"I am the reverberation of our ancestors' drums
my heart pumps time in the form of millenniums
I am the age of an age
time flows thru me. my name? Water Persun
our ancestors, known as Immortals, defended lands and kingdoms
their spirits still filters over I and you
they glow thru our hue."

his hand trembled, held out to me
searching for freedom while suffering slavery
physically resigned to here
spiritually we were eager to be free

so, our hands in union became a secret movement
like the waves of time on a current
our ancestors' alliance in resurgence
we speak in code
new words to mold
spells

TO ENLIGHTEN THE G.O.D.Z.

Act 1: Singing In Haunted Scales

to reclaim the 's' in our soul

we call it 'spiritual language'
used for a greater aim
we abbreviate and call it s'lang'

knowwhati'msayin'?

pardon me for prayin' on my own space station-airy
standing still on paper, my words are heavyweight
but light to levitate thru space
heavy? wait…
time drop my burden on page
we scratch spells
on the walls of this miss-edu cage
words reverberate
like bomb blasts
mask-air-raids camouflage my rage
in words that flip and spin

let me say again,

Kahm:
"who in with me
has no need to fear me.
for those who suffer in hue
– as I –
are hereby ordained an ally."

ꓔO ENLIGHTEN THE G.O.D.Z.

<u>Act 1: Singing In Haunted Scales</u>

"INSTITUTIONAL CORRECTIONAL FACILITY"

walking?
if we are the world's heir
then what carries us?
time's ashes and ancestral dust?
we inhale
our song
our own core-us
at center we sing as we march

one-by-1
march the children of the sun
lead by propaganda and guns
beaten out of proper grammar
we hold broken language on our tongues
but we ra-mold words from cryptic banter
and breathe soul from our lungs
turn the air into our whispers
playing the gust of songs we've sung
but our notes
too heavy to float
are played distorted in their lyceum

we are led
dome or jungle crown – shaved off head
minds bled and filtered with a lie
as the tired pray for sleep in hopes to die

this facility of higher learning
keeps warm with books burning
crosses bent and turning
twisted symbols clash
with modern translation and the ancient past

while ghosts and snakes split us up by class
my foreparents had the whip against their back
while it is my mind that receives every whip and lash
I am told it is my colour that will not last

while Persun is handed gun

TO ENLIGHTEN THE G.O.D.Z.

Act 1: Singing In Haunted Scales

yelled into his ear
that he is public enemy number 1
smoke in mind – polluted
thinking drunk
he's handed pills and lines of sand
and told to spread the funk

commanded to sell female saviors
and dismember train of thoughts
on arm tracks
programmed to spike stardust
and sacrifice cooked heroines
in the spoon of the big dipper – chasing the dragon
speak the drunkard's words
and stir them to ferment liquor
place jumping raindrops on tongue spot
and let rock pop, calling it 'trippers'

down-lock
Persun is supplied
by their cops
who re-wire tapes
to edit
charging Persun
to give him credit

Persun follows the law of the land
selling from his mouth
supplied by their hands
but that has been Persun's plan

so shall he wrote

Persun:
*"I'll make like the church
and sell back the indulgences to these ghosts
let their minds float in an illusion
as they keep doing
with their miss edu-cage, sun."*

and I told him

TO ENLIGHTEN THE G.O.D.Z.

Act 1: Singing In Haunted Scales

Kahm:
"if there is anything we do properly
it will be thievery to their property."

Snakes and ghosts celebrate, *"finally!"*
as we started to become the exact copy
of their sound blasted on stereo—typed up, amended
well learned slave – well behaved – criminally engaged
we thought we were rebelling
but we were still mist edu-caged
and we practice actively
in their institutional correctional facility

TO ENLIGHTEN THE G.O.D.Z.

Act 1: Singing In Haunted Scales

"MIST EDU-CAGED 1: UNDER OUTSIDE CONTROL"

anciently
I am physically and philosophically
ambidextrous
but both sides of my mind
could not stop the assault
coming from every direction

a council of snakes and ghosts
quietly spoke:

"first we peel their skin
and throw it into the sky
freeze their soul and tell them
they are a shadow that can never hide
then take the stars from their night
negate Sagittarius' light
so that his cold soul will filter thru the dark air
train his bow
to kill for us snakes and ghosts
and call him a night-mare."

ghosts preach and snakes teach
the sun would never set on them
and I was a black shadow
that would never blend with their nature
and only if I were blind
would I see the sun shine
and the moon's beam
would never touch my dreams
for I was the knight who rides the night-mare
climbing
eye
stare-ways
to no heaven
I drowned
held down
under
outside
deception

TO ENLIGHTEN THE G.O.D.Z.

Act 1: Singing In Haunted Scales

worshiping their conquest of me
without question

<u>"they will praise the day
we raised them as slaves
focus their eyes
until they are civil-eyezed
pacified."</u>

Bound and tied
watery with memory
as a one-sided history made me cry

<u>"they will be forced to look at our books."</u>

and the soul food you took

I tried to crawl into me
waiting patiently
looking for sanctuary
but myself
on the inside
was empty
and on the outside
there was nowhere to run
as even those with my face
spoke with a ghost's and snake's tongue

so I gave in
and I assisted them in their system
knowing that was the only way to breathe
to live
to blend
screaming to the heavens

Kahm:
"how dare I wear the night
I am the dusk of sunlight
a descendant of people
cursed at birthright

TO ENLIGHTEN THE G.O.D.Z.

Act 1: Singing In Haunted Scales

father-God cursed my Mother-land
into ash and barren sand
and I thank these ghosts for extending a hand
letting me wear their brand
for I should be burned of my flesh
seek their image and ways
as my dress code
under
       stand
the black hole time
where no thought slipped from my uncultured lips
or found a womb to grow in my ancestors' minds

we were a dying kind
with all the light of the sun
but still blind
off rhythm with nature
our beats never took shape
descendant of monkey and apes
there has never rested spirit on a black face

if only snow could drop
and melt its colour
on my woman's skin
to take away our black sins
shrivel away in cold winter winds
straighten the way our hair spins
thin the way our lips grin
and narrow our knowledge
of what we 'nose'
only then could I be happy
if you removed all the kinks and the nappy."

trap me in thoughts on how you perceive me
listen to the lesson as you deceive me
quiet my inner voice so I no longer believe in me

ghosts and snakes
their tongues rattle and shake,

"your lesson?

TO ENLIGHTEN THE G.O.D.Z.

Act 1: Singing In Haunted Scales

<u>you are sun less</u>
<u>no throne</u>
<u>no heir to breathe</u>
<u>no breath – *know your place!"*</u>

and I do – confused
as I look for a savior with their face
no space
by family
disband
without black whole
I am buried

held
down
under
outside
control

TO ENLIGHTEN THE G.O.D.Z.

Act 1: Singing In Haunted Scales

"MIST EDU-CAGED 2: DISARMING"

snakes and ghosts
in profess-sin-all cloaks
decide the vibe
on how our minds will die

"we begin
by removing their origin
done thru lies
we bend 360⁰ heartbeats into flatlines
mold false light into sunshine
and burn fire on the inside of their minds
until they speak flames
that burn their own names
stretch, extend, and bend
until definition descends
and they re-learn to write their names
with our pens — languished in anguish
their speech tainted with the hate in our language."

... and ...
I am kahm noiz
                (my name destroyed)
I BEKAHM NOIZ
I become noise

from black zion to a rabid lion's roar
separated from s'word
spiritual words
cut from tongue
syllables trickle and run
stabbing past
and cursing all descendants of the sun
until they set
in books that are burned or kept at bay

dying heartbeats
never again to play
lay in the earth beneath my feet
as I am handed shovel

TO ENLIGHTEN THE G.O.D.Z.

Act 1: Singing In Haunted Scales

and grave digger I become
for the words that set me free
and the glory I'm descended from

"next we preach their colour equals death
and we outlaw all forms of art
that will set them free
take their muse
poison it
make it sick – mu-sick
and crown our kings to their beats
take their roots
and hang them from their family tree
inject them with dis-ease
so they never step foot near their own history
take their ancient system
and distort it to a mystery they will never solve
let their understandings dissolve into dust
fill them with mistrust for one another

lighter against darker
mother against father
sister against brother

sexually exaggerate their women
until they are an object
remove them from goddess
and lover
remove the reflection of the mirror
sever to never see the Greater Gira

steal the thunder from the men
from plantation to prison
serving us, their new religion
craft for them heroes – control their narrative
make them believe only we can create their heritage
watch them drug one another
thru murder
intoxication
– genocidal killing –
the only way we allow them to make a living.

TO ENLIGHTEN THE G.O.D.Z.

Act 1: Singing In Haunted Scales

let them be at each other's throats
killing for pennies
from master snakes and master ghosts.

let them climb pedestals to fair maidens
as they drop their swords to defend their women.
and we will plant into them
a confused people

we will attack under the guise
that everyone under our 'god' is created equal

but keep them separate

while we continue to treat them
as 3/5ths of a human
twist the words of their martyrs
and make a king's dream
harder to bring into reality

bury their kingdoms
burn their books
we have the power to say
certain events never took place
keep them running in their own race
auction off their lands
place their history into the hands of another collective
the lie not inspected
the truth never detected
our insidious methods still effective
as homes become prisons
locked in illusions on the tell-a-lie-vision
our Romantic empire still in existence."

so, I become none
with all they took
as I search with anger,
screaming and beating women
and cursing those with my skin
I am cold as the wind

TO ENLIGHTEN THE G.O.D.Z.

Act 1: Singing In Haunted Scales

looking for my manhood
in rough neighborhoods
and slums
I am hoodlum
abusing my heart
and beating it
to reclaim the spirit of the drum
trying to give shout outs
and representin' places I'm not from
forgetting I absorb
not reflect
the heart of the sun
and I pimp my fear
      as anger
under the guise of manhood
and say it's all good
in the songs I've sung

with sun magic
I ra-spell 'sacred'
and multiply it by its square
and thru the voice
and thru its music
I share that I'm not a thug
I'm actually just scared

that's what it comes down to
in every hard beat I use to surround you

cuz at rates alarming
my name
my thoughts
my history
all go thru
a disarming

TO ENLIGHTEN THE G.O.D.Z.

Act 1: Singing In Haunted Scales

"MIST EDU-CAGED 3: NIGGER SHAPED"

I have been turned against me
turned inside out – now I shout
the word 'nigger' is part of the devices
that separates me like Osiris
when it was snakes and ghost pirates
that pirated even the titles
of snakes and ghost

where is my ancestral serpentine inner-g?
the true dark matter ghost
the binding substance that floats thru eternity
and beyond infinity?
the true Neggur God-King
and Neggura Goddess-Queen

these snakes and ghosts are but the noose
that choked my vocabul—airy
that took away my memories and the heir I breath
got me catching off-tempo syllables with my teeth

wait.

got me catching off-tempo syllables with my teeth?

nigga please!

The ancient word
neggur – nigga
is not my captivity
but my release
it's not my spilled blood
but my heartbeat
the attack on my heart
came from those unalike to me
those who needed to beat God
while invoking God in their speech

I am the Head Neggur in Charge

TO ENLIGHTEN THE G.O.D.Z.

Act 1: Singing In Haunted Scales

but I submit
because the stings of the whip
cut sharp
like a sword tip
and the origin of my Godhood
and Kingship
is ripped
and any form of spirit and royalty is stripped
tricked – tricked – tricked
trickled down
rooted in race cards
forged for me to play
and I'm hated when playing the cards
      I've been dealt
leave it up to me to kill myself

I hear their hiss
their rattle
morse code prattle

"if life is fire
wood a nigger burn?
if knowledge was a ray of light
from a less-sun
wood a nigger learn?"

and their syllables
an electrocuted prayer
sting and execute the air

nagas–neggur wisdom
of the true wise serpent
twisted into 'nigger'
they cut me with 'nigger'-knife
and it wood shape life
peeling ances-tree free
desensitizing me to the word
I now
wood use
to stab
another

ᛏO ENLIGHTEN THE G.O.D.Z.

Act 1: Singing In Haunted Scales

letting the dictation slick my lips
and hang at my side
as I justify its use as calling it 'hip'
lashed from tongue like a whip

1
word
1 way
spoken 'nigger'
nigg-er
        E. R.
to emergency room
to dissect word
keeping meaning
but surgically alter word

and
I say
it means
love
all becuz I end it with 'a'
"sup, nigga?"

the ignorant laugh
applaud and clap
their sound
bass trapped
in nigger-oxymoronic-syndrome

and I call it sweet
and use it in a wrap
exaggerate my walk
and tap
my language slang
no longer intact
broken
beaten
falling like a leaf in the dying season
bleeding
like the sun's light into the sky
as it dies

TO ENLIGHTEN THE G.O.D.Z.

Act 1: Singing In Haunted Scales

buried into night
this word has birthed stars
while dwindling their original light

driving in
           car tunes
animating heritage
into buffoons
sample my example
let me be yours

this isn't a cool limp
I just got ice in my legs
trying to freeze me
keep me in place
bend me to beg
to purify my tongue
and make it a sacred object

humble myself to Ixu and Gira – god and goddess?

on a cold tongue
nigga song
be the coolest track to play
let it reverberate and sway
into a breeze
let my sandy body freeze
cool down and glass shatter
and sprinkle nigger syllable matter
into pop and rock
so I can be hard
           rock
blast it thru gunshots
my hip-hopcrasy
will protest its use by snakes and ghost cops

wear nigger on my top
so that it blocks my thoughts
let it melt
and outline me in chalk
talk nigger

ᖨO EᑎᒪIGᕼᖶEᑎ ᖶᕼE G.Θ.Ɔ.Ƶ.

<u>Act 1: Singing In Haunted Scales</u>

walk nigger
sound like the massa (media) commands
given to me
when my thoughts and courage were bigger
so that I could stand up
fight back to a snake's slither and hissing

now?
my, nigga
I just listen

so concerned about my physical ego
and my softness below the shell
my strength fell
and I try to resurrect it with nigga songs
nigga psalms
told by nigger bard

doesn't matter how cold your words are
nigga,
you ain't hard
you just laggin' behind

light
whisper spirit:
[there are no niggers]

hol' up! ain't no niggaz?
then what the fuck am I?

[you are sunshine]

you crazy, nigga,
starin' at my kingdoms under the sun
is what made me blind
looking back
when I invented time
and dissected the cosmos
and preached: "those aren't stars
those are signs
and if you figure out their meaning

ꞀO ENLIGHTEN THE G.O.D.Z.

Act 1: Singing In Haunted Scales

and control your breathing
the shift of every hour will grant you power."

[oh! so, you do ra-member?]

there are too many chains
on my train of thought
ra-member?
I don't know how
I'm just their definition
of a 'nigger' now

ΤΟ ΕΝLIGHTEN THE G.Θ.D.Z.

Act 1: Singing In Haunted Scales

"WHY DON'T I SCREAM?"

belly whipped
scarred
lashed
memories burned into ash
'the property of snakes and ghosts'
branded into my back

here I lay
soul lost
tied to a burning cross

... so ...

why don't I scream?

I lay forgotten
and forsaken
forever forgiven(?)

wrists slit from a ghost's burning kiss
and drip sound from in between
every unsown seam
while moonbeams and the sun's gleam
dance happily in my dreams

and those dreams scream
quietly
under water
my sound traveling quicker and farther
in pools of thought
while I pool my thoughts
I am the exception that is destined to rule
the unpolished jewel
destined to discover its worth
to dig itself up – out the earth
and bathe until I drink myself clean

so why. don't I. scream?

TO ENLIGHTEN THE G.O.D.Z.

Act 1: Singing In Haunted Scales

body burning from light of less-sun
in kerosene
and snakes and ghosts
do no care-o'-this-scene

as my mouth bleeds bloody histories
chained to misery
sung in a symphony
my thoughts, a choir
I sing truth
while snakes and ghosts play the lyre

off key symbolic gestures for good measure
without rhythm
pseudo-realities of freedom
hidden actualities of my kingdoms

did they ever come?
not undone
I jog my memory
letting time run

future memories are a wish and a dream

why don't I scream?
becuz, coz, that's how I bug their thoughts

my an-ticks
my tac-ticks
my ploy

why don't I scream?
cuz truthfully.
I still ra-member.
my name be.

Kahm Noiz.

TO ENLIGHTEN THE G.O.D.Z.

Act 1: Singing In Haunted Scales

"FIGHT BACK?"

but I buried my spirit's name
down to a syllable
until no sound remained
and my heartbeat
tripped

tick
tock
cease clock
heartbeats
stop

but
        I
resonate colour
and vibrate tones in vibrant tones
stripped from burning cross
laid out on ancestors' bones
my thoughts roam in a future
without an ancestral past to call their home

my heartbeats quit
morse encoded
crypt-tick
tock
cease clock
heartbeats
stop
royal ghost's
reign drops
but I shimmer a faint sunspot
to battle with reign-bows
and fire heir-rows
inheriting nature's wind flow
I battle naturally – like the way my hair grows
stand tall – knee grows – fist up, golden shimmer
iron fist glows

my mind fights to save body

TO ENLIGHTEN THE G.O.D.Z.

Act 1: Singing In Haunted Scales

so my soul can glow the way it was born
instead of dripping minutes like blood
I am the scar
where time was torn
but there is a faint memory
telling me I am the thunders shouted
from Gabriel's horn

only 400 years of my past is playing in the present
my question in existence
this song is years long
and far from being finished
jazz improvisational and constantly ra-written
I freestyle under the guise of a ghost's image

I was even born in the year of the snake
I learned their tongue (properly)
so that mine can slither and shake
as I recite ghost histories
and bloody days
and glorify the foundation
of their nation's birthplace
pledge my allegiance to see how their words taste

I played part so well
the colour dripped from my face
and soon
my understandings were erased
my tongue laced with their words
their voices
all that could be heard

my eye on the mirror
and my thoughts to me
violent
my culture
silenced

hand over heart
reciting in their linguis-tick
      linguis-tick

TO ENLIGHTEN THE G.O.D.Z.

Act 1: Singing In Haunted Scales

          linguis-tick
                    linguis-tick
tick
          tick
                tick
tock
cease clock
heartbeats
stop

TO ENLIGHTEN THE G.O.D.Z.

Act 1: Singing In Haunted Scales

"ALLY VIBE: CID"

he was so seductively cool
autumn came early
with his vibe and breeze
stepping into summer's heat
thunder became envious
every time he tapped with his feet
and he blew clouds of smoke
with every word he chose to speak
he reflected the sun's inspiration
off his bald head and skin
stubbles of hair patched onto his chin

Cid:
"sup, my niggaz?
I be cid
life of thief how I live
I speak s'lang banter
walk on pillars
holding up mansions
in my style of 'manor'
I'm game planer
life an arcade."

and cid was the token
snakes and ghosts used for play

Cid:
"in this game? sheeeit!
I got extra life sentence
take sound stereo/type as my definition
standing at the foot of my own heart
I beat raps to keep life kickin'
on a mission to steal back
all the time
these fake-ass snakes and ghosts never gave."

he on trade with water persun
lap track circle business they run
and I was caught in cid the loop

TO ENLIGHTEN THE G.O.D.Z.

Act 1: Singing In Haunted Scales

roped into group
tied to definition
we march in triangular troupe

Cid:
"my boyz steal from 3 sides
we drink gin 'o' cide
numbing our mind
looking for forgiveness
inside this life sentence
throwing away minutes
just to reclaim time."

cid got us searchin' blank spaces
120 lessons written
looking to fill ourselves as blank pages
with what we define
but it was without the understanding
that we are divine
and so we swing
on d'vine by oppressive design
by our ...
... next heist
we fight to steal snakes' and ghosts' stolen property
calling it our birthright

looking for the spiritual inside stolen material
we become a circle trapped inside a circle
we scream revolution as cid keeps blowing smoke
and persun sells fog kept hidden on the inside of his coat

I walked in line
helping cid plan to steal time
we speak days
on what should be hours
singing in c-rhymes

and we wait
until early becomes late
and immortality thru immobility
becomes fate

TO ENLIGHTEN THE G.O.D.Z.

Act 1: Singing In Haunted Scales

it seems like forever

but cid say, **"we stall purposely
so our enemies will never see
how we came to find a plan
to steal back
our time."**

TO ENLIGHTEN THE G.O.D.Z.

Act 1: Singing In Haunted Scales

"STOLEN CHANTS"

from a distance
on the horizon
our prison looks like a palace
but in the hands of snakes and ghosts
it is a chalice where they drink us dry
and our crystal thoughts
melt into sands of time
and we think minute after minute
hour after hour
chasing our thoughts

cid's words
blurred into smoke
condensed as he spoke
writhed and danced,

**"what we steal first
is our chants**

**and we take it
and we speak it
lasso our chants to time
so that we can retrieve it."**

and his words inject
following flow, liquid
like water
each one after the next
parting the air
with his tongue
in every breath
syllables dangling
from his tongue's tip

**Cid:
"yo, peep this,
I've heard legends, rumors, and myths
that we as souls exist far past these bars
and beyond this prison's mist."**

TO ENLIGHTEN THE G.O.D.Z.

Act 1: Singing In Haunted Scales

and I listened closely
my ears like open palms
catching every word that dropped
as they dripped
listening to these myths
filtering into the air
seething from cid's lips

Cid:
"our time has not stopped
it lays captured
in the hands of snakes and ghosts
our Grandfather Clock
carved from the ances-tree
Grandmother B, Ourstory Book
suspended from a fixed support
swinging back and forth
under the influence of gravity
attracting you, persun, and me

like us, tragically
Grandmother B, Ourstory Book
and our Grandfather Clock
lay in captivity
telling time
to those whose time we serve
but it be our time
to free ourselves by way of the word."

and I spoke reason,

Kahm:
"though our minds
mist edu-caged
and caught
all we need to break and bend these bars
is a single thought."

and we pool our thoughts
and swim in chants

TO ENLIGHTEN THE G.O.D.Z.

Act 1: Singing In Haunted Scales

for this be our chance
to swim free
triangular thievery
stealing back our time in trinity
chanting in rhyme
speaking infinity
this is our chants
... forever ...

stall?
no.
we act now
or never

TO ENLIGHTEN THE G.O.D.Z.

Act 1: Singing In Haunted Scales

"BROKEN CHANTS"

it was just ... something in us
that caused us hunters
... to pray ...

cid
persun
and I
confessed
to the face of the sunrise
and we shivered with the wind
while swelling clouds began to cry

I hummed while persun drummed
and cid made confessions
to the heavenly bodies seated next to the sun

Cid:
"I thought all their property
would equal 'me'
and I studied actively
their crimes
just to steal back our time."

and then I spoke
and took over the chant
and rhyme

Kahm:
"and we humbled ourselves to them
thinking they were gods
trying to get them on our side
but they branded us with a title
that we waved
and now we've become princes
to a turning tide."

and as I took over drumming
and cid kept humming
persun chanted

TO ENLIGHTEN THE G.O.D.Z.

Act 1: Singing In Haunted Scales

held up by our vibe

Persun:
"I sold fog (well)
and smoked clouds (confess y'self, brutha)
trying to keep my thoughts in the sky (that's aw-ite, now)
trying to focus and never lose those dreams I had in mind.
but they just ... blurred with my crimes."

and we combed our hair
looking for wisdom
while burning sage's brush
filtering the aroma of dusk
we sing to the dawn
syllables humming in tune with our breath
we 3 become a triple son set

this is how we pray
letting our confessions burn
melt into smoke, swivel, and sway
growing upwards into space
the aroma of our sins
cast away
putting us in sense
we now think straight

cuz we be confessing to the sunrise's face
until we 3 sons rise
we warm the wind with our breath
never set
while nursing clouds as they wept

speaking under the sun
we **3 chant as 1:**

"WE HERE CLAIM
THAT WE PUMP MORE LIFE
THRU OUR NAMES
THAN SNAKES AND GHOST
DO SO THRU THEIR VEINS

TO ENLIGHTEN THE G.O.D.Z.

Act 1: Singing In Haunted Scales

WE BEG FOR FORGIVENESS
JUST TO STEAL AGAIN
UNDER THE SHIELD OF RIGHTEOUSNESS."

and we washed the lie
from our hair and minds
and we opened up a third eye
that would never go blind

righteous yet?
maybe…
but we still got one more sin to commit

and that
is to steal back
our time

TO ENLIGHTEN THE G.O.D.Z.

Act 1: Singing In Haunted Scales

"THE JOURNEY UP"

there was something in words
that allowed us to disturb
the snakes' and ghosts' unnatural order

we became recorders for the word
throwing our fists into it
to beat it
and fill the word with funk
for use of the word's power on our final hunt

persun and I
knelt – our palms open – facing the sky
persun sang moonlight
while I spoke sunshine
cid prayed for rain
and produced it thru cloudy thoughts
and the tears he cried

with the mix of these three elements
we were no longer weaponless
as from the root of our words did grow
mixed with moonlight
sunshine
and rain
came our reign-bows

and we spoke winter
until the wind forged into a quiver
as from the root of our words did grow
our heir-rows
we can now fire solid silhouettes of our ancestry
pass spirits with deadly accuracy – visionaries

forging our weapons from the sky
heaven donors
we hide our weapons
in the corner of our cell

handed to cid

TO ENLIGHTEN THE G.O.D.Z.

Act 1: Singing In Haunted Scales

by way of sun and moon
was an o-gun forged from Ogun
called a heater – loaded with stars

cid kept it close, tucked into his clothes
hidden from view of snakes and ghosts

we now
at least
under
          stand
we are more than man
gripping our weapons again
we folded our legs
clasped our hands
and prayed
moving the heavens forward
by 4 words
quickening – bringing the end of days

the sun ducked under the horizon
and it was now our time to rise up

we chanted words that rippled nature
and made matter bend
turning us into wind
we slipped through the bars of our cell
quietly crawling
with a low creep, using the shadows as streets
we mapped our way past ghost guards
and snake watchmen

far from where we were caged
at the center of this concrete stage
was a tower
carved from forfeit souls
molded into their reflection
a screaming mirror – extending upward
piercing the heavens like an unholy sword
standing over this concrete jungle
like an unholy lord

TO ENLIGHTEN THE G.O.D.Z.

Act 1: Singing In Haunted Scales

cid sang in a gentle chord,

**"our time is at the top
Ourstory book,
at the center of our plot."**

at the base
were snake watchmen
walking their beat

but with the power of clouds,
smoke, and fog
persun placed them in a sleep
and we slipped in
blending again with the shadows
our reign-bows worn close
locked with heir-rows
at the ready to battle ghosts

but the tower seemed empty

it started raining outside
every drop that dripped
trickled against the tower
like broken glass
and in hollow abode
the sound grew and echoed

snakes and ghosts
slithered from the ground

Kahm:
"here they come!"

we attack
our heir-rows hummed
cutting the wind
slicing through undead targets
that seeped through walls
and formed from demonic inscriptions

TO ENLIGHTEN THE G.O.D.Z.

Act 1: Singing In Haunted Scales

outlined in faded black souls on the floor

we shoot heir-rows like chords
strumming reign-bow strings
our weapons begin singing in falsetto
that speak to our soul
forming our ancestral black – whole
this is the bass and drum of our hearts

we journey up
climbing stairs
winding to the zenith of this tower

– *pursuing!* –
snakes and ghosts
glow dull, their power
shimmering on their swords
as they flood the stairs in hordes

we fire back
ascending the stairs
winding
bending
the walls reaching out to us
closing in on us
we fire downwards – down words
speaking spirals
carried by heir-rows
dissecting every syllable
yelled by false snake
or
false ghost
cutting their lies
lying deep in their throats

we ascend
fire back
and ascend
it seems
the climb
never ends

TO ENLIGHTEN THE G.O.D.Z.

Act 1: Singing In Haunted Scales

as our power
begins to descend

spiritual virgins
our power
has not yet blossomed

cid yells, **"conserve!"**
as we swerve
making the final ascent

with weariness battling courage on cid's face
with the last of his heir-rows
he fills the staircase with fire

he removes his o-gun
and with the power of thunder in his fingers
he thumbs back the hammer

4 steps forward
marching in line
we pace into room
that holds our time

TO ENLIGHTEN THE G.O.D.Z.

Act 1: Singing In Haunted Scales

"THE PULL IN"

and there was Grandmother B,
Ourstory book
pendulum hooked
swinging
silently
like a summer's breeze

outside
the rain sang
dancing
as it trickled
and dripped
Grandfather Clock
ticked-tocked
and my heart
slowly beat and rocked

cid knelt
dropped
and prayed
I bowed my head in silence
just the same

confessing
we threw away our sins
trying to ra-claim our names

persun turned away
he observed the cackling flames
that howled flares of snakes and ghosts
rising from the smoke of the burning stairs

persun locked heir-row
and gently strummed it back

Persun:
*"pray another day
we battle now."*

TO ENLIGHTEN THE G.O.D.Z.

Act 1: Singing In Haunted Scales

cid jumped to his feet,
moved persun aside

Cid:
"take the book
and get out.
I'll hold it down – shooting stardust
and blasting sun clouds."

persun slipped back
and he took
Grandmother B,
Ourstory Book

snakes and ghosts
slithered closer

Cid:
"I command, now!
kahm – persun – RUN!"

cid shouted war cries
shooting stars from his o-gun
and snakes and ghosts
retaliate with a host of shots
they fire twisted sunbeams
from sunSET-gun streams
that in the past have helped them kill dreams
but not for these knights
we've awakened
and we fight
our heir-rows glow
cutting thru the wind
racing with cid's stars
charging in snakes' and ghosts' direction
heir-rows and stars hit our targets
and cid backs up in farthest position
resting in front of Grandfather clock

Cid:
"I've got what I've come for.

TO ENLIGHTEN THE G.O.D.Z.

Act 1: Singing In Haunted Scales

I got time now. I got more.”

persun and I
stand still
as cid
begins to cry

“leave!” he commands
**“and if I got to tell you again
my next shots are in your direction.
now go!”**

we fire two shots of heir-rows
hit a snake
and two ghosts
then slip thru the window

and my eyes' last reflection of cid
watch as he speaks in haste
drawing a cloud
to mask his face
leaving no trace
the ghosts and snakes
will not know his true identity

... and I will never see him again ...

under the rain
persun and I do the same
we call the clouds
to mask our thoughts
faces and names

disguised
we use shadows to hide
and let snakes and ghosts
slip by us

we jump to a lower balcony
as ghosts and snakes
come slithering

TO ENLIGHTEN THE G.O.D.Z.

Act 1: Singing In Haunted Scales

we jump to the far side of the building
our powers fading
we search deep in mind
to find a soular miracle

we reach the ground
racing back to our cell

but hidden
slithering
closely creeping
in alleyway
letting hissing sounds escape
twisting the air to death
tormenting the wind's breath
our captors

snakes writhed from the ground
and ghosts reach for our ears
with glass shattering sounds
and we blast our way
with rounds of heir-row fire

ghosts' bodies ripple and bend
as snakes' tongues extend
wiring toward us
we dodge every grip
and lash every whip
one after the next
until persun is caught by the neck
catching him in place
near to removing the cloud that masks his face

ghosts and snakes
glide and slither
toward persun
standing over him
claiming victory

... but ...

TO ENLIGHTEN THE G.O.D.Z.

Act 1: Singing In Haunted Scales

with his last ounce of power
he tosses Grandmother B,
Ourstory book
over to me
and I catch the tome in my grip
blur into the wind
and run

... until ...

my power fades
far from where I was caged
and I hear the rage of my enemies
close behind me
their hissing and gliding surrounding me

but stepping from the darkness
into darkness
is an entity cloaked
neither snake
nor ghost
it steps close
reaches out a hand
gentle as it spoke
negating the slithering
and gliding moans
its voice
a feminine tone

Woman:
"take my hand, growing warrior,
and I'll take you home."

and I reach for her hand
and her power I felt
reshaping my body,
my spirit,
and producing
a fertile cell

and I was back

TO ENLIGHTEN THE G.O.D.Z.

<u>Act 1: Singing In Haunted Scales</u>

caged
but free
alone,
holding tightly close to me
Grandmother B,
Ourstory book

and I throw my reign-bow
into the heavens
for it to glow bright
in the hands of Sagittarius
and bring back his light

and when the moon's light angles
like movement of that angel
letting free its flow and glow
I hid Grandmother B,
         Ourstory book
underneath
a shadow

⊖ ENLIGHTEN THE G.⊖.D.Z.

<u>Act 1: Singing In Haunted Scales</u>

"I PONDER ANGELS"

I could see her stars brightly
even with the sun in the sky
virgo's eye
shined down on me
and rescued me from my enemies

I ponder angels in the mourning
a tear – a sunray
for every knight that was slain
for persun and cid
redeemed in their final actions
from the lives they lived

but I pondered angels in the morning
sunrays glowing
warming and caressing my face

for the first time
since I was blind
by less-sun
I saw sunshine

so I pondered angels in the morning
my thoughts swarming
on the hand that brought me home
her gentle voice – its musical tone

my back to darkness
in the corner of the cell
while my thoughts
face sunlight
and I dwell on angels
dripping time's leaves
from ances-tree

free from their lips,
their voices,
their kiss,
their skin,

TO ENLIGHTEN THE G.O.D.Z.

Act 1: Singing In Haunted Scales

I ponder angels
and wait to see her
again

TO ENLIGHTEN THE G.O.D.Z.

Act 1: Singing In Haunted Scales

"GARDEN WALK"

snakes and ghosts
could not live
on just choking us
they had to give us
some time

I spent mine
bathing in sunshine
and I walked thru gardens
looking to plant a thought
to grow ances-tree
back to my mind
and find my roots
in my hair-atage
and lock my thoughts away

I grow truth like fruit
nothing strange

my words roll
as I speak to flowers
and help them breathe
searching for angels
that would rescue me

I saw her
when I started to believe
she waved a smile
and a sly eye at me

in this garden
I saw Eve

black
butter
she be fly
her wings
attached to her mind
and she smiled

TO ENLIGHTEN THE G.O.D.Z.

Act 1: Singing In Haunted Scales

with her eyes

her hair
flowed
in spiraling whirls of wool
inspiring
whirlpools of thought

her body
                 – curved –
sensuously
draped
and caught
in a pink gown
that swirled like a cloud

and as I kept my eye on her
I wore thoughts of her
as my crown

when she walked
she danced
her feet
skipping
and tapping the ground
she was visual sound

and I heard the syllables
in my own name
begin to pound
when annunciated thru her lips

I became jealous of my name
spoken by her smile
it was giving her a kiss
fulfilling my wish
I live vicariously
thru my name,
vexed just the same

and I have the nerve

ＴＯ ＥＮＬＩＧＨＴＥＮ ＴＨＥ Ｇ.Ｏ.Ｄ.Z.

Act 1: Singing In Haunted Scales

to call myself 'kahm'

but I relax, fade to her black
while my heart beats tracks that I can speak over
but my tongue has trouble flowing

so I let the silent air keep blowing
allow it to speak for me
as I gaze into the eyes
of the angel who rescued me

TO ENLIGHTEN THE G.O.D.Z.

Act 1: Singing In Haunted Scales

"OHM LINGO SPEAKS"

this angel
had strong shoulders
that held up the burden
that holds her
her spirit rocked – **bolder**
but invisible tears
wrinkled time on her face

Ohm Lingo:
"I can save you from this place."

she speaks
creeps
and walks closer

Ohm Lingo:
"my name is Ohm Lingo.
I am an extension of the heavens
I came into existence between the sun's light
and the moon's beam
I've come to inundate streams of consciousness
to free you from all this
and place the proper words on your lips.

it was I who rescued you in your flight from the tower
I've come to help you speak your power
so that you may journey beyond the mist."

my ears
push my eyes away
and I gaze
my ear to her vocal-eyez

Ohm Lingo:
"haven't you tried
to climb
your 3rd eye's stare?
focused, it watches your soul
and becomes aware of the 7 divisions.

TO ENLIGHTEN THE G.O.D.Z.

Act 1: Singing In Haunted Scales

you have spoken the first,
separated your state of mind
from their church
you have spoken the 'khab'.
it corresponds to the physical body,
transforming you into other elemental properties.
that was how you could blend in to shadows
and turn into the wind."

I ponder the angel's words
and stare at my hands
gateway of my power
thru lips
thru throat
I am the well of words never to go dry
spoken by my 3rd eye

"all you need,"
said Ohm Lingo,
"is a guide
to ra-trace the steps
back into your mind
to remember the time
when you spoke all 7 divisions."

and her words
broke my concentration
... on her words ...
I stood perplexed

Ohm Lingo:
"you were not born in this place
you were conceived
soul wise
by the sun's rays."

I was silent
my voice
taken from me

TO ENLIGHTEN THE G.O.D.Z.

<u>Act 1: Singing In Haunted Scales</u>

Ohm Lingo:
"don't you ra-memeber?"

my heart aches
and my head shakes,
'no'

Ohm Lingo:
"then,
from what you've took
you must study,
Grandmother B,
Ourstory book."

and I reach for her hand
but
there is a wedge between us
a grip
that steals her kiss
lying
from the mouth
of a lotus flower

she sits
in a lotus position
as a haunting around her floats
she is bound
by the deceitful touch of a ghost

the wedge
between us
and she cannot move
away

in a whisper,
I say, "don't you know
deep in the mind
you don't need to spend your time
being the snakes and ghost's concubine?"

she gently replies, "you live vicariously thru your name

TO ENLIGHTEN THE G.O.D.Z.

Act 1: Singing In Haunted Scales

as it is spoken by my lips
giving me a kiss,
and I'll live vicariously thru you
when you journey beyond this prison's mist."

the ghost captures the angel
that freed, inhaled my name
and let me breathe

Ohm Lingo speaks
in tears
that seep
in a smile
that weeps –
she stands
and keeps her words
to herself
her feet
tipping
and tapping
the soil
she speaks words into her hands
condenses the air
melts syllables,
and turns her prayer into oil

she anoints my head
and rubs the words she said into my thoughts
restoring the memories I've lost
they swirl from my soul
spiral from my head
as my natural hair grows

but there is a wedge
between my lips and her kiss
she becomes bound at the wrist
her smile fades
but still exists in my thoughts

captured
Ohm Lingo wears a ghost

TO ENLIGHTEN THE G.O.D.Z.

Act 1: Singing In Haunted Scales

as her cloak

a feminine snake
wraps around my waist
and
carries me
back
to my cage

ᛏO ENLIGHTEN THE G.Θ.D.Z.

<u>Act 1: Singing In Haunted Scales</u>

"PIQUE TO PEEK TO PEAK"

underneath
shadow's
sheet
I look over
Ourstory book's
spine
and shoulder
and discover kingdoms
ruled
by my face
and colour

and every night
I would sneak a peek
at ancient kingdoms
ruled
by
me

soul matter
stirred
in the form of memory flashes
images crash
and shatter
the second they hit

and I prayed for sunshine
and some time to spend
walking in gardens
to speak to Ohm Lingo

but snakes' and ghosts'
strata
gem
glowed – brightly
shined
an idea

my speaking with Ohm Lingo

TO ENLIGHTEN THE G.O.D.Z.

Act 1: Singing In Haunted Scales

was a ploy
they wanted to show me
I would only get close
to myself
in memories
and the voice I trusted
they controlled

so I kept close
to Grandmother B,
Ourstory book
and tried to reconstruct
shattered
memories
and get back
to me

sleeping on book as pillow
learning thru cos-mosis
stars parted like moses
rearranged, constellating into lessons
be-knighted-mares chased away – on extended leave
finally, for this dark knight
caped in crusade
a peaceful night's sleep

TO ENLIGHTEN THE G.O.D.Z.

Act 1: Singing In Haunted Scales

"LAST CHANTS 1: THE MWINDO TALE"

I take part in my last chants
I read
closely
Grandmother B,
Ourstory book

I found my glory
glowing
in words
on the pages
of a story
whose hero
was me
searching for family
ances-tree
roots connected by cosmology
the hero battled
in an astrological setting

– mwindo-heru –
running thru
virgo-auset's womb
born to mid-knight
up from the horizon
to bring light
put breath into the sun
to give back its life
and sacrifice his eye
to give his people sight

by his mother's people
he was trained to reclaim his birthright
armed
with a ray of the sun
on his arm
commanding the wind and the thunder
speaking power in a single breath
battling the EMPIRE OF THE SUNSET
ruled by his uncle seth

TO ENLIGHTEN THE G.O.D.Z.

Act 1: Singing In Haunted Scales

who governed the sky
in the west — where sun-goes-down

allied with a beautiful princess
and brother an-ubis
and the rest of the stars
heru sought
to avenge the death of his father, ausar

battle one for the sun
ended with seth
and heru
becoming
stale-mates

battle two witnessed mwindo-heru suffer fate

he bled the dying sun
father's blood dripping from his face
pouring
from the loss
of his eye
crucified in the sky
dangling from a city of clouds
tempted by seth
to rule the sky
under the EMPIRE OF THE SUNSET

... instead ...
mwindo-heru chose death

but he was saved by the glow
fire
and wind
of sagittarius' reign-bow
and heir-rows
and claimed victory in battle three
screaming
while the sun rose in the east

TO ENLIGHTEN THE G.O.D.Z.

Act 1: Singing In Haunted Scales

Mwindo-Heru:
"I am king of the sky, like my father before me."

a perfect black's spirit lifted from the deep
and he became the king of heaven
mwindo-heru, prince of the sky
auset, queen of the dawn
mother goddess,
protecting her family,
no longer needed to weep

perfect black king
auset-queen
son mwindo-heru

the first family
the first trinity

and mwindo-heru's story
inspired me to be me

I wonder
letting my mind wander
and I think
on all of the possibilities within me
from this one story

under shadow's cover
I continue to study – and like an outlaw – read

TO ENLIGHTEN THE G.O.D.Z.

Act 1: Singing In Haunted Scales

"SEARCH 4 THE WOMB"

Ohm Lingo's voice
e c h o e s
her words ripple warnings that rain
and trickle
down
to
all
five
senses

"you were not born in this place."

and I yearn to see the smile
on my mother's or father's face

and I feel memories
in my hand
when I grip the pen
and hold the page

ancient stories inspire words to wave
and flood thru paper-mate
to inundate page

I see now that I found the womb
my mother – my creator

my pen – the father
holding his labors
to provide for his family

focusing pen and paper
I behold my makers
my saviors
I am the word neatly written
forged from two signatures:
father pen. mother paper.

TO ENLIGHTEN THE G.O.D.Z.

Act 1: Singing In Haunted Scales

"MOTHER PAPER"

my mother paper
was carved
from her own mother's nature
and I peeled a piece of her
placed it in the center of my cell
and burned it into vapors

from the core-us
of the singing smoke
I invoke
the image of my mother
dancing
while she floated on heir

dressed in a gown
the colour of beige
her hair
in waves
her skin
the colour of the sun's blaze
my image
caught in her gaze
and suddenly
happiness
dissolved
into a blank expression
on my mother's face

in her eyes,
there was surprise
          and wonder
as she beheld the thunder that was her son
long in lost, no longer lost

quietly,
she sung,

Mother Paper:
"my son,

TO ENLIGHTEN THE G.O.D.Z.

Act 1: Singing In Haunted Scales

rise and come,
scribe your father's words
onto me
so that I may help you
decipher each syllable
one-by-one

the 7 magical words of the sun
spilling
from your father's horn
the syllables
enunciating your physical form
scribing you into the word
where you were born

your father's imagination
dropped onto me
so that your thoughts
may breathe
and your father's words
may breed
swirling in my crease
you, a spoken word,
released thru my lips

I am the womb
where you were born
your Mother Paper."

and she disappeared into smoke and vapor
that slipped through my cell
and into the air it sailed leaving my imagination
to trail back to my mother's words

my eyes pulled toward my pen
and I placed my ear against it
to listen and see
if my father's voice could be heard

TO ENLIGHTEN THE G.O.D.Z.

Act 1: Singing In Haunted Scales

"FATHER PEN"

father pen
face toward heaven
his image
held up by a tunnel of light
robed in the night
the power of every word
that man has been known to write

        rippling strength
        channeling might

I saw him place thunder into the air
when his voice reached for the stars
filling space
he carried the rays of the sun's colour
on his face

         – my father pen –

his smile – a moon beam – spotlight on me

         – his son –

atop his head was a crown of wool
and I was caught in the gravity and pull
of his eyes

his voice
powerful sound waves
that could part the sea

Father Pen spoke to me, "my son,
you must speak to many
and add them all
to make one.

you must write on
where I left off
lead the lost from the burning cross

TO ENLIGHTEN THE G.O.D.Z.

<u>Act 1: Singing In Haunted Scales</u>

carved from our ances-tree.

continue to study
and listen
to the lovely words
of the angel Ohm Lingo

decipher the 7 words
given to you
by your mother and I
passed down from our ancestors
who reside in the sky

learn and escape from this place."

and then father pen laid down
on mother paper
and scribed his labor in 7 words

written
in a language
I could not
even
under
       stand

– these 7 words –

Father Pen:
"your mother and I
do not have the strength
to let our souls stay beside you,
to teach and guide you.

take these 7 words
to be deciphered.
you already know the first – the 'khab'."

twisting air
and
slithering rattles

⊤Ө ⴹNᒪIGH⊤ⴹN ⊤Hⴹ G.Ө.Ɔ.Z.

Act 1: Singing In Haunted Scales

cackled
outside my cage

father pen turned to mother paper
and scribed on her page
words
as maps
to a land
of 25,000 sages

mother paper handed to me
a parchment of my father's words
and with a wink of their 3rd eye
they dissolved into syllables
and floated into the sky

and although my body
stayed connected to the earth
my spirit
      started
      to lift
able to feel again
– with my soul –
I knew
now (nearly off the page, but loud and proud)
I truly did

EXIST

TO ENLIGHTEN THE G.O.D.Z.

<u>Act 1: Singing In Haunted Scales</u>

"PARENTAL GUIDANCE"

it seemed
as
my parents' smile
beamed
down
onto
me
my image was spiked with gin
and I began to imagine
I. Am. A. Jinn.
a creator

and when I studied
Grandmother B
Ourstory Book
my thoughts took shape
and began to multiply
ironically,
as they started to divide
they unified

what I imagined
became a nation
an imagine-nation
and I began creating a way
for me to escape
I meditated day-by-day
letting my thoughts spin

intoxicated
it seemed
as
my parents' smile
beamed
down
onto
me
it spiked my aura with gin
and I drank my own history

TO ENLIGHTEN THE G.O.D.Z.

Act 1: Singing In Haunted Scales

liquid memories
making my aura-gin
glow brighter

and I chanted thru
the annunciation
of the only word
I knew
and my hue
began to glow
the colour of soul

now I know where I come from

you've never seen black
glow brighter than the sun
be-cuz
you've never heard reverberation
like the sound of the perfect word
vibrating off
and playing on
your eardrum
you've never tasted soul
until you've kissed it off the lips
of where it aura/ginated from

all this time I've just been played
cuz I never heard
my own name sung

all this time
snakes
and
ghosts
kept us divided
but we knew
we all went thru this
as
one

and, so it seemed

TO ENLIGHTEN THE G.O.D.Z.

Act 1: Singing In Haunted Scales

as
my parents' smile
beamed
down
onto
me
it spiked my food for thought
my metaphysical rations
with gin
becuz it will be this food for thought
that will free my gin-e-ration

TO ENLIGHTEN THE G.O.D.Z.

Act 1: Singing In Haunted Scales

"LAST CHANTS II: SING MY WHISPERS"

caged
in their sentence
a broken syllable
unable to speak
and so I searched for a voice
to sing my name
or my emotions
just
the same

I
          found

there were flows
on the radio
negro-algo-rhythms
speaking my visions
in a finite number
of dance steps
a voice
looped
creating my personal circle
split thru a royal prism
against the reign
and producing rain that was purple

and it sang in whispers
that made heartbeats quiver
and life flow like rivers
and to touch true soul
the voice sang in falsetto
and black, baritone-low
scatting morse code
of prophecies
and odes
in the proper C, key
drumming and stringing
bass chants

TO ENLIGHTEN THE G.O.D.Z.

Act 1: Singing In Haunted Scales

whispering my heartbeat to life
and making heart dance

I turned the dial of my heart low
so no snake or ghost
could hear the beat
and stop the flow
but I had to let the jam grow
so I tossed the voice to the sky
so that its vibe could play
whenever the breeze beat
and the trees swayed

I listened closely to what the voice sang
and it rang inaudibly
its range falling
like autumn leaves
the secrets of its change,
just for me
I listened closely
as I lost myself
in the image of someone else
this voice kept me
close to me
I listened
secretly

and I found
there were flows
that grow
in the halls of my house
bruthaz singing softly
substituting for a violent shout
and
bruthaz sang,
        "listen,"
fire trembling from their throats
words musical,
rotating like wheels
as they spoke,
        "listen to me,"

TO ENLIGHTEN THE G.O.D.Z.

Act 1: Singing In Haunted Scales

they sang
as their bodies became
consumed by ghosts,
their music choked
infected
mu-sick
but they sang

"we may die
straighten our vibe, our DNA
and our thoughts
with their lie
but you must sing battle cries
let the standard be set
so you can rise
fiery eye
son, you belong in the sky

what are you still doing
walking to their tune
when you know damn well
you can fly?
beyond the border of high
between the universal thighs
of the sun and moon
is the womb where you were given birth
why just fight to reclaim heaven and earth
when your real estate is the entire black universe?"

and before I knew the voice's worth
snakes surrounded its flow
and breathed snow into the air
freezing every harmony
every musical note (written to me)
forming lifetime
ice-cycles on the ground
the voice lay in time, frozen
never again to open

snakes circle and surround
ghosts sing off key

TO ENLIGHTEN THE G.O.D.Z.

Act 1: Singing In Haunted Scales

to mock
the voice's
never-again sound

but it's too late
my heartbeat
pump!
pump!
and pounds

more than a voice
it was a little bit of myself
that I found

TO ENLIGHTEN THE G.O.D.Z.

<u>Act 1: Singing In Haunted Scales</u>

"LAST CHANTS III: JUNCTION"

equipped to speak
I could now seek
the land
of ancestral sages
and I scribed
onto many pages
eulogies
for cid and persun

I composed their soul
down onto paper
so that their labors
would always be ra-membered
sun and moon engendered

and I knew there were other allies
who needed to lie down
on this paper

in chant
I whisper,

Kahm:
"if I could combine time
       – I would –
put every inspirational ally
on the same point and line
split their image
and create light
let my mind flow
as I begin to write

question: what is my life?
answer: the allegory of my own story."

I combine mwindo-heru's glory
to an angel's words and image
and a voice
that travels beyond a calculated distance

TO ENLIGHTEN THE G.O.D.Z.

Act 1: Singing In Haunted Scales

sound
that in an instant
lights the path for me to follow

I compose my life
in the sum of every novel
writing my name is prince
down on morning papers
I create a blue light
that melts with you
        – my language and lingo –
sweet baby,
our combined words
are the flow of 7
and I learn to speak
to seek
translation
search to shift gears
my trans-mission."

and as I write
I transform
      my voice,
      my soul,
      my name,
have been ra-born

I am kahm noiz *(black zion)*
my syllables no longer destroyed
the space where my soul resides
no longer an empty void

ㄒ⊖ ENLIGHTEN THE G.⊖.Ɔ.Ƶ.

<u>Act 1: Singing In Haunted Scales</u>

"CHILD SPEAK"

I AM the voice of gabriel's horn
and I recite how I was born
so that a crowd can form
        – like a cloud –
and I can rain on them

some of my people
were too busy handling their labors
or
disrespecting their
father pen
and mother paper

snakes and ghosts
corrupted my people with promises
stuffing them into cosmology machines
trying to turn them into stars
but my voice would touch their ears
no matter how far

and they gathered around me
searching for true cosmology
and I spoke to the light crowd
glowing bright and black

Kahm:
"if you could speak back
to every word you read
you would understand
how we as warriors
were conceived

not from a maiden's womb
but from her smile
to the way her 3rd eye blinks
you see
we were not brought into this world
by the way you think

TO ENLIGHTEN THE G.O.D.Z.

Act 1: Singing In Haunted Scales

penis-pen
ejaculation
DNA description
swirling thru
paper womb
going thru ovulation
no question of exclamation
no abortion thru period-menstruation
no jail sentence
we run on
speaking 1 - 2 - 3 - 4(words)
march!

February – march into spring

as we are spoken into spring waters
key notes: C-Sons and Daughters
for we are the words of life you read
populate spiritual speech
with syllabic-seeds
free you from writer's cellblock

      eye
hair
lock
      believe

this is how
and why
we were conceived
so that you may change like leaves

we are the proper annunciation
for communication
13 cycles of ancestry
is our period for gestation
father pen
and mother paper
gave birth to our imagine-nation
entire black population
we defend in an army that is ancient

TO ENLIGHTEN THE G.O.D.Z.

Act 1: Singing In Haunted Scales

with black women, day soldiers
and black men, knights
                    – that are long
we as warriors were spawned
thru the scribing of scriptures
and the reciting of psalms
our heart beat syllables and songs
our description held in our parents' palms
and thrown into the dawn
for a new age of Black to be drawn

as soular clouds formed our names
letting these royal morning sons reign
and daughters drip
against their mothers' lips
inheriting their spiritual and physical image
and running away with it

blowing in the wind of trend setters
is how we became our ancestors
the kahm heirs to the weather
we need no feathers to fly upon hour wings
levitating minutes
we made time fly
quietly speaking invisible battle cries
against their lies
snakes and ghosts
those who re-wrote our story
and used it as a rope
to choke those whose spirits we invoke

ancestors hang, gently
swinging on 11 branches
of the ances-tree
our spirituality
dying

and we've been so miss-edu caged,
we've been barred from the truth
blinded by someone else's view

TO ENLIGHTEN THE G.O.D.Z.

Act 1: Singing In Haunted Scales

buried under me
our own story
dated by carbon – copy
the ancient words that make up our bodies

but I no longer see an illusion
as I see thru real eyes

I realize
       I am my ancestors of old
dressed in armor that is new
golden-brown hue

and so is my quest
to connect me-to-me
and 3rd eye-to-you."

... but there were other eyes spying ...

TO ENLIGHTEN THE G.O.D.Z.

Act 1: Singing In Haunted Scales

"THE DEFIANCE"

and my words
spurred minds
thinking
and eyes
began weeping
lies began bleeding
trickling from the body

but my words fell on those
who wore my face
with their original minds erased
their thoughts too close
to a snake or ghost

they were led by a black man
shaved of head
named eye-van, the all too terrible
advisor to the snakes' and ghosts' king

Ohm Lingo
raced to my cage
to say, "please, be careful."

Kahm:
"why?
becuz my freedom of speech
is a disturbance to their piece
of the pie?
I will not apologize
for putting bass into their vibe,
exposing the rhythm
of their lies."

Ohm Lingo spoke
in a whisper, "this is no way to fight.
you must time your words
— *and your actions* —
make them precise."

TO ENLIGHTEN THE G.O.D.Z.

Act 1: Singing In Haunted Scales

but the tremors
in Ohm Lingo's voice
were heard
and there came
a slither
and twisting of air
approaching near

Ohm Lingo:
"I have to go!"

Kahm:
"no!"

Ohm Lingo:
"I'm not supposed to be here."

Kahm:
"none of us are,"
I said
holding her hand thru the bars
"none of us are supposed to be here.
just hold my hand
wonderful angel
and give us the power to disappear."

speaking sorrow
she let go
and floated away

there I sat
alone and caged
back against a shadow
when snakes and ghosts passed
I covered my naps
up into a wrap
protecting my thoughts
and keeping them intact

words began to spread
from face-to-face

TO ENLIGHTEN THE G.O.D.Z.

Act 1: Singing In Haunted Scales

and little-by-little
we began to escape

I stayed behind
preaching more vibes
ra-storing more lives
helping them flee

           ... until the day
           it all came back
           to haunt me ...
           literally

eye-van
and several snakes
surrounded my cell
I was placed in chains
to drain my name and fill me with shame
I was paraded around like a criminal
bound
but my family ances-tree ties
were too tight

           I looked at eye-van
and began to recite, "y'know, brutha
you see the world thru a blue eye.
you believe in who you are
only thru their lies."

he was silent
speaking louder than I ever could
and I would remember that tactic
(even my enemies seem to teach me)

           Kahm:
"I saw you
from your point of view
when I meditated
I saw thru space.
I felt every emotion
on your face

TO ENLIGHTEN THE G.O.D.Z.

<u>Act 1: Singing In Haunted Scales</u>

as you sold my name
to ghosts and snakes."

silent. he remained.
as our captors dragged me
to the center of a burning stage
surrounded
by snakes and ghosts – all cloaked

shouting
turned to whispers
turned to silence
as heads turned
from me
to
him

NEMTUSAR, the ghost in the flesh

he had become deified
thru the spinning of thousands
of coiled rattling tales and lies
his smile protruded
– curled in grimace –
the rest of his flesh dripped
as if melting, running from his bones
a ragged beard
coiled
from his chin
the hair atop his head
oily and stringy
a tattered tuft
dimly lit crown

I lay at the center of his eyes
and I hoped he would cry
my image free

I bent my knee
and bowed

TO ENLIGHTEN THE G.O.D.Z.

Act 1: Singing In Haunted Scales

Nemtusar:
"<u>why do you speak lies</u>
<u>in my kingdom?</u>"

Kahm:
"I speak wiZdom."

Nemtusar:
"<u>you speak foreign histories</u>."

Kahm:
"I speak Ourstory
so that my people
have a foundation
to succeed."

Nemtusar:
"<u>what good are your stories,</u>
<u>when your people can't even read?</u>
<u>don't believe</u>
<u>in your Grandmother B,</u>
<u>Your Story Book.</u>
<u>burn the words you've looked upon</u>
<u>your people</u>
<u>in soul</u>
<u>do not exist</u>
<u>look away from your 'myths'.</u>
<u>away from your past</u>."

Kahm:
"I ... _we_ study
our story
our past
so that our present
may last
and become a future.

and we'll sample
our ancient civilizations
thru our modern day creations
if you won't let us build new ones.

TO ENLIGHTEN THE G.O.D.Z.

<u>Act 1: Singing In Haunted Scales</u>

it ... it's been
no mystery
the ghost writer
who spreads lies
and misery
thru
our-story."

I lifted from my knee
and looked him in the eye
when I defied
he, the deified lie

I peeled away my wrap
and awakened my naps
letting my natural hair
flow
free

and the chains
began to glow
burn
and
scratch
my soul

– but again, did my knees never bend –

Nemtusar
"remove him!
and let him suffer in descent."

whipped by unholy glow
the blow of snakes and ghosts,

eye-van, that terrible house nigga
dragged me to my destiny

TO ENLIGHTEN THE G.O.D.Z.

Act 1: Singing In Haunted Scales

"DESCENDING UP/READING BACK WORDS"

triumphant.
depths
the
from
up

descendant
this

east
the
in
again
rising

leaves
the
ruffled
they
as
tickled
thoughts
my

breeze
new
every
of
pass
the
with
breath
my
resurrecting
trees
by
surrounded

nature

TO ENLIGHTEN THE G.O.D.Z.

Act 1: Singing In Haunted Scales

of
greenery
the
on
settling
west
this
in
set
I

glide
could
ghost
any
than
better
floating

reside
to
meant
was
son
this
where
was
that
knowing
not

sky
the
to
me
tossed
they
so,

TO ENLIGHTEN THE G.O.D.Z.

Act 11: The Order of Maa Tru Ark

"GRANDMAMA NATURE"

wrapped in rags
breath fresh and new
in the view of the moon's light
and the sun's might
I am held inside the arms of the heir
swept up by the fresh, mystic brume
– this be grandmama nature in bloom –

she nurtures me to health

her breath, the wind
against my chest
and my breath speaking back to her
my words. just. chill.
grandmama's words warm
our breaths mix and create thunder

grandmama speaks loudly my name
her words condense into clouds
and produce rain

I am cleansed by her tears

grandmama nature – on my mother's side

I dance in her rain and natural vibe

TO ENLIGHTEN THE G.O.D.Z.

Act II: The Order of Maa Tru Ark

"VISITATION RITES"

curses kiss my lips
and drip onto the grass

Grandmother B,
Ourstory Book
lay inside my cell
in reach of a snake's
or ghost's grasp

and although free
I wish to dive into time
and plunge into the past

liquid memories stream from my eyes
and they carry the image of Grandmother B,
Ourstory Book
and I look to the grass and see my thoughts
floating
glistening thru my tears

crying a thousand pieces
until my tears make a puzzle of a single thought
crying as a sum of one
my tears
digested by the heat of the sun
run to the heavens and hide in a cloud

they move thru the sky
and drip
drop
as the cloud cries
to water Ohm Lingo's mind
speaking my thoughts aloud
as they are allowed to speak
silently
whispering
clearly
to the angel who rescued me

TO ENLIGHTEN THE G.O.D.Z.

Act 11: The Order of Maa Tru Ark

Kahm:
((I'm alive))

and as my tears loudly brushed
against her mind
like the wings on a butterfly
Ohm Lingo, too, cries

Kahm:
((Ohm Lingo,
I'm alive
and there's something
you must do))

Ohm Lingo:
"what?"

Kahm:
((creep inside my cell,
and walk to the corner
where no light dwells
or glows
there,
hidden underneath the shadow
speaks
Grandmother B,
Ourstory Book.
bring it to me, angel))

Ohm Lingo was silent
and I lent her a prayer
exhaling my spirit into the air

Kahm:
((please, angel.
I beg you
use every ounce of your power))

and there was silence
running as minutes
growing roots

Act II: The Order of Maa Tru Ark

and sprouting hours

…there was silence…

a circle burned on the grass
Ohm Lingo magically stepped free
her image shimmering
close to fading
holding Grandmother B,
Ourstory Book
she placed it gently in front of me

Ohm Lingo:
"it's gotten worse…
every righteous name
spoken like a curse.
they've made our minds a hearse
driving our thoughts to the grave.
snakes and ghosts have formed a frontline
casting illusions into our minds that we are free.

they've created a cracked-brained class
of our kin and kind
broken the family ties that bind
and watch us swing by the neck
from what's left of the rope.

we kill ourselves to look like ghosts
slit our tongues to speak like snakes

we have become frustrated slaves
crawling back to the plantation
letting our masters know we'd rather be in chains

and as for _your_ image and name?
–kahm–
they've negated your image, black man
they plan to shake you from their hands
wash your image away
if you can't be a slave
then you are not needed.

TO ENLIGHTEN THE G.O.D.Z.

Act 11: The Order of Maa Tru Ark

they open our minds and bleed it
if we think about you."

her words touch my brow
I sweat her thoughts
that drip to my lips
and I speak, "I preached once
that our people should hunt for their meaning.
now people who think clearly
have their minds stabbed and left bleeding.
but I know a safe place.
– a haven –
Ohm Lingo, let me return,
and free you from…"

she placed a finger to her lips
and kissed she me a smile

Ohm Lingo:
"remember our agreement?
I'll speak your name,
kissing its syllables,
while you run free?
all I ask, in return
that wherever you go
you inhale life and think of me."

she faded like a ghost
her image dripping time's leaves
from ances-tree
bound were her lips,
her voice,
her kiss,
her skin,

I ponder angels
and wonder
if I would ever
touch
another
again

TO ENLIGHTEN THE G.O.D.Z.

Act II: The Order of Maa Tru Ark

"TRAINING GROUNDZ: MEDITATION OF THE KHAB"

I sit in a clearing
until mind is clear

I kahm
myself
until
I am a single
word

and I speak this word
repeat it like a verse
until I have a conversation with it
holding the word between tongue and lip
bury it
onto these training groundz

I cry sounds that water
the word's burial mound

and the planted word grows roots
sprouts syllable petals
that open like a net
releasing an ancient alphabet

and I speak this 1 word
until I curve its syllables
to help more words grow
resurrecting ancient syllabic souls

my hue glows thru my being
I birth words
thru the womb of my lips

ancient words,
spoken new
I create nativity
combining syllable matter
overcome by my mind
I bind *creatively* with *nativity*

TO ENLIGHTEN THE G.O.D.Z.

Act 11: The Order of Maa Tru Ark

and birth *create-tivity*
spiritually, I now glow with the soul
of my own inner-g

and I know believing in 5 senses
is only a myth
becuz I have found the 6th

and now, able to explode
thru my own energy
I can float on my ancestral heir
and lift

back flip
kick
into a split
fold my legs
and sit

quietly meditating
training on these groundz
I become the sound
of this single word

my aura curves
and ignites my nerves
as I jump into the air
and speak this 1 word
as a whole uni-verse

I absorb all elemental matter
between heaven and earth
and shatter
stars
I let their sparkling debris
fill my body with inner-g
Ixu-god inside of me – Gira the cosmic adhesive
keeps me together, I blend into weather
become the breeze
combining syllable matter
with 'free'

TO ENLIGHTEN THE G.O.D.Z.

Act II: The Order of Maa Tru Ark

I free-ze
solid
again

suspended in air
I ball my fingers into a point
like a pen
firing all celestial inner-g
back into the heavens
I mold stars
back together again

back flip
kick
into a split
fold my legs
and sit

quietly meditating
training on these groundz
I become the sound
of this single word
at. rest. Breathe. Easy. just. BE. me.

practice is over

tomorrow, I journey east
while the sun jumps over me

I will find
my elders
to teach me

for now, I sleep

TO ENLIGHTEN THE G.O.D.Z.

Act II: The Order of Maa Tru Ark

"TAKE A RIGHT 2 PASSAGE"

I know better now
not to journey
thru
the middle
passage
I journey
just
rite
of passage

walking east I step into a past age
a city where pyramids still stand
and blaze with the reflection of the sun
time's sands run like a river
while at night the stars twinkle and glitter
off windows on domed towers
that stretch like arms
to praise the heavens

boxed houses, windows stained with color
clouded with laughter on the inside
celebration
giddy, sexual elations – hollers of freedom

personally
my 'I' – not dotted –
sees clearly

I walk like I float
and cross every universi-**T**

their walls glimmer like the stars
and they hold the knowledge
to unlock the same heavenly bodies
turning the stars into signs
to guide our lives
and provide 12 houses for the sun to reside

this city is my home

TO ENLIGHTEN THE G.O.D.Z.

Act 11: The Order of Maa Tru Ark

I hear air billowing
like thunder whispering
seeping from lips that are reading each other
speaking as sisters and brothers
dressed in the proper leaves of the ances-tree

hair locked or braided
bushes of fire twisted
bald headed or faded
brothers
         and
sisters
crowned properly

I drop to my knees
and bow my head
humble to be here
my troubled footprints
         now behind me
fill in
fade
...and disappear...

TO ENLIGHTEN THE G.O.D.Z.

Act II: The Order of Maa Tru Ark

"HOUR COUNCIL"

dark
15 degrees apart
24 elders levitate
as they meditate
connected as 1 mind and 1 heart
their bodies glowing soul
each 20 and 4 are sacred gems

time stands still thru them
they have seen rotations
and divisions
of stars split into constellations
cos-mystic-politicians
governing the heavens
these venerable warrior sages
have witnessed the passing of 12 ages
25,000 revolutions around the sun

and these elders know
that before a greater kingdom arrives
it will be a change in time that comes

I step into the center
and place Grandmother B,
OurStory Book
down on the floor
bend 1 knee
and bow my head
to the 24 elders

they speak in two voices
masculine and feminine
the sound
echoing
inside my body

SPEAK YOUR NAME

ꟘO ENLIGHꟘEN ꟘHE G.ꟳ.ꟳ.Z.

Act 11: The Order of Maa Tru Ark

Kahm:
"I am kahm noiz
my name once destroyed
has resurrected thru the void,
and become black whole again.

I have already learned the khab.
used it to blend with the wind
and all of natures elements.
I solidified my family from vapor
met my father pen and mother paper
they scribed inside me majestic magic, like the picatrix
they instructed me to journey thru prison mist

but, sadly, prison has not missed me
nor I it
as it sits
on the outside of my forehead
clouding my thoughts.
my mind still caught in its mist edu-cage.
I seek lies to be erased
so that my mind can find a gentle page
for its thoughts and words to rest on.

great hour council
please, free me."

WHAT MUST B, WILL B

my eyes glisten with tears
as the council disappears
and I am left alone in the center of light
surrounded by the dark

from my left
walks a man dressed
in black robes and black sashes

he is not death
but life at the beginning

TO ENLIGHTEN THE G.O.D.Z.

Act II: The Order of Maa Tru Ark

"TIDE TURNER"

his name filtered
from the scented waft and flame
of incense burners
he greets me, "well,
I am mystagogue turner
teacher of ancient arts
I speak in the language of lightning and thunder
when my lips part

bellowing words
blowing in the wind
I send
bolts of electrical syllables
from heaven down onto you
erasing the lies from your eyes
and scripting cosmic truth."

I stood enlightened
the lightning of his words
lighting the room
and mystagogue turner
formed from a shadow
to a venerable figure
caught in my view

the wool of his crown
was like ash and smoke
as his seering thoughts
and visions
sear from his head
spiraling. locked. and dread.

he was a godly
golden-bronzed
vision
the visage of this sage
rippling with woolly smoke and ash
crowning his lip and chin

TO ENLIGHTEN THE G.O.D.Z.

Act II: The Order of Maa Tru Ark

his knowledge
rested inside
both eyes
and they burned
searing visions

though light as air
his thoughts weighed heavy
his eyes were separate worlds
with their own gravity
pulling me in

worlds
too heavy
for atlas to hold
or move

and here was I
muscular
but slender
and ready
(hopefully)
to hold all the knowledge
that mystagogue turner knew

TO ENLIGHTEN THE G.O.D.Z.

Act II: The Order of Maa Tru Ark

"RA-BIRTH"

I float
dangling from an invisible rope
connected to the sun
held in the space
of where I am descended from

slowly,
gently,
I brush my back against the sands
slowly,
gently,
my body lands

mystagogue turner chants, "child running to man
born of the woman's verse
inside her womb-a-verse
we will cast away your physical
so that you may search
for celestial materials
that will fill the empty space inside you
and reclaim your spiritual birthright."

mystagogue turner
turns the earth
casting dirt to my body
and I witness the sky melt into night
and the sun dissolve into stars
while black holes raise the temperature
and burn the sands
my physical body dissolves
from being a man
liquefies,
spirals,
and begins to dance

I spin thru black loops
and spool thru the earth's spine

I outline the earth

TO ENLIGHTEN THE G.O.D.Z.

Act II: The Order of Maa Tru Ark

as the earth out lines me
speaking in phrases mortals call the breeze

(never battle the earth
the origin of verses' birth
thru poe-a-trees)

I am pulled towards earthly elements
and the gravity of 1000 celestial bodies
I am
s t r e t c h i n g
into infinity
the sun rises from inside me
kicking like a newborn to be free

the **hue** of this young **man**
trying to be
in a constant state of **being**

every lie becomes a tear I cry
that drips back down onto me
bursting in 1000 degrees of heat
I produce an atmosphere
from my lips and introduce space
to the sound of an earth shattering
scream

stars shoot and fall
drown my sound
whip,
tie,
and bound me to space
lies melt and erase
soul forms from this womb-a-verse
and finds its place
as the mentality of mars
drips
          drips
                    drips away
I am original soul at peace
held inside a physical body

TO ENLIGHTEN THE G.O.D.Z.

Act II: The Order of Maa Tru Ark

the night molds into morning skies
while the stars solidify into sunlight
I am black whole again
black holes
close off and fly away in the wind

I float
dangling
from an invisible rope
connected to the sun
held in the womb-a-verse
of where I am ra-born from

nature's
great
womb

slowly,
gently,
I brush my back against the sands
slowly,
gently,
my body lands
kissing the hands of the earth
lies erased
replaced with a soul
gone thru
a ra-birth

TO ENLIGHTEN THE G.O.D.Z.

Act II: The Order of Maa Tru Ark

"DEAN RUTHER"

in myself
back again
soul,
with body,
and mind
all 3 blend seamlessly
my eyes reflect me
becoming a heated image
burning 1000 degrees

and from there,
mystagogue turner
takes me to a room
filled with chants and tunes
lit by the light of the moon
where warriors called oluso
feast
as they give praise
to the sun's womb in the east
and speak,
like masters,
all 7 words perfectly

and I wonder
which oluso priest
or priestess
will teach me
properly
these 7 words

and then I saw darkness
stepping in physical form
emanating soul
and casting nubian light
like his fellow warriors
he blinded you with blackness
that glowed bright from his flesh
his hue constantly blazing
and burning kinetic-ali

TO ENLIGHTEN THE G.O.D.Z.

Act II: The Order of Maa Tru Ark

his title
was dean
        his name
        was ruther
chiseled and sculpted might
brought to life
flesh
echoing night
eyes speaking the stars' light
his voice like a potential fire
ready to ignite

his brown sashes and robes
flowing like melodies, musical odes
floating on the wind
stretching like wings
fluttering to sing in morse code

but when he approached
he never used his lips when he spoke
like his fellow warriors,
his voice was heard
when his words like the wind
curved and bent in electrical strands

the twists in his hair
and the lock of his eyes' stare
landed in your hands
seeped into your skin
and kissed the inside of your mind
like the gentle touch of the wind

like many before him
he was nurtured in the arms of grandmama nature
birthed thru the womb of his own mother paper
taught properly
by Grandmother B,
Ourstory Book

I would not learn 7 words

Act 11: The Order of Maa Tru Ark

but the proper truth
spoken thru the 7 kheru

Ruther:
**what is your ren?
your true name,
the way your soul
from dark matter and dark inner-g
was sent.**

Kahm:
"my name is kahm noiz.
soul resurrected from the void."

hands on my shoulders
eyes on my soul
ruther,
again,
thru his mind
spoke:

Ruther:
**all here!
listen to my reason
for I declare in rhyme
for you to bear witness
I take kahm noiz
as my apprentice
to learn the 7 kheru.

child-running-to-man
you will speak truth.**

TO ENLIGHTEN THE G.O.D.Z.

Act II: The Order of Maa Tru Ark

"REST THRU CELEBRATION"

I rest when my eyes blink
kick back with stardust and drink
swim thru the black sea of my people
and flirt when my eyes wink

I mingle with stars
when the day fades
and continue to ball
even when the night
shrinks

this black machine
runs best on kinks

feet moving like water
when I tap
dance close to a feminine soul
and hold kinky thoughts back
in nap-sacks
my wild
divine hair
never relaxed
kick back
stardust – drink and feast

for the first time when I rest
there are no nightmares when I sleep
and when I'm awake
it's like I've always dreamed
surrounded by freedom
feminine and masculine souls
black shining righteously
their caring arms
embracing and holding tight
to me

cuz I fight for them
as they fight for me

ᖶⵔ ᴇNᒪIᏀᕼᖶᴇN ᖶᕼᴇ Ꮆ.ⵔ.Ꮻ.Z.

Act II: The Order of Maa Tru Ark

"TOURING THE ANCIENTS"

I'm clothed respectfully
robes and sashes
flowing
like my tongue
ready to practice
the 7 kheru

ruther speaks
guiding me thru the city
on words
and heir

Ruther:
**this is Maa-Tru-Ark
covenant and womb
where knowledge blossoms and blooms
we the people are the Paa-Tru-Ark
we build to maintain her balance
it is peace solidified
like daydreams coming true—

Ah! forgive me. I'm no poet

however,
it's a black city where we build thoughts into reality
and where bruthaz and sistaz
rome free
studying actively
the 7 kheru
to battle snakes and ghosts
for the soul of our Ances-Tree

we meditate on the day when we escape 3rd density
forming into a triple trinity
involuted into ourselves
the four elements boiling over in us
angling light on a 90 degree plane – diagonally, like heru ptah
we fly just the same
to evolve into a star

ΤΟ ΕΝLIGHTEN THE G.Θ.D.Z.

Act II: The Order of Maa Tru Ark

to dissolve and fade
against the blackdrop of space.**

I am overwhelmed
and warmed over
the city stands bold
like a protector
and I am to be trained
to defend her
and the wonderful
natural
element of nature
that stands tall in the distance

the Ances-Tree

I can feel its power
beneath the earth
its roots
connecting to me
while the sun's tendrils
touch every leaf

the pyramids of the city
pulling on my breath
every time
I breathe
in sync with my heart
every time it gave a beat

inside the chorus
of this city's song
is where myself
as a word
belongs

there were meditation chambers
digi-glas, combat simulators
airship hangars

ruther told me

TO ENLIGHTEN THE G.O.D.Z.

Act 11: The Order of Maa Tru Ark

in order for him to feel alive
he needed to fly
and touch the sky

I remained silent
as he recounted
countless adventures
as a pilot
against snakes and ghosts

Ruther:
**we are able to blend
technology with our power
plus nauture's wind.
we create balance.**

he looked closer at me
almost ... thru my body
and felt what I was feeling

Ruther:
**you're anxious to learn
stay inside your namesake,
kahm.
you've had a hard life – to this point.
enjoy your safety – this, your sanctuary.
your first lesson: know when to rest.**

I smile, feel blessed
...and safe.

TO ENLIGHTEN THE G.O.D.Z.

Act II: The Order of Maa Tru Ark

"KHEMI-LOHIM"

black diamond
shaped spades
in the heart of the city
I enter this club

khemi-lohim

I step into lights and laughter
a gathering of 16 shades of black
in all styles and patterns

I wonder
which feminine saturn
I could slip my rings onto
dancing and singing
in this atmosphere
with beats that surround you

– but masculinity would distract me –

an ally created water in his own vibe

leaning over the railing
I see a rally
of heavenly student bodies
circling
a single
son
his robe
            dangling
feet
crossed
and linked
as he floated
and recited words
in meditation

Floating Poet:
"I am like king saul,

TO ENLIGHTEN THE G.O.D.Z.

Act II: The Order of Maa Tru Ark

floating thru meditation
between floor, ceiling,
and these walls.
even without the earth beneath my feet
I can feel my connection
to the Ances-Tree

and with its power
nothing around me
can battle me."

Kahm:
"really?"

eyes, sharp like swords
point in my direction

hop. over railing.
my robes sailing up – I drop down
and meet the floating poet
in the center of the room
his smile blooms
and his voice billows and booms

Floating Poet:
"if you got words for me ...
... then I suggest you speak."

let's see if I can make his smile
fade back into his black
and fade to blank

I whip crack my lips

Kahm:
"your style is like the emperor's new clothes
transparent and see thru
and even if you performed
1 of jesus's miracles
I still wouldn't believe in you!"

TO ENLIGHTEN THE G.O.D.Z.

Act 11: The Order of Maa Tru Ark

and there's nothing
but *'ahhhs'*
and *'oohhs'*

but this mysterious floating poet
just bathes in lyrical waters
and lets his words flow and cruise

Floating Poet:
"naw, kid
I'm the emperor's new groove
bald headed and smooth
my heart's got rhythm
with its beat
to make you move
I dissect lies from the truth
the telephone tone of my voice
is filled with fax and proof.

I'm a heavenly angel
with a beautiful angle
that's why the women call me a-cute."

his feet meet the floor
and he battles me with words
in colours I've never seen before
blinding me in an array of divine light
stopping me in this verbal fight
but my tongue has yet
to reach back
and throw all it's might
in a single breath

Kahm:
"when I sing into african sands…"

blank verse

Crowd:
"c'mon now, sun.
bring it!"

TO ENLIGHTEN THE G.O.D.Z.

Act 11: The Order of Maa Tru Ark

Kahm:
"when I sing into african sands…
I feel time run backwards into my hands
and begin to flow and roll with soul
I'm so cool
my presence can make summer seem cold
my thoughts are so concrete
you believe you can actually hold
any 1 of my rhythms and rhymes
catch this entire crowd of fish
and reel them in
with just 1 of my lines."

and the crowd lights up in a flash
we cast our robes away
and our words continue to clash
but we move from the flow
let our souls
and true intentions glow
we roll with the wheel of our words
while we spoke
we talk about our attacks
on snakes and ghosts

we crowd of students
our feet become drum machines
and our hands clap
with a spastic beat

I scream, "snakes and ghosts
are copy cat killers,!"

the poet yells back,
"we'll be their grave diggers."

and thru the kheru
we conjure christ figures
writers of the isis papers
we sing well
and well-sing

TO ENLIGHTEN THE G.O.D.Z.

Act II: The Order of Maa Tru Ark

browder
diop
and epps
john henrick – and all the rest
their spirits swirl inside vapors
our breath beginning to condense
and we speak to our ancestors
with a 6th sense

the poet concludes,
"we'll set time straight
and every line they've bent
we got the true 7 kheru
words heaven sent
formed by our tongues
as they melt into our bald heads or locks!"

Kahm:
"and we'll reconstruct the fire inside our center
like a modern day cheops."

our dances rock
growing root words
thru the 7 kheru
and we digest food for thought
cultivating our syllable crops

and when all but one letter of the alphabet disappears
and drops
our groove stops
on Q
and every glowing hue
all shades of black
embrace 1 another
beautiful sistaz – beautiful bruthaz

TO ENLIGHTEN THE G.O.D.Z.

Act 11: The Order of Maa Tru Ark

"ALIK KEEM"

clothed with his warrior's robe
the poet introduces himself

Alik:
"I am alik keem."
he points out,
"that woman,
in the corner,
with the locks
is my queen.
her name is MooRah.
her beauty is the daughter
to every angel and god.
they call her, 'pretti-lox'.

and what is your name and title?"

my broken record
continues to spin
on my lips
in the same place
in the words

Kahm:
"my name is kahm noiz
my name
once destroyed
has resurrected thru the void."

Alik:
"you escaped prison mist?"

Kahm:
"yes. no myth.
our people
trapped inside
by snakes and ghosts
question whether or not
they even exist.

TO ENLIGHTEN THE G.O.D.Z.

Act II: The Order of Maa Tru Ark

they are trained to cower
when a ghost glides by
or a snake speaks with a hiss.

their hopes
like their backs
are bent
and they believe
they can set themselves straight
thru ghosts' and snakes'
false knowledge
tunneled thru false universities
mist edu-caged
to set themselves straight
with 90 degrees.
far from the 720 and 120 they need."

Alik:
"what was it like?"

and I begin
my head spins
I recount the daze clearly
days
I spent in the prison's mist
hazy-day dreaming ways to escape
I speak thru tears
that spell cid
and water persun
I exhale the image of the maiden
Ohm Lingo
accosted of her innocence
I inhale life
and think of her again

silent

remembering my promise
I battle and push away
violent thoughts of revenge
and speak about the guidance of grace

TO ENLIGHTEN THE G.O.D.Z.

Act II: The Order of Maa Tru Ark

I received by my parents
the brilliance of their words
leading me from the dark
to this city
Maa-Tru-Ark

I feel their souls embracing me
I inhale every name
cid,
persun,
Ohm Lingo,
father pen,
mother paper,
I exhale another description
and use the khab
so my words can properly beam
and enter the mind of alik keem

this new ally
beams back thoughts
connected
to my train-of-thought-tracks

Alik:
**we're all here for you, brutha.
learn your words
speak like lightning
and boom like thunder.
let the dying leaves
of our Ances-Tree recover.
we'll exhale life to our roots
and touch every leaf
like the gentle hand of a lover.**

we embrace with glow and hands
as we understand
we are a part of a greater plan
I am kahm noiz
young child becoming young man
an age at its end

TO ENLIGHTEN THE G.O.D.Z.

Act 11: The Order of Maa Tru Ark

(now all I truly need
is the wonderful touch
of a beautiful
black
woman)

TO ENLIGHTEN THE G.O.D.Z.

Act 11: The Order of Maa Tru Ark

"HAUNTED AURA-GIN 1 : RUEBUE"

we sit
students in class
listening
mystagogue turner
speak of snake histories
and their haunted past

Turner:
"perfect black lost his grip on his son
and the sun dropped to set.
light was caught
in nighttime's net
and ice formed from the wind

it absorbed the colour of the moon
split in two
and slipped inside
a black man's seed
and a black woman's womb

from our righteousness
came foul sin when the sun rose again
black man and black woman
conceived a dead child

black
but lost of soul
born of flesh
but still a ghost
able to absorb
the heat of the sun
but still produced
words that were cold

solid in physical form
but there was something about him
that you could see thru

his name was Ruebue.

ＴＯ ＥＮＬＩＧＨＴＥＮ ＴＨＥ Ｇ.Ｏ.Ｄ.Ｚ.

Act II: The Order of Maa Tru Ark

he spoke foul words
and curses to his parents

Rubue:
'I will create creatures
of haunts and slithers
that will rule you.'

and he grew to study the soul
its glow, aura, and magnetic field
its ever coming light
its strengths
and its shields
and he studied ways
to manipulate it thru steel
to steal the power of soul
extract from black whole intact
and turn a righteous spirit
into a ghost."

taking notes
as turner spoke
he paused
while we students
wrote

then he continued, "he separated all from allies
and created all lies
in our 'ies' speaking deceit
spinning his words like silk
the spider snared time flies
biding time
converting those
with a naive ear to his side

his trail of tricks
leading back to his lips
empty words filled with
hollow promises

TO ENLIGHTEN THE G.O.D.Z.

Act 11: The Order of Maa Tru Ark

ruebue reversed
the knowledge we kept
plotted carefully
and preached
to put his plans in effect

a false king on his throne
by a Black King and Black Queen
he was thrown in prison for his haze
blurry visions

with his followers
he was cast away
thru the african atmosphere
in the patmosphere
on an island of revelation
where his plan of black annihilation
took on its special effect

a 666 year plan
beginning at the day's end.

ruebue taught his top scientists
all the magnetic properties
of soul
how to de-melanate it
and dull its glow
freeze ice to it
and slow down its growth

generation
to
generation
all that were generated
     thru father
     thru mother
     from child
were ghosts."

TO ENLIGHTEN THE G.O.D.Z.

Act II: The Order of Maa Tru Ark

"DE-CYPHER 1: KHAB, KHAIBIT, SAHU"

I trained
where quiet
speaks
in anograms
– to listen –
silent
carefully
as ruther taught me
the 7 kheru
and their branch
(association) to
the Ances-Tree

the wind was still
and the grass
glowed
green

ruther
'spoke'
properly:

Ruther:
**the khab
divides your physical body
and bleeds you into the wind
and all earthly elements

it stores inner-g
connected to the trunk
of the Ances-Tree
linking its roots to your feet

stepping in the earth's words
walk and listen to what the earth has said
– its name is osain-geb –**

so this energy
walked with me

⊤⊖ ENLIGHTEN THE G.⊖.⊃.Z.

Act 11: The Order of Maa Tru Ark

wherever the earth
touched my feet
and even
beyond
to the sky
when I learn to fly

Ruther:
**bubbling,
burning
in the middle
you will feel the sensual,
and speak to your soul
mating with
your own feminine aspect.
the **khaibit** will teach you
to speak with your heart
and see a respected
Black Goddess
as respected
thru
a third
and single eye
on head.**

I meditate
on the words
that have been spoken
and said

more syllables
are bled by ruther:

Ruther:
**both these two kheru
can be connected
by studying the **sahu**.
— all 720 degrees — 120 in lead
— of your physical body
placed together,

TO ENLIGHTEN THE G.O.D.Z.

Act 11: The Order of Maa Tru Ark

all three will guide you,
on a thousand journeys
and a thousand lifetime trips.
now, with what you've learned,
begin to practice.

the lesson, over
class dismissed.**

⊖ ENLIGHTEN THE G.⊖.Ð.Z.

Act 11: The Order of Maa Tru Ark

"SAFI-OYA"

I saw sun light
shine down on midnight
when she walked in rhythm
from the bass
of the pyramid
she glided gently on the wind

her hair, natural
weaves into a crown
an extension of her thoughts
never relaxed

her dress,
patterned with flowers
outlining the delicate
flower that she is

her strength
vibrates like a drum
and I come to believe
its her blackness
that gives light to the sun

and as her image makes my thoughts flow
her sensuality makes the syllables of my khaibit
EE RR EE CC TT
and begin to grow

I moisten the air
with my tongue
letting the space
between us become wet
rub my head
with her image
to make my thoughts erect
and slowly
words –
harden –
straight –

ꓕO ENLIGHTEN THE G.O.D.Z.

<u>Act II: The Order of Maa Tru Ark</u>

my thoughts
a continuous line
I penetrate her mind
and she reaches back
touches me
and holds time

this Black Woman
stops
rubs her belly
and tickles her inner-G spot
and what we hold that is special
is more than an effect
when our minds connect

Kahm:
my name is kahm noiz.

Safi-oya:
**I am safi-oya.
commander of over a thousand oluso.
and to a thousand students
I am a professor.**

and enter safi-oya
into my life
as I wish
to enter life
into safi-oya

she looks to me
and smiles
walks away
turning my inches
into miles
and extending my thoughts
farther

let me step away
into safi-oya
my future

TO ENLIGHTEN THE G.O.D.Z.

Act 11: The Order of Maa Tru Ark

away from my past
this
wonderful
Black
Professor
walking onward
with nothing but elegance and class
that I. need. to. attend.

TO ENLIGHTEN THE G.O.D.Z.

Act 11: The Order of Maa Tru Ark

"LISTEN, AS I DESCRIBE"

I step back into shadow and blend
become the wind
and end up
four domed towers down from khemi-lohim
where alik keem and his queen
– moorah, the pretti-lox –
dine and eat

and their eyes
nibble on my appearance
but my eyes
smiling and shining on them
still see safi-oya

Kahm:
"friends! friends! friends!
throw my heart into the sky
let it pump the syllables of her name
and let love reign – pull me in and rein
pouring her image thru my veins
so that I may always
feel her image inside me.
or just rain into my eyes
so that I could always see."

and two friends
as 1
begin to tease

I step to them, take seat
and exhale relief

alik kickstands
and gives me support

Alik:
"all right, man!
give us the name of your future queen."

ƬO ENLIGHTEN THE G.O.D.Z.

Act II: The Order of Maa Tru Ark

Kahm:
"ahh, the future is too far away
even if it's just a minute

I need her image in my arms
right here
in the present.
this beautiful gift of the heavens."

alik's eyes, boulder
roll on the wave of emotion
carved into his visage
until they land
on a teasing smile
while low
rumbling wind
as laughter
escapes his lips
and his body quakes

Kahm:
"come now, man.
just ... listen, as I describe

she's a drop from the galaxy's midnight sky
I would take the colour of all four seasons
but only paint springtime in her eyes
so that flowers blossom and bloom
nurtured by the tears she cried
and I would break her heart
just to see that magic occur
time after time.

her name is safi-oya.
she is—"

Alik:
"—commander
of over a thousand oluso!
and to a thousand students
she is a professor.

TO ENLIGHTEN THE G.O.D.Z.

Act 11: The Order of Maa Tru Ark

oh, kahm!"

Kahm:
"calm???
no, no, no, my friend

she excites every syllable in my name
and I cannot remain that way."

Moorah:
"it's like music
when you speak of her."

Alik:
"yeah! muse-sick.
ahh,
my queen,
pretti-lox,
have you fallen ill to this?
safi-oya is a commander,
a professor.
there's no way for a union!
        – of course, age means nothing –
safi-oya is but a few cycles older
but rank…
his muse-sick is poisonous."

Kahm:
"I found the cure to muse-sick.
she is now a muse."

Alik:
"how a-muse-sing."

Kahm:
"pretti-lox,
my words have value with you?"

Moorah:
"yes, they do.
just

TO ENLIGHTEN THE G.O.D.Z.

Act 11: The Order of Maa Tru Ark

turn a blind eye
and deaf ear
to my husband
please, continue."

Kahm:
"yes,
let me say I imagine safi-oya's smile
so much
that it has become my imagination
adorned with bright thoughts
and colourful creations
safi-oya has become my 6th sensation."

Moorah:
"alik, what would be the trouble
if this black knight
and black queen
found love?
battling side-by-side,
saving future black lives,
and **procreating** as much?"

Alik:
"these two?
black knight?
black queen?
check mates?"

and I retaliate
with moor words,

Kahm:
"if only I could speak
the word 'knight',
to carve it from my breath
right in front of your eyes,
so you could realize
the word 'knight',
is actually
'king' in disguise."

TO ENLIGHTEN THE G.O.D.Z.

Act 11: The Order of Maa Tru Ark

Alik:
"don't even start
a battle of words
you can't finish.
I've been nice so far."

Kahm:
"no drama of words—
not today.
peace has entered my heart
that had been broken into 14 pieces,
but my crisis is now mended by this isis."

I leave
to think
to study

… to think …

safi-oya,

I wiish to study thoughts of her
closer…

⊤⊖ ENLIGHTEN THE G.⊖.D.Z.

Act II: The Order of Maa Tru Ark

"HAUNTED AURA-GIN 2: GRADIOUS"

seated
again

silent

listening to mystagogue turner
as his lessons on snakes and ghosts
continues:

Turner:
"ruebue died at the age of 152

his legacy and insanity
passed down
to his descendants

a ghost named Gradious
heir to ruebue's foul winds

he was re-molded without soul
in the image of his lesser father

trained, shaped,
and ready to finish the plans
to diminish our hue
and cut
the Ances-Tree from its roots.

these fixed people,
drafted, sterile
ruled by ruebue's top disciple,
were now see-thru
lost of soul – ghosts.

and lies were born inside them
death, murder, mayhem

gradious studied his lesser father
– closely –

TO ENLIGHTEN THE G.O.D.Z.

Act II: The Order of Maa Tru Ark

all of ruebue's lessons
genesis
now twisted
lost
in dementia

with the mind of a snake
gradious would take to the tree of knowledge
and leave its fruit raped
plucked,
not ripe
but rotted
he and his people plotted

gradious added tricks
to knowledge
and created tricknology
fused tricks
to ma'at
and created
a ma'atricks
surrounding our people with dreams
he carved magical wands
from holly trees
and with these holly-wood staffs
he would lead our people
down an illusionary path

gradious knew how to spin spells
and with these holly-wood wands
we
would
wander
twisting
trying to be cast
loudly
in stero-type-cast
by
holly-wood staffs.

armed with tricknology

TO ENLIGHTEN THE G.O.D.Z.

Act II: The Order of Maa Tru Ark

and holly-wood wands
– all weapons in his hand –
gradious led these ghosts
back to the original lands
to burn the sands
instead of caressing them
and letting them run
burning sands
unlike the sun

and with fine smiles
these ghosts glided
trustingly
back
into our kingdoms

possessions would come
our nations
undone
as ghosts possessed sistaz and bruthaz
putting us at war with one another

in those deceitful days
civil war reigned
blood spilled from clouds
lies tickled our tongues
to dance and swim from our mouths

united in war
to kill sistaz and bruthaz

all original tribes against one another

ghosts were possessing us
doing themselves justice
but what about
just
us?
black figures
to crystallize our mindz

TO ENLIGHTEN THE G.O.D.Z.

<u>Act II: The Order of Maa Tru Ark</u>

gradious, the ghost leader,
this war's creator
stood
to control us
acting
as a benevolent mediator

always the snake

this ghost's quest
was to resurrect
to feign an injection of life
as he sprinkled death
over the beds
where we warriors slept
content
and
complacent with rest
the theft of our knowledge
was something we never did expect
wavering on the words
we swore we would serve and protect

multiplying our distrust for one another
we were easily ruled
once we were divided

but nerves were struck
deep down
there was a saving song
in all of us
militant messiah sequence
black dot
melanin drop
daath ele-vator
lay deep inside warriors' chords
and these
bless-ed
Black men
and
Black women

TO ENLIGHTEN THE G.O.D.Z.

Act II: The Order of Maa Tru Ark

gripped their swords
and made war
with gradious and his ghosts

these warriors
quickly
severed
dis-chord words from gradious' throat
black warriors increased the gravity
so that these soulless spirits
could no longer float
absorbed the shadows' might
so the ghosts could no longer hide
inhaled universal winds
so the ghosts could no longer glide

these ghosts' power faded
no longer able
to possess our people
or
seed us from within

they were driven out
cast toward the clouds
to allow the sands to burn them
for the mayhem
they brought to our lands

cast out
burned by sun-above
and from below, by the sands

but the ghosts were still protected
by the hand of an ungod
and ungoddess
these ghosts were pushed
to a frigid land, not promised

they fell upon the face of the full moon
swirling
in

TO ENLIGHTEN THE G.O.D.Z.

Act II: The Order of Maa Tru Ark

a
void – an infertile womb

this not-promised land
possessed by ghosts
while Black Warriors
cut them off from knowledge
by lightning woven into a rope

some ghosts became solid
others melted into dead water
forming burning lakes
some ghosts developed
slithering tongues
and devolved into snakes."

TO ENLIGHTEN THE G.O.D.Z.

Act II: The Order of Maa Tru Ark

"DE-CYPHER 2: AB, SHEKHEM, KHU"

> back
> in clearing
> back
> against the wind
> facing forward
> as I send thoughts
> into natural elements
>
> ruther continues
> to guide me
> in the 7 disciplines

Ruther:
**have you studied, kahm?
have you studied, calmly?
patiently,
not anxious?**

> **Kahm**:
> **yes, I have.
> I've let my khaibit
> extend
> to kiss the mind
> of a Black Woman
> placed
> in my destiny's
> path.**

> ruther smiles

Ruther:
**well,
you will learn
3 more of the kheru today —
next class, the last.
and then,
you will be tested
in 7 Physical Essays.**

TO ENLIGHTEN THE G.⊙.D.Z.

Act II: The Order of Maa Tru Ark

he wipes a hand,
gently,
before my eyes
and I close scenery
to emptiness
and I concentrate
on the magical darkness
dancing in my mind

Ruther:
the **Ab,
associate of the heart,
the truth,
controlled by balance
beating
like a warrior's drum
pumping bravery
for you
to become
the mwindo-heru,
thru this kheru.

you will feel faith
pouring onto you
drowning you in a warm light.
you will feel the chaos
of the battlefield,
the fight.
but as a warrior
you will see this chaos
as if it were paradise.
you as the warrior
will understand
sacrifice, for future life.**

and I am reminded
of situations
where I have felt blinded
and overwhelmed with the fight
battling for Grandfather Clock
and Grandmother B,

TO ENLIGHTEN THE G.O.D.Z.

Act II: The Order of Maa Tru Ark

Ourstory Book
but something kept me ...
as my namesake

something kept me
battling

my mind clear for battle,
clear for the fight
auras of past
oluso
dispersing a blinding light

it seems
these words
— these kheru —
were always
with me

Ruther:
**and the kheru
could not exist
without
tongue
or
the lips
and we celebrate this
through the **Shekhem**

this is your voice.
it guides you to speak these kheru
properly.

you will have
your enemies
fear your voice
and pray
for gunshots.**

mold my words
as weapons?

TO ENLIGHTEN THE G.O.D.Z.

Act II: The Order of Maa Tru Ark

have them be
weighed
upon
a balance, the sacred scales
to speak the truth
and fire them
thru
snakes' and ghosts' lies
wherever
they may
lie?

Ruther:
the **Khu
is your 3rd eye.
it allows you to see
even when you're blind.

but
beware those
with the power of
Yah-Khus.
they will graft your perception
into the illusion of their deception

when you learn this kheru
you can converse with the future
in the present time.
then time your actions – perfectly
re-write time's line.**

Eye script. Eye speak. Eye learn.

I will study closely
and be like a master
when I return

TO ENLIGHTEN THE G.O.D.Z.

Act II: The Order of Maa Tru Ark

"RUNNING AFTER NOON"

waiting
chasing
safi-oya
was like
running
after
noon

so first, my fixed earth
would have to wait
until her venus
was at my zenith
and I could
penetrate space

… and there she was …

walking
or rather
dancing

beauty
dripping
raindrops
from her face

art in motion
that not even the most skilled painter
could trace

her body curved
to excite my nerves
jerking
and
jumping
in a manner
no drug could imitate
no matter how it was laced

TO ENLIGHTEN THE G.O.D.Z.

Act II: The Order of Maa Tru Ark

natural hair
up in an african wrap
a moorish sword strapped to her back
this woman was 'moor'
than I could imagine

I place my study-books in my pack
latch it over my shoulder
run – quickly – and bravely
stand
before
safi-oya

losing an internal
verbal battle
I am at a loss
for words

safi-oya smiles
waving my words
onto her landing pad

and I speak
carefully
but still
foolishly

Kahm:
"if you…
if you…
if you could speak back
to every word you read…"

no! no!
I've already said that

Kahm:
"if I could speak words back in…"

what. am. I. doing?

TO ENLIGHTEN THE G.O.D.Z.

Act 11: The Order of Maa Tru Ark

remember my namesake!
(inhale)
remember my namesake!
(exhale)
remember my namesake!
(inhale)

relax
and
concentrate

– fighting battles
is easier than making love –
but volcanically,
my words errupt
orgasm raised
to come
up

Kahm:
"if I could put you on the spot
every time I opened my mouth
I'd speak your name
in every corner of my house."

Safi-oya:
"young student,
I would wrap my lips
around your forehead,
and just blow your mind."

surprised, I back up
as my words get backed up
clog my throat for me to choke
but I'm hanging
on every word
hoping to find the time
to drop a single line

but she continues to speak, "my heavenly body
would eclipse your son-light

TO ENLIGHTEN THE G.O.D.Z.

Act 11: The Order of Maa Tru Ark

melt into midnight
and let the stars begin sweating
as I continue melting onto you
and blend
as the melanin in our skin.

I am black
and cool as the wind
I can pull righteousness
out of a sin
put my arms
around my grandmama nature
and blend

as mother nature
I gave birth to the sun
put the rhythm of my heart
inside an african drum
and gave it its beat

I've melted from a queen
and have been every profession
– respected –
most likely
invented it
as a judge of words,
I've taken every curse
and sentenced it."

I rub my hands
in front of my lips
to warm my words

she wants to battle? … okay … this is only a test …
this professor will find out
I have been studying yet
and so, I profess

Kahm:
"your words twist my tongue
letting my imagination

TO ENLIGHTEN THE G.O.D.Z.

Act II: The Order of Maa Tru Ark

r u n
so vividly
until you come
or day becomes void of light
bringing your shadow
into my sight
star gazing
my comet breaking
and penetrating your night
as I lick in between the breath of your voice
until, yes,
I confess
you give birth to my son
and I kiss your belly
until our child
humz
kicks
and
taps
against you
for his mother's heart will be his drum.
playing on his umbilical *chord*
and striking soul with every strum

allowing you to breathe music
and let you sing
every time you exhale that cool air
from your lungs to fan you
— but remember,
it was my breath and thought put up in you,
course thru the obstacle
making sounds full of your cool, musical voice possible."

this
court-ship
is fun to fly

safi-oya continues to speak
flirtatiously cold
while at the same time
she motions for me to come closer

TO ENLIGHTEN THE G.O.D.Z.

Act 11: The Order of Maa Tru Ark

thru morse code gestures
with her eyes

*(and don't think this line-pitcher
missed this feminine catcher's signs)*

Safi-oya:
"foolish,
young,
student.
child becoming man
always trying to light
your life
thru a son.

I don't need a son to shine.
I can spend bath times
bathing in the darkness
of my maternal waters
and fertilize my seed
to resurrect me
in the form of my daughter

would you like to drown in my waters?
you couldn't
not if you just spoke my name
for it would be like
coming
up
for air
without the need to inhale
you would constantly breathe
possessing yourself with me.

all your thoughts
orbit me
because I am like gravity."

Kahm:
"I have been studying longer
lifting heavy and ancient dictionaries

TO ENLIGHTEN THE G.O.D.Z.

Act II: The Order of Maa Tru Ark

to make my vocabulary stronger
y'see
you are definitely
caught in my attraction
and pull."

Safi-oya:
"you are as stubborn
as the fixed earth,
like the smell of your words
produced by the bull."

I yield my thoughts
and my tongue

Kahm:
"humble to you,
I must agree,"
I said to safi-oya
painting footsteps
in her direction
and drawing closer,
"gravity may have given my body
                    a reason
to trip
but it has been your smile,
knowledge and kiss,
that my heart has fallen for."

and our egoes
go
we have spent too much time
seeing how long we can ignore each other
trying to hide the fact
on how much we adore each other

Safi-oya:
"I want to know all you have been
thru a kiss.
I want to journey
to the center of your mind

TO ENLIGHTEN THE G.O.D.Z.

Act II: The Order of Maa Tru Ark

and touch its deepest abyss
don't you want to feel … my bliss?
penetrate … my lips?"

Kahm:
"you damn right I–"

wait!
wait!
wait!
let me handle this …
play it cool,
let my body turn
and twist
my back facing her,
my hands on my hips
and let my head
shake

Kahm:
"I dunno…a kiss
could ruin the moment…"

Safi-oya:
"it doesn't have to be long,
as long as it's with you.
and we be-long to each other."

her sincerity
is clarity
and this
is clearly my moment
to seize

I glide on the breeze
and we embrace
hands exploring shape
resting
on our waists

we waste no time

TO ENLIGHTEN THE G.O.D.Z.

Act II: The Order of Maa Tru Ark

and we kiss
perfectly
by quietly
reciting
poetry
on
our
lips

silently
and
orally
massaging
each other

when we kiss
we taste
the beginning of time
and our time has begun

my heart is healed
from being broken
and both sun and moon
shine down on us
to spotlight
this beautiful moment

and we speak
silently
and free

free inside our lips,
our voices,
our kiss,
our skin,
I ponder this angel and swim
in a pool of wonderful thoughts
again

TO ENLIGHTEN THE G.O.D.Z.

Act 11: The Order of Maa Tru Ark

"2'S (DAY) OF UNION"

2sday
was 3 months
long
condensed
into these
stanzas

safi-oya and I
exchanged lifetimes
stories of past allies
adventures,
rebellions,
and movements
all in verbal union

we studied each other
learning of one another

safi-oya told me
of her father
great warrior,
commander,
defender
of the Ances-Tree
becoming one of its leaves
as he passed on
by way of the battle

and she spoke
of her mother
diplomat
and healer

both parents
carved from pen
and paper

and I spoke
of being mist edu-caged

TO ENLIGHTEN THE G.O.D.Z.

Act 11: The Order of Maa Tru Ark

locked by prison
and bars
not thru my hair
or to my roots

I spoke of cid,
persun,
Ohm Lingo,
and the fight for our truth
I spoke
of my father pen
and mother paper
how they
guided me to the kheru

and from there
we practice our words
doin' flips
and afro-batics
flipping the first six kheru
in a verse

we run thru natural elements
feet and chest bare
dancing merrily
speaking pleasantly
our bodies
blending with our words
into the afternoon air
only to reform
beneath a tree
(physically)
to twist
each other's hair

now our naps
lay awake
twisting
like fate
down a less traveled road
we use our knowledge as a map

⊤O ENLIGHTEN THE G.O.D.Z.

Act II: The Order of Maa Tru Ark

hair locked
keeping our thoughts intact

this 2s (day) of union
comfortable,
beautiful,
thru this route
we let days pass

we sleep,
in peace,
beneath a tree
my head
in safi-oya's lap

TO ENLIGHTEN THE G.O.D.Z.

Act II: The Order of Maa Tru Ark

"DANCING AS US"

safi-oya dances so close to me
she becomes me
I dance so close to her
I become her
we become one another

the stars form into lightning
as bass pumping
from khemi-lohim
becomes thunder

safi-oya and I
vibe
under the star's light
dancing to the bass' might

and when we kiss
the war we fight disappears
ceases to exist

I dance so close to her
I become her
and she to me
we become one another

we two black bodies
blending,
twirling,
twisting,
as khemi-lohim's music
is released

we 2 black bodies
safi-oya and I
we – as 1 – dance in peace

TO ENLIGHTEN THE G.O.D.Z.

Act II: The Order of Maa Tru Ark

"HAUNTED AURA-GIN 3: AZA THE SNAKE"

mystagogue turner
like thunder
spoke our final lesson
on snakes and ghosts

Turner:
"trapped,
cold,
bare of soul
and barely of flesh
savage without rest
swarming around
hives
caves as their nest
these ghosts
dripped off them what was civilized
centuries hardened by the wind

oluso kept them at bay

no guide
to keep them
civilized
in this cold land
bound and tied
deprived of guidance
that was divine

the sentence – for their lies
for these words
without syllables
naked
shameless
with pride

learning to dance
with wolves
what was once god
                    – to them

TO ENLIGHTEN THE G.O.D.Z.

<u>Act II: The Order of Maa Tru Ark</u>

became a dog
instead of exhaling the wind
they blew fog
with their foul speech
rugged
raw as the meat they would eat

their unnatural state
raping mother nature
making her bend

there was one
named aza
who held sympathy
for these ghosts

he sang
in the harmony
of the scales
that made up
his flesh
civilized
and properly dressed
underneath
he was a snake

the descended seed of gradious

living among us
he was biding his time
to strike with this
venemous,
created
nation

he believed his scales
could climb
and bring
an imbalance to ma'at
diminishing the order
of the warriors

TO ENLIGHTEN THE G.O.D.Z.

Act 11: The Order of Maa Tru Ark

known as asir-ites
auset-ites and seth-ites
which gave birth to us
as mwindo-heru-ites

vowing to tame the ghosts
he scaled their rugged homes
he slept in a ring of fire
to keep them at bay
as they bayed at the moon
soon
he led a team of converted snakes
to haunted regions
where in 3 unholy years
aza civilized them

those ghosts
who remained
savage
were deemed
gladiators

those who devolved
into snakes
whose tongues
would slither
and shake
would make
our ways
and
philosophies
quake
until they would break
into separate religions

and on these bastardized
                    – doctrines
these snakes and ghosts
would setup nations
planning their invasion
of original nations

TO ENLIGHTEN THE G.O.D.Z.

Act II: The Order of Maa Tru Ark

putting our people
under subjugation

taking away our arts, our sciences
unrightful heirs
claiming all was theirs
while continuously leaving us to graves
even when we kept bringing light
to their dark ages
we ancient sages
were put to the sword
by who **they** now deem
saints
who dared to call us snakes

and we constantly believe
bringing them light
will make them
conscious
and awake

they only honor us with graves

don't let them dull your mind
while they sharpen their swords

my students,
do you believe
with all this genetic mapping
that ruebue's plans of grafting
is not still practice? these diabolical tactics?

we have been brought thru
a middle passage
only to be brought
back to the beginning

we are the heroes to this plot
we are — *unfortunately* —
the reason snakes and ghosts
started to murder

TO ENLIGHTEN THE G.O.D.Z.

Act 11: The Order of Maa Tru Ark

but we will be the reason
they stop

and here we are
seeds of the Ances-Tree.
defending its 11 branches
and every last leaf."

and mystagogue turner
looks to me

Turner:
"kahm,
please speak on your captivity."

and I rise from my seat
and spin tales
that put me
in a tail spin

crawling from my lips
names of allies
who just remain
names
(once with bodies)
only thru memories
do they appear again

Kahm:
"but I am here,
Maa-Tru-Ark,
where my soul began.
bare feet
running thru sands

I say to you,
my fellow students,
my allies,
we hold our destinies
in the palm of our hands."

TO ENLIGHTEN THE G.O.D.Z.

Act 11: The Order of Maa Tru Ark

"DE-CYPHER 3: BA"

> we study
> under
> the sanctuary
> of the stars

Ruther:
**you must learn
to wear your soul
atop your head.

(I see your hair
is locking).

every molecule
every atom
aligned
with atum
you,
the universe,
your queen,
all souls
as one.

and you will
insperince
all this
thru the **Ba**, black sheep.

like the stars to you,
these lessons
are now
over.**

let the essays begin

TO ENLIGHTEN THE G.O.D.Z.

Act 11: The Order of Maa Tru Ark

"TRAINING GROUNDZ 2: PHYSICAL ESSAYS"

for luck
safi-oya
left a kiss
right on
my cheek

Safi-oya:
"relax,
concentrate on your kheru,
and for good measure,
think of me."

I dress
in warrior sashes and robes
gently glide thru streets
and roads
until I come across ruther

we walk
silent
for miles
thru the city
until the sun
chills at noon

we step into dinclinsin's illusion
ogun's tarot-made fabrication
and the essays begin

I am placed
in the center
of darkness
in a room
that stretches
to the far reaches
of space
but in here
no stars exist

TO ENLIGHTEN THE G.O.D.Z.

Act II: The Order of Maa Tru Ark

the scenery is mist
and I become nostalgic

and then the fog
begins to condense
into a scene of battle
fire enters thru
my visual sense

Ruther:
**your objective,
is to use all 7 kheru
properly,
to guide you from mission to mission.**

I close my eyes to the scenery
but the scene is still open to me
made possible thru the 3rd vision
…it's like breathing
using the **Khu**

ruther blindfolds me
but with the kheru
I fold blindness
back into sight
so that I can see the fight

I dash forward
(speaking four words)
use the **Shekhem**
and let my voice flow
to conjure
at my command
heir-rows
and a reign-bow

I target these illusions
ghosts

but they target me
firing unholy sunbeams

ꓔO ENLIGHTEN THE G.O.D.Z.

Act II: The Order of Maa Tru Ark

burning streams

I speak the **Khab** (silently)
break into brilliant light
and gleam
letting their weapons
streak thru me
I blend into the wind
dive into shadows
and send a barrage
            of heir-rows
cutting thru snakes and ghosts

I mold back together
and stand in front
of a fellow oluso
and his Commander

Brutha Mel:
"diplomat **Ifa** is trapped
inside the white pyramid.
find her to secure our future."

I nod

again I shift and become the wind
I inhale my own essence
and with heir-rows and reign-bow
I defend

the **Ab** disperses fear
keeps my mind clear

it's clear to me
in battle I may die
but thru battle
I live
I am the warrior's spirit

slipping thru
natural elements

TO ENLIGHTEN THE G.O.D.Z.

Act 11: The Order of Maa Tru Ark

I bring the kheru
together
thru the **Sahu**

and its with this
the combination
of these kheru
like a verse or lyric
I am able to find
the white pyramid

using its own shadow
I slip in
from underneath

rising
from room to room
encountering
snakes and ghosts

danger after danger
rising thru
the 36 chambers
and 360 rooms

I have come full circle

standing in front of me
are two women
with equal beauty
twins in shape
form,
      and
mind,

but one
was without soul

I speak the **Khaibit**
place my palm toward them
and it begins to glow

TO ENLIGHTEN THE G.O.D.Z.

Act 11: The Order of Maa Tru Ark

and then I know…

so
I load light into reign-bow
and hit the 1 on the right
with two heir-rows

>*the illusion disperses in the wind*<

the true ifa
congratulates me

I remove the blindfold
open my physical eyes
and the scene of dark inside
dwindles into a clear day

Ruther:
**remember,
real battle
will not be that easy.
but you did wonderful,
my student.**

I catch my breath
it's rhythm forms my name

Kahm:
"but I only used 6 kheru."

Ruther:
**you believe the essay is over?
there is one more test.**

to the air
ruther throws
a heavy sword
and it floats

I feel this sword in an invisible grip

TO ENLIGHTEN THE G.O.D.Z.

Act II: The Order of Maa Tru Ark

or possibly, it has me

the sword's shade
brightens blue — from hilt
to crossguard
to wide blade to tip
cosmic inner-g twists
thru the power of the darkness
surrounding the sun
dark matter
       and
dark inner-g
shining in
from above

the sword's blue
bends to a black hue
a cosmic shade encircles
outlined in humming gold and purple

Ruther:
**this object is held up
by the mind,
the body,
and the soul.
but whose?
yours or mine?**

I concentrate
feel a connection
with the blade
and say, "both minds.
yours and mine.
united as one."

Ruther:
**Partial credit.
you used the **Ba**
for your answer,
but let me tell you

ᛏO ENLIGHTEN THE G.O.D.Z.

Act 11: The Order of Maa Tru Ark

the true manner
of this sword.

this is a dark matter blade
carved from the melanin
that swirls thru space
it is thru this
you will feel a connection
to all natural elements,
supernatural
and even
unnatural.**

so, as my reward
a dark matter sword

its energy writhes
the blade
touches my chest
melts thru me
and finds my soul
as a nest for it to grow
my arm begins to glow
and a beam extends
with all the colour of the heavens
reflecting darkness
as all colors fade to black
the sword grows from the lines
in the palm of my hand
connected to an inner-g
writhing on my back
I hold hilt, soul extended
to crossguard
to wide blade to precision
pin-point tip

... this ...
dark matter sword
... this ...
dark inner-g ...

TO ENLIGHTEN THE G.O.D.Z.

Act 11: The Order of Maa Tru Ark

I open my palm
and the dark matter blade
retracts
back – black
into me

knowing who I am
gets better. every. day.

ꓔΘ ΣΝLIGꓕꓕΣΝ ꓕΗΣ G.Θ.Ɔ.Ƶ.

<u>Act II: The Order of Maa Tru Ark</u>

"ON THE HORIZON"

they came
like drops of hail
and hard rain

flooding the horizon
and even corrupting the sky
ghosts and snakes tried to blind mwindo-heru
by eclipsing the light of his heavenly eye
marching in troops and fleets
burying themselves into the soil
to attack the roots of the Ances-Tree

but they kept at a distance
and we constantly flew missions
to keep watch
mwindo-heru eye blessed
to see if they would progress

but until there was war
I studied
more
with
dark matter blade
(my beautiful Moorish sword)

until the day
words flew in and came to say
that time was a luxury
we could no longer afford

sista ifa came into the training room
and took safi-oya away from me
there was a call for conferencing
decision making
on the ghosts and snakes
who lay in the distance

I retract my blade
dark matter and inner-g

Act II: The Order of Maa Tru Ark

flowing back into my body,

I turn to face my allies
alik and moorah
could see anxiety
creep onto my face

Kahm:
"it's like this day after day
snakes and ghosts stay at bay
and safi-oya constantly in conference

is my thinking off track?
why do we train
if not to fight?"

Moorah:
"please remember,
we train
to keep our life on track.
battling snakes and ghosts
we are to defend – never attack."

for what it's worth
moorah's words
makes little sense to me
so my thoughts
do not make change

Kahm:
"switch the situation.
put us outside their prison.
you know snakes and ghost
wouldn't even let us start
what we would be there to finish.

they would dig their claws into us
and us into a grave
in less than a minute.

they, to us, should be no different.

TO ENLIGHTEN THE G.O.D.Z.

Act 11: The Order of Maa Tru Ark

to wait
is not righteous
but foolish."

Alik:
"I feel the same.
supplying negotiations
to snakes and ghosts
should not be in demand.
we need an army to command."

Kahm:
"what!? you and I aligned in words?
stardust for celebration
mark it like a target
pen and paper,
for us to remember,
alik and I agree."

>*slight laughter*<

humour lives uneasy
its intensions
battle poorly with the tension

alik applies the fatal blow

Alik:
"however, kahm,
we are not empty without command.
– we have our orders to stay at rest."

Kahm:
"well,
I'm going to investigate this situation further
I'll go to ruther and turner.
they'll have better sense."

Moorah:
"whatever happens

Act II: The Order of Maa Tru Ark

will have to be discussed,
thru Hour Council."

Kahm:
"I just don't have a good feeling
our thoughts on war cowering and trembling,
we warriors
ready
and tested
to make war
just sit here dry and waiting
while the opportunity of battle
keeps raining

and them
making
an offense
while we
just speak
of defense
is offensive to me.

and it
takes away my queen —
it plucks her from my daydreams.
like an imagined flower

and my thoughts' garden
remains frozen
hardened
… for war …
barren
unable for her flower
to grow any Moor.

so she withers in thought
and I battle thoughts of war
charging violent imagery
that swirls like heavy winds
trying to make her image grow again.

TO ENLIGHTEN THE G.O.D.Z.

Act II: The Order of Maa Tru Ark

but all I see is him.
something you have not gazed upon
as of yet…
dull light
but
he still thinks himself a star –
… nemtusar …
the bastard king.

and his image
reigns
dripping sterile drops
on barren thoughts

his image
reigns
over my queen.
and she is unable to grow
and his light
dulls my reign-bow
and
heir-rows
and this son's sword
becomes eclipsed
… by his war …

I cannot
remain still
but here
I still
remain

still I am
unable to prove
I am Moor than a man.

birthed from
a lion's lips
which
is how
I stole its roar

TO ENLIGHTEN THE G.O.D.Z.

Act 11: The Order of Maa Tru Ark

with them on the horizon

here I stand
still
and just
only
prepared for war."

ᛏⵔ ENLIGHTEN THE G.ⵔ.ⵔ.Z.

<u>Act II: The Order of Maa Tru Ark</u>

"EVERY MINUTE, HOUR COUNCIL DECIDES"

students gather as oluso
inside this pyramid
that ached
with contraction pangs
pregnant
and birthing
the mind of heroes

elders gathered around us
they as teachers
multiplying courage
and dividing fading images
of
mother figures
and father figures
now
before their children's eyes
they were forming into warriors

and the 24 elders
levitating
15 degrees apart
spoke as 1 mind
1 soul
1 heart

Elders:
**your learning
will now be applied.

the sun has set on peace
and your lessons
have come to an end
as here
war begins
and your new objective
is to defend the Ances-Tree.

now ask yourselves,

Act II: The Order of Maa Tru Ark

who here
will make war
with the beast?**

and there is silence
created thru eternity
but I time it perfectly … to interrupt
with noiz

I raise my fist
to declare
into the tense air
– unity –

Kahm:
"I will!"

alik
speaks
as well,

Alik:
"I will!"

moorah joins his side
and students begin to sing
I will
and it begins
like a rhythm
creating its own vibe

I will' – two words
spoken
over
and over
creating multiple verses
and now our elders and the 24
have to split us up into separate forces
and ask themselves
who will be sent first

TO ENLIGHTEN THE G.O.D.Z.

Act 11: The Order of Maa Tru Ark

and safi-oya steps to the stage
stepping from my imagination and dream

Safi-oya:
"I volunteer my team."

24 Elders:
**the height
of the number
of your oluso
is short.**

I point to myself,
alik and moorah
then carefully speak,
"will three extend her army?"

Safi-oya:
"not in the least.
elders – please,
I can do without these oluso
they are just students."

what!?

alik
teases,

Alik:
"I didn't know you were born from your future queen.
she's your mother as well, huh?"

Moorah:
"kahm,
she's just being protective."

I speak

Kahm:
"oluso commander safi-oya,
I am a greater oluso than most here.

TO ENLIGHTEN THE G.O.D.Z.

Act II: The Order of Maa Tru Ark

I have dispersed fear
traveled miles thru mist
and conquered trials.

I have gone inside
the unified hive
of the snakes' and ghosts' mind
and have seen things
that could make even your 3rd eye go blind.

ra-born as oluso
as a dark warrior,
you cannot
deny me my battle.
Grandfather Clock ticked and tocked
to watch me fight."

24 Elders:
**there will be no fight,
anxious warrior.
this is just to keep an eye
on the offensive line of snakes and ghosts.

oluso commander safi-oya,
your team will keep an eye on the matter.
you will have these 3 oluso
and 10 more to look after.**

and I look closely
safi-oya's concern
bent into angry eyes
aimed at me
her tears
could easily be traced
and I never saw more love
– disguised as concern –
on this Black Woman's face

ΤΟ ENLIGHTEN THE G.O.D.Z.

Act II: The Order of Maa Tru Ark

"KNIGHT TIME DISCUSSION"

I walk
under
stars
and know
the influence of mars
is not just on battlefields

– so I write a letter to venus –

and when she receives it,
I want her to whisper
my love into safi-oya
kissing each shoulder
and tickling her neck
send a breeze to swirl
underneath her dress
and kiss her where our future life
will be born and blessed

and I walk under stars
as they light my path
to safi-oya's quarters
speaking my two cents
at her yard

I let my body fade
become the wind,
ascend and flow
materializing – solid
on the balcony
of safi-oya's window

she prays at her bed
african wrap atop her head
and a gown covering her syllables
sensually accenting her marks
voluptuous
she sparks thoughts in my head

TO ENLIGHTEN THE G.O.D.Z.

Act II: The Order of Maa Tru Ark

Safi-oya:
**I sensed
you would be
here.**

and as her words are spoken
her window
opens
and I glide inside,
as gentle as my name

she turns to me
eyes glowing wide with tears
that only add to her beauty
she removes the wrap
and allows
her locks
to flow
swinging
seductively
absorbing the aroma
of incense in the air

she tries to speak
but her words hide inside her throat
the syllables
caught inside tears
safi-oya's heart beats her emotions in morse code
a code of moorish odes
sad ballads of lost love

Kahm:
"I'll be all right out there.
there is …
actually …
no reason
to be scared … I …"

words
come to her
spurring

TO ENLIGHTEN THE G.O.D.Z.

Act II: The Order of Maa Tru Ark

and sprouting
rushes of syllables

Safi-oya:
"oh, kahm.
I'm cemented in emotions
my heart
like soft concrete
can only be impressed
by the hard rhythm
of your heartbeat.

you don't have to do this for me."

Kahm:
"safi-oya,
to fight alongside the righteous
… that's all I've ever wished …

and to know my back
will not be against a wall
but against yours
as we have
each other's back …

beautiful black woman
you and I can do no wrong
by each other's side."

you may not believe it
as such
but even
with all the months passed
safi-oya
and I
have yet to make love

we begin to kiss with our minds
and make up for lost time
as our bodies shed clothing
our souls speak to each other's body

TO ENLIGHTEN THE G.O.D.Z.

Act II: The Order of Maa Tru Ark

and we swirl into the rhythm of a flame
black love, phoenix ra-born
wild and untamed
we sweat incense vapors
I lay her against the bed
where she becomes my paper

and she
felt
tip
pen
where I scribe
inside
and she sends
music
that vibes
in our minds

and
she
felt
tip
      – I –
pen – a – trait, genetic traits
our bodies
sweat
and
incensed laced

we switch positions
thru intermissions of kisses
discover our black soil and oil
and all our riches

scented candles send our aroma
to be inhaled as the syllables
of other people's wishes to be us
embraced in complete love

and far from where our love began to run

ᴛᴏ ᴇɴᴌɪɢʜᴛᴇɴ ᴛʜᴇ ɢ.ᴏ.ᴅ.ᴢ.

<u>Act II: The Order of Maa Tru Ark</u>

our souls arrive, and our bodies come
undone – physical flesh to spirit
heaven sent lyrics – we are the word
and in the beginning there was nothing but us

and where the moon
was our spotlight
we are now
spotted
by the sun

two bodies
in each other's arms
holding
as
1

TO ENLIGHTEN THE G.O.D.Z.

Act II: The Order of Maa Tru Ark

"JUST US VS. VENOM US"

snakes and ghosts
march on the horizon
an empty sky behind them
cuz … the sun had *our* backs

our 36 oluso
march as one
in hour 36

snakes and ghosts continue
rising from their horizon
marching
for our horizon-line
to meet theirs

prepared
I pray
using the kheru
as my only words
to compose an appeal

safi-oya reads my thoughts

Safi-oya:
"careful of your tongue,
lips,
and mouth.
we are just here to scout
– not for war."

I nod,
but still feel the inner-g
that writhes in my arms
ready to ignite
my dark matter sword
to deal with these dark matters

our bodies
rain

TO ENLIGHTEN THE G.O.D.Z.

Act II: The Order of Maa Tru Ark

and spill
atop a hill
to glance down
on a haunted area
– a slithering terror

thousands of them
their venom
poisoning the land

a haunting mist
spilling
from the ghosts
as they float
over nature's body
burning her – calcified

grass shriveled
roots wrinkled
as mist and venom rippled
withering mother nature

Kahm:
**by my words! can you believe this?
this scenario is now war.
let's leave orders behind
and turn this into something Moor.**

Safi-oya:
"kahm, I empathize with you –
but
please,
divine yourself –
instead of **defining** yourself
thru their savagery."

the kheru
opens my eyes
– all 3 –
and I quietly apologize
to safi-oya

TO ENLIGHTEN THE G.O.D.Z.

Act II: The Order of Maa Tru Ark

the others she guides

alik and moorah
surround me
one at either side

Alik:
"well, commander,
do we speak prayers for peace?
or greater words for war?"

Moorah:
"all of war's thunders
cannot silence words,
nor make them great;
and prayers spoken silently
can deliver peace.
remember, my husband
the kheru
are but prayers."

Alik:
"yes —
but whose?
mine
or theirs?

for these snakes and ghosts
better know them.
at least
under
          stand them
speak them,
and if at all, respect them
for the kheru will be their last

even if their words are lost
trapped, blinded in their mist
poisoned by their forked tongue and venom
are carried away from Ixu's and Gira's ears
these villains should know the kheru as prayers."

TO ENLIGHTEN THE G.O.D.Z.

Act II: The Order of Maa Tru Ark

safi-oya
connects
eyes
and words
to moorah

Safi-oya:
"speak the wind
so that these men
will cool
their hot heads."

and I connect
with smooth butter
fly
words
to alik's ears

Kahm:
"my hot head
created heat,
last night."

Safi-oya:
"excuse me, kahm …
speak your words,
again."

Kahm:
"goddess, my words
were like the ghosts in front of us –
they were nothing."

my right eye
folds quickly
at alik

Safi-oya:
"keep in mind

TO ENLIGHTEN THE G.O.D.Z.

Act 11: The Order of Maa Tru Ark

and remember,
I am still *your* commander."

I shift my thoughts
and settle back into the grip
of the situation at hand

Kahm:
"well, goddess
it is your command.
there are thousands of them down there.
so
do we move forward
or report back?"

before she answers
the khu reacts
becomes a scanner
and thru the scenery
paints and begins to trace
finding a familiar
unfaithful
traitorous
face

eye-van
the terrible
house nigga

Kahm:
"nobody send.
nobody use your mind to speak.

there is someone
down there
who can peek
into our thoughts,
and gain our position.

has anybody
spoken

TO ENLIGHTEN THE G.O.D.Z.

Act 11: The Order of Maa Tru Ark

thru the mind?"

and then I think

Kahm:
"damn!
in haste –
I have made
this mistake.

when I first spoke,
I sold our position."

safi-oya
our commander
quick
on decisions

Safi-oya:
"moorah,
keep your mind clear.
if we need reinforcements,
it will be your power
that calls for them."

we gather
ready to make
a journey back
but as we turn
we realize venom and mist
surround us

Eye-van:
"a foul kiss
from acrid mist
burning tongues
striking
venomous.
oh! kahm!
you would excite my heart
if a heart

<u>Act II: The Order of Maa Tru Ark</u>

inside me
still did exist;
and I was not
nigga-are-dly,
and allowed
my heart to give"

Kahm:
"you only pump
lies from your lips
face split in two
traitorous.

come, eye-van —
move your vision
and look upon me."

safi-oya and I
back-to-back
1 body as 1 mind
our hearts ready
for this battle

Kahm:
"well, alik
we got these snakes and ghosts
attacking from either side."

Alik:
"well … if this is our last day
and tomorrow no longer exists for us
then you and your queen
take 1 side as you die
as my queen and I
take 1 side as we die."

and as the battle begins rockin'
and powers begin poppin'
I wonder if death is our only option
we rush forward
ignite dark matter swords

TO ENLIGHTEN THE G.O.D.Z.

Act II: The Order of Maa Tru Ark

and disperse ghosts
like clouds
speaking the kheru
mentally loud
heavy mental
our words drop
on snakes
and crush them
under syllabic weights

moorah –
puts her thoughts
in clouds
that rain back
on Maa-Tru-Ark

and with safi-oya at my side
I carve a path to eye-van
and stare him eye-to-eye

he's dressed in tight clothing
holding
his thoughts of escaping the mentality
that ensnares him
he dances foolishly
but
confuses me
with his sambo dance
and his unintelligible rants
talking in beaten words
broken language
that falls in shards from his lips
tattered
as his hair
– unkempt locks –

he swings a dull sword
and I never before
imagined
I would be fighting
1 of my own

TO ENLIGHTEN THE G.O.D.Z.

Act 11: The Order of Maa Tru Ark

held by the tongue of snakes,
erased from spirit,
possessed by a ghost

we swing!
battle!
and clash!
cut and slash
hoping to drive
sense and heat
into each other's minds

and I reach into his mind and connect
to make a special effect

Kahm:
**if only you knew
your history—
our story.**

Eye-van:
"I know our story —
kept in my locks.
I know the betrayal
of perfect black-ausar
thru his brother set,
I know who we were
back in ancient Moorish lands
such as
kush,
nubia,
abssynia,
and kemet … and even beyond.
yeah, Hausa nigga – field this
I'm Dog-on sirius, black
I sing songs high
kiss both earth and sky
all the trade routes of mansa musa
drink with the orisha
right at home with the Dahomey
I am the heart of them that sold their men

TO ENLIGHTEN THE G.O.D.Z.

Act II: The Order of Maa Tru Ark

I know the western nations, amexem indigenous
I know the kemetic elements
and the science of her-ehm-akhet;
our ancient ways,
robes,
and dress
– our sashes
our journey thru the middle passage
and the reduction of our kingdoms
so how dare you curse me
speaking that I know nothing of them!"

his attack
knocks me back
I roll and twirl with the wind
catching its beat
jumping back upon my feet
I take stance
keep my roots under me
and plant

Eye-van:
"I serve the power that rules –
not the exception destined to be ruled."

planting impatience
I grow tired – sick
of what his speech drools

I attack

snakes and ghosts surround me
but safi-oya has my back
and I keep slashing at eye-van

I become the definition
of my own name
and look for the kheru
to guide every attack
and stride made towards eye-van

⊖O ENLIGHTEN THE G.⊖.D.Z.

Act II: The Order of Maa Tru Ark

thunder and lightning
make love above us
and the day bleeds red

humming effects
as technology
driven by african spirits
fly overhead
firing beams
that tear thru snakes
and dissolve ghosts
into vapor and streams of mist
— afrikan killer bee airships

they come in swarms!

12 have fallen
from our 36
       we are down
to our
       final hours

leaves begin to grow
warriors slain
their spirits
blossom on the Ances-Tree

but our numbers increase
with the warriors flying technology in the sky
but snakes and ghosts
have their own sky assault
and our technology
— with spirits —
collide with twisted metal

I continue battling eye-van
and his terrible ways
slashing uncontrollably
until nothing but his ugliness
is carved in scars on his face

ᖶO ENᒪIGᕼᖶEN ᖶᕼE G.Ө.D.Z.

<u>Act 11: The Order of Maa Tru Ark</u>

Eye-van:
"you can drink
from a one thousand
african queens,
ancestral drug laced
but I know, by force
how Ohm Lingo tastes."

and with the kheru
I search his words
for truth
and
detect
no lie
— it appears
even with all my actions
he is able to wound my pride

I slash again
the power of Set swirling inside
and as if he were Mwindo-Heru
I remove him of his eye
then, with a fist
void of the energy of my sword
I knock eye-van to the earth floor

but he slithers back to his feet
calls for retreat
and escapes
to save what is left of his face

… the scene takes on my name …

afrikan killer bee airships
land from out the sky

safi-oya and I
as battle allies and lovers
— along with other sistaz and bruthaz —
hold one another

TO ENLIGHTEN THE G.O.D.Z.

Act 11: The Order of Maa Tru Ark

retracting the blades
of our dark matter swords
victorious
in the first battle
against the snakes and ghosts
and all their hordes
we are in celebration
and in peaceful prayer
we prepare
singing in one harmonious chord

Wariors:
"let our spirits guide us
speaking rhythmically
properly
in these Spoken Wars."

TO ENLIGHTEN THE G.O.D.Z.

Act II: The Order of Maa Tru Ark

"DAZE OF WAR"

… the spoken wars …
they began with a whisper
and would end just the same
but in between
there were screams so loud
they could be seen

I passed on ranks
keeping myself an oluso
and traded for my thoughts
to be respected
on how to wage war

alik, moorah,
and safi-oya
would tease me
and say that I should be a general
and I would retaliate
that in general
I was an oluso

but
my ancestral sister
was in danger
and captured images
of Ohm Lingo in captivity
held my mind captive

I spoke all this to safi-oya
about Ohm Lingo
the angel who rescued me

from quivering lips
seep shaken words
on how eye-van's tongue
cursed me like ghosts
haunted me like snakes
fill my heart, off beat wish shakes
pumped within – venom

TO ENLIGHTEN THE G.O.D.Z.

Act 11: The Order of Maa Tru Ark

writing notes
to an imagined Ohm Lingo
was my antidote
but sending them nowhere
kept my heart in despair
even on bright and clear days
I saw haze polluting the air

safi-oya comforted me
beautiful, understanding,
and as gentle as a breeze

on a clear day
with sun smiling
and a light wind
tickling the leaves
I told safi-oya, "Ohm Lingo
is like a sister to me.

I've spoken
to the branches
of the Ances-tree.

looking to see
if Ohm Lingo has found peace
and connected as a leaf.

she has not.
which means
she is still caught."

safi-oya
head
on my shoulder
arms
around my waist
she wastes no time
soothing the hurt
in my heart and mind

TO ENLIGHTEN THE G.O.D.Z.

Act II: The Order of Maa Tru Ark

Safi-oya:
"like water touched by the sun's rays
dwindling into gas and dust
and flying back into space
in all stories
the hero must return
to their birth place.

black man,
we'll try something
in balance's view
you have followed I –
now it's time
for I to follow you."

Kahm:
"are you sure you can do that,
'strong – independent' woman?"

laughter escapes her

Safi-oya:
"Black Men and Black Women
do not have the time
to be independent of one another
we live in harmony with each other,
building balance together

that other philosophy
of separation of our body-church
from our states of mind?
well,
that is feminine ghost philosophies
that continue to divide
sistaz and bruthaz.

let us let go
of ghostly principles
laced with venom and sulfur
we need
to hold tight

<u>Act 11: The Order of Maa Tru Ark</u>

to each other.

that independent game –
kahm –
you know I don't play that
black man,
I got your back."

Kahm:
"good, becuz I got yours.
with reign-bows, heir-rows
and dark matter swords.
black woman – I got yours."

I pause for breath
and effect
hoping a kiss is next
but another thought
grows

Kahm:
"what of Hour Council?
they'll never agree to send
a small team to–"

Safi-oya:
"you let me worry about that obstacle
alik, moorah, you,
and myself will strike force
into prison mist,
– our aim on target.
and free Ohm Lingo and a 1000 souls
who believe they do not exist."

Kahm:
"will we win the war with this?"

Safi-oya:
"we will have at least
given ma'at's scales a tip."

TO ENLIGHTEN THE G.O.D.Z.

Act 11: The Order of Maa Tru Ark

I turn to my goddess
and give her a summertime kiss
knowing now
it's time to reclaim balance

TO ENLIGHTEN THE G.O.D.Z.

Act II: The Order of Maa Tru Ark

"WITH RUTHER, FLY"

in stanzas creating syllabic breath
I confess to ruther
his ears, like vibrating wood
my sounding board

I wondered
as these thoughts and plans swirled
could this pilot navigate
thru my thinking

hard hitting plans to hit hard
were suddenly becoming
punch-lines as I spoke them

but ruther
planting thoughts
grew interested, telling me, **meditate for three days
let burning power raze
and rise to three points of your mind,
conserve your inner-g and store it
where your heart resides
to pump it later
on this mission to free
those inmates from prison mist
and your angelic savior.**

3 days later
we ra-group for our labor
alik, moorah, safi-oya,
ruther, and I
gather in hangar

we ascend into the sky
in afrikan killer bee airship
we
butter
fly
away

TO ENLIGHTEN THE G.O.D.Z.

Act 11: The Order of Maa Tru Ark

"EYE MIST PRISON"

on the boundary of colour
devouring clouds
churning them into mist
reflecting sunlight
eclipsing space
there grew dull towers
spitting up
strangling, choking fog

it was here
where drifting thoughts of hope
were lost
and lost hopes found graves
decomposed
by way of less-sun rays
or evaporated into mist
and became rusted chains for slaves

carrying hopes like burdens
to funeral pyres
where in the afterlife
they were told
they would urn all their hopes back
burned into ash

its here where the past
stings my eyes
it is many of my people's
present
and so, we bring the gift of hope
descending from the heavens

afrikan killer bee airship
glides thru mist
lands undetected
we birth ourselves
emerge we, young killer bees

safi-oya, alik, moorah,

TO ENLIGHTEN THE G.O.D.Z.

Act II: The Order of Maa Tru Ark

and even ruther
– their eyes inhale the scene

a glorious
magnificent
dull colour
this mist had swirled
and smothered
inside my memory
but now it breathes again

inside the prison's breath
I can feel the presence
of eye-van
and his master: nemtusar
this time,
I time warnings perfectly
and warn ruther
to talk when he speaks

Ruther:
"all right, kahm,
it's your lead."

Kahm:
"eye-van's dull aura
summons me. I follow."

ruther waves a hand
his ship's image
dissolves clear, disappeared

creeping
on misty streets
silently
we hear haunting moans
and slithering

with the kheru
we compose ourselves against the mist
blend, hoping not to be drawn in

TO ENLIGHTEN THE G.O.D.Z.

Act II: The Order of Maa Tru Ark

sketched eternally emprisoned
our connection to the Ances-Tree
winters with the misty winds
snows statics – we are on our own

our power, we carefully conserve

I lead them to the cage
where I spent days
being reduced of time

it's here
where I lead these new allies
all-in-with-me
to the institutional correctional facility
– and our eyes capture the captured –
chained
bound
tied
caged
minds erased
bodies laced with ghosts and snakes
constantly raped of soul
black bodiesm, dull of glow

I sense a presence
a haunting voice
e c h o e s

"<u>they will be let go</u>."

and mist walks
gliding on flesh and pride
hanging from his smile's tip
tongue, slithering with every word
spoken from his lips

nemtusar

on 1 side
close to him

TO ENLIGHTEN THE G.O.D.Z.

Act II: The Order of Maa Tru Ark

eye-van, lost of eye
(taken by I)

it was to him nemtusar spoke
plus another
who was neither snake or ghost

this second, wore a rope
around his throat
tied up – wrapped
to cover his face

I whisper words
light as the air, "stay close
and with the shadows."

nemtusar
and his house niggaz
glide into the next chamber

we flow after them
diving into darkness
the **khu** lights our path
and we travel beneath
the underneath
slip into depths of barren space
– and I have returned –
there in front of us
the burning stage

a lesser council
of ghosts and snakes
await nemtusar

silent, we listen
an age
counting its own days
to an end

TO ENLIGHTEN THE G.O.D.Z.

Act 11: The Order of Maa Tru Ark

"UNVEILING UNGODZ"

syllables stand
up
tight
in nemtusar's speech

Nemtusar:
"the Ances-Tree
is truly asleep.
in its slumber
we will possess
every last branch
and leaf.
we will tear out its roots
and supplant it.

from its trunk
that touches earth
to its tip
that touches the sun
we will climb its power
and rule its truth
with our lies.

we will bury its guardians
underneath it
let our ungods
reside in its body."

and ghosts
poured
from every corner
snakes
slithered
from the air
and the two bodies
formed the despair of 10 minds
dangerous and un-kind
these snakes and ghosts
began to bind into something

Act II: The Order of Maa Tru Ark

far from divine

and thru nemtusar's speech
they were each defined

Nemtusar:
"<u>Et – enemy of Osain-Geb
ruler of the lower
Ances-Tree –
trunk and stump,
sprouting weeds
to attack the roots
and strangle the spirits
of every leaf
burning the grass beneath
and rotting the soil
removing riches and oils
never to touch
the original guardians again.</u>"

and Et
rose
to set
and to betray
the opposite
of his name
and crown

Nemtusar:
"<u>Ah-Dunah
bastard creation,
killer of auset;
whore that wept–
she will tickle virgins
and veil her intentions and lies
under the number 1515;
false ruler and queen of heaven
her deception will kiss the beast
and ensnare the image of mwindo-heru.</u>"

and the light

TO ENLIGHTEN THE G.O.D.Z.

Act II: The Order of Maa Tru Ark

of a whore
was har-lit
burning
desire

Nemtusar:
"<u>Remeh
set to slay
sebek –
ruler of order
with his key
you will open chaos
and strangle syllables
from becoming words
– and thoughts
from becoming birthed;
people will enjoy screaming
unintelligible curses
lost of meaning.</u>"

and there formed wind
void of a drift
breathing chaos
from his lips

Nemtusar:
"<u>Sluh–
beautiful
eyes blue
swimming
in Oshun's spirit
holder of the venus stone planet
sensuality will flirt with lechery,
so much
that lust will become envy
and the body will become the pride,
disconnected from soul and mind
lips caressing the khaibit-by-bit
distorting rhythm.</u>"

ᛏᴏ ᴇᴎᴌɪᴦʜᴛᴇᴎ ᴛʜᴇ ɢ.ᴏ.ᴅ.ᴢ.

Act II: The Order of Maa Tru Ark

and an image
seductive
crept from the mist
flesh of the mist

Nemtusar:
"Zammu,
avenger of Set.
catching mwindo-heru
and the pine crystal in your net;
eclipsing the son
with your hands
covering sun disk
painted into religion
and worshipped

huemans
will never know the difference,
although quite different –
we will inject them with your religion."

and the face
of a snake's cousin
was painted over
the true mwindo-heru

Nemtusar:
"Liyer –
in a court
of our law
you will be truth
ogun will hang
from your pendulum
like a noose;

your speech
twisted
and let loose
a thousand criminals
overseer
of huemans

TO ENLIGHTEN THE G.O.D.Z.

Act II: The Order of Maa Tru Ark

keeping them in place
in prisons –

you will make them
charted flies,
nats,
stat-tis-ticks.”

dripping oil from his suit
this snake could never shed
his skins and past labors

Nemtusar:
“Asfet –
ruler of corrupted law
chaos
woven with lies,
and imbalance
worn as your garments.

leaving a tip
on ma'at's scales
screaming disaster into the wind,
your judgment will reign
and all will hail.”

and justice
opened her eyes
tired of being blind
she would judge
thru weighted scales
that no hueman soul
could balance

Nemtusar:
“Wes,
the skulls of the dead
worn around your neck,
slayer of obaluaye
guardian to the deceased

TO ENLIGHTEN THE G.O.D.Z.

Act II: The Order of Maa Tru Ark

he will lay where souls weep
and scream
for life
eternal.
closing the cycle
making death final
without transition."

and an infernal ungod
was born from the waters
wearing the skulls
of deceased
dark sons and daughters

Nemtusar:
"Croia,
my wife —
feminine lies
burning
djehuti's book
de-ciphering wisdom
into ignorance
the omnipotent thot
closed off
from the 3rd eye
reducing the 360 degree sight-divine
one train of thot
on 1 track mind
tunnel vision
narrow minded prison
trapped in loop of 1 thot;
caught forever
kept in a prison wherever they walk."

her DNA was straightened
hanging in strands
scales, the flesh on her hands
while the rest of her flesh
was see thru
her eyes dull
and with little light

TO ENLIGHTEN THE G.O.D.Z.

Act II: The Order of Maa Tru Ark

her sight
narrow minded

Nemtusar:
"I will kill olorun-ausar,
the perfect black
and remove him
of the force
generated
by the djed
wear its corrupted power
as a crown
and its electricity
as dreads or locks
I will rule the second branch to the top
and wear my ruler
as another crown."

nemtusar
a dull sun
surrounded by
his ungod planets
and the souls of snakes and ghosts
as their stars

on this burning stage

they gripped
their power
together

we stood as witness
as they brought into existence
a giant snake
a spiritually inept inner-g
with the anchored physical number
of 666 inside him
(but not true carbon)
trapped in the physical
beating as his heart

TO ENLIGHTEN THE G.O.D.Z.

Act II: The Order of Maa Tru Ark

Nemtusar:
"my master,
my beautiful,
master
you will split prayers
of atum
slay prayers
of amen
and speak sin
separate huemans
the alpha from the omega
tearing apart the heart of the ankh
the transistor of electrical spirit-receptors

blind these black men
and black women
bind them
to blindness
soothe them with kindness
thru the spell of your name,
unspoken. unnamed and unborn
an abortion hanging in judgment. "

and he came
from the flames
of the depths of the stage
his mouth
like a cage
holding devoured souls
lost of glow
slowly becoming ghosts
the syllables of his words
corrupted feathers
flying foul

Qnu-Tansey:
"I eat bowls of flies

to levitate my lies

to dance in front of your eyes
to float

and possess your throat

as ghosts

TO ENLIGHTEN THE G.O.D.Z.

Act II: The Order of Maa Tru Ark

so you will speak them.

          ingest them,

               let them flow thru your veins

so that when I cut you

          you will bleed them.

and I hold sin

          in the palm of my hands

               and manipulate it

          so that a woman

will feel liberated

          only when she commits

               the sins of a man – kind.

          we will continue

to remove them

          of their hues

               and stuff scales into their eyes

          until they go blind

and their tongues slither;

          let their Ances-Tree burn

               and wither."

Kahm:
"ruther,
we must leave
ra-group
at the Ances-Tree
ask who will make war
with all these beasts?"

we disappear into the wind
slip
back
to the afrikan killer bee airship
and ascend

TO ENLIGHTEN THE G.O.D.Z.

Act II: The Order of Maa Tru Ark

"WE CALL 4 HOUR COUNCIL"

closer to the sky
I gave a silent prayer
while we used clouds as roads
I spoke silently to the air
as if it were Ohm Lingo
telling her I would return

we were awaited
when we arrived
and for our flight
we were chastised
by Hour Council.

but our information
kept our punishment
verbal
and ruther's presence
deemed the mission
official

I stepped forward
and spoke Moor words, "under
Qnu-Tansey's name
a pact has been made

and the house niggaz
gave up soul
in trade
to be Qnu-Tansey's advisor
dressed in hiS thoughts
and attire
tired of struggle
they would live single lives – double

in appearance they look as allies
but their tongues
slither lies
and shake as snakes
and their hues are see thru

TO ENLIGHTEN THE G.O.D.Z.

Act II: The Order of Maa Tru Ark

never to be touched by the sun
they're cold

their intentions as intangible as ghosts
their hue no longer gold
but dull, rusted
russet
the talented 10th
up against 5 percent
and all allies that are heaven sent."

the decision was easy to capture
and the 24 elders
displayed themselves
as masters

speaking to the branches
of the Ances-Tree
and the 11 spirits
who governed
the 11 principles of wisdom
divided among different minds
that in time
would be unified

but we warriors
would cultivate millenniums
so
until then
we would still defend
this age at an end
all before an imbalance
governing our Ances-Tree
would begin

TO ENLIGHTEN THE G.O.D.Z.

Act 11: The Order of Maa Tru Ark

"TIME MOVING IN"

time
was moving
in
weighing itself
on haunted scales
and slowly becoming
thin
tomorrow would never begin
and every day would just
end

hour council
14 and 10 strong
their spirits
glowing on their arms

24 hours for the day
we were surrounded by time
as haunting minutes
crept away and moved in
slithering like snakes

all we could do
with thinning patience
was
wait

and as I paced
safi-oya stepped into her quarters
with concern etched on her visage

Kahm:
"my queen,
do you bring bitter news
on your sweet tongue?"

Safi-oya:
"great, black warrior
I bring words of a final mission

TO ENLIGHTEN THE G.O.D.Z.

Act II: The Order of Maa Tru Ark

that you must be brought to."

Kahm:
"please speak."

Safi-oya:
"there are 11 tokens
held by the guardians
of each branch
of the Ances-Tree.

onyan-atum's loop-cross, adinkra
perfect black's king piece
djehuti's book
obaluaye's skull
ma'at's scales
ogun's pendulum
mwindo-heru's sun disk
oshun's venus stone
sebek's key
auset's veil
and osain-geb's root

we must become guardians for our guardians;
and lead their totems from Maa-Tru-Ark
and defend until this age's end."

eye
accept
this task

Safi-oya:
"at this moment
vibrating
with all their power
in every key,
in every hue,
and tone,
the 24 elders
of hour council
re-create these totems

TO ENLIGHTEN THE G.O.D.Z.

Act II: The Order of Maa Tru Ark

as simple tokens

re-created perfectly
with polarized energy
to seduce and trick our enemies

nemtusar wants
the Ances-Tree?
he can have it.
but not at full blossom
and power
as will be seen
thru those
who make up a day
and all its hours."

Kahm:
"I'll steal suggestion,
it will not be just us
on this great mission."

safi-oya smiled
and music played
thru the sun's rays

Safi-oya:
"you, myself,
alik, moorah
and ruther.

the rest,
will defend our mother's womb
our libraries
our ancient tombs of Ma-Tru-Ark."

I reached for her
my goddess,
my commander,
my queen —
kissed her with ease
and we made love

TO ENLIGHTEN THE G.O.D.Z.

Act II: The Order of Maa Tru Ark

to one another
until we be-came
a gentle breeze

I come in pieces
only to be restored
by her isis
when we climax

TO ENLIGHTEN THE G.O.D.Z.

Act II: The Order of Maa Tru Ark

"THE GATHERING OF TOTEMS"

24 elders
stand
before me
their time
born
far
before me

11 totems
before me
their time
eternal
spinning
thru infinity

and here
at the burning
cross —
        — roads
of infinity
at a moment
where 1 decision
has been made for me
I have become the guardian of the guardians
who played chess with time
moving pieces of its line
to secure my birth
so they would have a guardian
ages
before their spirits
protected the earth
our Ances-Tree
its branches
and leaves

and I hold
the worth
of this task
calculated time —

TO ENLIGHTEN THE G.O.D.Z.

Act II: The Order of Maa Tru Ark

these circumstances
with the truth of building
adding
and multiplying
math
the days of this age are numbered
not to die, but to become forever
and re-engender
in another time

safi-oya, alik,
moorah, and I
we gather the totems
and with ruther
fly

TO ENLIGHTEN THE G.O.D.Z.

Act 11: The Order of Maa Tru Ark

"3RD EYE VISION"

we trace clouds
and draw attention as a moving star
allied with the night
we are guarded
from the sight of snakes and ghosts

ruther allows us to float
and guides our killer bee to the earth

we slip from the ship
and bury the totems
inside
and under
consecrated soil

all 11 hidden

it was here that heat
scratched my 3rd eye
and made an incision
with a vision
of Maa-Tru-Ark

twisted metal descended from the sky
and fired twisted, polarized sunbeams
from burning crossed eyes

thru straight 3rd eye
I could see afrikan killer bee airships
they like the moon
turn the attacking tides
as the 24 elders spoke fire
they wielded lightning
and clapped thunder
— all as 1 mind
while oluso
pouring from Maa-Tru-Ark's womb
battled with dark matter swords
each kill

TO ENLIGHTEN THE G.O.D.Z.

Act 11: The Order of Maa Tru Ark

purchasing minutes
buying us time

I was not the only 1
who took witness
to this experience
this scene
poured over all our senses

with this vision
we slipped back into ship
but moorah's lips
spoke
and caught us like a whip

Moorah:
"I can't return.
my womb
has earned life.
and my fight
must be for this child."

she felt her belly
and felt
inside her belly
her power
echoed the child's heartbeat
in our ears

that's all
I needed to hear
for me to speak

Kahm:
"alik,
guard your queen,
your child, our totems,
and our future.

I promise a return."

TO ENLIGHTEN THE G.O.D.Z.

Act II: The Order of Maa Tru Ark

alik and I
connect with mind
and shake hands

Kahm/Alik:
goodbye

Alik:
**my friends,
may our ancestors
guide you.**

Kahm:
"that will be difficult,
when they will be by you.

don't worry
our story
still holds
many chapters."

Safi-oya:
"and characters
yet to be born."

Kahm:
"and some waiting to return."

Alik/Moorah:
peace be unto you – even in war.

as duty rises
and war dawns
our eyes hold memories
and these two friends
are forever gone

waving us away, the wind in their face
alik and moorah
watch us fly into the night
to secure future days

TO ENLIGHTEN THE G.O.D.Z.

Act II: The Order of Maa Tru Ark

"WHAT FATE DECIDES"

in the distance
Maa-Tru-Ark
limps
not stands
buried
under crimson flames
her knees
scraping the sands
her inhabitants begin to star-alize
involute to become a star
to populate the safe haven of the sky
while polarized sunbeams dance
against our killer bee airship
– ruther shifts
our flight curves and twists
but too many blasts rip
and tear thru to us

ruther fights
to keep us a-lift
hoping the wind will assist
and drifts us closer to Maa-Tru-Ark
but instruments that keep us flowing
floating
begin to spark and burn

like the daughters of babylon
our wings of flight are clipped
the killer bee
stings
giving
1
last
kick
spraying true sunbeams
before we collide with the earth
and hit

on our feet

TO ENLIGHTEN THE G.O.D.Z.

Act 11: The Order of Maa Tru Ark

quick
we charge our dark matter swords
and charge into battle and war
tight with action against this unholy faction
moving closer to our home city

ruther scans Maa-Tru-Ark

Ruther:
**our people fight
to cast light over the city.
there is an orb of inner-g
hidden
underneath.

if touched by a heart in sync
a shield will burn the unholy
and heal every crack
and tear
on every building,
home
and city street.**

safi-oya and I
once again, warriors
at each other's side

and now
it's time
to end
time

we rush forward
in a trinity's line

but –
safi-oya can feel her mother's spirit
passed into a leaf
and something stops me

my eyes fill with water and swell

TO ENLIGHTEN THE G.O.D.Z.

Act II: The Order of Maa Tru Ark

– for I can feel
– another
– has passed
– as well

and though
tears
warp
reality
I can see clearly

(though my eyes
scream and cry)

on giant cross
Ohm Lingo
crucified

safi-oya embraces me
so that I may hide
but I can still see her
my spirit-sister
I pray for her

safi-oya holds me close
this beautiful
queen,
goddess,
commander,
she commands the wind
and allows
Ohm Lingo's body to descend
and become 1 with the earth

I break from her

Kahm:
"spoken wars!?
I have spoken too much of war
so, I speak of war no more.

TO ENLIGHTEN THE G.O.D.Z.

Act II: The Order of Maa Tru Ark

I study war no more
for I have been tested to make it.
and all that I love
is eaten
and disintegrated –
and for its life
it is turned against me
as an image of death and hatred!"

Safi-oya:
"oh … kahm …"

Kahm:
"will I ever be me?
never!
you help me get to this beast,
open his neck
and sever."

and enter
eye-van

Eye-van:
"oh! how clever.
look at your soul sister…
how rood of me.
but what a plan.
shame,
that Ohm Lingo's last feeling
came thru my forceful hands."

Kahm:
"why do you do this to your own people?
what raped your spirit and birthed evil?"

snakes and ghosts
come from the earth
and make war
ruther and safi-oya
negate them

TO ENLIGHTEN THE G.O.D.Z.

<u>Act 11: The Order of Maa Tru Ark</u>

Eye-van:
"your words
are irrelevant to the times.
they burn behind you,
with Maa-Tru-Ark."

we are back in battle
the earth
like snakes
rattle
our swordz
cackle
as they crash
against one another

I am
against
one
of another

Kahm:
"I'll take your other eye!
and nemtusar,
when finished with you,
will take your life
and find another slave to control."

and his smile spoke
thru smoke

Eye-van:
"I'm sure he will."

we fight
swing
and fight
until
we are backed up
into the night
and surrounded
by the flames

TO ENLIGHTEN THE G.⊖.⊃.Z.

Act II: The Order of Maa Tru Ark

of Maa-Tru-Ark
our fight
has taken us
this far

eye-van turns and disappears
beyond the burning city gates

safi-oya takes my side

Safi-oya:
"we must rush in.
ruther has given me
a mental map of the city
to find the orb hidden beneath.

we might even be able to save
the Ances-Tree."

safi-oya rushes in
unscathed by the flames
that torture the city
I step quickly to join her side
but the earth shakes
and cries
splits
and opens
allowing the buried ungod
named liyer
to rise high into the sky
carrying his book of lies

he opens to a single page
and blows the words into the wind
firing loopholes that attack
and bind me
separating me from my queen
who has been allowed to slip thru easily
by her workforce
into the workforce

ⴺO ENLIGHTEN THE G.O.D.Z.

Act II: The Order of Maa Tru Ark

I am attacked by snakes and ghosts
I sever the loopholes
obey the lies
and carve my way to the city gates

closer
to safi-oya

ruther takes my side
battling liyer's lies
and ghosts
that glide
and snakes that slither
close

nemtusar
descends from the sky
behind safi-oya
and encases her
in a misty cloud
that rains inter-fear-ence
safi-oya freezes
stopped in time
her locks
unable to receive my thoughts
picking up
this heavy inter-fear-ence

nemtusar gathers the four winds
and makes them collide
up
into the sky
where they are digested
by Qnu-Tansey
the beast exhales them
into Maa-Tru-Ark

with these combined winds
he dives
and explodes
with an out-of-tune vibe

TO ENLIGHTEN THE G.O.D.Z.

<u>Act II: The Order of Maa Tru Ark</u>

… and how cruel
of what fate decides
Ixu and Gira
without mercy
only
allowed
myself
to survive

the charred
scenery
searing vision
branded into my eyes
at my side
there was safi-oya
still and lifeless
… still

quickly –
– slowly
slowly –
– or quickly
I reached for her body
and held it close to me
as I cried and screamed

and I gave her a kiss
on her appoca-lips
brought revelation
to our relationship
and tattooed her name
on my arm
again
done
my body fading
as her body faded
I bled into the wind
reformed again
and buried safi-oya's image
as a memory

TO ENLIGHTEN THE G.O.D.Z.

Act II: The Order of Maa Tru Ark

deep
under
my mind's soil
watering it with a 1000 tears
and swirled in that fateful memory
for 80 years…

the memory of her lips
her voice
her kiss
her skin

I ponder my angel
and see
that I have lost her
twice
again

TO ENLIGHTEN THE G.O.D.Z.

Act III: Heart and Shadow

"80 AND 24 YEARS OLD"

locks left open
mumbling slurs
not words

death does not see fit to take me
mold me into a dried leaf
on the withered Ances-Tree

I remain remembering
the imagery of what she meant to me
knees bent
begging Ixu and Gira for an answer
why this was meant to be?

but locks left open
mumbling slurs
not words

time makes up
my flesh
wrinkled
like choking breaths
dim
as the sky
bleeding a sunset

flashes of imagery
of what she meant to me
flashes of her smile
that gave the flow
to the river nile
asfet
brought into our court---ship
and our love
placed
on trial

placed
on hold
without a grip

TO ENLIGHTEN THE G.O.D.Z.

Act III: Heart and Shadow

reality slips
slurs kiss my lips

locks
left
open
I
left
alive

flashes of turner pulling me
from Maa-Tru-Ark's burning tides
flashes of me
taken from s-f-y-a's side
leaving behind
an echoed scream
thru decades of tears I've cried

soul-sister
Ohm Lingo
crucified

flashes of heat
tearing thru ruther
and the way he died

flashes of the Ances-Tree
withering
and the ungodz victory
and the guardians
and their power
all mimed

and here I am
frozen
in time's line
stubborn
as the fixed earth
not willing to die

80 years
suffering from 1 memory

TO ENLIGHTEN THE G.Θ.Ɔ.Z.

Act III: Heart and Shadow

1 moment in time

Kahm:
"... the spoken wars ...
they began with a whisper
and would end just the same
but in between
there were screams so loud
they could be seen

and vicious imagery
that shined
so bright
all sight would go blind..."

nothing but explosions
her imagery
eroding --- shattered ---
all her matter
of what mattered to me

remembering imagery
of how turner nursed me
in this hideaway
day
by
day
soothed

but my body
my spirit,
my mind,
never moved

my eyes
always staring into nothing
seeing something
remembering the imagery
of what she meant to me
the sway in her hips
how she kissed culture on my lips

TO ENLIGHTEN THE G.O.D.Z.

Act III: Heart and Shadow

but
locks
left
open
mumbling
slurs
not words

80 years covered my body
the burden of allies
on top of me
I am
buried by burden, the dead

mother paper and father pen
speaking into either ear
telling me to awaken

but if I did
could something
104 years old
ra-mold this world?

so they just sit next to me
patiently
waiting
to see as I do
what's the next move
for destiny

TO ENLIGHTEN THE G.O.D.Z.

Act III: Heart and Shadow

"ANCESTRAL VOICES"

just as I was led thru the paper's womb
my thoughts drifted
led to an ancestral guardian's tomb
my ear tickled by an ancient tune
that crept into my room
harmonized by the moon
centered in the sky
eclipsing the sun
blowing clouds at high noon

and as my thoughts drift
my eyes
for the first time
in 80 years
shift and connect
with the man in the moon

eyes focused – I realize
it was actually a woman crying
hiding her face in shame
her tears fell as rain
while she used a cloud as a veil

Gira crawled
and hid inside her own womb
eclipsing her husband and their sun

Kahm:
"Ixu ...
my example ...
I have ...
failed you ...
my mother pen ...
my father paper ...
and the rest
as they rest in peace

I come to pieces
without my goddess
--who holds your wife's spirit--

TO ENLIGHTEN THE G.O.D.Z.

Act III: Heart and Shadow

to put me back together."

and appeared
the spirit of a teacher
glowing next to me
as dark matter soul

Turner:
"you have not failed
you have been covered
and hidden by Gira's veil

and your parents have spoken
for all these years
whispering your name into each ear
keeping you whole
thru your ren (your name's essence)
so that you would never be forgotten

time has not forgot you,
time has preserved you,
reserved you
to set its line straight.

the Ances-Tree still sings
harmonizing ourstory;
and Grandfather Clock
still keeps time,
while Grandmother B,
Ourstory Book,
keeps the memory
written in the pages of her mind.

you,
with your friends' descendants,
must raise our guardians
to bring back
our time."

Kahm:
"I can't even
raise my legs.

TO ENLIGHTEN THE G.O.D.Z.

Act III: Heart and Shadow

and my spirit carries 104 years on it
nothing
weighs more heavy than time.

I am older than you,
turner,
when your spirit
ascended to the ancestors."

Turner:
"my eyes
focused
still see a child I taught
to be a man, a warrior."

my eyes are attacked
with tears I thought
I no longer possessed

Kahm:
"how holy does water have to be
to wash away 80 years?"

Turner:
"how much does your spirit
have to believe to make time
disappear?"

and next to turner
stepped
the lord
of the perfect black

my eyes
so wide
they swallow
too much
and I breathe
rapidly
breath entering me
fresh

TO ENLIGHTEN THE G.O.D.Z.

Act III: Heart and Shadow

something I never thought I'd feel
for an eternity

Kahm:
"pardon
my blaspheme,
but my lips
are not worthy to kiss
your name."

The All Black (in masculine):
"you may speak
my entire spirit, mind, and body
sing all 3 in a key with soul
I am before the gods given to you
I am the all black
with blood of gold."

I exhale 80 years of grief
and find relief
hidden in spirits
that have become a leaf

Kahm:
"oh ... sire ... us
great guardian
noble,
black king.
I have failed your family
The first trinity."

his smile chases winter away

The All Black (in masculine):
"you have come well
and are welcomed into our plan.
failed us? no, kahm.
you have played
right into destiny's hands."

I now believe
that I have enough inner-g

TO ENLIGHTEN THE G.O.D.Z.

Act III: Heart and Shadow

to stand on my feet

and I lift
supporting myself
with a withered hand against a shelf
tilting my weight
on books of past ages
I am held up by written time
tomes
not tombs
I rest on time
as my time of rest has come to an end

Kahm:
"my teacher,
my guardian,
where do I begin?"

the all black
and turner
as well
as my father
and mother
smiles combine

The All Black (in masculine):
"you will begin at the root,
find its truth
take away the lie,
and from there
kahm noiz
– warrior preserved in time –
climb and rise."

TO ENLIGHTEN THE G.O.D.Z.

Act III: Heart and Shadow

"RA-4MED"

the four spirits gather me
carry me
to outside scenery
where the wind
touches my skin ---
skin that barely exists
as I
with it
hang on the tip of life

turner casts the earth
to my body
so that my hue
can sing on Q in perfect tone
and echo the night

while mother paper
and father pen
ra-write my image
and I am
once again
dressed in young flesh
inhaling fresh breath
a young spirit
resurrected from the west
rising
with a turning tide
from the east
while young body
re-nude
and young spirit meet (again)
my mind cleaned of tragedy
now dreams of heaven

ra-born and ra-formed
80 years slip from me
and I am once again
adorned with youth
my hair
locked tightly, neatly

TO ENLIGHTEN THE G.O.D.Z.

Act III: Heart and Shadow

at the root

my eyes shimmer with colour
no longer winter white
but swirling with new life
of spring and summer

my robes
tattered and old
remold
into something new

and my voice
opens
speaking
words
not slurs
I can form speech
without thought
(as it was meant to be)

my beard slips from me
and youth caresses my face
80 years leave me
without a trace

Kahm:
"I am kahm noiz
my name once destroyed
I have once again
resurrected from the void

I am that word spoken
with rhythm
that makes your tongue roll
I am black whole

I am ra-born
I am no longer the scar
where time was torn
I reclaim my name
and billow it thru Gabriel's horn

TO ENLIGHTEN THE G.O.D.Z.

Act III: Heart and Shadow

let the angels
announce my arrival
for all my rivals
I walk with psalms on my feet
as my heart speaks the bible
let the tides flow
when my dark matter sword
like the moon, glows.
let peace reign
when I make war with my reign-bows
let the ghosts and snakes tremble
when they inhale my heir-rows."

the all black, in feminine,
descends on the wind
kisses me on the cheek
and I feel safi-oya's spirit in her lips

the mother of creation hands me a gift
plucked from the Ances-Tree
annointed in gold
dangling from a chain
safi-oya's spirit leaf

I thank Gira
and place
safi-oya's spirit
around me

The All Black (in feminine):
"her life will be with you again
when you complete your task
and restore the 11 totems and keys
to the Ances-Tree."

The All Black (in masculine):
"even as a single man
you carry the spirit of an army
in militant harmony."

and from locked hair to naps

TO ENLIGHTEN THE G.O.D.Z.

Act III: Heart and Shadow

these five guides place in my mind
a mental map

I can feel all 7 kheru intact
although
weak
with no use
practice will be
when I fight each enemy

I bend a knee
to my teacher
my guardians
and parents

Kahm:
"I know where I must start—
past the city of Maa-Tru-Ark
where we left hidden
those 11 totems

it is there
where I will meet
the descendants
of my friends

their children's
children."

I grip the leaf I wear around me

safi-oya's spirit
incased in gold

I wear her soul
and pray

Kahm:
**safi-oya
you have never been
more closer in 80 years
my goddess,

TO ENLIGHTEN THE G.O.D.Z.

Act III: Heart and Shadow

my commander,
my queen.

no matter what snake
slithers and shakes around you
no matter what ghost haunt
and surround you
your spirit is with me
and I will see you
when this journey is complete
and if there is nothing else left to pray on
it is in that notion, I truly believe.**

I stand
turn
and walk
toward destiny

5 spirits'
combined smiles
shine on me

TO ENLIGHTEN THE G.O.D.Z.

Act III: Heart and Shadow

"SHADOW DRUMS"

the journey's length
is shortened by the kheru

blending into natural elements
I billow as smoke
towards a people
whose father pen
and mother paper
wrote in a time
known as my past lifetime

the sun holds itself still
for a few minutes longer
sweating daylight
with its own heat
I greet the sun
on the opposite horizon
rising from the east

and as the sun sets
I am met by two figures
who figured I would be here
something destiny
scribed for them 80 years ago

the locked haired leader
was dressed in the age
of my appearance
24
he was the sight
of a shadow's dream
battles scarred his face
his years matured and aged
thru war

a tall dark tree
he was the roots
of this underground family
bathing himself in midnight
eyes brighter than stars

ᴛO ENLIGHTEN THE G.O.D.Z.

Act III: Heart and Shadow

his name was Amar

and left of him
was the beauty of an african desert
molded in feminine form
eyes adorned with amethysts
rubies melted onto her lips
birthed
from the earth
this natural gift
made up of every element
--- her name was Norah

I form
physical
solid

Amar:
"you have been news spoken
by our clan's prophets
you are kahm noiz?
hero of a time long destroyed."

Kahm:
"no. just a survivor.
the heroes died."

Amar:
"well,
I hope you don't mind,
being a hero with us
in our time."

Kahm:
"not at all,
if that's
what fate decides."

norah speaks
defining their power
still connected
to an ancient

TO ENLIGHTEN THE G.O.D.Z.

Act III: Heart and Shadow

Ances-Tree

Norah:
"thru soul and lyrics
we invoke the shadow's shaded spirit
for we are the silhouette formed from rays of light
the black specters, fiery solid shapes, that mimic
the dark matters and inner-g of the cosmic night."

Amar:
"I am the grandchild of alik and moorah
they spoke
and wrote inside us
a power to mold ourselves into solid shadows
standing tall on two legs
and strike like lightning rods

our heart beats on drums made of shades
We are 16 tones – sharpened as blades
we fight against nemtursar
until all is one and won
until his daze be numbered and done
and the Ances-Tree
glistens healthy with every leaf."

--eyes focused--

I see around amar's neck
his grandparents' spirit leaves
I quickly rush to him
and take his hand

Kahm:
"your grandparents
were great friends,
and meant so much to me."

Amar:
"both passed in peace, not war.
it was my mother and father
who served to fight
with shaded cosmic might.

TO ENLIGHTEN THE G.O.D.Z.

Act III: Heart and Shadow

they passed on thru battle
I was barely a rattle

although you have been released
from time's shackles
you will still feel a heavy burden

time has not adapted well to the weather
only storms have been born in time's womb."

and we were warned
by norah's words

Norah:
"the horizon swallows the sun
let us return to sanctuary
where we can recreate the day
with our words."

and I followed them
teamed again
with allies

╪O ENLIGH╪EN ╪HE G.O.D.Z.

Act III: Heart and Shadow

"WORDS AROUND THE CAMPFIRE"

their clan is barely an army
but each one makes two
with the spirit of the cosmic tones, dark hues in tune
drum-beating in their hearts
in between the pages of their martial arts

I am welcomed
as fire ignites and makes daylight
stories start
air condenses into verbal art
the first to speak is amar

Amar:
"destiny has only written one book for me
one book for us as 'we'
and we must keep it from being re-written
by our enemies

for 80 years our clan has wondered
who was the man who lived inside eternity
trapped inside time's faint memory
one thought that kept him alive
reliving agony constantly

and here time has sung in a heroic chord
bringing us an ancestor of the Spoken Wars.
he is here to take back the Ances-Tree
every branch and every spirit leaf.
he is kahm noiz."

I am referred to as an ancestor
by life just made new

and a young warrior
seated next to me
speaks with jest, but elegantly

Muur:
"time has treated you well, ancestor
no wrinkles, no scars.

TO ENLIGHTEN THE G.O.D.Z.

Act III: Heart and Shadow

you look no older than amar."

Kahm:
"not every scar is physical."

amar sits and motions for me to stand

I plant my feet
feel my roots, weak
I feel the Ances-Tree
breathing only faintly

my old eyes, made new
scan each new face
they are too young, too willing to die
I as a student
must now be their teacher and guide
and there's nowhere to hide from responsibility

my syllables crawl with 8 legs
and my words spin web-like-tales
of prison and nemtusar's mist-filled jails
and how I (and two allies)
came to realize our souls' glow
how we could conjure nature
and battle with reign-bows, heir-rows

I speak on angelic saviors
the history makers
that these young warriors
only know as 'history'
history that I knew as friends
that once battled alongside me

alik keem
moorah
safi-oya
ruther
turner
Hour Council of 24 elders
a great city – Maa-Tru-Ark –
whose sun set on her

TO ENLIGHTEN THE G.O.D.Z.

Act III: Heart and Shadow

left her in the dark
while she burned in the flames
created by snakes and ghosts
10 ungodz
and nemtusar

Kahm:
"but we'll throw our words, celestial ropes
over the horizon, lift her sun out of the east
while we as warriors make war with the beast
every branch of the Ances-Tree
will shake off every rattled snake
and exhale these ghosts for relief

so when you enter thru war's door
it's not that you must think of death
and not care
but you must climb your 3rd eye's stare
step-by-step
until you are aware of your power
at the tip of your spinal tower
that reaches up towards heaven
and down into the final hour

when you reach heaven
turn the moon like a knob
so that you will be cleansed thru a sun shower
take the sun's seeds
plant them into the earth to grow sunflowers
so that emptiness will never touch the earth again
and the light of these petals
will never be extinguished
no matter how strong
qnu-tansey blows his four foul winds

and no matter how strong
qnu-tansey increases the gravity
to hold down our thoughts
we will always ascend

there are no such things as descendants
nothing is separate

TO ENLIGHTEN THE G.O.D.Z.

Act III: Heart and Shadow

neither the moons, stars, or suns
those before me,
you,
Ixu and Gira,
time and I,
we are all as one
who invented who
is not even the question

uniting our minds
binding them to Ixu and Gira
purpose,
ancestors,
and time,
is our quest, sons
drink me as water
and bathe me in my daughters' speech.
I as syllables will exhale peace."

I plant into young minds
ease
and they sleep

amar and I take time to verse

Kahm:
"a lot can happen in 80 years
so what has happened on this lot?"

amar shifts
almost as if
he doesn't
want to speak

Amar:
"Maa-Tru-Ark
is now named in shame
as the Compli-City
faded beauty
where only we can speak
thru our minds
but not speak our minds.

TO ENLIGHTEN THE G.O.D.Z.

Act III: Heart and Shadow

we are in collusion to serve the illusion

eye-van the gatekeeper
keeps his mind open
to hear every thought
and report back to nemtusar."

Kahm:
"are there others like you?
spirited with cosmic shades
souljahz as one who walk as two?"

Amar:
"if you dig deep enough
you will find those with our face
speak with the tongue of a snake
and connect themselves
to the command of nemtusar

he uses them
so that trapped slaves can pretend
they are free
and have someone speaking
for the ways they cannot express

personally, I ask
how can you know someone is speaking for you
when you don't know how
to form words with your own breath?
that's another reason we remain silent

all we can trust
is just us."

Kahm:
"I have an understanding.
do you know how to use the kheru?"

Amar:
"they have no effect
in the Compli-City.
when we enter,

TO ENLIGHTEN THE G.O.D.Z.

Act III: Heart and Shadow

you will be powerless
so,
instead of your dark matter sword
learn to use your fists,
close it like this
place it in the air
it's more powerful than any prayer."

Kahm:
"yes.
we use to do that in my time.
but don't worry,
I know how to turn Compli-City
back to Maa-Tru-Ark.
let me be the fire and spark
to put things back in order."

norah looks on
admiration dawns
and curiosity piques

Kahm:
"a lovely woman."

Amar:
"an orphan
she just learned
how to invoke the cosmic shadow.
her spirit is now twice as vicious."

I take witness to every word
and circle back to a familiar name

Kahm:
"eye-van still exists?"

Amar:
"kept immortal by the miasmic mist
his concept lingers on
but it's the warrior
—the house nigga—
known as Nuus

TO ENLIGHTEN THE G.O.D.Z.

Act III: Heart and Shadow

that we fear

even nemtusar trembles
in this warrior's presence

he is the extension of the sun
backwards.

if you are to fight him,
you must battle far from Compli-City,
so that your power is at full essence.
he's dangerous
and he will take you as a word and sentence you."

and there, in memory, are flashes of imagery
I have met this 'nuus' before
and I hang from his image

rope
around his throat
tied up
wrapped
to cover his face

he sings in the harmony
of every snake
a fight between him and I?
it can't wait

some things are still young in me

the noiz in my name will never change
or remain completely silent

TO ENLIGHTEN THE G.O.D.Z.

Act III: Heart and Shadow

"TOURING THE CONTEMPORARY 1"

what little light
the sun had to spare
on these dark times
shined
dull
to take away the night

this new sun was an old man
limping into the sky
every ray
was an exhaled sigh
a heave
from a heavenly body
that could barely breathe
coughing light and heat
to warm what was left
of our people's heartbeat

but all our heart could do
was bleed
all our Ances-Tree could do
was choke
without heir to breathe

Maa-Tru-Ark did not stand
it did not limp,
crawl,
or sleep
it just lay in the distance
broken
our city lay on her back
the Ances-Tree
withered and sapped

the dull morning
pulled the night away
like an unwanted wrap
but darkness
stayed intact

TO ENLIGHTEN THE G.O.D.Z.

Act III: Heart and Shadow

amar traced the emotion
writhing on my face

Amar:
"that's the Compli-City…"

I will journey in
to see beauty
turned to sin

as for now
my eyes gather images
of my clothes
sashes and robes

Kahm:
"my clothes will put us
in dangerous waters
setting us for sale
they will sell us out."

Norah:
"don't you wish to make an impact?"

Kahm:
"I'd like to keep our purpose
and our lives
intact.

for some reason
our guardians
(along with the fates)
have decided
that I will carry out this mission

I vow to honor their decision.

above that
I will not fail becuz of pride
wishing to make an impact.

gather yourselves

TO ENLIGHTEN THE G.O.D.Z.

Act III: Heart and Shadow

       or just yourself
to head back
and gather clothes
made for deception
and lies
for us to blend in
and spy with eshu's trickster eye."

norah disappeared
into thick environment
and thin air
leaving us
in the middle of our nowhere

amar and I stayed silent
expensive time spent
on staring into our hands
trying to etch a plan
into the winding roads
where destiny drove

our lives mapped out on our palms
we two sons sat wondering
if we held enough light
to bring about a new dawn

Kahm:
"did you know your grandparents?"

Amar:
"not like you—
they were warriors
forced to conceive peace
       too early
the battle still inside them.
but from them came my mother
and their duty shifted
to the protection of just one potential leaf
out of the whole Ances-Tree

I was written in prophecy
and with their protection to secure me

TO ENLIGHTEN THE G.O.D.Z.

Act III: Heart and Shadow

they believed they were selfish

like these ghosts
it haunted them
like these snakes
it was venomous

my grandparents wanted to be by you
but when life began to glow thru
my grandmother's womb
and hue
they knew their destiny
was tied to another root."

Kahm:
"if they were in that battle,
I have to say,
they would have been killed, too.
your birth would be worth nothing
the potential of what time could have been
a wish carried in the wind

they may have figured
their actions were worthless
but they were a part
of fate's greater purpose and plan."

norah echoes from the shadows
with bundles of deceptive clothes

we switch our dress
and suppress our intentions
wrapped in these broken syllables
and ragged sentences
we are words disguised
dressed up to deceive the naked eye
and under the shadows
is where our ancestral clothes hide

my power stays behind
as the Compli-City's aura
circles my spirit and mind

TO ENLIGHTEN THE G.O.D.Z.

Act III: Heart and Shadow

(my body feels empty)

at the gates of the city
there was eye-van,
ragged,
old,
his destiny
taken from his hands
he was unable to speak
unable to see
unable to hear audible words
he barely
breathed

Kahm:
"I see nemtusar has taken your other eye."

my speaking captures amar by surprise
I assure my new ally, "oh, I figure he can't hear me,
unless I speak thru the mind.
his power
concentrated
too much
on those inside
keeping our people in line
taking away destiny from time."

I wave my hand
in front of his face

Kahm:
"he can't even see me."

I stand on a single knee

Kahm:
"hey! eye-van!
you would excite my heart
if my heart inside me
beat only to be your gift
and I would fill your heart with my beat
if your veins were not filled with mist

TO ENLIGHTEN THE G.O.D.Z.

Act III: Heart and Shadow

here, my brother
I give you this razor
so that you may cut yourself
and bleed the ghost that possesses you
from out your wrist
along with the snake's venom and hiss

I would even grow love on you
by planting a kiss
if these ghosts
had not grafted your lips
and made them too thin

no wonder you can't speak!
how can you form words
when your lips no longer exist?"

we leave him to the curse
of being him
while he sings haunting hymns
to justify his sins

colours of ghosts
dance in his arms
and snakes
slither from his throat
his rusted locks
trying to dig themselves
into the ground
to amplify that he makes no sound
but he has secret hopes to connect with his roots
but no matter how wild he sprouts his thoughts
they will never grow truth

Eye-van:
**you ... think ... I can't hear you
... my friend?
here, I think I can.
so I see,
you continuously ignore me

TO ENLIGHTEN THE G.O.D.Z.

Act III: Heart and Shadow

I might be blind ...
but you can't see who I really am
I might be white- and brain-washed
but I am still...
a black...man...?
but...
so what?
so I poisoned the Ances-Tree
making it grow strange-fruit
blood on every spirit-leaf
blood on the roots
so what?
so I scrape my ancestors
with the bottom of my boot
so what? isn't that where sole is?
isn't that what soul is?
dancing on the bottom
of what I called a spirit?

promises make me live

AND these SNAKES AND GHOSTS
promised me THE WORLD
every time they spoke!!!!!!!
so what?
so they took my innocence
while our guardians
gave you back your youth.
so what?
so no matter how thin I got
obeying their lies,
I couldn't slip through their loops.
so what?
who cares if I've been blinded
by their point of view.
so what if soul has slipped from my hue
and has been taken by the confused ... ? so what?
what the fuck you gonna do?
save ... this ... wretched ... world?
with so-called knowledge and truth?
fancy words like 'ances-tree' and 'roots'?
nigga, please.**

Act III: Heart and Shadow

trust me, black man ... I can hear you.
yes. I can.
but ... as you say, so what?
who cares if you and I
are 1 and 1
and can't make two?
so what?
so what if you let these snakes and ghosts
hang us by our roots ---
neggur, who are we
to judge you?

ꓕ⊖ ЕИᒪꓲᎶᕼꓕЕИ ꓕᕼЕ Ꮆ.⊖.Ɔ.Ƶ.

Act III: Heart and Shadow

"TOURING THE CONTEMPORARY 2"

have you ever
had a nightmare
follow you
out. of the dream?
that. was the Compli-City

Maa-Tru-Ark's ashes
had condensed into mist
proud warriors
brothers
sisters
and teachers
dissolved and became
the sambo-coon and the harlot witch
unholy magic
disguised as nemtusar's and qnu-tansey's gift
sin made righteous
and the worship of snakes and ghost
turned into bliss

women wore their DNA straightened
and only ghosts and snakes
would forgive them
when they wore themselves naturally

bruthaz walked castrated, casually
with broken language
and sambo feet
dancing on the graves
that were this Compli-City's rusted streets
these warriors' hearts were offbeat
kicking nothing 7 days
their thoughts constantly weak
and serving the purpose of snakes and ghosts
who served them an image that was worthless

and these sambo-coons and harlots
knew less of their worth
honoring the image of snakes and ghosts
inside their own church

ꓕO ENLIGHTEN THE G.O.D.Z.

Act III: Heart and Shadow

singing ghost-spell songs
of a great ship to take them away
named jesus
his true name
was zammu
slayer of yeshua and mwindo-heru
he controlled every church
preaching his curse as righteous verse
so when they died in their smell
and pews
there was no need for a hearse
bury them
right there
in the stench of venom

my people's souls would no longer ascend
to the Ances-Tree, become a leaf
they would hang in the air
unable to be moved
by the strongest of winds
our people's spirit would bend and twist
and become one with the mist
fueling the prison in the distance

it now has a name
NahtShay
a city
built backwards
draining
and withering
our Ances-Tree
a city built by our minds
our own kind
built on the reversed images
of our ancestral signs

and with every step
I heard the children of what was left
laughing

the punchline
leaving our people

TO ENLIGHTEN THE G.O.D.Z.

Act III: Heart and Shadow

verbally unconscious
and physically
and mentally in bondage
while sambo-coons and harlots
tried their best to pay homage
to ghosts and snakes
while wearing their hoods and capes
living in a confused vacuum
sucking on phallic images of ghosts and snakes
pleasing the masters
                        my people
unable to see they were being raped
and run over
in ghost and snake attire
while trying to win over our enemies' love
thinking nemtusar was god
just because he ruled our Ances-Tree
from above

and my people took pride
in these ghettoes
these dead
man-made mountains
holding us down
and my people sing proudly
screaming
without making a real sound
my people have been thrown
to the face of the full moon
and all of its values
as volumes of valium slow reality
my people escape
by false dreams
selling each other weeds that choke
as we speak haunted smoke
in a broken language
that snakes and ghosts wrote

castrated men
search for manhood
trying to define themselves
through the definition

TO ENLIGHTEN THE G.Θ.Ɔ.Z.

Act III: Heart and Shadow

of a savage
who calls himself
civilized
*(but empty seeds
only sprout a haunted phallus)*

while women
with DNA intact
are shuffled like marionettes
locks wrapped around
the fingers of a ghost
and strummed like strings
by a snake's tongue

my people
have disconnected themselves
from the sun
only to serve a father of lies
without a mother
or feminine guide

I see a woman eating garbage
and she speaks
thinking her speech
makes her justified
(but just in who's eyes?)

Woman:
**I eat the best they give me

once and a while
they let me think
of a time
when my culture's rhythm
made the sun shine.

so, I eat the best they give me.**

I wish I could make her creativity bloom
then she could see
that she possessed the power to birth
her own culture

TO ENLIGHTEN THE G.O.D.Z.

Act III: Heart and Shadow

thru her own mind's womb
but her memory
has died
too long ago to remember how to fight

Kahm:
"cook for yourself, sista.
the best of garbage
is still garbage."

she chooses not to hear me
my image,
a black man,
has her only fear me
becuz of what someone else
was trained to do to her

these snakes and ghosts
knowing our strength
had to make us our own killers

Kahm:
"I'll win back your soul, sister.
give you back some of that glow,
sister…"

TO ENLIGHTEN THE G.O.D.Z.

Act III: Heart and Shadow

"TOURING THE CONTEMPORARY 3"

the soil is soiled
mother earth unable to breathe
smothered by an unnatural paving
that covers her as streets
the soil is soiled
ruled by et
no longer osain-geb
and by the rules of asfet
her court-ship
run by liyer
bruthaz are constantly
under
and in
the fire

khemi-lohim
now named shuckinjive
a dive
for those
who swim
in cesspools

this is a place
for sambo-coons
and harlots to rule
under the rules
of the ghost-ungoddess
named sluh

she rules thru the distortion
of the venus stone
my people shake thru body and bone
and not thru soul
but with the khabit
they still glow
for satisfaction and entertainment
of snakes and ghosts
no longer to teach thru their artistic gifts

and I watch as harlot hips

⊖⊖ ENLIGHTEN THE G.⊖.D.Z.

Act III: Heart and Shadow

shake and quake
deep inside
my khabit quickly awakes
and the rhythm creates confusion
I am torn between eyesight and insight

the beats of my heart accelerate
an over abun-dance of melanated gyrations
fast moves and inhalation
I breathe thru my eyes
my khabit burning my insides
but my heart is the nose
as it smells deception
and knows
this is not the way
that my bruthaz and sistaz
were meant to behave
under Ixu and Gira
they will be saved
and their manipulator slain

for now
I pray
leave the room and wait

amar takes me aside

Amar:
"I know.
it's too much
for even the most
experienced of eyes."

I decide to look around

Kahm:
"where is norah?"

Amar:
"somewhere,
if not everywhere.
she can't stand the sight

TO ENLIGHTEN THE G.O.D.Z.

Act III: Heart and Shadow

of this place."

norah slips from a shadow
the hurt of her people
dripping from her face

Kahm:
"let's be out."

we gather
to plan
to avenge
and I look back
and send a prayer
to my people

Kahm:
"I love you. even when you sin.
even when you're as cold as the wind.

snakes and ghosts?
you bastards killed dreams
your venom
has torn us
so it seems
but I'm going to win my people back
and if your haunted thoughts
and your venom tries to set in
I'll fight against that."

I turn
to leave
to plan
to turn
the tide

ＴＯ ＥＮＬＩＧＨＴＥＮ ＴＨＥ Ｇ.Ｏ.Ｄ.Ｚ.

Act III: Heart and Shadow

"AROUND OUR NECKS"

my eyes regurgitate the sins
of Compli-City thru tears
while dark shaded drums
fill my ears and my heart
beats to rhythm and my prayers
beat away the visions
that poisoned my eyes

back in ancient robes
amar, norah, and I
sneak back to where hide the shadow tribe
their campsite
the undaground
drums beating from the ground
up

I rest in their rhythm
the vibrations a bed
some of the women
light incense
and amar begins
to chant with them

we rest – chant – and feed into separate activity
the rhythm and the shadows disperse, taking leave

Kahm:
"I battle with Compli-City."

Norah:
"there are brighter visions,
dispersed along the lands."

Kahm:
"no, young woman
I must see reality
keep the illusions away from me
concentrating on the effects
of the beast

TO ENLIGHTEN THE G.O.D.Z.

Act III: Heart and Shadow

to battle this beast – that is my need

I ponder unity."

Amar:
"our people are split into gangs
they battle for illusions
they are made examples
for the delusion
of the snakes and ghosts.
a political rope
wrapped around our necks.

unity bleeds.

our people believe in the hope
to battle for the values
and love for snakes and ghosts.
they know
our Ances-Tree withers
and they look to nemtusar
and his ungodz
as christ figures

but snakes and ghosts are cursed figures,
grave fillers
blood spillers
who only deliver hate

unity just bleeds.

nemtusar
even created villains
worst than him

this was a ploy

he came in to save our people
making him appear less evil

when we try to restore our views and values
we are counted as villains

TO ENLIGHTEN THE G.O.D.Z.

Act III: Heart and Shadow

becuz they had been made notorious
under him and the villains he created."

the kheru
as the khu
rises from my hue
and scans the area

Kahm:
"something amiss
is about to hit."

norah chants

Norah:
"my heart as the drum
calls the shadows and shades
to become as one."

my dark matter sword ignites
my heart pumps AB for the fight

we hear slithering
haunting moans
dripping
from shadows
laughter
that is a battle cry

amar allows his power
to be his guide
with norah at his side
the two shift into giant shades
right before my eyes
standing solid, blackness stretching for days
pillars as legs
tall and towering
I thought they touched the sky

and as the snakes and ghosts
attack from foul mist
the rest of the souljahz

TO ENLIGHTEN THE G.O.D.Z.

Act III: Heart and Shadow

come from the undaground
their power
unable to hide

Amar:
**show no mercy!
no more shall we see an oppressive regime
no remorse for these snakes and ghosts
let them choke on our power!**

black shadows and I
jump to battle
dark matter swords and kheru
shaded claws
a giant, shadowy maw
hollering and pushing back the attack
made by these venomous figures

until
thunder triggers
and rain
pours
when a moonbeam
CRASHES
against my sword

I turn
with flips and loops
dodge these haunting troops
and battle the one they call Nuus
his weapon, a moonbeam
it SLAMS against my dark matter sword
the colours converge
and become as one
but when my blade separates
it glows like the sun

the night
glows bright
and our battle gleams

Nuus:

TO ENLIGHTEN THE G.O.D.Z.

Act III: Heart and Shadow

**I have waited 80 years
plus several more
taking a thousand lives
wishing they were yours.**

my speech is baited
as he taunted

Kahm:
"why thank you,
it always feels good
to be wanted

eighty years
plus several more?
you should be careful
as to what you wish for, my friend."

I THRUST!
attack
and RUSH!
our fight erupts!
we kick, dodge, and SLAM!
the night glows like the day
as our weapons touch

this brutha,
this house-nigga
this hueman killer
throwing the weapon
that is his name
we battle
baptized by a gentle rain
that reminds me of tears

even the sky cries
when brother fights brother

Nuus:
**let me toss books
and my name as a hook
to snare your neck

TO ENLIGHTEN THE G.O.D.Z.

<u>Act III: Heart and Shadow</u>

and choke all heir and breath

oh,
kahm noiz,
you have filled
an empty void.

my life,
has meaning,
to end yours.
to extinguish the light of your sword
but ...
we battle
no more.**

nuus
his eyes on norah
smiles
and chuckles
his pupils
undressing her
she as sister dark in hue
attracts him
and he knows a true woman
when he sees one

maybe
there is still light
inside this burned out son

nuus calls for retreat
the rain ceases
and amar and I figure
the battle was too easy

Kahm:
"we better move your camp."

shifting back into man
amar replies, "right
I feel they were here
just to see

TO ENLIGHTEN THE G.O.D.Z.

Act III: Heart and Shadow

if their prophets see well."

Kahm:
"nemtusar knows I'm here. good.
then there is no reason
to hide our intentions
of ending his dying season."

Norah:
"we need a plan."

Kahm:
"gather yourselves
to make haste
to plan this night
and attack by day."

TO ENLIGHTEN THE G.O.D.Z.

Act III: Heart and Shadow

"BREAKDOWN CHANT"

amar and I gather the souljahz
for a battle chant and cry

Kahm:
"let me breakdown chant
this is how we plan
there is an orb
that can restore the essence of Maa-Tru-Ark
lift all souls from the dark
where inside their minds
will spark an independent thought
and these ghost-nets
will no longer have them snared and caught
this orb is hidden
deep
underneath
the Compli-City

combined
with the power
of the 11 totems,
this orb will restore
all that is broken."

Norah:
"who do you believe
will dive deep for this orb?"

Amar:
"the question is,
who won't?
when we expose those
        as traitors,
we will march and chant
continue with this plan
to restore Maa-Tru-Ark
and the Ances-Tree."

I touch safi-oya's spirit leaf
and feel a memory

TO ENLIGHTEN THE G.O.D.Z.

Act III: Heart and Shadow

kept intact

swirling
inside the spirit leaf
was the map of Maa-Tru-Ark
and how her underground was carved
the image of the orb
swirling in the colours
of red, green, and black
but from feminine mind to mine
it would take
a feminine third eye
to read this map

I motion to norah
and she steps in my direction
I place a finger to her mind
palming the spirit leaf
and my finger breathes
blowing the winding curves
of the underground nerves
beneath the Compli-City
and she can see clearly
our destiny

Norah:
"I can lead you back."

Kahm:
"just you and amar.
I'll create a diversion in words
to distract."

Amar:
"are you sure you can handle that?"

Kahm:
"I have more burdens to carry
than speaking words.
now, let your shades disperse
in groups of three
forming separate trinities.

TO ENLIGHTEN THE G.O.D.Z.

<u>Act III: Heart and Shadow</u>

tell your shadows to stay ready,
willing, able
and most of all,
stay black
because when we return
we will have the might of nemtusar at our backs."

we celebrate our duties
by screaming ancient words
first formed
by cosmic background sound
we drum,
dance,
and chant
we sleep over earth
under our plan
and understand our destiny

TO ENLIGHTEN THE G.O.D.Z.

Act III: Heart and Shadow

"TRADE ON TRAITORS"

we are carried
on the syllables
of the kheru
I make our bodies
see thru
as we are now the wind
ra-formed again
in front of the Compli-City

this is where my power leaves

eye-van
sits
nowhere
and we enter
quickly

norah and amar
blend into daylight
disappear from sight
and find their way
to the underground

I walk thru crowds
that part
when I pace
in rhythm of heart
and art

my people throw their best jeers
and I hold back tears
swallow them
ra-form them into words
and talk in the way of child speak

the innocent tongue of the beginnings
origins
coming toward the end
of an age of ignorance

TO ENLIGHTEN THE G.O.D.Z.

<u>Act III: Heart and Shadow</u>

Kahm:
**if you could speak back
to every word you read
you would understand
how we as warriors
were conceived...**

and I lay upon their minds
the knowledge they need
empty belly-minds I feed
but stopped
in the middle
of my lesson and speech
someone yells, **to depend upon ourselves
would be too much a burden;
you speak as a serpent! you, a hypocrite!
born glorious in the prison mist!**

Kahm:
**in our ancient kingdoms
serpents first symbolized wisdom
and not lies
thrown over your eyes
by those you believe are allies

they use you on their deceptive stage
my people, for you, I say
draw back the act
and close their curtain."

my people can't truly interpret
the words I've revealed to them
casting open the curtain of deception
they toss rocks in my direction

knocked off my feet to the city streets
but I'm up in a beat – dashing toward the exit
running from my people
who have a lust and fetish
for melanin
black
seen as death finite

TO ENLIGHTEN THE G.O.D.Z.

Act III: Heart and Shadow

not daath infinite
as their minds crush the remembrance
of our ancients

oh! my people
you believe snakes and ghosts
give you peace
you believe
that you live in peace
while the deceptive serpent
takes you
piece
       by
peace

I escape the Compli-City

my people do not follow
too scared to leave
an environment
that has become scary

I scan for amar and norah
and they are nowhere

Kahm:
**come on!
we must escape from here
where are...**

and her feminine voice
dances in my mind
like a chorus
over and over

Norah:
**let's go, kahm...
...let go, kahm.**

in the distance
norah holds the orb

TO ENLIGHTEN THE G.O.D.Z.

Act III: Heart and Shadow

I am in front of her in several strides
look deep into her eyes
and feel the pain of time
it swells as tears
ready to be free
and cried

but a feeling
taps against my mind

Kahm:
"norah…where is amar?"

Norah:
"he has died.
snakes and ghosts
attacked
and he sacrificed
for my life."

I step farther away
from the Compli-City
and the khaibit alerts me
to deception

Kahm:
"let's get back to the undaground
this place will be crawling with ghosts
and snakes."

norah curls her lip
balls her fist
and throws her spirit
I am knocked thru the wind
and soar as if I'm made of it
I crash
earth against my back,
I jump to my feet
only to be attacked again
foot against my chin
body lifted back up into the wind
I tumble to the ground

TO ENLIGHTEN THE G.O.D.Z.

Act III: Heart and Shadow

my lip bleeding sound
heavy heaves
as I gasp and wheeze
norah makes another attack against me
using the shadow claws on her feet
she scars my cheek
and throwing a fist into my stomach
—a fist that swirls with electricity—
the power twisting me
weakening my body
bending to despair
norah knocks me back through the air

she tosses the orb aside
I stare at this broken woman
thru bloody and tearful eyes

Norah:
"and now,
kahm noiz,
you will die!"

she stands over me
in victory
but amar
—wrapped in the body of the cosmic shadow—
strikes like a shooting star

Amar:
"she hangs on her orders from nuus!

this traitor,
this woman,
no more than a ruse."

Kahm:
"amar,
call her not a trick
norah is no harlot witch
she is just confused."

the woman shifts her body

TO ENLIGHTEN THE G.O.D.Z.

Act III: Heart and Shadow

now molded out of the shadow spirit
and the two shades battle each other
sister and brother

norah — traded — traitor — betrayer
but ... did we be-trade-her?

as her cold attitude thaws
I can observe her hypocritical flaws
I can see she's third over on the Revolutionary scale
psuedo africanus
throwing her fist up only to us
trying to give the air a pound
believing whispers make no sounds
and thoughts are deep and heavy
only because they fall and hit the ground

a voice crawls into my ear
and I turn to see eye-van,
his broken eyes
hoodwinked
but ... I feel a 3rd eye in him
beginning to blink

no matter...
I ignite dark matter sword
my grip
clutching the blaze of its hilt

eye-van borrows my name
he speaks to me, calm and serene

Eye-van:
**my concept was allowed to survive…
just a stall tactic for all this to happen.

didn't you find it odd, kahm?
norah's body language
a difficult read
it didn't translate well with her emotions
-- withered her emotions --
and I could feel you doing your best

TO ENLIGHTEN THE G.O.D.Z.

Act III: Heart and Shadow

to find the spirit of oshun or oya or auset
swirling inside her
but you could draw no better a blank
than the finest painter

as I did with Ohm Lingo
I did with norah.
I threatened her at pen point
to pin point her emotions on paper
predicting her dictation
and scribing every word
as her voice became fainter

I divided this orphan by her thoughts
holding her conscience as a remainder
and now a corporation
of corporal thoughts
have claimed her

do not blame her for this end
where we are all heading
blame me for my sendings
blame me for giving up
on soul – on our people – on black love.**

and there stands eye-van
his eyes remold
by the power
of Ixu's and Gira's hands
and his flesh is renewed
            against his black drop
behind him
is the Compli-City
and instead of anger
I feel pity

my name leaves its letters
on my spine
and for the first time
(toward eye-van)
I am kahm
I show peace

TO ENLIGHTEN THE G.O.D.Z.

Act III: Heart and Shadow

and retract the blade on my arm

Kahm:
"eye-van
slowly,
child,
you become a man."

he drops his face
and speaks his words

Eye-van:
"it's taken 80 years
a long walk in time's sands."

I turn back
to amar and norah
they attack one another
I hear laughter
echoing thru silence
and my real eyes
see the situation

black-on-black violence

blak woman torn from blak man

Eye-van:
"too little too late
for me to pray

my actions
have negated
the sun's rays.
our people will never shine."

and a voice tears thru the air

Nuus:
"you are no more a man than I! *DIE!*"

I rush to eye-van's side

TO ENLIGHTEN THE G.O.D.Z.

Act III: Heart and Shadow

and as nuus throws his whip
I shield eye-van and take the hit
My body jives, but doesn't shuck or buck
I remain up on my feet
my arm lights up with dark matter sword
shimmering a blazing stream

I attack nuus
he parries with his moonbeam
and screams, "haven't you heard, kahm?
I am the extension of the sun
backwards
added with a little bit of you
I am the sun's reflection and hue
I am the per-centage of its light,
mixed with the flow of the water's might
I am the moon
  and have you ever known
  the sun to eclipse the moon?"

Kahm:
"Yes! You brainless knight
with brilliance – abundance of light
raises your lunar intelligence
making you bright – your sacred satellite
the representative of day at night – the moon!"

fierce! our weapons hum in tune

he attacks as winter to make me fall
while I throw the heat of summer and spring
I thrust another attack upon him
dodge
move
and bend
silently at the command
of Grandmama Nature
to move like the wind

I take her advice
like imhotep to zoser
I attack again,

TO ENLIGHTEN THE G.O.D.Z.

Act III: Heart and Shadow

knock nuus back,
wink,
and give sly gesture
for him to come a little closer

Nuus:
"you might've been trained to kill
but I was BORN to kill
training in my mother's womb
I cut myself free of her tomb and culture."

Kahm:
"yet your 'moon' continues to steal the light
from your mother's nature
you still need the warm glow of her sun
to act as your cold-nature's savior."

we exhale fatigue
and inhale bravado
neither of us will allow
our weak state to show

even without clouds
it rains above us
a spirit
still cries in shame

his moonbeam
SLAMS!
against my sword
this, our own private war
where we dance,
throw curses as chants
and play right into nemtusar's hands

we back away from the fight
trying to gain sight and breath
fighting with what little strength we have left

my sighs are a rant

nuus can see me tired

TO ENLIGHTEN THE G.O.D.Z.

Act III: Heart and Shadow

he spots his opportunity and chance
and he backs farther away
instead of leading to an advance
he retracts his moonbeam
and SLAMS! his fist into the earth
knocking the wind out of it
taking our breath in the breeze
I try to hold tightly to reality
but I,
as well as amar
and eye-van,
lose consciousness,
and fall back into the hands of our enemies
as traitorous allies
— *nuus and norah* —
stand over us, claiming a victory

TO ENLIGHTEN THE G.O.D.Z.

Act III: Heart and Shadow

"RA-UNION OF NAME"

I awoke
chained to smoke
my DNA captured in a cell
my arms bound by mist
this gaseous chain
scraping my wrists

amar and eye-van
at either side
I look closer to eye-van
and contemplate
...*new ally*...?

Kahm:
"you're dead as you speak,
eye-van."

Eye-van:
"by whose words?
nemtusar's? or yours?"

Kahm:
"I'll consider you an ally."

Eye-van:
"as you should
nemtusar wants
the trinity of black men
dead.

his destiny
will stay even
while we are at odds."

confusion kisses my thoughts

Kahm:
"explain your speech.
what is this trinity?"

TO ENLIGHTEN THE G.O.D.Z.

Act III: Heart and Shadow

eye-van's words
hung
as if captured by nuus
his mind
the epicenter of fear
as his body trembled
as his tongue held revelation

Eye-van:
"the three elements
speak thru you,
myself,
and another man's hue.

and with the mix of our elements,
you know that you would never be weaponless
added with rain,
sunlight,
and the moon's light--"

and the words
of a traitor
haunt me
like my enemies

--I am the extension
of the sun
backwards
added with a little bit
of you--

nuus
suUn
sun

--I am the sun's reflection and hue
I am the per-centage of its light,
mixed with the flow of the water's might
I am the moon--

and it connects
like the sun

TO ENLIGHTEN THE G.O.D.Z.

Act III: Heart and Shadow

on the horizon
when it sets

water?
per-centage?
suUn!
nuus!
suUn!
water!
per!
sun…?

and his name
water falls
from my lips

Kahm:
"water persun
is nuus…?
then
that means
you…?"

the illusion
that was eye-van
drops from my sight
and view
and all that is left
is an old ally
in his original hue

his voice was silent
but his face
spoke of guilt
his eyes
hung
waxing the floor with tears

I realized thru real-eyes
nuus the moon(beam) as a weapon
while my dark matter blade
blazed the colour of the sun

TO ENLIGHTEN THE G.O.D.Z.

Act III: Heart and Shadow

and when we fought
and our elements clashed as one
thru cloudy thoughts
tears were let loose
and rain was produced

eye-van
this traitorous man
who caused his people pain
was once an ally
who could make it rain

Eye-van:
"kahm, please
say
my
true name."

Kahm:
"how can I…?
you bastard!
you left time
and a goddess tattered
raped
and battered
you killed
and helped shatter
your people's dreams
and everything that mattered.

now you beg me to feed you
your true name?
feeling that my ears
have taken pity
by sipping your whine

you sold your people out
just to hold time!"

Eye-van:
"kahm…"

TO ENLIGHTEN THE G.O.D.Z.

Act III: Heart and Shadow

Kahm:
"you're lucky I am – and chained to mist!"

but I can also see
how his soul has dimmed
and I know *(even without the kheru)*
saying his true name can redeem him

Kahm:
"cid…"

a single breath
condenses
and spells
how cid confesses

time
comes
full
circle

Cid:
"when I acquired time
I became immortal
but snakes and ghosts
injected time into my veins
removed me of my name
and put my mind in chains

my weakness
was time
and to be kind
snakes and ghosts
gave it to me
but they were not
my kind

but it was too late
I had walked from destiny
and entered a different fate
the mask I wore became the face
and myself reversed?

ҬΟ ΕΝLIGHҬΕΝ ҬHΕ G.Ο.Ð.Z.

Act III: Heart and Shadow

that became my faith

persun had been captured, you escaped…
although it was my command for you to run
I had become…jealous

I watched you bloom
Ohm Lingo assisting you
and you began to glow
day by day
inside a cage
as I was made to nurture my rage,
my hate
for you,
myself,
all of our kind and hue

it was I who whispered to nemtusar
to allow you to leave
to throw you away from this cage
so that you would be our lead
as we followed you to Maa-Tru-Ark
and the Ances-Tree

I am truly guilty

ah!
o-gun still in my hands
aimed at my people
and my temple
where I minded my worship
instead of worshipping the knowledge
in my mind
my temple desecrated
by these thoughts
against thot;
these actions
against thot
against the wisdom of my own culture."

I try to stop my heart
and reverse its flow

Act III: Heart and Shadow

so that I could smother soul
and produce hate

this is the 'man'
who left safi-oya to die
and Ohm Lingo raped
who helped burn Maa-Tru-Ark's city gates

but it's all too different

I try to cry tears that will switch reality
make these circumstances
change
this would be different
if not cid and eye-van
were one and the same

now I'm pulled in two directions
by one man with two names and faces

Amar:
"I'll kill him for you
tear him with my shadow claws
and watch him bleed
his hue

this is the man
who took away the pledge
my parents and grandparents made
took them away from the duty they had sworn."

Cid:
**"watch your mouth, kid.
if it wasn't for my actions
you would never had been born."**

Amar:
"never to be born?
I could live with that
becuz thousands of lives
wouldn't have died.
Maa-Tru-Ark and Ances-Tree

ᵀᴼ ENLIGHTEN THE G.Θ.D.Z.

Act III: Heart and Shadow

would be intact!"

I quickly fill the situation with my name

Kahm:
"we can all contemplate
would-be destinies
and fates
but we're here in our reality."

they inhale their emotions
as cid exhales a plan, "**I say I play possum
while amar plays shadow**

**nemtusar is soft-minded
easy to impress**

**my words
may not be kheru
but
they will magically
paint a false reality
for nemtusar to trust me**

**I'll keep kahm in my sight
while amar
as a shadow fights
and steals the orb,
blends into the night — and escapes."**

Kahm:
"where does that leave us?"

Cid:
"well,
you decided to make war with the beast
now it's time to rest in its belly."

Kahm:
"and start kicking like a newborn to be free."

TO ENLIGHTEN THE G.O.D.Z.

Act III: Heart and Shadow

we relax
memorize the plan
from behind our eyes
drench ourselves
in a pool of thoughts
and dive
perfectly
executed
cid feigns his other lie
and becomes eye-van
just
one
more
time

this time
for the sake
of time

TO ENLIGHTEN THE G.O.D.Z.

Act III: Heart and Shadow

"TO ESCAPE FATE"

changing cid
was the smartest thing
nemtusar
ever did

he put the elements
against one another
if heat
smothered the cold
there would be no thunder
and if the sun did not compromise
with the clouds in the sky
there would be no rain
just the same

without the mix of black souls
nothing that touches the earth
would grow
so he figured
he'd create slaves
castrate their hair
and twist their reality
graft their mentality
and the outline of allies
would shadow me
their reversed fates would battle me
cuz these snakes know
their venom could never rattle me

cid informed me
that nemtsar
kept Ohm Lingo raped
extracted her suppressed emotions
and created hate
forming norah
cid added to the mix
eclipsing her mind
from the knowledge that resided inside us

norah

TO ENLIGHTEN THE G.O.D.Z.

Act III: Heart and Shadow

orphaned
and the product of slavery
was a facade trapped inside a facade
inside a facade, inside a facade

it seemed
the trinity of black women
was also in danger
natural safi-oya dead
the spirit of Ohm Lingo raped
and norah
consumed by her own anger

Cid:
"you don't have to worry
about your hue
nemtusar does not want you dead

he just wants to control you
otherwise
he can't survive."

Kahm:
"then let our rebellion be his suicide."

cid closes his eyes
his thoughts
roll back into his head
as he rolls back into a role
from cid – eye-van remolds
and as dull as it may be
his soul begins to glow

I keep inside my name
I have to remember
cid just plays a game
(and all too well)
I wonder…

cid forms words
into a deceptive breath
that tickles the ears

TO ENLIGHTEN THE G.O.D.Z.

Act III: Heart and Shadow

of our captors
he is released
while amar and I
sit in the belly of the beast

minutes transform to hours
as hours swirl in haze
and transform into a daze
that our eyes cannot shake
light enters our room
and we are taken from our cage
amar is lead down a separate hall
surrounded by snakes
while I am led by cid
back to nemtusar's burning stage
a glowing chain
suppresses my power
but not my rage
even though,
I remain as my name

nemtusar tries to stab me with his eyes
my gaze shifts
and hangs with the image of nuus
he is seated to nemtusar's left

(my friend
stolen of soul
name
and flesh
a great sun,
inhaled for a villain's breath)

Kahm:
"a prison full of spades is a full house
let me be the ace speaking my black people
and free them thru the breath out my mouth
let me be their voice when I shout

let me exhale fountains of youth
so my people can breathe the truth
that can't be killed

TO ENLIGHTEN THE G.O.D.Z.

Act III: Heart and Shadow

no matter how many times you shoot
and even if you try to drown me
let me remind you that I'm waterproof
and no type of nuus can hang me
cuz my thoughts are too loose

nemtusar,
you couldn't buy courage
no matter how great your wealth
I know you're too much of a coward
to kill me yourself

unbuckle my Orion's belt
and suck on my phallic constellation
so I can ejaculate comets in your eyes
and black holes of whole blacks into your mind
maybe then your thoughts would be solid
and maybe then you wouldn't slip off the knowledge
living life on the edge of your thoughts
trying to build a web thru my people's culture
just so soul can be caught

I know our hue is priceless
and truly can't be bought
those who sell out
will only have their souls lost

and to you house niggaz
who think I'm on a soapbox
just remember
it's you that have been brainwashed

being free is my cost."

nemtusar breaks out in emotion
boils
over
cid steps closer

Eye-van-Cid:
"you see,
my master

TO ENLIGHTEN THE G.O.D.Z.

Act III: Heart and Shadow

he'll never change
like his hair
he'll remain
a natural disaster."

I believe I've angered the 'god'
his eyes burn and inhale
the tension in the room
silence smothers snake hisses
and the haunting drip of ghosts

Nemtusar:
"you believe yourself a word
ha! a word!
I'll beat you
and leave you in syllables
scattered all over broken language."

kahm:
"your actions
will be like the blood in my body
            all in vain.

I see you can only curse my name
while I am bound and powerless
I dare you to do the same
when I am released of these chains."

nemtusar whispers a chant
that does not have enough breath
to reach my ear
he waves a hand
and the chains fade, disappear
my power rushes back into me
but before I can strike
nemtusar lifts safi-oya's spirit leaf

(my hand sweeps my neck
and I feel that her spirit is no longer by me)

safi-oya
from the flames

TO ENLIGHTEN THE G.O.D.Z.

Act III: Heart and Shadow

and mist
condenses into flesh
resurrected from eternal rest ... ? ...

my khaibit
cannot feel
the difference

is she real ...?
my goddess ...?
my commander ...?

tears burn mist into my eyes
as I gaze on a truth and detect lies
I rush to my goddess' side
waiting to inhale her like a breath

closer to safi-oya
but her image
knocks the power of the stars
into my chest

I drop to my knees
she fires vapors that tears at my flesh
as I am surrounded by an infernal breeze
this illusion keeps me caged inside heat

and nemtusar knows
I cannot fight back
I cannot lash and attack
for this illusion
is made up
too much
in the image of a black woman
that I truly love

and that damn snake,
nemtusar,
stands smug

but although on my knees
I hold my own smile

ꓔO ƎИLIGHꓔƎИ ꓔHƎ G.O.ꓷ.Z.

Act III: Heart and Shadow

as I see behind nemtusar
there stands cid
holding two o-guns – double the wrath

(even when our enemies hold 95
cid's 5% was always the better odds with math)

cid fires
shooting stars that knock against nemtusar
pushing him forward, opening his hands
and spilling free safi-oya's spirit leaf
the flames leave my body
and safi-oya's illusion dissipates
as I roll with soul and catch
the falling
golden
ornament

nemtusar turns and commands, *"finish him!"*

Kahm:
"finish me?
you don't even know
where I begin."

Nuss:
"I care only for your end.
and the end of your life
is where I will begin!"

into the air
nuus jumps to the burning stage
he ignites his moonbeam
and attacks
every swing
filled with years of suppressed rage
I step away
ignite my dark matter blade
attack! parry! and sway!

my secret weapon
I battle nuus using his true name

TO ENLIGHTEN THE G.O.D.Z.

Act III: Heart and Shadow

Kahm:
"water persun! turn your moonbeam inward
attack the demon and snake
that holds you at the center of your consciousness
free yourself from this mental bondage
you only hang by this false name
this nuus is not you."

water persun's voice
surfaces from the deep
crying
like a newborn to be free
but…faint

Nuus:
**they ... have ... made me ... less a soul
and more ... of a man ... of their kind ... and mind.
I am
buried
under
          stand
sandstorms ... are what ... snakes from my eyes
when ... I have wept ...
my spirit ... held down ... by the paw
of her-em-aket.**

Kahm:
"my friend
fight it! curse it!"

Nuus:
I'll fight you!

he flips and kicks
as I dodge and split
defending with my sword
as our weapons hit

cid trapped in a corner
firing the heavens from his o-guns
each star pounding like a drum

TO ENLIGHTEN THE G.O.D.Z.

Act III: Heart and Shadow

in sync with our hearts

norah,
leading snakes and ghosts
marches into the room
I cannot bare to look in her direction
this misguided woman
turned nemtusar's deadliest weapon

I find a single moment
dodge from my fight
and into the sights
of cid's o-guns
covered by the stars
I take cid's side

Kahm:
"together again, huh?"

Cid:
**"let's use the khab
and blend into the wind."**

our bodies become air
dissolve into the syllables of our prayers
and drift into the night

Nemtusar:
"let them go. it's no loss.
I'll show kahm noiz
that I will own all the heavens,
the Ances-Tree and the souls of its leaves
at all cost."

TO ENLIGHTEN THE G.O.D.Z.

Act III: Heart and Shadow

"UNDAGROUND PLAN"

flowing thru the air
we two sons
cast light
allow syllables to dance in prayer
while we form from out of the night
escaped from prison mist
met by amar
who quickly lets his story
fall from his lips

Amar:
"cid's tears dispersed the cloud that kept me bound
my body became the shadow, letting loose my might
I could roar chants that tore thru the mist and fog
cutting rattles and hissing tongues
by way of the shadow's claw and maw
and exorcising the ghosts
by way of chants and breath
given to me by Ixu and Gira.

I prayed for your escape."

Cid:
"you have the seed of Maa-Tru-Ark? the orb?"

taken from a shadow
in all its might and glow
was the orb

the seed of Maa-Tru-Ark

its light hummed in a red, black, and green tune
ready to restore Maa-Tru-Ark's children
waiting in her womb

with this seed's power
the Compli-City would be no more
instead
it would be
filled with descendants of Moors

TO ENLIGHTEN THE G.O.D.Z.

Act III: Heart and Shadow

Kahm:
"let's bury ourselves in the shaded undaground
so that a plan can grow from its fertile soil."

we use the khab,
ascend into the wind
and form again
in the circle
of black shadow warriors

we explain our story
and the need of a wanted plan

Kahm:
"our greatest army
comes from the gangs
inside the Compli-City

we must help them
nurture themselves
worship themselves
for inside them
is where Ixu and Gira dwell

we must free them
from the thought
that they are of nemtusar's
DNA and cell

they must turn their o-guns
on oppressive ghosts and snakes
who create a police state of confusion
an illusion that our people are dogs,
not Goddesses and Gods.

we must show them
they are the new warriors
the new protectors
the resurrectors of Maa-Tru-Ark,
and the Ances-Tree
we must help those souls

Act III: Heart and Shadow

that are caught in between death
to become a spirit leaf."

Amar:
"how many prayers
will it take to accomplish this?"

each of my words
mirrors my name

Kahm:
"19 – 7 kheru, 11 totems,
and the seed of Maa-Tru-Ark.

they will pull the light from the dark
bend time's line
place the end back at the start
for us to come full circle
and start all over.

now
do I speak to cosmic new beings
who have lost the roar of their shades?
or shadows who can't keep down
the spirit of a good souljah?"

voices in sum
become a dark, glowing sun
causing cloudy silence
to dissipate like fog
— shadows begin to chant

THE SHADED TRIBE:
"we will take down those who robbed us!
with shaded cosmic spirit that glows inside us
for we are the hue-man form of Ixu and Gira!"

and they chant
over and over
until all gathered are no longer sober
but rather
intoxicated with these words

TO ENLIGHTEN THE G.O.D.Z.

Act III: Heart and Shadow

that keep our minds satiated
and we speak words into our hands
so that we can hold our faith
put them together
pray
and lift our words into space
let them form into clouds that rain
so that we can give our own words a taste
and we can drench our bodies in words and bathe

and as we celebrate
amar takes me aside

Amar:
"I tremble when I think of norah."

Kahm:
"I know."

Amar:
"she ... cides with nemtusar
she has chosen death
instead of the fight
nemtusar has seduced her might
and placed it against us…

I too hold shame

y'see,
croia,
nemtusar's wife
struck
at the life
of black men
using them for their hues
she sat confused
trying to use us
becuz nemtusar abused her
and neglected her with a word
he never knew
which was 'love',
and…I use to…lay with her

TO ENLIGHTEN THE G.O.D.Z.

Act III: Heart and Shadow

before my mind was cleared again
I was fogged from my destiny
her addictive venom
made me unable to see…properly…
I thought I could teach her
to sing our love songs

I was wrong…
croia had been an agent
all along…

oh! these damn snakes and ghosts!

they have healed the hurt
of the daughter of my people, slightly
saying peace, peace;
when there is no peace.[1]

for when they shall say, peace and safety:
then sudden destruction cometh upon them,
as travail upon a woman with child:
and they shall not escape.
thus saith the lord god:
woe unto the foolish prophets,
that follow their own spirit,
and have seen nothing!
because, even because they have
                              seduced my people,
saying peace; and there was no peace:
and built up a wall, and lo, others daubed it with untempered mortar

because with lies ye have made the heart of the righteous sad,
whom I have not made sad:
and strengthened the hands of the wicked,
that should not return from the wicked way,
by promising him life.[2]

norah is my fight;
a wrongful passage

---

[1] Jeremiah 8:11
[2] Ezekiel 13:3, 10, 22

TO ENLIGHTEN THE G.O.D.Z.

Act III: Heart and Shadow

looking for its right

I feel, as if, in this struggle
I have ignored her
so, let it be me who restores her
let me be the masculine auset
putting back together a feminine ausar."

I nod
we two suns
join the celebration
and dance as stars

TO ENLIGHTEN THE G.O.D.Z.

Act III: Heart and Shadow

"RESTORATION"

our mother covenant
sleeps with a drunken mind
swirling with ignorance

we march in line,
amar, shadows,
cid, and I

old friend and me
we relive memories
of when we stole back
our time

the Compli-City in the distance
we stop
pray over the land
to create a sacred spot
hold the seed of Maa-Tru-Ark
inhale our own prayers
so that sacred air can be caught
and we birth sacred thoughts
a rainbow
of three colours
(red, black, and green)
they sprout from the orb,
descend down on the Compli-City
and restore it to its true form

time begins to flow backwards
as tattered temples
fix and mend
pages and libraries blend back together

burned books form from ashes
and we inhale the essence
of smoked syllables — a real habit
we knowledge addicts
here to push our practice
on the Compli-City's in-habit-ants

ᴛᴏ ᴇɴʟɪɢʜᴛᴇɴ ᴛʜᴇ ɢ.ᴏ.ᴅ.ᴢ.

Act III: Heart and Shadow

our emotions run in the present tense
watching Maa-Tru-Ark's temples erect
from being flaccid, bent
align with the stars in the sky
resonating with the reflection of nature's vibe

our people will pay tithe
by just giving up time
to give knowledge a rhythm
inside their hearts that beat
from being a flatline

the rainbow's three lights
becomes a wave and tide
that turns to burn
those who have lied
and haunted our presence
and put venom
in the syllables of our true names
making these snakes and ghosts
burst into flames

asfet's court-ship crashes
her gavel burned down to ashes
while liyer
receives the scars and lashes
given to our people
that his mentality kept inside
the triangle of the middle passage
and sluh runs
as our people place upon their frames
ancient clothes
zammu and ah-dunah
run from their church
to escape their curse
that has turned against
their tide and deceitful tithe
…they barely escape being crucified…

the seed sinks into the earth
and births the ra-birth of its own mother
and we can feel the rhythm of the heartbeats

TO ENLIGHTEN THE G.Θ.D.Z.

Act III: Heart and Shadow

of resurrected minds
of 16 shades of black sisters and black brothers

we march in and inhale the scene
as if it were the wind

Maa-Tru-Ark glows so bright
the sun shines at night
we Paa-Tru-Ark
to protect with spiritual might

we quickly let our words connect
to make a special effect on the gangs
them that call a truce
aim their o-guns at the one
who wrapped them in a noose
and ruse

tears of joy create rivers
soak the soil and swirl into roots
we can hear the Ances-Tree
slowly resuscitate
with heir to breathe

I know the final battle
will be at the roots
and go from the ground up
as we take the battle to the stars
and are heaven touched

for now
with a shield surrounding the city
we ra-educate the miss-edu-caged
in the resurrected libraries

hours of knowledge
remove our people from the daze
spent walking in hazy years

lies drip away in tears
and we unite to fight

TO ENLIGHTEN THE G.O.D.Z.

Act III: Heart and Shadow

in the morning
the 11 totems
will resurrect
our guardians

TO ENLIGHTEN THE G.O.D.Z.

Act III: Heart and Shadow

"GUARDIAN MODE"

this morning
there will be no more
mourning
and the spirit-leaves
of the Ances-Tree
will glow brightly

in rhythm
we march toward the prison
where mist swirls
and blurs the vision
of our people trapped inside
their thoughts
perverted
with the view of another's eye

standing
withering
is our Ances-Tree
our roots absorb
not the earth
but venom
and mist
its leaves shake
by a haunting breeze
and rattle with a snake's hiss

amar, shadows,
cid, and I,
the gangs of the Compli-City
allied by our side,
we place the 11 totems
in a circle at the base
of the Ances-Tree

we stand in the center
to make the 12th hour
to re-claim time
and all that is ours

TO ENLIGHTEN THE G.O.D.Z.

Act III: Heart and Shadow

we black men and black women
pray
our thoughts
fueling the sun's rays
strengthening this brand new day

together:
**we are here to defend you
with our words and hue

with our knowledge
and the truth of who we are
connected to you at the roots."

the 11 totems glow
seep into the earth that begins to quake
and birth 11 guardians
as the power of the totems
bleed into them
they rise again
and we name

together:
**of ever blak man and blak woman
body of stars run thru me
and the words you give to me

allow my soul to stay
makes death just a phase
for me to resurrect like the sun
each and every new day

all the truth you got
wrath thru you makes the thunder boom
may our spirits emulate you
may we swim in your water and love when our day is done
put order in our breath
we are the tears you've wept and the love you kept
to help our people resurrect

for you as the earth
may we defend with blood and tears shed**

TO ENLIGHTEN THE G.O.D.Z.

Act III: Heart and Shadow

and from the earth
our guardians were born
coming in swarms
like killer bees

ᴛO ENLIGHTEN THE G.O.D.Z.

<u>Act III: Heart and Shadow</u>

"TO BALANCE THE SPIRITS"

four winds
billow
above us
while we watch
below

the Ances-Tree
shakes
exorcising
haunted leaves

from the top
drops qnu-tansey
weak
as his name is miss-spelled
he is de-spelled
his power taken
from those still imprisoned
within NahtShay
ancestors attack him
with the power of the sun

the birth of 10 ungodz
from 10 possessed branches
glide down
to meet the opposite
of their name, spirit, and sound
and when they collide
thunder cries and lightning strikes

nemtusar
sits
perched
atop the Ances-Tree
using his mind
to call his snakes and ghosts
norah
and nuus to choke

souljahz mold

TO ENLIGHTEN THE G.O.D.Z.

Act III: Heart and Shadow

into shadows
and gangs
hold their o-guns
ready to shoot stars
reign-bows glow
firing heir-rows

norah,
in shade of shadow
appears at amar's side

Amar:
"you! sista!"

Norah:
"sista!? I represent you
only in hue!"

they battle
and rhythm becomes laced with venom
as it rattles
off key
as brutha and sista are at each other's throats
one possessed by a ghost

I rush in haste
but a moonbeam
wraps around my waist
and I am kept in place

I turn and see nuus
my dark matter sword ignites
my arm
bright
with its soul and glow
I use every ounce of my spirit
to hold my power steady

Kahm:
"are you ready?
I'm going to cut the snake from you
so that you can remember

TO ENLIGHTEN THE G.O.D.Z.

Act III: Heart and Shadow

the responsibility
of the power
that glows thru your hue."

the moonbeam retracts
and I attack
fierce,
deadly,
quickly,
but as my name
I strike,
only to slay the enemy
that possesses an ally
to remove him of the point of view
that possesses his eye
and stings it with venom

amar and norah
nuus and I
we battle,
flip,
kick,
and split,
circle one another – and switch opponents

I swing at the woman's feet
she jumps into the air elegantly
lands
and connects a fist to me
I roll with the hit,
twist like my locks
and kick
connecting with her stomach
to remove the ghost from it
to stop her heart from pumping it

we pause for effect
to throw out a net
and catch a breath

Kahm:
"sista,

TO ENLIGHTEN THE G.O.D.Z.

Act III: Heart and Shadow

how could you give up?"

Norah:
"I have been fighting so much
and fighting for the both of us.
I was tired,
and so it was easy to give up."

Kahm:
"tired as your excuse."

I twirl away
and roll back
into my fight with nuus
while amar
battles again
norah

Amar:
"sista,
I know you feel abandoned."

Norah:
"being abandoned
does not come with feeling
it's void of such a thing."

they continue their melee
as nuus and I kick,
parry, and sway
he battling with moonbeam
I
with sunray
each
trying to eclipse
the other's
weapon
I shine a series of thrusts upon him
but nuus,
quick
and loose,
dodges my attacks

TO ENLIGHTEN THE G.O.D.Z.

Act III: Heart and Shadow

strikes back
fast
and furious

from above
nemtusar spies
ally against ally
and a plan
forms in his mind

Nemtusar:
**<u>wes,</u>
<u>resurrect death.</u>
<u>and make these cursed children</u>
<u>fight their parents,</u>
<u>ancestors,</u>
<u>and teachers.</u>

<u>well, kahm.</u>
<u>now you will become</u>
<u>a sun</u>
<u>that has sunk</u>
<u>beneath my western horizon.</u>**

wes kneels
guarded with a misty shield
his power touches the spirit-leaves
to awaken the resting ancestors as enemies

cid blasts o-guns
but the stars dissolve
into the misty shield

with spoken kheru
I knock nuus away from me,
thunder erupting from my hands
knocking him to the earth

I, amar, and cid
rush toward the ungod named wes
who is ready to put our people
at odds

TO ENLIGHTEN THE G.O.D.Z.

Act III: Heart and Shadow

with our ancestors
who soundly rest

but norah stands in our path
a dull glow of the past surrounding her
she drips with emotions: hate and anger

and it is poetic justice
that we 3 men are to die
by a premenstrual picaso
going thru her blue period

we 3 black men stand
only to fall victim
of this black woman scorned
for hell hath no fury
like a black woman raped and unborn

Norah:
"when I speak your names,
you will feel them grinding
against my teeth.
as your syllables I eat
and your pride I swallow."

my eyes in two directions
the physical eyes spot norah
the 3rd
thru the khu
split-seconds ahead of time
can see the fate of ancestors
resurrected as enemies
all in mind

we can barely breathe
and I can see
this woman is barren by name
there is norah
no rah --- no sun inside her
past anxiety
to live presently extracting revenge
on the men who failed to protect her

TO ENLIGHTEN THE G.O.D.Z.

Act III: Heart and Shadow

who abandoned and left her
to taste the scales of snakes
attempting to fly
wearing a ghost's feathers

the guilty party rises
the manipulator
croia
shadowing norah
a smile attacking amar

Croia:
"do you remember me,
my black shadow beast?
may our past
always stab your heart

and look at your heart
she now stands to pump
hatred back to you
nothing but the anger
for the men who share her hue."

Amar:
"you beast!"

Coria cackles
her image a shackle
binding amar to the past

Croia:
"go on, norah.
tell these men
what they did.
tell them how--"

Norah:
"-- you black men left me to die.
choosing their cide
feeling justified
that obeying their lies
would give you life ---

TO ENLIGHTEN THE G.O.D.Z.

Act III: Heart and Shadow

what life is their to breathe
with this beast without form
who can take 1000 cultures' form?
what does this monster speak
but fire,
this dragon with ten horns?"

it's too late
our ancestors awake as enemies
our culture cides with snakes and ghosts

and we don't know who to fight first

Cid:
"beautiful,
black woman…!"

Norah:
"oh! now I'm beautiful!
now I'm your goddess.
I! the one *you* fathered
you never
said
so
before
in these past years
I have been referred to
as hooker, bitch, and whore
possibly hoe
to cultivate dirty deeds
on my own earth
my body hurts with the words
you used to cultivate it

and you dare to call me
hooker, bitch, and ho'
becuz I took the brunt
of the master's blow
when he raped me
over
and

TO ENLIGHTEN THE G.O.D.Z.

Act III: Heart and Shadow

over.
my taste touching the lick of his whip,
taking me on a false trip
my mind made to believe
that I was a queen when he raped me ---
thinking this beast was saving me
bathing me
to make me clean
while I only became more dirty ---
left hurting and bleeding

I let this bastard use my royalty as a bribe
as he took me for his bride.
and I married myself to the twisted words
of his pedestalized woman
a sisterhood with her as a burden."

Cid:
"so, abandoned sista
we have both suffered
from taking these snakes' and ghosts' cide
both guilty of this crime against our people."

norah transforms to heated rage
born from a cold stare
knocking cid into the air
and screaming,

Norah:
"since when are victims guilty?
I'm tired of being guilty!"

my eyes float to nemtusar
and they swallow his image
wide with surprise
unable to see anything but his visage
my eyes are fixed on his face
his expression, fear and sadness laced

it doesn't make sense
until I figure out
what fate decides

TO ENLIGHTEN THE G.O.D.Z.

Act III: Heart and Shadow

how the rest of nemtusar's time
will be spent

it seems
nemtusar cannot digest the situation
his pride has been swallowed
and he cannot stomach his own fear
as our people's problems
mixed in blurry visions to become clear
focused

with all our troubles in the open
nemtusar knows
that the next step in thought's evolution
is to present itself with a solution
so he keeps blowing steam
tricks, and confusion toward our people
trying to keep each other at our throats
using his snakes and ghosts to play mediator
so that we will forget him as a dictator
and we will look upon him as a christ figure

but his equation
never calculated
or figured
us
it never added up
to us
as the figures
these determined
16 shades
black bruthaz
black sistaz

however, at the time
unwanted gift of the present situation
norah's glow becomes stronger
holding us back and blocking our path

Kahm:
**amar, jump left.
I'll go right.**

TO ENLIGHTEN THE G.O.D.Z.

Act III: Heart and Shadow

there are no questions
no hesitation
just an execution of plan
as norah's power strikes
I use the kheru
and blend with the wind and light
forming behind wes,
and dissipating the misty shield
as my dark matter blade ignites

I roll with soul
as cid
blasts light from his o-guns
each star
pounding like a drum into wes' back
heavy attack
I twist, thrust, and connect
throwing my blade into this ungod's chest

I back away
as obaluaye
uses his power
to disintegrate
the opposite of him

wes turns to ash and rust
that swirls into the wind
and nemtusar knows
through all his shields of trickery
and lying
he's 9 ungodz away from dying

olorun-ausar gives a command
for obaluaye to lay his hand
upon the Ances-Tree
and form safi-oya's spirit
from out of the breeze

and she lays upon the earth
on the soil where she was birthed
and conceived

TO ENLIGHTEN THE G.O.D.Z.

Act III: Heart and Shadow

scribed by her father's pen
and mother's paper
this word – this beautiful word
brought to life thru a name

safi-oya

it comes in tears
that seeps through my breath

her name

safi-oya

and I am not the only one touched
norah's eyes stand still
as hardened images of time
run away from her
norah watches closely
in her eyes
safi-oya's image
--- a true black woman ---
norah
knees bent
begins to repent
for her sins --- we all bend for our sins

amar strikes at croia
every ounce of his power
tossed with every scrape and claw

I rush to safi-oya
and feel
thru khaibit
that her image is no lie
but there is still no life
her eyes, closed like curtains

the earth rumbles
the battle around me
but I am blind to its danger
I remove her spirit-leaf

TO ENLIGHTEN THE G.O.D.Z.

Act III: Heart and Shadow

and place it gently on her body

... my goddess ...
... my commander ...
her eyes open immediately

we embrace
face-to-face
our tears streaming
and running into one another
twirl and twist, DNA helix
our tears make love
as they nourish the ground below us
we hold each other
until we glow each other

the light of our union,
black man and black woman
strengthens us

Kahm:
"I speak of war no more."

Safi-oya:
"just let us speak our names
until they rearrange
and spell our sons and daughters."

nemtusar jumps to our union
and tears us apart

Safi-oya:
"nem-tu-sar,
do you really think
you can stop my heart
and its connection
to the black man of my art
the other half of creation?"

safi-oya ignites dark matter sword
and is once again an ancestral oluso
battling nemtusar with a fury that has been at rest

TO ENLIGHTEN THE G.O.D.Z.

Act III: Heart and Shadow

for 80 years

I jump to her side
so that she can remain
as my name

cid turns his o-guns to et
and blasts the ungod
with shooting stars

Cid:
"the earth is ours!"

the ungod dances
as each star crashes against his body
osain-geb overpowers et
with the earth's natural magic

cid rolls our way
shoots down a ghost
and 3 snakes
places his o-guns on nemtusar
and is well aimed

nemtusar
(battling safi-oya and I)
dodges each star
aims a glowing palm
toward norah, cid, and amar
he traps them in a net
made of bi-polarized beams of light
he catches safi-oya and I
within the same reversed glow of soul
and we struggle
with this haunting, venomous might

we begin to believe
his strength is too much
which depresses us ---
suppresses us ---
oppresses us ---
caresses us

TO ENLIGHTEN THE G.O.D.Z.

Act III: Heart and Shadow

with thoughts that turn our locks to rust
and fills our heir with dust
cutting the roots of the Ances-Tree
blocking heir to breathe
robbing us of memory
his web spreads —
catches the shadows and gangs of souljahz
choking them of breath

until a moonbeam —
no — a nuus
catches nemtusar
by the neck

the bi-polar power fades
and our souls fill our bodies

nemtusar reaches for the moonbeam

Nuus:
"how does it feel to choke?
how does it feel to inhale nothing but smoke
and false dreams
strangling you like a weed?

that is what you have done to me
and all my black people."

Nemtusar:
"wh-wh-what
ha-ha-have
you done?"

Nuus:
"I have returned to my purpose and name
I am water persun
I glow gold when nature rains."

cid fires his o-guns
while amar and I
fire darkness and shade

TO ENLIGHTEN THE G.O.D.Z.

Act III: Heart and Shadow

the power
of strong-minded black women,
norah and safi-oya
attack with soul and mind

and thus
the power united as us
enters nemtusar
he explodes and crumbles to dust
blown away in the wind
along with his prison

our people run free!

the guardians gather 1000 winds,
lightning, thunder,
dark matter and dark inner-g
all the stars we stand under
and incinerate every ungod,
ghost and snake

clouds form, drip tears of joy
allowing peace to reign

we bathe in the victory
that destiny forged us to claim

TO ENLIGHTEN THE G.O.D.Z.

Act III: Heart and Shadow

"THIS MAN'S EYES"

I am kahm noiz
black zion
my name once destroyed
I allowed love to fill the void
and found my name
inside love's frame
and rejoiced in the picture of peace

the Ances-Tree glows brightly
re-nude, all the spirits united
in the distance
there sighted
was Ohm Lingo
planting peace into the soil
for it to grow
and glow with soul

her smile meets my eyes

Ohm Lingo:
"just inhale life,
and think of me
keep me in your heart
as a memory
your sister in soul."

Ohm Lingo disappeared
to wander and find her daughter norah
to repair her
by finding her lost tears
and soothe the anger she used
as a weapon

amar embraced
the broken black woman
--- norah ---
both repented
minds together
united forever

TO ENLIGHTEN THE G.O.D.Z.

Act III: Heart and Shadow

safi-oya in my arms
and her voice in my ear

Safi-oya:
"it seems
you were not sedated
to undergo star sterilization."

and she rubbed her belly

Kahm:
"inside you glows a son?"

her eyes
and smile
roll with laughter

Safi-oya:
"kahm…noiz.
will you ever find balance
between your names?
still trying to light your life
thru a son?
well, ra-joice
becuz of all the stars
and their signs
I hold inside
gemini.
twins.
daughter and son alike"

Kahm:
"so, this is how we begin?
80 years past
where I thought
we came to an end

I thank destiny,
my parents,
my teachers,
and our guardians.

TO ENLIGHTEN THE G.O.D.Z.

Act III: Heart and Shadow

and greater than them,
Ixu and Gira."

we look to the Ances-Tree
water persun
formed into his spirit-leaf
deserving rest
cid continues to live
on quest to find peace of mind
on the deeds he'd done
to be forgiven by norah and Ohm-Lingo
create a broken family
back together as 1

there among the stars
glow with the spirits
of alik keem
and his queen, moorah
friends
watching us always
from the heavens
sided with ruther, turner
mother papers
and father pens

Kahm:
"we will be with you in the end
let us live a life and resurrect our images
thru sons and daughters."

Safi-oya:
"let us now relax in your name, kahm.
and behold a 24 hour dawn."

24 new Elders
descend
to once again
fill Maa-Tru-Ark
and govern

we journey back
to Maa-Tru-Ark

TO ENLIGHTEN THE G.O.D.Z.

Act III: Heart and Shadow

to unlock our locks
and let them flow naturally
with nature's musical keys

to build a nation
a family
and cultivate peace

we are now true
and free to sing
to ring the ra-bell

free to love
inside our lips
our voices
our kiss
our skin

let us ponder angels
as we find eternal black love
and never lose sight again

THE SUN DIAL TONE

(Featured in Fable Avenue Book I: The Ghost of Gabriel's Horn)

THE SON DIAL TONE

<u>Act 1: Eye & The Family Tone</u>

If Adam existed literally
In the flesh physically
Instead of meta-euphoric
      Allegoric-scientifically
I would be his flesh flickering
      Candle sunlight quivering
      Perfect molecular molded rendering
      Second manifestation
For on the Eve of my birth
I fed on information
And this is how I knew I was a male child

Not through the illusionary flesh fallacy
      Of the phallic waving serpent
      Of condensed masculine energy
      Swinging between me
But by the piece of the apple
      That would forever reside within me
The compiled music – the lump in my throat
So, I ink penned, cried signature-signed and scribed a song
Scribbling rhythm on the inside of my mind

I began to take notes of the harmony vibrating
      Down my umbilical 'chord'
And there it roared – soared up from drowning
In the watery waves of the musical key C
Up and down into my mother's deep, dark Oshun
Where I lay surrounded 9 months, watery moist
There came the thunder of my Father's Voice

His music rolled on paper and lit this new joint
      with the spark of a pen's point
Poetry piled up in ashes
As he smoked shades of himself
Exhaling shadows of a former existence
Spooling and spinning into spinal energy
Standing on the corner of the galaxy
And suddenly, there came the breath that was me
Leaving ether winds as a trail, I wore 12 songs as my tail
To tell a tale made of 26 notes – 13 days and 13 nights
That my mother would take to compose and write – trials and crucibles

THE SUN DIAL TONE

<u>Act 1: Eye & The Family Tone</u>

Time spawned metronome into psi-click [tick] intervals
My shadow casting its light onto me

Then my father's fingers snapped, and his hands clapped
And he sang me to life
There to throw back words working backwards into the past
So that we may move forward
Past the horrors – mirror spinal-dimensional spiral
Reflected through the dark corridors
Filled with the final note melodies of my father's memories
Tickling me in my mother's belly. Mother Harmony.
My parents' story was a melody played on guitar strings
Floating and singing
All the way to their beginning
Of first kiss and serenity
To the conception of me, swirling inside
        Watching these memories
Vibrating past realities from my Father's Voice
        And Mother's Harmony

Etched in glowing hieroglyphs on the inside
        Of my mother's belly
My father left graffiti to speak to me

Father Voice:
"We met in a square
Your mother's admiring stare
Watching the words forming, the poetry I shared
Recite, syntax flip, verbal gymnast
Poetry swirling between Arabic and African language
Add Italian, French, and Greek
Dazzled crowds seek every language shift
        Inciting puns, irony – tongue and cheek
My arrogance praised and encouraged
My poetry flourished
Piqued passion plucking a crowd's 'hurrahs'
I, the Sun, audience my solar system orbiting
        Caught in the warmth – the heat of my stanzas
Your mother a distant moon
My words' gravity pulled her higher to my noon
My words my tendrils of light offering a syllabic boon

THE SON DIAL TONE

Act 1: Eye & The Family Tone

A bold balladry birthing a lyrical atmosphere
Spread and domed
We admire one another long after crowd and applause
          Disappeared. Dispersed into the al-Andalusian night
Initiate, neophyte – neo-poetic Mason
Standing on this Moorish square
I, your Father Voice – she, your Mother Harmony
Calculating Maat-hermetic, mathematic future possibilities
We kissed destiny into existence – love into continuance
Life into remembrance, the present into future reminiscence
Circling love embraced there
We slow danced to intimacy's song
          In an al-Andalusian square.

She told me in passing
She held the secrets to life everlasting
Crafting cures – this immortality nurse
Mother Harmony's poetry scripting medicinal herbs
Her intelligence lured out into the open
Cut purses armed with needles and hexes
Hoping to be blessed with
Her alchemical equation for resurrection

They cursed your Mother Harmony
To believe her beauty was off key
Hiding herself behind a veil
She hid herself from me

I
Unsheathed
Variant pen
Moorish sword
Coupled with
Physical acrobatics
I assailed and blessed
The anti-equation of your Mother Harmony's life
I became death
I felled the ill omen, diabolical men
Seizing your Mother Harmony's equations for creation

THE SON DIAL TONE

<u>Act 1: Eye & The Family Tone</u>

With a kiss
I resurrected your mother's vision
She saw herself – in my eyes – her true beauty
Its reflection
Her cracked perception restored
Our first life – love of black to ancestral core
Praise be! Ixu, me and Gira, she –
Amen! A-Moor!"

Hours fade
Churn time and make years from days
Father Voice and Mother Harmony
Continue a black love story
      In new bodies
Wobbling waves of African dunes
Blazing beige and burnt by the sun
Or turned snow white by the blaze of the moon
Here nature, man, and woman croon
Rising from a musically measured desert
Sings a kingdom's sandy song
      Of sunbaked mud bricks
Mixed with mud-based mortar and plaster
Sculpted smooth designed holy edifices
Towers placed at every corner of the city's wall
Coral stoned tiles bathing building interiors
Africa's Rome
Grand palace constructed from imported limestone
Wondrous worlds, family defined
      Residential homes

Father Harmony:
"I, alone, walked the streets in the morn'
Coupled with thoughts of poems
Your Mother Harmony, I met her while she read an ancient ledger:
      Metu Neter
Mathematics spoken as sacred letters
Musical words conceived out of ancient breaths
She, your Mother Harmony, composed these lessons
Enunciating numerical syllables with the power
      Of the third card in the tarot set
Possessing the look of all four queens

THE SUN DIAL TONE

<u>Act 1: Eye & The Family Tone</u>

In a fifty-two deck
Her voice was as sweet as the scent of flowers
    Though
She issued warning
Trickery trickling off the tongues of scholars
Scriptures infected, spoken inverted
Spiritual retrograde, regressive
Seventy-two holy names turned negative

On these incantations we prayed too long
    Off key songs
Prayers answered by sins turned flesh
    Foul and hateful
Created creatures, conjured ghosts
Smothering dreams and hope
Nations bleeding – bound
The sounds of muffled music jammed into boats
Notes sing melodies of slavery
Booming bondage verse-us freedom
Marching from kingdom to kingdom
    Until it burned into our kingdom.

We fled the violent deluge
And moved east
Behind us
I saw the rockets' red glare
The debris of earth's torn body
Turned foul and filth
    Deviant
To contaminate the air
The discharge of dis-chord
Offbeat pop that rocked the airwaves
Exhaust raged, flared, and fumed
Misguided alchemy consumed the sky
The smoke biting and devouring the golden eye
These gray and misty ghosts twirled and swiveled
Throwing obscene gestures to the sky as smoke signals
Choking the blue so the day could speak no more
Air smothered
The face of the sky suffocated into purple
The sun's warm intent extinguished

THE SON DIAL TONE

Act 1: Eye & The Family Tone

Its tendrils limp
The off-rhythm bombs birthed minstrels
        Strolling streaks of erratic beats
Some of us plead, plead, plead
Marched into slavery
Some bodies melt into the earth
Notes once singing life, decomposed of their melody

Your Mother Harmony leading us to safety
        Or so we believed
Her brother's kingdom a poisoned leaf
        On the family tree.

A kinsman. A scoundrel wears royal robes
With a silk tongue salivating
        Odes to lies
Backward speech seeped
        A secret oath
Family bonds, in his heart
Bankrupt and broke
Family ties now a loop knotted rope
Mother Harmony and I
Took asylum in this madhouse of mirrors
Reflections, reversed heart, bad-blooded interior
The Governor, brother-in-law that was broken
Brother to your Mother Harmony
He opened his kingdom's gates with a perfect perfidy
        A lie hidden in his smile
While we came baring warning,

        "Violence across our African land ensues
        Nights of unrest have turned to mourning
The fetid aroma of war has left sacred land acridly perfumed
But, the dead lay fortunate
        While the living, chained together, by boats have been consumed
Wooden monsters make meals of us
Fed to them by the world's youngest children
        They tempered in tantrums
Are taking us across once charted waters
Our sun, rising since the first millennium, has set
The dark hour of alchemy

THE SON DIAL TONE

Act 1: Eye & The Family Tone

*Will transmute us to be
As slaves in the hidden land to the west."*

Brother-in-law gave us refuge and rest. Kindness. Comfort.
He hummed the song of deceit. Your mother and I
      Could not sense its rhythm or beat
But hidden behind curtain, pallid, profiteer Polonius
Plucking chords, playing him as a puppet
The foreign tongue, Captain Iago
      Speaking to this Othello

African sands freeze when he speaks coldly
Every limb of brother-in-law at his command
      A hold in his grip
Brother-in-law, on unkind command, turns kin into profit
First, molds deception, kissed on the lips of kith
We were seduced with wine and meal. Sanctuary.
This safe haven laden with traps and tricks
The deception revealed after the second day of reception
Citizens gathered, I among them, in exchange
      For the currency of gold and weapons
Brother-in-law a tool,
He preps us for slavery and rule

We the people would not go without fight
And the kingdom becomes a familiar sight
      Worse. Civil strife.
War among one another. Family blood spilled.
I take advantage of the confusion with quick movements
I compose myself a song
      And sing myself into the wind
With nature I blend, wind, and bend
Looking for Mother Harmony to put my notes at peace
I team with three to breach a wall of enemies.
      African with sword, a woman.
      African with spear, a man.
      African with bow and arrow, a woman too.
Band together. Short blades caressed in my grip
      I play a song with the rhythm of my body

I move in a warrior's grace and manner

THE SON DIAL TONE

<u>Act 1: Eye & The Family Tone</u>

Carving a path through adversaries
      Like the heroes in the Legend of the Alchemist's Hammer
Throne room. Mother Harmony bound and sitting
Brother-in-law is left to die by my hands
Slave-capturing captain cowardly leaves his side
He hides away, but this act all a play.
Survivors of this civil fray will be made slaves

There stands an army, African and foreign
I twist my body to dodge the arrows and bullets coming my way
Loop, turn, cut and sway in a single breath
Arrows seem to pass through me, as I twist
      Body shifts into air as I run my blade
      Along the necks of my opposition
The warrior's song plays through me
      Moves me forward
I cover Mother Harmony's eyes from a gruesome sight
I stab her brother's chest with all my might

Mother Harmony explodes in pitch. She cries!
The palace cracks and crumbles from inside
I cut her from her ropes
She continues to scream
Force greater than thunder
      Erupting from her throat
She screams the palace and city into ash
      I hold her
She weeps a rainstorm over my shoulder
Her torrent tears collide and form a tidal wave
Everything is washed away
      Away. Away. Away.
We continue moving east
      Trying to recapture the day
A betrayal and war behind us
Laying in a pile of mud, ash, fire, and haze

In a safe
Quiet place
Mother Harmony sings
      Like a candied dream
Original melodies

THE SON DIAL TONE

<u>Act 1: Eye & The Family Tone</u>

Her supreme mathematics
Team with my supreme alphabet
    And there
Syllables and numbers turn
    A pirouette in the air
Coiled to build the anatomy of the
    Original prayers
Your Mother Harmony made me orgasm birthdays
    So that I would come of age
This lovely, mathematical sage
Her + time x 9 + coincidence = fate
She kissed my chest as I kissed her neck
Love leaks from her breast, her treasured chest
The milk of her honey, consecrated – blessed
I form a circle for our ritual

I compose your mother's beauty on my lips
Kiss her with closed eyes
    So that she may experience
    On the inside of her mind
What she means to me
Always locked in her memory
My words and breath
So that she will never forget
    My love to her, your mother
Forever be, etched on the inside
    Of her belly
If we give birth to a son rise
This feminine imprint I leave
    To study with your developing eyes
And later recognize
To choose the perfect woman to be at your side
    As a lovely bride
And if we give birth to a daughter
This feminine imprint I leave
    To study with your developing eyes
The way of which you carry yourself
Understand all the treasures of the world
    Do not add up to your wealth
I compose in the key of the watery C
    My legacy

THE SON DIAL TONE

Act 1: Eye & The Family Tone

Your mother's harmony adds rhythm
      Mathematics and precision
Split the light of music through our prism
We score ancient symphonies
Commit to memory a language that would
      Forever rest
      In Her and Hymns. Our Story.
All as we. Passed through our seeds.

Love in night glides, and our spirits fly
Day rise.
      And we wait for this new day
      To break back into night
We align with twelve tones residing in the sky
This specific time of day
We chant to signs, harmonics in disguise
And the four elements must obey
      On command
The stars dance
My breath carried by seagulls
Three dots. I hum the dark sound
      Played in the background of Heaven

I breathe for my body to create a perfect seed
Our child. Cipher, circled perfect. 360 degrees.
I breathe in. A beat drops.
Heart. Half the song composed by Mother Harmony
The other by me
Beat. Beat. Heart. Breathe.

Invisible swarm. Electric fusion.
The gods strum life on a newborn's heart's movement
Guitarra moresca
Life amps. Lightning necklace, precious joule. Light watts.
Night watch

Your mother's earth forms the natural elements
      Of precious heavy metals and rock
I sample. Ample. Two lovers, music adorned."

This was music composed – for me to be born

<u>Act II: Singing In Harmony Over The Dis-chord C</u>

Mojuba Kimoyo:
"I am void of physical form
Soul cosmos-black
Inhaled through my father's breath
While my mother prepared in prayer
A place of rest

The might of my rhythm sung
      When my father kissed
      My mother's lips
Lifetimes ago on this spiritual trip
To the present of this reality where we exist
Sang to her when he described her beauty so precious
      Sang my future lessons
      Future sermons
Keeping determined the brave turned slaves
Pulled from the Heavens, temporarily leaving perfection
      That above world
      When I was inhaled
Caught by my father's voice like a whirlwind
I swirled like a mist-I-call a haze
Condensing into physical form in twenty-nine
      And one-half days

I am the Jesus Seed of antiquity
In my father breathes, believes, and prays
I possess the rhythm of a cannon to translate
      What the thunders say
I am the muse-I-call a breeze that makes a people
      Dance and sway
I as breath can breathe as I travel through my father's body
Sit at the right side of his creativity
This is the beginning of my journey
My rhythm. My flow. My name is *Mojuba Kimoyo*.
      My black body shaped as soul
Wearing a white robe
I speak musical odes that break down God's name
      To seventy-eight codes
My father's body a humble abode
Reproduced in his masculine image
Conceived through the love of Gemini

Act II: Singing In Harmony Over The Dis-chord C

Fused as my father and my mother – plus "I"
Wearing their combined image in the flesh
As my soul's physical clothes, my code of dress
Future events
For now
My black glows the color of gold
Floating above green grass while seeking my spiritual task
The wind as my shoes
No need to use my feet to move
I glide on the wind, playing the breeze like an organ
My destination is the River Jordan
Travel halfway – meditate into space
Seated under the sun, I float in time and stay
      My father abstinent for three days
I absorb all darkness to wear every shade
Where all righteousness fades
Peace in God's final hour

Meditating in my father's world
Seeking my mother's womb-a-verse
Meta-terrain. Mother Earth.
My physical form given birth
Do I sit at the right side of my father's creativity?
      Or do I drown in my mother's musical key?
Her Meta-terrain-ion C
It's my father's choice on which gives birth to me
Eternity already knows of which way
      My fate sways

I continue my journey
Three days of adrenaline rush
Traveling up the River Jordan
      To receive God's touch
I sing in the key of inner-G
Condensed by my own gravity
I am the nexus
Ordained as my father's sun in the solar plexus
Under the heart's beating drum
I don't beat freedom. I caress freedom from the drum.
Musically eating this feast of bread in Bethla-hummmm

<u>Act II: Singing In Harmony Over The Dis-chord C</u>

I travel up the tree of life
I receive judgment's light
Where Jacob matched the angel's might
Penuel. Where all is penned.
       O-penned at the Face of God
Mounted on skulls
I cross two thieves ready to judge me
On humble knee I bend
And I sing graciously, in my voice, and the proper key

"I am
In no sense
Aware of guilty actions
      You call sins
Because my childhood has yet to begin

My mother, the virgin
She still bleeds the backwash
      Of future life
I as her son will give her light
Menstrual tunes from the womb
My father, he has yet to stop her waters
      And make her flower bloom."

And here am "I"
The Jesus Seed
Ready to see in which direction
      I breathe
Judgment received
Do I sit on the right of my father's creativity?
Or mature through birth in my mother's soil
      And earth
Watery rhythms of her Meta-terrain-ion C

The thieves give judgment
I am judged
1000 petals unable to open up
My lotus flower closed and shut
Time locked vault
My knowledge held at fault
My spirit churning into a body of salt

<u>Act II: Singing In Harmony Over The Dis-chord C</u>

Blazing like a comet – all the fire of heart and hearth
Tunneled from my father's body into my mother
To be as life, on Earth, as it was not yet to be
In Heaven
        And so…
From my father's body
I was gala-x-haled
A comet of thunder
With lightning for my tail
The winds of ritual and prayer
        Guiding my sails
Led into a trail of mother's womb-a-verse
To sing spiritually inside her seed
Until I am born physically
As rhythmically I sing in the Anu-Na-Key
I am the Anakim here to descend through black hole
Message on black radio – into black womb
Played on space's black winds
My body, now a comet is the essence of Seraphim
Here to negotiate in space with the Elohim
Creator of the sun's race
Their bodies split into stars to constellate

I watch as foreign seeds conspire and contemplate
        The burgle of my mother's egg
It blazes bright in the center of her space
The warmth of my birthplace
Disturbed by a paler race

How could my father have let these foreign seeds penetrate?

No matter
This Jesus Seed must protect destiny and fate
I define my namesake
I am Mojuba Kimoyo
I flow with stealth
Discover language in star formations
Speak to the constellations, pleading for help
I am imbued with the power of Taurus
        And the passion of Aries fills my heart
I, comet, a spiritual dart

THE SUN DIAL TONE

Act II: Singing In Harmony Over The Dis-chord C

I blaze quickly as paler seeds fire Cancer toward me
I weave through space's field using dark harmonics
      And large lodestones as my shield
Sagittarius fires air-rows from rain-bows, dissolving foreign seeds
Virgo sings righteousness into space
Leaving my mother's womb-a-verse to heal

Paler seeds come close
But I hold the proper keys
      To break my mother egg's seal
So, I may rest, expand into a physical form
      From a single breath
Deep in this egg's core
As a comet, I soar
Lead paler seeds to be ensnared
      By Leo's roar
Paler seeds continue to attack in hordes

But I got it
Keep my rhythm on topic
Duck, dive and weave
Straight through space
To make these paler seeds understand
And truly believe
When it comes to me, they can't stop it
I'm sailing with the physics and tidbits
      Of Afro-nautics

My rhythm truly natural
All original
Black magical
Giving my speed a boost
Soaring through my mother's space
Paler seeds giving chase
Their rhythm a limping bootleg
Taurus imbued
Rhythm of my hue
I sing to penetrate my mother's egg

The reverberation
      Of comet-sun

THE SON DIAL TONE

Act 11: Singing In Harmony Over The Dis-chord C

     Penetration
Creates a dazzling light show
Bass flow, guitar rave
Sound and shock waves
Burning throughout the womb-a-verse and space
Paler seeds crumble to dust
And by the waters of Aquarius, they are washed away
     On the surface…
Waves of aqueous reverberations
     Rise and dip below us

Father Harmony:
"Boats dance saturate rhythms
While Yemaya sings somber
     Our chorus
Swelling cadence, crying chained
Caustic acoustics
Foul odors wail like banshees
My eyes become blind
Caused by effect
Harmony becoming off key
     I drown in C
Diving to search for me
Splitting my trinity
Self, sitting lonely on shelf
Purchasing me alone – I buy myself
We are currently currency

Buried under me is me, buried atop I
Black sea of bodies cry sweat
Wept, wicked carried away – captivity
Divided, but chained in unity
I swallow the collective, humming moans
     And breathe out mutiny
My voice rolls through the mass of packed
     Flesh sea of black

Captured hymns and hers, off rhythm words
     We curse instead of sing
My voice caresses the bruised cheek of she,
Mother Harmony

<u>Act 11: Singing In Harmony Over The Dis-chord C</u>

She sings, and our breaths connect
      To life past death
The effect, black turns rainbow
      And King Alpha's song resurrects
A cosmic kiss falls from the Heavens
      Down to our world
Twist, twirls, and swirls into the East winds
      Settling gently on the green of our heart
Beat. We hum a collective cosmic stream
The dead speak hauntingly as they cast ghost spells
      Rumored spirituals
We sing in the key of the deceased, gospel songs
Quietus psalms
Humming resonates, and a light the color of dawn
Burns in our palms
We clap sunshine and cry sunbeams free
      To drain the color in our eyes

Clap and cry until the sun rises back into the sky
And the stars' little cousins drink our tears
      To become fireflies
The vessels shift and lift, floating over the sea
We sing, we sing, we sing!
But slavers bring winter when they enter below
Our warm glow cannot be cooled by the cold
But somehow, they know
      All the breaths flow from me
I am the epicenter from where the music breathes
And so, these slavers scream!
They cut, whip, and grab me
I cry one last note to put Mother Harmony at peace
      No protest. She drifts to sleep.
Color fades to darkness. The nightmare resumes.
Slavery over the watery horizon
Looms…

      Father's last verse
Fettered. Plucked like feather.
I, Father Voice, am made to fly
Shoved until above

THE SON DIAL TONE

Act 11: Singing In Harmony Over The Dis-chord C

Beaten until I feel nothing
Thrown overboard to sing
      In the sea as I sink
Wine and wafer for sharks
Poseidon's communion
I am now the voice of the sea untamed
One day, I will be a hurricane
My scream moves the waves
Settling in the belly of Mother Harmony
Whispering my voice
As my son's heartbeat

His new life sang in bloom
Inside my wife's womb:

Mojuba Kimoyo:
"I was born twice in one life
The first started with a recital of tears
When my eyes were hit with light
Signal, push, pulled from the cosmic womb
Into a new space – my mother's trembling embrace
Dirge of fright playing on her face
An apology in her eyes
Mother Harmony, not off-key
But beauty withered into sadness

I knew her eyes
Because
I saw the world through my mother's eyes
9 months blossoming inside – wide and watching
Heaven breathing a gentle breeze
A tickle of air greeting long feathered,
      Fan-shaped leaves
Where earth, coastal sand touches Iemanja's sea
Babalu Aye sickened her hydrous belly
The sea rolled sickly and the horizon regurgitated vessels
Stockpiled with human cattle
I, my mother's fruit, watered with this imagery
And eyes see
As eyes wide cry
Try to blur

Act 11: Singing In Harmony Over The Dis-chord C

So, eyes become blind
But I see faces of me chained
      And walking limp like nzumbi
Stench of death and waste, walking rot
A pale man commands, "Let the pregnant women watch."
As the system – the machine – is oiled with captured ichor
Pale men and women flush, drunk as if off liquor
I saw this through my mother's eyes
Trees were garnished with new leaves,
Bloodied, hanging bodies
Pregnant women beaten until birth came through stress
The strongest of men castrated and made genderless

Children shot, bodies boiled in large, ominous pots
Rivers of blood slither like snakes
Punctured corpses and severed heads adorn stakes
When my mother breathed in the scene, I could taste
Sated for gestation, this indoctrination
A meal that lasts for the rest of my days
How to make a slave
Obedient
Spirit broken, bent
Survival depends on obedience
And obedience is suicide

But my mother hummed witchcraft
Caressing me deep, a musical bath of protection
The only thing these tragedies did for me
      Was make me anticipate antipathy

My skin hardened
The light I was born into darkened
And there came my second birth,
Pulled away from my mother's embrace
Mother Harmony became a universal song
And pale men shared her chorus
But their voices could not reach her incorporeal notes
I heard her singing to me
As if she was there on that boat
That journey
Taking me as sold property

THE SON DIAL TONE

Act 11: Singing In Harmony Over The Dis-chord C

These young hands
would be made to work
another

far

away

land

THE SON DIAL TONE

Act III: Sing. Song. Son.
Ring. Roar. Rah-Bell-Lion.

N-Word
Inward
To ourselves bound
New word in New World – put us in Order
Brewed war
Yester-millenniums ago
Time remembers history
Speak it not to heed it
But to repeat it – the war of one word – for one word
N-Word Wars – inward wars
Battle with ourselves
Neggur, my king – Neggura, my queen
God and Goddess – Ixu and Gira
Repeat through breath the decayed distress of history
Words as effective as chains – the static beat of repetitious beatings
R to blame

Rastus, tar baby, pickanniny, nigger (what?)
Rastus, burrhead, coon, shine, monkey, (oh…)
Sho' nuff nig-berry

I don't have a name – I have titles
Work boy, slave
Fingers rave, work land by hand
Slaves in droves as drones
Singing with moans, earth tones
Open field picked by day – till until noontime, then a house slave
And I see slave women sewing new seeds to reap
A new tradition of nursing the master's children
Mother Harmony's song a distant dissonance
Dismissed
Her song now tends to the master's wish
The commands from his wife's lips
Men work, whipped for sport
And for good measure, women whipped for pleasure
From 9 to die, sun up to life down

Loop, loop life, cycle, pattern
Continue 'round like the rings of Saturn
Retrograde action
A little black boy now

THE SON DIAL TONE
Act III: Sing. Song. Son.
Ring. Roar. Rah-Bell-Lion.

12 years a spirit Earth bound, bet placed if I become a man
An endangered species I am
They skin pieces of me to see how the sun
Kisses tenderly my skin
So to them I must be little boy
Beaten black and blue
My hue not considered being
My black mixed with red, bleeding
Whips lick my back. One. Two. Three.
All to keep as a memory
A reminder, emasculating menstruation, once a month
But at least I get to bleed – Our slave minds admire palien artistry
They draw our black blood to breathe

I see a black man upset. He's put to death.
Hanging after whips and lashes
Castration, more lacerations
When his stench is a well-planted memory, his body
        Is removed from the tree

A woman goes missing, returns bleeding
Blood streams, ripped seams down her legs
She begs the gods in the sky to let her die
But 9 months pass her by,
She is taken from life, and her song fades
When she gives birth to a lighter shade

And even when black conceives black
There is love and mercy. It happens
Like virgins fed to volcanoes and dragons
The innocent are heaven sent
Instead of sacrificing them to live life
Under the actions of whore-able monsters
Up, freed from being earth bound
Smothered or drowned
Love's complexity

I see and live this reality
And I wonder if my Mother Harmony truly loved me
And in that thought I think
All the days I sing dirges

THE SUN DIAL TONE
Act III: Sing. Song. Son.
Ring. Roar. Rah-Bell-Lion.

Mother Harmony and Father Voice
Conceived and birthed me for a purpose
I was put here for a reason, to change the scenery
And call out a new season

I think and gaze at the sky
Once a day as 2 years flutter and fly
On a noontime
There flickers a figure in my eye
I spy a little girl behind the slave shack
She black and bright
Hair wild,
Like lightning tussling in a tornado with night
Smile beaming back to the sun,
Her cocoa-colored eyes
Wide enough to swallow the sky
She talks up to the air as I approach and stare
Wonder tickles me
I am close
She still talks up to the air
I am there but she does not see me
The slave master and his overseer freeze me
Late, not in my place for house duty
My fate an example
Dragged and trucked to a newly bought stock
         Of young bucks – slaves my age
Whipped and beaten in front of them
And among them, a friend

Him called Li'l Chew
Spunk that sparks life
A smile that brightens the night
A dance to his struts and step
The last of life that is left

He tells me after house duty,
"I take these beats the master gives me
Turn them into music that will free me from slavery
I am the artist always known as an African Prince
So, let's go crazy
Morning is my glory

THE SON DIAL TONE
Act III: Sing. Song. Son.
Ring. Roar. Rah-Bell-Lion.

I have the power of Anansi's stories
I'm the cosmic spider, man
We be that Eshu trickster clan
I see that gleam in your eye, your purpose for this life."

I remark, "This world is off balance,
Unmoving. Iku's night freezes
And creates plight. Ojo's concentrated light
Keeps half this world burning
Shackled by shine and shadow,
How do we get the world turning?"

Li'l Chew replies, "Don't let this phase
    As slaves faze us.
We'll get both the night and the day's light
To chase us. Run. Run. Run. Step up.
Let our enemies try and catch up
We trickster gods, let our plots evolve
Our circular momentum will once again
    Get the world to revolve
We no slaves, we are salve
Salvaged parts of Osirus' whole
Wearing Isis' love as a cloak
Set hides the sun for us to plot
Keep secrets in song, tucked in blue skies
    And under rock
Anubis' sickles help us till the land
Let this slave master villain challenge me
    Cultivate me
Until I am unmade his slave
    And become Anu hue man."

"I saw a maiden," I tell him.
"A little girl – a ghost speaking to heaven.
Bright and black. Her glimmering shadow
    Haunts behind our slave shack.
I believe she asks Heaven if she can come in.
Her spirit trapped
Chained to what she knows."

Li'l Chew says to me, "Wish her well this night

THE SON DIAL TONE

Act III: Sing. Song. Son.
Ring. Roar. Rah-Bell-Lion.

And talk to her tomorrow."

I remember Father Voice's graffiti
Etched inside Mother Harmony's belly
I close my eyes and see that script in me
Gypsy, glyph poetry
I close my eyes to sleep
And I see the script in my dream
I read a story etched inside me
And I learn a trick
Watching Tehuti pluck a little time from the day
As the story went, he split seconds
Hid them in a circle
Elongating rotation through the heavens
Then he pocketed time
And he had a day to himself, and let the gods be born here
Every leap year
I awoke and stole time, picked with my fingertips
And I saw the ghostly girl wandering, talking to the air
Head looking up, eyes in a stare
She only in my eyes
And when I captured enough time
I crept behind the slave shack to ask,
"Have you died? Go, go. Go to Heaven. I bless you."
Little black girl, with wild hair like black lightning
Turned to me and giggled as little girls do
"I have not died. I am in between time.
Blessed and protected by Mamma Iyansan
No villain can touch me, no slaver can slave me
Don't you
Have an angel too?"

She sees the scars through my shirt
Snakes tunneling through earth
Keloid tracks
Like lightning on my back
And she can see the words choked and trapped
In my throat
Little black girl knows my answer is, "No."

But she wiped away sadness

THE SON DIAL TONE
Act III: Sing. Song. Son.
Ring. Roar. Rah-Bell-Lion.

Painted a smile on her face and bragged,
"My people can fly. Mamma and Papa flew away.
Brother and sister went with them too.
Up into the blue, they kissed the sun
And hugged the moon
My heart was heavy, chambers echoing
A melancholy melody
Nothing happy to make me lighter than gravity
My baby eyes had seen too much

Smothering my imagination,
I just see the tragedy surrounding me."

Little black girl grows up faster than most
She boasts maturity mixed with naivety
She can't fly, but she floats
Giggling happily

"Mamma Iyansan protected me
When the slave master wanted me
Beat me
Head under water
Beaten for being my father's daughter
Beat with a collective jealously come from generations before
Angry years in this slave master's might
Beaten for being the last of my family's light
They escaped, magically flown away
And here I was, a dove plucked of its feathers
A symbol of peace come to pieces
The slave master on top of me, ready to take me
Then Mamma Iyansan kissed me invisible
Kissed me from existence
But I saw many killed for my sudden disappearance.
Now, here I am. 3 years past ten. Whole again.
Mamma Iyansan told me about you. Mojuba.
I know your name. You will help me reclaim my family
Reconstruct my invisible wings, and
Fly to an invisible island and reunite with them."

My time runs out. I walk to the master's house.
Work. My hands. Work house and land

THE SON DIAL TONE
Act III: Sing. Song. Son.
Ring. Roar. Rah-Bell-Lion.

To take up time and create space
Chase minutes and pocket them
And stow away to be face-to-face
     With the little black girl
But I just wait.
Night, watching the moon

I talk to Li'l Chew
And he knows myths and legends
That extend to the world's end
He's heard of invisible islands

"I've heard of a haunted ship
Created from the heaven's firmament,
Silver, and haze
Captained by a fierce African maiden
Conjured by a runaway slave – a gravedigger
With his shovel the ground bubbles
And he raises the dead, stirred like lilac brew
Presenting to the African maiden captain
Slain, resurrected African slaves for a crew.
Rebellious! They fled to an invisible island.
The slave and the maiden married, and carried
     Themselves back to the cosmos."

I don't know if it's true
But next afternoon
Time in my pocket and hand
I speak again to little girl black behind the shack
She makes me smile,
Her voice is the gold to her black
She doesn't talk, she sings. Harmony.
Inspiration for me to become the Voice in this story

She sings her name. Mwana. She gives me a kiss,
Transfers protection through this bliss
I see Mamma Iyansan floating
Her image eclipsed by a voice
"Aren't you so precious."
I turn, fluid like water and stare
Tall, wild red hair

THE SON DIAL TONE
Act III: Sing. Song. Son.
Ring. Roar. Rah-Bell-Lion.

The master's daughter

No need for water, this shark lives on land
She beams seductive,
Interested smile aimed at the slave-hands
Intrigued black men found dead in the field
When their thoughts bleed her
And she entertains their flesh and thoughts
Her smile stands over me
Red, gleaming glow glittering from her lips
Flat stone pendant speckled with red markings
Dangling from a necklace, twirled through her fingertips

But she was not speaking to me
She grabbed Mwana with smile and hand
"And where have you been?"

Gods and Goddesses forgive me as I question
The effectiveness of Mamma Iyansan's protection
But chin up, I become brave
As Mwana is back in the hands of her enslavers
Little black girl, once again a slave

Time moves by daze. I dig graves.
I talk to the dead — skitter and scat
My chit chat with them
My breath carried by seagulls
3 dots, hip-hop jive from the heart
4,4 my 6,8
I'm conversing with those
Referred to as 'the late'

"How have you been, my brothers
You now emancipated slaves?
Your afterlife is better than this life.
Tell Mamma Iyansan that I wish to see her soon
Send my prayers up into the air and whisper, 'hello'
If Mwana too is there — she disappeared so long ago
I can recall her melodic screams' echo
Dragged to the master like a convict to the gallows
He made her scream. And then he screamed curses

THE SON DIAL TONE
Act III: Sing. Song. Son.
Ring. Roar. Rah-Bell-Lion.

Again, she disappeared before her violent sentence
Four black slave girls of the same age took her place
Relentless punishment upon them
You remember, don't you? Those four,
Four of many that went to the afterlife before you.
Give my prayers to them too."

Six feet deep. I tuck my brothers into an eternal sleep
Just so their souls can seep
And creep through the ground to soar heaven bound
The day bleeds black into routine
I believe, we've died to the dead

There are no days of the week
Weak and dazed, us as slaves
"Live loop, loop life, cycle, pattern"
Guessing and hoping games
On who will be freed from life today
I've lived this life since the first day
18 years have all been the same
But on the first day of 19,
I come clean as it rains
Standing outside the slave shack
Drizzles drip and outline an invisible, feminine frame
Giggling happily
Invisible eyes stare at me

Mwana, a year younger than I, but
Matured, aged womanly grace
With an ethereal, flirtatious grin on her translucent face
Mwana returned to me, unseen and ghostly
She looked both ways
Mamma Iyansan's rain washed the presence
Of the slave master and his associates away
And so, she steps from out of the mystery
Physical black, arms around me

She whispers,
"My shadow swallowed me and my scream followed me
Peeling my flesh from physical reality
Before the slave master bit into me, took my body

THE SON DIAL TONE
Act III: Sing. Song. Son.
Ring. Roar. Rah-Bell-Lion.

I drowned in waves of invisibility
And fed on the music of my own inner-G
The goddess within

Mojuba, I am alive, and I have music to teach you
Unheard harmonics that will release you when spoken
Open the four chambers of the heart to climb the throat
Focus the vision of the blurred eye that lies
          On the inside of your mind
And let bloom the flower wide atop your crown
I can teach you sounds that can pull thunder from the clouds
          And bury it into the ground
To make the earth rumble and bubble
Mamma Iyansan gave me these lessons
When I was cloaked invisible."

Her lips kiss my cheek

She exhales relief,
I no longer hold my breath either
Mwana has returned to me
I too can now breathe
I lead her into the slave shack
All the way into the back, into a corner
Eyes and whispers loud
Shining on us, flickering stares resonating
Wonder
Mwana, the whisper and shade – the missing girl
The subtle harmony, volume raised in our presence
Music underneath her footsteps
Everyone is silent
The sun's clouded song dims below the horizon
And the rain continues to play into the night
Mwana hides invisible, covered in shadow
House slaves give daily bread to us
Overseer, Curly, watching

Gone. Away. Safe. Mwana appears
Like lightning out of the blue
She asks all to gather,
I, with Li'l Chew peep outside through the doors

THE SON DIAL TONE
Act III: Sing. Song. Son.
Ring. Roar. Rah-Bell-Lion.

Save the clouds in the sky, and their rain, all is clear

Mwana's voice is like a hum
Sweet, singing
"Listen close
I bring mystical, musical notes
Spells as ballads
Tapped from the heart
Magic spoken when lips part
When you sing harmonies as spirit
Prayers in lyrics
There, manifested, rah's hymn. Rhythm.
Words made physical
Manifested to create a vision
I call forth Mamma Iyansan
To put an end to these days
Heart of truth extended like the sun's rays."

Mwana pounds her chest,
The men beat with her
We surround her as warriors
Soldiers
We give words anu tone and breath
The seventh sun of the 7th cycle
Sets
Anu day rises
Heartbeats resurrect
The women's voices harmonize
Coil and spiral, rising into the sky
In the electrical palms of our hands
Swirling with the wind and condensing into thoughts
The men hold red, the women hold blue
We come together,
I hold Mwana – her blue mixed with my red
Hand in hand
We perform a purple rain dance

Mamma Iyansan condenses in the center
Of our festivity
Plucked from our mythology
She vibrates beauty

THE SON DIAL TONE
Act III: Sing. Song. Son.
Ring. Roar. Rah-Bell-Lion.

Resonates harmony
And she speaks to us,

Mamma Iyansan:
"I blew out the 3 sources of light
Contemplated that my physical form would be
Partly day and partly night
I gave birth to my own life
And brought back the day with an idea 1000 times bright
Equaling 3, putting back the trilogy
1-by-1: the stars, moon, and sun
I sung the sunrise chorus in an off-key sunbeam
When my voice was Horus

And I pulled from space's womb the new moon
And I threw the stars in your eyes to keep my thoughts hidden from you
And always in d'skies
Forcing the conscious and curious to study astrology
To know more about me – but it ain't that easy

Forgive me when I don't appear when you call me
I don't come at a moment's notice
I come when I notice moments drawn as time's line
And line times 'I' without the proper prayer and song
Can equal a divide
So, I make time flow with a musical sequence of thoughts 'I' cry

Dripping time in a matter of seconds
Where in seconds matter explodes
And reality and time erode away
I can drown you in a lake called life-stream
And it seems like so that as life flows
It grows into memories – harmonic, musical keys
'I' swimming in 'C' playing Sirius in 'E'

Naturally, my thoughts have been nurtured by nature
I tell you to keep your windows open
Even on cold, winter nights
So that you can get a rough…draft
Of thoughts to compose on paper later
Drop verses because the burden

THE SON DIAL TONE
Act III: Sing. Song. Son.
Ring. Roar. Rah-Bell-Lion.

Of your negative thoughts
Are too heavy to hold
So, mold them on paper."

I'm brave to speak to Mamma Iyansan,
"I apologize. Forgive my outburst and cry
But we draw blank stares from blank paper."

But Mamma Iyansan has an answer,
"Then declare yourselves abstract painters
Divide the time between 'me,' 'myself,' and 'I'
And give no thoughts about the remainder
Sooner has left with later
And all that is left is now
Humble yourselves. Bow at the bass of musical bars
Swirl in the 'C' of electric stars and fill space with silence
This slavery is not your life
All of you are who I am
We are an hour past 11 p.m.
I know because I timed it
And the Orisha, Lwa, and Neteru signed it

It's true! You are both Heru and Eshu
Please to meet you – I am Iyansan, Mother of 9 Rhymes
Rah's hymn, sun- and shadow-shaded children."

So, night after night
We danced as our magic produced
A spiritual light
Mamma Iyansan gracing our presence
With anu lesson
A supreme musical alphabet
We learn to sing this language,
Uplift with voices winged and feathered
If English could speak or write, it would compose 26 letters

A is the All. B is the key of Being. C is where music floats and swims
D is the key of Divinity. E is our key of Equality
And we sing and we sing. F is our Flow, how we move and go.
The key of inner-G, our god inside. We sing in Harmony, H our key
Key, I, the self. We sing as we say, 'No Justice, no peace," in the key of J

THE SON DIAL TONE

Act III: Sing. Song. Son.
Ring. Roar. Rah-Bell-Lion.

The constant state of prayer, Kinetic, K musical key, inner god, inner-genetic
L, l-evates to the key of M, magnetic of which we N-joy
O sung to Open—ciphered filled with bliss
A seed from a single flower resonates the key P, our Power
Hitting every note, holding until timing is perfect, signaled all on Q
Our nation, Rhythm, Rah's hymn, sun drenched—key R, a blazing star
The key S-ence, the royal, mother's Truth—key of T—anointed oil
For the next key to reflect U, become you
Sing to make all things Visible, V for Victory—reclaim our true history
Increase you, sing you twice and W, and fold you
Until the unknown X blooms, and the great mystery is revealed
As we ask in the key of Y—how can we zigzag-Z through All this?

And with these new notes we sing
Harmonized with the faint, lingering screams
Of the dying
With these anointed, mystical musical notes
The slave master cannot hurt us
We sing with purpose
Communicate in the field by way of a supernatural chorus

We knead these blessed keys
Massaged with throat and tongue
Capture the warmth of the sun
When the day is too cold
Mend the bones of those too old
Slow digestion when our belly's ache
And food is scarce or light
We sing to use the moon's beams to keep us warm
Through the night

These are nu days—no daze
We sing chance, make moments dance
Song notes become circumstance
We swim in the musical note C
And see time at a glance

We slaves no longer need to walk
In that old way
One knee bent, pimp limp
Slow stroll,

THE SON DIAL TONE
Act III: Sing. Song. Son.
Ring. Roar. Rah-Bell-Lion.

While the arms swing and sway
We've been released
From carrying the burden of yesterday
Even if the scars still remain
Handed down like family heirlooms
As the past's air looms over us
When we dream it tries to choke us
Hang us by our roots from our ancient
Family tree
But the space in the sky is for rent
And so many stars are selling out
We all know this man builds on land to take up space

Curious eyes peep our celebrations
Red hair sneaks a look,
We dance as the light of stars swirl around us
We are living constellations
Many among us believe our music
Can soothe the master's savage lacerations
Herkus Bar is one of them
Scared, but intelligent—fate has him wait
For his moment
That sadly comes through tragedy

Over the weeks
Sister Ure and her Brother Nat
They store lightning
And thunder
In their bodies, readied for attack
On a clear day destined for a bloodstain
A field woman was out of place
A whip crack cuts into her back
And tensions snap
Brother Nat and Sister Ure act
Lightning uncoiled and cracked
Thunder rumbled
But first, Brother Nat simply cursed
No enchantment spoken through syllables and breath
Just a simple word – frustration expressed
      In a statement
Overseer Burneside, had words of his own

THE SON DIAL TONE
Act III: Sing. Song. Son.
Ring. Roar. Rah-Bell-Lion.

Descriptive slurs, and a whip at his command
Surprised when cracked, that Brother Nat
Took no lash, but grabbed the leathery cord
With his hand, unscathed – no wound, cut, or brand

Sister Ure releases her words
She sings her verse to wield
The force of thunder as a shield
Brother Nat's movements
Fluid like water and lightning
Pulling overseer Burneside close
And striking,
Quick, deadly
A martial medley
Two men creep forward, pistols at the ready
I come from the shack,
Hear two gunshots aimed for Brother Nat
His retaliation striking
His movements like lightning
Sister Ure, the thunder – her power
Overseer Burneside's two men
   Become a memory
A tone resonates at the center of me
Ringing – a whisper, *"Ring the re-bell."*
And I want to dive into the pool of violence
Mamma Iyansan, naked of flesh and form
   Tells me to be silent
Let the voice just whisper
"There is no need to let the whisper scream."
I stay my hand
Herkus Bar watches next to me
He shakes anxiously – his expression uneasy
Desperate for peace
A possible reality that dies quickly
The slave master joins the fight
And he's quickly struck down by Sister Ure's might
Dead – hope in our eyes as the slave master dies

Summer becomes colder than ice

Wide, curious eyes peep

THE SON DIAL TONE
Act III: Sing. Song. Son.
Ring. Roar. Rah-Bell-Lion.

Red hair sneaks a look
Moves closer – confident glow on her lips
Flat stone pendant speckled with red markings
Dangling from a necklace, twirled through her fingertips
The slave master's daughter
Brother Nat and Sister Ure move to attack her
Her charm abrogates their power
Wounded, Overseer Burneside
Troubles our rising water and tide

Rebellion's song
Proud and strong
Improvised
With hopes to echo
Eternally
Becomes a threnody

We bear witness
As Brother Nat and Sister Ure
Are subdued
And under control
Tied and beaten
Bloodied
Awakening memories
Stirred in all of us
An old song and chorus
Mundane music makes us obedient

My re-bell whisper is mute
Drowned by overseer's shouts
Yelling
As Brother Nat and Sister Ure
Are hung on a tree
A reminder that keeps us from rebelling

A sly man
With a plan to make a slave
Behave
Fellow Fallows, he invited to restore order
He calmed the plantation's feud
He and the late master's daughter, intertwine devious smiles

THE SON DIAL TONE
Act III: Sing. Song. Son.
Ring. Roar. Rah-Bell-Lion.

Flirt, enthrall as we are in thrall,
Married, bonded to keep us in bondage
Order is in order for us
The crime of rebellion, still in judgment
Hanging over us
Brother Nat and Sister Ure in the distance
Swinging, swaying – behaving properly
Decorated tree holds the new master's property
Our verdict came at night
Chained and barely clothed
Lined in front of the slave shack
Plucked like crops
Four males and four females
      From our stock
A young woman of Mwana's age,
A thirteen-year-old girl
And two elder female slaves
The chosen men picked just the same
I want to fight
Red hair, the slave master's wife
Twirls pendant
My spirit and inner-g dampen
I again become a spectator to torture

We only hear screaming
The doors of the shack closed
Tearing and stripping of clothes
Then cracks of whips that give us a hint
But the screaming is dominant
Scratching and tearing, penetrating the night
Beyond the doors,
Overseer Burneside and his horde
Ravage the women and the men alike

Red hair stares at us, still curious
Twirling her pendant

The shack doors open

Overseer Burneside's artistry
On display

THE SON DIAL TONE
Act III: Sing. Song. Son.
Ring. Roar. Rah-Bell-Lion.

Stripped, broken, and bloodied
On their knees
Shamed
Then set aflame

…The burning bodies seared my eyes…
A brand on my mind
The plantation is reorganized
Fellow Fallows creates a hierarchy for us slaves
Titles as a wage
That makes us claw over one another
To reach the top
Our mystical harmonies, Mamma Iyansan's lessons
Fade to forgotten
As we struggle to keep from being at the bottom
Of Master Fallows' plantation
The women's minds broken – and she do cry

The climb and strides in the hierarchy
Of slave men is frozen
Only some of us make it up, as its purpose
A solution to the rebellious slave problem
Keep the restless at the bottom
Separate
Create an illusion of inclusion
Unbalanced, uneven
The women selling the 14 pieces of the men
No attempt to recreate them – recreate us
Osirus
The beam of Master Fallows' smile considered sacred
We dance and jive to be his favorite
Work hard for his prosperity
Argue among us who is the greatest of his property

Li'l Chew and I remember
The reality
The brutality
Brother Nat and Sister Ure
Magic preserved bodies
Still hanging from the tree
If this decoration is a reminder

THE SON DIAL TONE
Act III: Sing. Song. Son.
Ring. Roar. Rah-Bell-Lion.

Why not remember

Herkus Bar re-collects
The memories of being forced
To whip his mother to death
Crimson life dripping from his father's neck
Gasping for words, telling his son,
"Bring peace. Bring peace, so that I may rest."
With Li'l Chew near,
Herkus Bar tells me in a desperate plea,

"I can bring real peace.
Master Fallows' wife is
   Like us
She wields glorious magic
Brother Nat and Sister Ure
Frightened her. Killed her father. But I can talk to her.
There will be no more tension
   In this so-called order
A spiritual emancipation
Imagine real freedom on this plantation."

Herkus Bar wanted freedom in slavery
I plead that peace without struggle
Would continue the disharmony
"Herkus, I understand how you believe what you say is true
Brother, I've seen this through your view
Deciphered with both my eyes
One as Eshu the other has Heru
But those thoughts have set sail
I've whispered mystical, musical scales
Observed wails in this musical note 'C'
And like Moses I divided the 'C'
And split the vibe
And played the hidden, musical note of 'I'
And 'I' am as 'U' 'R'
And we 'B' rockin' in these notes on air guitars
These thoughts are so loud
I got them blasting from passing shooting stars
With observers shouting from afar:
'Man, turn down the Rah Dios station

THE SON DIAL TONE
Act III: Sing. Song. Son.
Ring. Roar. Rah-Bell-Lion.

I'm pickin' up vibrations of cosmic sensations
That are breaking the beat down soul low
I'm able to hear the grass grow and cultivate
And the beat be breakin' down culture soul low
I'm able to hear my knee grow shufflin' with the flow
Playin' that natural music – soul funky you can dance to it
Liquid flow playin' on water flu-ids
And jamming on the organ-ics
An earthly instrumental with wind instruments
And thunderous percussions
That are brushing through my ears and hair."

Herkus Bar smiles
An infinite beam stretching for miles
My words comfort him
But his ideals are too much a part of him
Night after night
Herkus Bar meets with the master's curious wife
But only words exchange between them
The slave master's wife listening
To all the mystical lessons Herkus Bar offers
A coffer of old-time magic
Passive Herkus Bar soothed his master's wife
Telling her, "We all cried when your mother died."
And she, teasing, replies, "Don't lie. Those were
      Tears of joy in your eyes, as cruel as she could be."

Herkus Bar
Would instruct her curious eye
To stay hidden and spy
To try and imitate our dances
Our magic wrapped up in prances
We caught up in ancestral trances
Herkus Bar stealing glances
Eye on the shadow where she observed us
We felt her presence
Our power, running rampant,
Would dampen
And her pendant was the only answer

But there were things she couldn't see

THE SUN DIAL TONE
Act III: Sing. Song. Son.
Ring. Roar. Rah-Bell-Lion.

My attempts to bring Mwana out
      Of her invisible haze
I spent days composing to Mwana
I left her love letters

Then burned the paper
Flicker and flame back into vapor
Think me less of a man,
But when she did not appear, I cried
And when my tears dripped into the flames
I heard her reply:

"Black prince
Listen to this
Wade in the water
Of our streams of consciousness
Through ritual and prayer
Meditate on the time before space shattered
Into material matter
And all that mattered was spiritual
Before black cosmic Ixu and Gira's copulation ritual
Whole as one – holding conversation in the original embrace
Planning the birth of their children – suns, moons, planets, and stars
And the origins of themselves manifested multiple
In Man and Woman of the black race."

Something touched my head
And baldhead sprouted hair of wool
A black halo

She sang, "Hello. Hello. Hello.
Your hair of wool, curled galactic swirls
Intense twists, DNA helix
With all the power of gravity's force and pull.
The slave master has set us aflame
Our burning bodies angry, incensed
And myrrh
Burned and burned as the slave master
      Gathers with his family
To breathe in our sixth sense."

THE SON DIAL TONE
Act III: Sing. Song. Son.
Ring. Roar. Rah-Bell-Lion.

I speak, "But this makes no frankin-sense to me
Because even if you burn me at an excess of 1200⁰
My spirit will retain at least fifty percent
Of its original properties
Absorbing all forms of energy
Light – Heat – Sound – Electricity
Charge like cavalry – horse-powered battery
Because actually
This black body has been here for eons.
Let me sit back and think upon."

I can see Mwana's faint form
Her smile breathes
She pleads, "Yes, sit back with me
Recall every part of your memory
Before you were born in what is called physical history
Reflect on our mystery system. Cosmo-politicians.
We governed the heavens
Cruising through gala-x-seas
Astro-afro-nauts
Singing in perfect harmony with musical keys
That tightened our locks – only we can open them
We screamed! Screamed! And we screamed to the heavens!
We sang the entire musical range
Through black hole ankh-rah-phones
Until physically we took on the universe's color and tone
On our backs, scratches and scars are just shooting stars
For we are the black drip of the black backdrop
The world our private square
Soul locked, unable to think outside the box
Broken down, now lost of crowns
Our pyramid blocks
Have become our slave master's city blocks
And these city streets surround black family trees
While corporate branches steal their leaves
Because we now live in a spherical world
With corners on every block
Piled on block-by-block
And I see slaves hanging at the corners of these blocks
Trying to claim these blocks
Until we have enough blocks to rebuild our pyramids

THE SON DIAL TONE
Act III: Sing. Song. Son.
Ring. Roar. Rah-Bell-Lion.

Back to the top
To let our black drip up to our black backdrop."

Mwana pulls me into her ether
We kiss
And we cry sunbeams free
Draining the multiple colors in our eyes
Until the sun rose back into the sky
And the insects drank our tears
To become the stars' cousins, we call fireflies
We intertwine and add rhythm and reason to our rhyme
We compose a love song as our spirits fly off into the distance
Toward our newborn sun
The sky resonates our daughter
Dawn
Mwana tattoos the Earth on her belly
So that 9 months from now, when pregnant and round
                    Like a drum
She will hum a reminder of where we all come from

I fold back into reality
Mwana with me
She hides in shadows
Our power swirling inside one another
I've found my harmony
Mother to my songs
My sun and dawn

I sing to my family seeds
Brother Li'l Chew and I
Speak in 360⁰ of revolutions and loops
We are festive with rebellion
All of us
We ignite a ruckus
We make combat into an art
Kicks, jabs, stabs
Disguised as chants and dance
Make the slave master and Curly laugh
When they see us wild in whirl
Pirouette and twirl – butterfly float
African killer bee sting strike, a dance stroke

THE SON DIAL TONE

Act III: Sing. Song. Son. Ring. Roar. Rah-Bell-Lion.

Li'l Chew drums
He hums a new name,
"Irakere! Irakere!
Call me! Call me!
I pound djembe, djembe!
My sound, my sound!
I am Irakere."

Mamma Iyansan sings,
"Ring the re-bell! Ring the re-bell!
Sound through the horn can dispel
Her spell – her spell."

Li'l Chew renewed as Irakere
He pounds sounds
From his bare hands
He screams, "Let the red hair spy
Let her curious eye watch
But her movements
Will never have rhythm with our rhyme!
We call her Sarah! Sarah!
We call her Sarah the Pantomime!"

The curious eye flees
We whisper her name in the field
We tease, and we tickle the air when we laugh
Speaking her name into the breeze
Even nature chuckles
But Herkus Bar tells her of our laughter
Our numbers fall at the hands of the master
Paying too much attention with amoral intensions
To his wife
Burnings, whippings, death – the rough taking of our flesh
Master Fallows, Herkus Bar at his side, points to the west
The strong tree with the bodies
Of Brother Nat and Sister Ure,
Rope around their necks
Bodies, magic preserved, serve as a reminder
As do the burnings, whippings, death – the rough taking of our flesh
We sleep with nightmares choking our breath

THE SON DIAL TONE
Act III: Sing. Song. Son.
Ring. Roar. Rah-Bell-Lion.

It's the same all over again
Sun up to sun down
We are complacent
Herkus Bar walks adjacent to Master Fallows
Dressed in better rags

I disappear into the ether
Spend time with Mwana
Cosmic flora and fauna
Surround us
I spend my time with her
In the ether
I-spirit put on my physical as a garb
And manifest back in the slave shack
Irakere dragged away
Whipped and whipped
And whipped and whipped
For giving the pantomime
Her name
Spared from death
But beaten, broken
Open wounds draw blood
As he can barely draw breath
Mwana, wearing a shadow as a dress,
She puts a hand on Irakere's chest and mends his flesh

In the night, it's there. Just sitting.
A haunting. A tension.
At any time…ready to break

Morning opens wide
There's a pitch that breaks the sky
I hear her. Mamma Iyansan.
"Ain't nothin' new here to see.
Heartbeats done stopped,
But not the spirit of the drum.
Ain't nothin' new here to see
'Cause there ain't nothin' new under the sun.
This ain't my beginning,
But I've seen this so much

THE SON DIAL TONE
Act III: Sing. Song. Son.
Ring. Roar. Rah-Bell-Lion.

I believe this is where I come from."

A tree branch snaps me awake
I walk out and walk west
Brother Nat and Sister Ure
Crumpled on the ground
Mamma Iyansan floating above them
I run and run,
I kneel over Nat and Ure's bodies
I wipe my hands over the branch,
Look over my shoulder
No sign of the slave master or his soldiers

I sing a soft prayer
Mamma Iyansan beaming
Her eyes bright
She winks
"I will dream of this moment in the dreaming
I will dream when I am no longer aware of this moment."

I gather all the sounds
And I sing
My voice carving out of the branch
Borne a new form
A horn
I run to the slave shack,
Jump into a shadow
Swallowed by the ether
I breathe through the instrument
Inhale. Exhale. All the musical properties of the galaxy
All the universe's harmonies
The horn, reborn as cosmic mahogany
Anointed by the infinite ebony

Mamma Iyansan and Mwana bless the horn with their voices
I step out of the mystical
Rejoin the physical
And attend to my slavery
Sun and lash against my back
Hair pulled for its burst of fiery wool
It's the same all over again

THE SON DIAL TONE
Act III: Sing. Song. Son.
Ring. Roar. Rah-Bell-Lion.

Sun up to sun down
We sing the master's religion
Until our spirits are bound
And our ancestry is drowned in myth
Work. Work. Work.
Paid the bare minimum slave
We are punished for speaking to the air
Our spoken prayers
To the unseen, Mamma Iyansan or Mwana

We communicate with brother and sister slave
They allocated to the house
Our dealings cloaked
By myths that are soaked
In rumblings that we don't get along
But it's just for convenience
We keep the master unaware
Use these myths to our advantage
We communicate in slang and song
Through the anguish
We sing and sing and sing
Our voices ring and ring and ring
The re-bell, Rah's bell
The sunshine harmony and tone,
Twinkling cosmic foliage
Our locks unlock us from bondage
We sing together on this plantation
In coded language

We told the wind not to sing
We told the clouds not to gather
Or cry
Time was all that moved,
And that was only by very little
When the sun crept up into the sky

No one would work for the master today
Not even nature would be his slave
Neither he nor his wife
Would pluck us from stock
And savor our tastes

THE SON DIAL TONE

Act III: Sing. Song. Son.
Ring. Roar. Rah-Bell-Lion.

We would wait
And wait
And wait

The doors opened
And entered Herkus Bar

"Should everyone
Who works in this land
Stay their hand?
The master employs
People of his collective here too
Indentured like you
For the right to work
But they dance grateful with gratitude."

I tell Herkus Bar,
"They enjoy employment,
The indentured report also as soldiers
Extra pay given
Even if just pittance
It's their reward for keeping us submissive
We wallow in servitude
With no chance to move or grow
Unless we take your method
And sell out our own."

Herkus Bar takes offense
"My methods are a means to an end
I spared you and your friend
Outside, now, overseer's soldiers march closer
Let me extend that mercy again
To curb their violence."

I hiss my frustration
"You are an off-tuned spectator
Dancing unaware
You stand there and just stare
And blare witch projects
That throws your own people off topic
And you've believed you've rocked it

THE SON DIAL TONE
Act III: Sing. Song. Son.
Ring. Roar. Rah-Bell-Lion.

Because you've fooled a few to follow it
To search the floor below them
For a deep thought once you've dropped it.

We are the real gears of the machine
Abused in our rotation
Abuse our payment for keeping in order
And moving the currency of this plantation
Our spirits mop your mess up
Our spirits restore natural order
It is our original thoughts
The stone warriors that rock
Chiseled down at the writer's block
On a chronological spot far before you were born
Even with no physical form
We play the wind through a metaphysical horn
Our blessed music, the ripple that makes waves for the waves of today
Not just the new waves
But the all-present waves that bathes you in yesterday
To make you think you got flow
And I throw you a meta on your shore
And you have the nerve to ask, 'What's this meta for?'

I'll tell you
It's a key to a door
That keeps thoughts you can't afford
Consciously deep, unconsciously low."

Irakere booms from the corner,
"Man, this joker is only impressed
When you dress things up with the number three
I'm not talking about trilogies
But the trickery of unholy trinities
Herkus Bar believes he's a part of them:
The slave master, his wife, and him
The hat trick — the matrix
All that neo, new wave bullshit
I'm talkin' about substance substituted with the obvious
And on top of this
You be insultin' my intelligence
With that shallow puddle you defined

THE SON DIAL TONE
Act III: Sing. Song. Son.
Ring. Roar. Rah-Bell-Lion.

As deep thought art
The spell the master has you under
Is designed to make ignorant fools like you think they smart
But your final objective has made me cry
Until my tears rise and I finally sink
Brother, all we're askin' you to do is think."

Herkus Bar barked, "Please,
I'm thinking more than you ever did
My thoughts' tone Saturn's rings cosmic
They ring Sirius."

Mwana speaks herself into existence,
"You just don't get it
We were at the beginning of all this
I have a lock for every life I've lived
Me and the Aztecs use to hold think tanks
At each other's pyramids
While writing lyrics that reflect
Our philosophies and dance steps
Surviving in pictures, depicting scriptures
Is how we transcend death
My thoughts are a story for your vision
And I wrote the same story perfectly
But I distorted the same story purposely
Just so you would believe it was a religion

I don't mean to offend you, my brother
Just your blind service to this man
But maybe the best way for you to have a clue
Is if I wrote it in the palm of your hand
But you still wouldn't have it
No matter how many times you try and grab it
But for now, that's my only plan
So just sit back and relax
Let yo' belly shake like jelly
And you can listen to us real masters
Jam."

The plantation's soldiers flood the shack
A storm of threats

THE SON DIAL TONE
Act III: Sing. Song. Son.
Ring. Roar. Rah-Bell-Lion.

Rain hectic
One of them grabs Mwana
And I react
Beginning the dance electric
Irakere pounds the air solid, not hollow
(What's the use of war drums if a battle doesn't follow?)
Thunder's sound strikes
Our kicks and jabs cut like a knife
Mwana sings and becomes the air
Wind whirls and wobbles the plantation soldiers
Our partners in this artistic, martial dance
The tools we use to till the land
Now weapons in hand

The fury of our flurries sets the barn blurry
With blaze
Plantation soldiers lay dead
Our fire spreads to the field
The horizon births more soldiers
They fire lightning and thunder
And our numbers litter the arable land
Mamma Iyansan
Sings them back to life
Our fallen numbers spring upright
No bullet or whip
Delays our strike
We are the gods' and goddesses' might

I dance and take fight with Herkus Bar
His rhythm drenched
With the master's lashes
He scars me, scratches
His fists crash against me
I duck his fury
Clutch his next potential pound
And strike
He slips – loose
We move and shake
Every hit makes the earth quake
I attack his physical
He bombards my spiritual

THE SON DIAL TONE
Act III: Sing. Song. Son.
Ring. Roar. Rah-Bell-Lion.

Each hoping our kicks and jabs
Will break spirit or bone or the energy coiled around our spine
Winding up our backs

I'm grabbed!
A haunting chokes me
A phantom dampens my power
Pantomime twirls her pendant
Negating and subduing our advantage
The soldiers lightning and thunder kills us again
Mamma Iyansan's wings are clipped
Our Great Mother stripped
Herkus Bar seizes this moment
And hits
Scars scream on my body
And blood pours and drips

Master Fallows
His whip like a serpent
Attacks
The venom racks my body
The agony brings me to my knees
Master Fallows lashes me
Again and again and again and again
Curly's whip, more devastating
Than the soldiers' lightning and thunder,
He fells six in our number
The pantomime's trinket
Mutes Irakere's air drum vibration
The phantom borne of her pendant
Grabs Mwana
And chokes her until she turns to glass
Squeezing and squeezing
Ready to shatter her body to small shards of ash

I swallow my voice
Put all the mystic notations at my finger tips
Reach back
Call the horn into my grip
And with its mouth against my lips
I scream with the keys

THE SON DIAL TONE

Act III: Sing. Song. Son.
Ring. Roar. Rah-Bell-Lion.

Of all the cosmic harmonies

Herkus Bar
Skin of burnished brass
Turns to ash
I sing loud through the horn
Its melodies clash with cracked-brain
Slave drivers
I scream with the horn
Create pressure and wind
Mystical notation lessons
When properly played, form compression
Sounds resonating ancient
Shatter Pantomime's pendant
Dissolve her phantom's menace
And restores Mwana to her natural, spiritual state

Tornadoes mend Mamma Iyansan's wings
The horn sings rainbows
While the air makes thunder that screams
From Irakere's hands that slams against soldiers
Makes us slaves fluid like water
Fighting for future free black sons and black daughters
Led no more to the slave master's slaughter

Mamma Iyansan
Sword in one hand
Whip made of horsetail in the other
Her eye spies the Pantomime
Curly rushes red hair away
Mamma Iyansan gives chase
The master's lash wraps around her neck
And keeps the angel in place

Mamma Iyansan's arm twirls and spins
Her sword cuts the master's lash in half
Horsetail whip shifts into a snake
It eyes the master as prey
And strikes as its body ignites
Coils around the master
Keeping him stiff and frozen

THE SON DIAL TONE
Act III: Sing. Song. Son.
Ring. Roar. Rah-Bell-Lion.

Mamma Iyansan takes the moment,
Swipes her sword
And takes the master's head

The snake jumps back into her hand
Horsetail whip at her command
Mamma Iyansan turns to take
The master's bride
In 9 strides
Mamma Iyansan flies,
Her body twists, turns into a tornado

The pantomime waits for her
Holding a pound of pendant rock
Red spattered and blotched
No knowledge, wisdom
Or understanding
No philosophy reaped or sown
In this grand piece called a skeptic's stone

The master's bride
With her pound of stone
Vomits ghostly rumors and lies
That attack Mamma Iyansan

From inside the plantation house
Mamma Iyansan fights and strikes
We hear her cries
As she's overwhelmed by the ghosts
The lies
I howl the horn to push back the desperate attack
On our Great Mother

As I exhale melody and sound
Mwana inhales
Mamma Iyansan turns into feathers
And clouds
Spiraled, spun and siphoned down
Through all chambers of Mwana's body
She exhales, breathes
I play my Father's Voice

THE SON DIAL TONE

Act III: Sing. Song. Son.
Ring. Roar. Rah-Bell-Lion.

And connect with her Mother Harmony
Our bodies shift
No longer slaves, we are all free
We fly up into the breeze

Mwana sings happily,
Smile brighter than the sun's beam
"I fly, Mojuba! I fly!
The breeze we ride."
Up, we are, in the sky
Dwindled to fourteen pieces

We soar south
To the shore
We meet land
And water waves to us
Freed woman and man
Gospel ghost spells
Turn to spirituals
And we hum in harmony
As the waves' sound
Crash on the shore

We shout
Exorcise the devil's ghost spells out
Call and response with nature, our mirror
We speak to us, glorious
Our knowledge, culture, and power
Drinking in four bars
(Blues)
Our pen and tonic
Two subdominants to tonic to dominant back to tonic
We cry freedom
Our tears, the ghosts of those slain
They too are now free
Fighting for one last chance to be heard or seen

We hear our tears sing collectively,
"Don't forget
Always remember me
The condensation of a memory

THE SON DIAL TONE
Act III: Sing. Song. Son.
Ring. Roar. Rah-Bell-Lion.

Feel the way we flow
As we pass through your eyes
Rushing like a river at 33^0
On a square like pyramids of Masonic imagery
We are the voices tossed overboard
Into shark infested waters
We will be the emotion of recycled oceans
That wave goodbye with bloody hands
Held down, whipped and bound
Our voices will return crippled
Walking on hurri-canes
Waves that first rippled in Africa."

We amplify
We amp, and we be fly
Increase our tears' sound
And make the whole crowd 'def'

Irakere say,
"I remember this
Tapping on a tree's hip
When I heard the beat flip
I caught it on my lips
And called it music."

The women belt out a note so high
It rattles the sky
As stars pour over us fourteen
Burning black
Whole
X
And internally
This power burning in us
We become the ON of eternity
Mars combined with Venus
The heroes reborn as the phoenix

Irakere pounds the air and drums
I hum thunder through the horn
The water swirls angry
And from its depths emerges

THE SON DIAL TONE

Act III: Sing. Song. Son.
Ring. Roar. Rah-Bell-Lion.

A silver ship born from Irakere's myth
I play the horn
And we fourteen lift,
Landing on the deck of the silver ship
We sail away into a cloud of mist
Celebrate with an abundance of food and drink
While hours fold over one another
The ship provides, and we nurse one another
Back to health

Voices sing from beneath the sea
Stir the water and make it breathe
Their sound, through water, waves
Mwana's eyes see on the horizon
An invisible island coming into focus
Solid
Like the sun shining light
To open the day
The island is there, and we give praise
A council of eight awaits us
The Ogdoad
And behind them, a council of nine
Mamma Iyansan's rhymes
Her children, the Ennead

Disembarked
Mwana's heart
Hugs her mother
Mamma Asase-Anc
She leads us into a mystical
Tropical forest
Where frolicked freedom
And where we bathe in waters
That wash away our scars
But not the pain of their memories
Done purposefully
So says Mamma Asase-Ane

Then she directs,
"We must compose with haste
No minute made waste

THE SON DIAL TONE

Act III: Sing. Song. Son.
Ring. Roar. Rah-Bell-Lion.

Fifteen and Fifteen and Fifteen ships
Approach on hurried pace
The population here, this island of freedom
A target to be enslaved
Music, your mysticism at your command
Come together and band
The Ogdoad and Ennead that I lead
Will make this island visible
For this last stand.

My daughters, with me
We must pull Mamma Iyansan's spirit
With ritual through your father's Voice
And my Harmony

Irakere, the boom in your hands
Pound and pound
Until this sound shields this land
Mojuba,
Your horn must play
Call upon nature
To make all four elements wave
The rest of your fourteen
The remaining eleven
Take weapon
Join the rest of our army
Our deities
And should any slaver land upon our shore
Make war and bring balance."

Sadly,
We believe
Even if we embrace victory
This will make no difference
For a long time

But we take stance
We are the holy ghosts
We are the sun's tone
The cosmic dance
The universe's rhythm

THE SON DIAL TONE
Act III: Sing. Song. Son.
Ring. Roar. Rah-Bell-Lion.

Croons through us
Baritone, bass, soprano
Falsetto
We stand ready and mellow
In melody
We are something new
Our mutation is the separation
And differentiation
In time and space between the tones
Without us, there is chaos
We are the proper keys and harmonies

We march toward the shore
The voice of four winds
Mwana and her sister's ritual begins
Breath, balance of
Vocal chords, vibration of
Her M (magnetic) Ahket
Upper and lower sounds

Irakere drums
Hands rattle the air
Until collective prayer
Creates a sound barrier
We dance on the shore
Freestyle, our style is free
We chant collectively
Twelve tones from sixteen shades
God's 78 names interchanged
144 – thousand
Our spirits housing the open lotus flower
Our might and power
Chanting on this specific time of day
Chanting to the twelve signs in the sky
Light value emanates and synchronizes
Manifest triangulated thought
The four elements must obey
Different styles of music play

Fifteen and fifteen and fifteen ships
Approach

THE SON DIAL TONE
Act III: Sing. Song. Son.
Ring. Roar. Rah-Bell-Lion.

Hurl cannon fire at our coast
That knock against our sound barrier
And explode
Mwana's voice moves the tide
Waves climb and crash
Dash against the attacking slave ships
Mwana harmonizes tornadoes
Hurricanes and whirlpools race
The sea's mouth opens
And satiates her body with a fleet's taste

But they come back up
Irakere, distracted with victory
Ceases his percussion
The sound barrier drops
Cannon fire rocks

A concert of explosions
The island left vulnerable and open
Mwana and her mother and sister
Fly and sail
Sword in one grip,
In the other, a whip of horsetail
Mwana's father and brother lead a charge to the shore
They speak spells through ankh-rah-phones
Incant the proper tones
To nullify the effects of the Pantomime's hex
But a pound of pendant rests
Nestled aboard an attacking vessel

Horn to my lips
I breathe out all my energy
My body shifts
Funneled through the horn
The horn breathes me
Exhaled and streamed through its bell
An audible runnel, a booming beam
The universe at the center of me
I take the sounds of Irakere's hand pounds
Collect the harmony of Mwana,
Her sister, and Mamma Asase-Ane

THE SON DIAL TONE
Act III: Sing. Song. Son.
Ring. Roar. Rah-Bell-Lion.

And absorb the voice and tones
Of the ankh-rah-phones
Imbued with galactic hue
I dive
From high up into the sky
Down into the pound of pendant
And shatter it from existence
My physical beam twists and twirls
Swirls and funnels back through the horn
Kissed into physical form
I return
And amplify the harmony around me
The pounds, voices, and tones
Circle
Revolution
A tornado digs into the sea
A whirlpool opens
Iemanja feasts again
Without the ships' resurrection

The island remains free
A small area of peace
Mwana glides next to me
We embrace
As the island population celebrates
This small victory

Sarah the Pantomime
Is in the wind
And we know we would confront her again
We are prepared
With tricks of our own
Mamma Asase-Ane declares,
"We will be our own descendants
On our family tree
This will all be locked in our memory
Resting in her, hymn, and our story
All of us as 'we'
Passed on through our seeds
For a while,
This will be like repetition

THE SON DIAL TONE
Act III: Sing. Song. Son.
Ring. Roar. Rah-Bell-Lion.

But don't we find joy in that?
Rough drafts to rough tracks
Slave chains like hands clap
On the final
Cut
Wrists
And bleed sap
From the tree of knowledge of good and evil
Hold onto cross atop the cathedral
Preach and sing broken words until old and feeble
As works of encoded art
We will take care of our people, be as all forms of expression
As under the guise of cloud and sky
We will become wise and one with sunshine and fly
Talk about the days beyond when we die
Glide into heaven's eyes and see more than we ever could
When we were alive
Now our birthdays are every day and our age is eternal
Forever X and internal
Heave no sigh
Everyone returns to the elements in time
Reduce fraction of soul/body/mind
      Down to soul
      Soul low down
      Into earth's soil
      Down so low
      That soul begins to grow
      Again, by resurrection
Like what should be done with time
      Instead of killing it
We should be willing it, fulfilling it like destiny
And no longer riddling over the question that cannot be
Solved
Under the canopy from creation to creation
Our spirits will evolve
Frustrated that nothing will be resolved
360^0 revolve to the bullet in the next chamber
The thief in our temples
Losing our minds by gunshot
Pondering the difficult and not the simple
Life in danger

THE SON DIAL TONE

Act III: Sing. Song. Son.
Ring. Roar. Rah-Bell-Lion.

Danger in life
Releasing not through anger but in chorus
We don't have to steal our fire like Prometheus
We unwrap all talents and gifts
Shift
Return package in better condition than when we received it
       Used
No longer shall we ponder, "How strong shall we be?"
What the ego said and how the id replied
That conversation is hazardous, words are pollutants
Hallucinogens
Dangerous secret agents – our holy word is our bond
And tomorrow never dies – it's resurrected every day like people
Because we are everyday people
And I want to take you higher
My, my, my. Ain't that sly?"

Mamma Asase-Ane takes my horn
She sings our story's notes
Into its bell
Mystical harmonies
Turn the horn's body
Into faerie-like notations
Fluttering and flapping sprites
They anoint the end of a spear
Mamma Asase-Ane tosses it through the atmosphere
Up, beyond the sky
To reside and open
At the proper time on cue of collective cry

Mwana and I
On the shore
Hand in hand
There is freedom for us
But we pray for more
It can't be just us; there must be justice
Our spirits remain as music
Playing
From existence fades the island
The sun, ready for bed, on the horizon
Our music will evolve

IN 13 PIECES

(Featured in Fable Avenue Book II: Brooklyn's Lilac Brew)

IN 13 PIECES

Act 1: Epoch's End

Here. We. See. Sand.
Pregnant belly dunes
The horizon, our Caesarean
Cut
We up, over
A thousand clamors
Shuffle, shuffle and ruffle the calm
The heat sighs. A low wind sings and a swirl tumbles
      Billowing down these rolling, sandy hills
Here are we. An army of horses, fish, and rams
We walk the lion's land, surveying golden, crushed waste

Alkebulan is not the same. Not even in name.
She has become finely divided rock – nature mirrors us
Sun scorched instead of kissing us
This land is now Osiris in the Ament, a furnace
Without cold – Af-Ra – Heat, reeks our motherland
Basilisk licked into granular particle, sunny quartz bits
An abandoned place, once glorious face, a desert
This is how home looks now
Forestation receded – by angry war and nature's wound, retreated
Only sand ripples where we step and breathe
This golden sea bleeds proof of nature's gentle creativity
Even as motherland weeps wounded
Her tears turned to waterless, sandy reefs
There is so much beauty in this endless
      Golden, natural scrap heap

Our cavalry wears the desert – browned, tanned robes
Rain-bows in our hands. Air-rows on their breaths
      And quiver
In rows of ten, our thousands trot

The fishers, ferocious, wear the sea as their color
Waving in waves. Their feet drip footprints on dry motherland.
A moving oasis, an army of aquatic life breathing words
For weapons or blessings

And the rams wear green. Left wing, their armies flank.
Emerald horns adorn helmets
In hand, weapons gleam, glimmering
      Flushed,

IN 13 PIECES
<u>Act 1: Epoch's End</u>

The faces of blades blush with the stains of sacrifice
And strife

But war is behind us, faded
Peace, loosely woven and braided
War will come again, as consequences intend
Tock-tick, the cosmic clock, flipped backwards
The ages are confused. Twelve in our Father's house
       Are doomed to be disguised from our eyes
The war we walk away from, over foresight interpretation
Has more to say
War pauses only to prep – practice its speech, until the need
For War to speak again. Scream.
Louder

For now, an emancipation from war – we have come home
Both she, motherland, and we
Her children
Desolate
Seared
We return to her,
The last of a failed generation

We come bearing uncertain alchemy in our speech
Prayers laced with pleas
Our frames may extend to the heavens
But our spirits crawl the Earth. We are gods, humbled.
Motherland. She. There. A lone, sable maiden sitting on ebony chair
A high priestess
We bow to her, come to ask for forgiveness
"State your business," she says
Disappointment possesses her tone

"We are a reaction. This faction. The world population.
Kings and queens. Warriors. Scholars. Artisans. All class of citizens.
We. Observed. The Wall.
Every scratch, every etch that was sketched
We saw its mouth
Opened
Screaming our future
And we. Will. Be. Broken.
Our crowns will crumble

IN 13 PIECES
<u>Act 1: Epoch's End</u>

The Wall speaks, of bumbling, broken speech,
Created sentiments, harmful prayers
      From the caves of our mouths, learned upright
On two syllables, walking. We will serve the cursed words' dictation.
So, has it, in stone, been writ

Mother, we of your matter, made war against this
Our future. Carved on a wall.
We could not figure its all in all this
Was this just a warning? Can we fight the storm?
Embrace it? Civilize it. Turn it. Or, treat it kindly like family.
We had no answer. No one agreed.
So…we made war with one another.
Scared, we scarred the land, weaponized egos in hand.
You, motherland, spirit once whole
      Divorced, broken into seven. We know you suffered the most.

Peace only stalls our disagreement
Egos are dressed in different sects and factions
Philosophies, made mockery in council
The dissatisfied will rise,
And war will reign again among our people
The storm will be made physical, literal
Three thousand miles across the sandy paved way
Barren mountains will roar
We will fall to sword. Broken more and more.
Little-by-little until shipped away as slaves.
So sayeth The Wall. Its hands, that we into, played.

Every kingdom we now create
Will only serve as a grave
      Reminder
      Faintly lit
To echo once brighter days."

Motherland, our high priestess
Speaks silence
Louder than my pleas
Her Medusa gaze
Reversed to self
Her visage is stone
Her face. Becomes. The Wall.

IN 13 PIECES
Act 1: Epoch's End

If only her anger was a façade

We wish she stayed this way
Silent. Stone.
But her tone makes desert heat turn tundra
Dictating our dejection, our judgment:

Mother Covenant, of Motherland:
"Fate's scripted-sketched wall is built only of stone
If made of air, script unseen, there would be an issue
But stone is grown. Sketched. Crafted. Shaped.
With great force, can pressure crumble – break
Nothing set in stone is set in stone for you
Never did you wear fate's woven cloth
The cosmos your skin: proud, heavenly black body – live freely
Naked, you've pranced playfully through life picking profitable prophecies
Fate to you is a suggestion. You are a spirit separate of its lattice.
You, first-born children, are risen – The Wall was only heeded warning
But now from this conduct, wars erupt
          Stirs virgin lands to wake for lust
The sacred text of the Earth, no longer scripted
In the cosmos' free-willed ink
This world? Its spirit sinks. Its three moons: red, black, green
          Look! As now, like eyes they blink
          But from existence. Faded into one, ashen, blanched body. Neglect.
And this one sickly moon, Earth shall she reflect

But even while barren, there in Her are treasures still
Made claim by warring, whorish Barons, who wanton in their want
Will want to chain you
Subdued for duty – from here to the world,
You will build kingdoms for Tantalus, and never satiate him
Over and over
He will attempt to drink, to eat
Just a carrot waved in front of an empty sole purpose
You, an ass to follow

Tantalus will make you work for wages absinth of your reflection
He will paint images of you and call them mirrors
Muddled, mocked, misshapen silhouettes
Epileptic shadows stretched to represent you roped up
Dangled, puppet, Marinette

IN 13 PIECES
Act 1: Epoch's End

For your ill comport: You. Will. Hang.
By the fingers of Tantalus; or so help me gods,
In a Northern wilderness, your shade will decorate my trees
And when my clouds rain down on you, swinging ornaments
Do not mistake that for you, I as your Mother Nature weep
My disappointment in you, my natural children, is too deep

Jealousy taints your vain
Proudly pumped pride through all four chambers of your heart
Day-by-day, chains upon chains you will pray
If then you beg to be a slave
   Let your kings and queens forget their crowns
   Let your warriors lay down their swords
   Let your farmers inhale the smoke of poisoned land
   Let your scholars and priests sing corrupted, foreign mythology
     In perfect harmony – if indeed you believe your pitch cursed
Fall down! Lift sword only to one another! The ripe bounty of the Earth be damned!
Double, double—meaning—your coiled hair be trouble, spin, spun – ruse!
I will have you confused!
You think you've seen war? My script is heavy with it. Just wait.
Hordes of a horrible plague carried on two legs from the mouths
   Of lateral mountain graves
   Will come
And you will serve the sound of Tantalus' command
So, forget, forget, and forget. Your black fleece made golden.
Coveted by interest piqued men; piqued women.
Love of self, experienced vicariously through cursed vocabulary
So, go! Love those words, and know thyself.
Then you will remember
Your covenant to me. Motherland.

So, let the hanged man haunt you
Anger sever you
Only through this alchemical fission, properly applied
   Mathematical equation
I pronounce
Your vision will be new, clear
For all the generations you rebirth blind
You will see, on your final return, with lilac eyes
Open and bright. Clean. – By the womb of the Cobalt Flame
Three moons returned. Red. Black. Green.

IN 13 PIECES

Act 1: Epoch's End

Surrounded, shimmering halos gleam, circled, cipher stream

And as you will not mistake my rain for tears
Do not mistake my punishment for lack of such
My first children, born out of the black
And into the blue
I bestow this fate out of love for you

For twenty-five thousand years you will birth
A versed lineage
And in each of those years construct you will a fraction
Of a new language to speak a grand wish
Here are your pens. Get started. Good speed. God speed. Leave me be.
I have my own script to draft."

Motherland drinks a parting glass.

Then, her hand and head lift
Fingers twirl, making the cosmos swirl
And writ upon the cosmic fold's brilliant assemblage,
Bright cosmic script, there do the stars shift
Heavy, heavenly planet bodies drift, weightless – then still, remain, fixed
This new celestial rotation makes black cosmic waves ricochet
And we weigh heavy with burden

A heavenly menagerie holds back our dark energy
          The embrace of our dark matter
Our cosmic cloth torn
Fate now our vestments
We seek sacrifice as a birthright
Under these new stars
Born
Ritual now our guide to the fabric of the heavenly sky
Anansi spins our tale as Milky Way silk. Star connected to star.
His widowed mother wears an hourglass on her back
She mourns while poisoned stardust pours through her
Empty one glass. Fill the other. This, our time.

Tock-tick. So, shall it be writ. Under foreign, celestial penmanship,
Our story is told. This is not stone. In the stars, fate is set.
And we stand here ill, littered and 'ret to go. Our judgment come.
"Let your story unfold and be done," says Motherland

IN 13 PIECES
Act 1: Epoch's End

The horizon swallows the sun,
Thus, adjourned are we

End act one

IN 13 PIECES
Ritual Interlude

The nighttime animals walk the cosmos-pasture backwards
A maiden and water bearer as their shepherds
They hide behind the sun's shine, high in the sky
Glittering pricked out points in the firmament's cloth
We watch and decode their glimmer, eyes like moths to their flames

Them animals frolic with the sun and the moon's movement
Earth's rotation, we evolve around their influence
Degeneration after generation, them animals' emotions mock us
As they play tricks that pluck the chords of heart strings
Bubbling music bursts too loud for the soul to sleep
Single eyes, blurry with dust not blessed from the desert golem's touch
Wide awake, we shake restless and go breathless
Pondering the proper rites to help dim the nighttime animals' influence
Make starry animal sacrifice
We even look to the water bearer and his virgin wife to get the knife

Work, work, work to please the heavens and ease the ego
Make the most of the desert, tilling and tempering civilization
Architecture aligned properly with astronomy
City buildings' shapes and interiors mirror the body
All sounds ring through our temples
Perfect pitch and harmony
Clothes stitched to display the soul and humor the body
In mythology, we speak simultaneous – of gods and goddesses
Astrophysics and biophysical equations
Double triples the meaning, interpretation after mathematical interpretation
Methodical is obsessive. Meticulous mocks intelligence.
Nothing is done unless it pleases the heavenly black body
          Or Her stars, the moon, and sun

For this work, we drink our smiles. Pride becomes drunk.
Stumbles our ego – vanity remains among us – restless
The heavens gasp and are breathless
Thousands of tithes have us swimming against the tide
But in time, we spread our mathematics to the world
Civilization blossoms high and perfumes the heavens
We believe, without bended knee, that charity is in our presence
And the nighttime animals continue to frolic and mock us

We forget punishment
Neglect of Motherland covenant

IN 13 PIECES
Ritual Interlude

Magic squandered. Magic only flickers. Sputters soft.
We sow our oaths
Growth civilized pride
We shed responsibility
And give culpability to superstitions
The ego blamed on bipedal reptilians
Tsetse, the leopard of Mbomba, from sky to earth
The clever leopard puts fire into mountains
Where birthed and set free, Tokoloshe and the red-eyed wolves
Our monsters in past, now in myth, star-studded brilliance

Cursed language created, banished and isolated
Unspoken in the cold, desolated – civilization disrupted
By spotted lambs fleeced of black wool
Superstitions take the physical
Mitered materiality – the reality of the matter at hand
          That rocks the cradle of our civilizations
Open mouth, from the mount, pale shadows march as whirlwinds
With heart, we give lessons to tame them
Overtime, we are paid with enslavement
Chained to pale shadow system – our rebellion only changes the scenery of the
system
A concrete jungle springs up among us
A grave where the living dead reside
Hollowed buildings, unaligned, stare blank with glassy eyes
A city of puzzles and mazes and tricks and riddles
Boggled dance, we limp and trip as pale shadows shade black from heaven's light
Further unravels the degeneration – black generation after black denigration
                              (de-nigger-ration)
Whether absent or present, scarred black parents maim their children…

IN 13 PIECES

Act II: Starry Eyed and Pessi-Mystic

Here I stand as tall as I sit, back bent
Watery, weak conjures as tricks
I daydream and grin
Of superstitions as a wish
Infatuated, I think of the water bearer's daughter, and I wish her no harm
She is heir to his firmament flagon of fermented waters
Her steps are dances, prancing across the sky
She smiles the sun and she exhales the stars in a breath
She wears her mother's cosmic color as her flesh
Her hair is a locked mystery with many twists
Black, puffy smoke that reflects the universe's abyss
They say
       she will one day
            dance with a king
                  as black as me
This story keeps my head and glory above the clouds
But I see the city riddled with puzzles when I look down
And the height of my circumstances scares me
I come down to Earth
Birthed through the clouds
My eyes pry answers from my environment
A puzzled city stares back at me, oblivious
Its bloodstream: confused colored citizens
Little black boys kill their youth to become men
Their speech a chorus of revenge on fathers absent
Little black girls too young for pangs of labor
Mimic absent father and absent-minded mother's behavior
A prison cycle worth its weight in slave wagers
Other colors are given green to grow in our gardens
While we sleep and eat our daily bread – baked in savagery
The lack of nutrients poisons us deep
Buried is the history. The system of slavery. The pale shadow's trick and ruse.
Buried so low as our souls hang low,
Our history can no longer be used as an excuse

I escape the city's loud landscape
And go where the traffic travels slow
Too much pride in the city's vibe
Keeps other black minds tied to the city
I ponder the water bearer's daughter's mythology
And so, my mind grows. I come to know:

IN 13 PIECES

Act II: Starry Eyed and Pessi-Mystic

There is something better than the current weather

Here I stand as tall as I sit, back bent
The sky, filled with turbulent clouds, assists the wind
      with haunting the trees in the background
Shake! Shake! Shake!
The sun and the blue peek to give beauty to the day
Rough waters stream – scream tumultuous energy
A conflict outside
And within me
I am surrounded by passion and enthusiasm

I carry heavy sword that weighs more
Than my wiry frame
I, a slender black flame
Doused in doubt from the words
Dripped from my Father Zero
And my Mother Nothing's mouth

I stand youthful as The Fool
With sword instead of stick
No home and parentless
The silence is loud
Far away. Here. The city is quiet.
I can think
So, I drink and eat inspiration
And I vomit plans and ideas

I spy behind the blue
The twinkling hues
Of nighttime animals
I tame them with a glance
Instead of frolicking, they dance
More rhythm in them to move
And I'm in sync,
      rather than at odds,
With their groove

Up to the sky, through the air
I, to the maiden and water bearer, declare
"I will serve your daughter. She, conceived in Heaven,

IN 13 PIECES

Act 11: Starry Eyed and Pessi-Mystic

Born on Earth, the perfect Queen.
I will wear the galaxy around me and be
The blackest of light – I will become her knight.
We will walk hand-in-hand, civilizing the untamed land."

Too much past time – daydream pastime
Too much past the city's line
Devil swine take me away

I, surrounded by coppers
My mind thinks mercury and silver
My thoughts shine like a mirror
Conduct electricity, stir alchemy
I think of myself as deadly poison – I am five deadly venoms
       And the proper medicine
My wiry, weak frame is not the true temperament
I am candle and wick. I am a slender, black flame
My black is gold
I know my proper rites
I lift eyes to the sky and declare,
"I will find your daughter. I will walk hand in hand with her,
And I will become her knight."

I arrive
Inside the city
With devil swine
I am calm. Not kicking.
Delivered to my cage
Disguised as a building
It houses so many

In house. A cage. In room. Just the same.
My thoughts sweat my brow
Wet weather knocks on window
Drops from sky, I believe the tears
In my eyes are distant cousins to the rain,
The clouds cry for reasons just the same

I understand. I am.
A wiry frame of a man.
I am. My circumstance.

IN 13 PIECES

Act 11: Starry Eyed and Pessi-Mystic

Circumcised blind of my manhood
Mother Nothing and Father Zero
Broke my hands good
And they healed limp

Mother Nothing shouts obscenities
That sound as absurdities
She walks away, nose up at her history
Skeptical that she was ever a queen
Her head hangs and swings low like a sweet chariot
It's humility of slavery that possesses her memories
She bows to pale shadow authority
And asks how much they're willing to pay
For all fourteen of her husband's pieces
His penis is priceless
Mother Nothing walks backwards through the story of Isis
Littering the world with her husband's parts – mocking man and wife
One flesh, my mother

Father Zero believes himself a circle
A revolution
He is a cycle of abuse
A black, paler shade of shadow
Double duty, acting like devil swine

He polices family
Iron fist, and I know personally
His alchemy makes me golden
Shine black and blue
The system injects him with possessions
Breaking his family earns him protection
A good example, outstanding black citizen

I count my blessings
At least my Father Zero is here
Other father zeroes are superheroes
With powers to disappear
But still I blush green with envy

Maybe I should be grateful
For the lessons my parents taught me:

IN 13 PIECES

Act 11: Starry Eyed and Pessi-Mystic

Question no authority
The foundation here is family
Slavery is not slavery
Bow gracefully to my enemy that shows no mercy
Only attack when the perpetrator looks like me

I take seat – rain-blurred window
I have a first-class view to watch
Black cage-city residents walk in sleep
Speech, in circles – feet walk the same pattern
My throat cries a soft sigh

My heavy sword
Hidden before
Devil swine marched me
Here

My imagination donates a sword to me
Same make and shape, but lighter in weight
I swipe the air and watch the mirror
Warrior pose perfect
Reversed reflection, I begin to question
Is the world beyond the mirror perfect?

Right hand is left hand
Sleep walking, sleep deprived black citizens
Conscious and rested?
Father Zero
Mother Nothing
Less of the same; more of their forgotten titles
And names?
Pale shadows, ghosts and memories
For this I melt the mirror to a liquid
And drink the reflection for inspiration

Liquid looking glass refreshed
I see all that came before me – our story
Forgotten covenant to Motherland
I understand now that I am the mystery
      I am the deeper meaning
      Locked inside all mythologies

IN 13 PIECES

<u>Act II: Starry Eyed and Pessi-Mystic</u>

My body, the temple, I stand at my altar
Change through ritual, and alter my image
Electrolyte liquid looking glass candle magic
I sweat oil, lather baldhead
Liquid mirror inside me
I reflect on tangled, dreaded thoughts
Set them ablaze
My sprouted puffs of smoke scream coiled
Natural hair hollers tangled, dreaded – loud
Makes black hippie-gypsy guitar players proud
I beam sunshine all the same

I look through rain that stains
The windowpane
The blurry cage-city sleeps wide awake
No light, even with sunshine
I gaze up into the rainy, gray sky
I wait. The clouds part before my eyes.
Sunshine bows humble, stepping away
The day fades to night
And I ponder, curious, the stars' light
Still configured as is
To the agreement we live under,
And have cosigned with
But I decode a new alignment

The stars' light glows
A soft voice
No shouts. No growls from nighttime animals.
A pleasant purr
Voices sing, softer
A new testament from the stars
Their light croons a conjure
They chant, "You see us stars as we are.
Who are you?"

I think in mind
Song and rhyme
Up to the stars
Little daughters and suns of night

IN 13 PIECES

Act II: Starry Eyed and Pessi-Mystic

"I am Kibaru."

Clear in my name
New daze behold this knight
Time flows through haze
My eyes ponder all in sight
Father Zeroes are too absent for me to find an ally
Even when at side
Heart gone. Ab. Sent. Away.
None in the cage-city can I spy
Comrades of mine, Bwa, Phour, and Cimetiere (we call he, Baron C)
Too many spirit-drinks haze their eye

So, I look for a feminine eye
To see eye-to-eye
Detect like minds
I look for black's harmony
In a proper, pitched queen carved of cosmic ebony
To rule the state of lonely with me – equal by my side

I wander riddled streets for answers
Cracked, broken – leeks like flowers
Power potential pedestrians planted seeds
Cemented – stiff competition
Medusa gazed madam-damsels
Stoned distress signal
Stagnant even in movement
Destiny tells me I have appointments
With four disappointments

The first. I enter her web.
Bow and pay respect to her shadow
Though her memory is pale
And dead
Maybe she will remember
Sun and moon romances, civilized dances
On bare feet against the sands
Covenant to Motherland
Rituals to the stars – diadems, singing jewelry and hymns
Hair locked with secrets

IN 13 PIECES

Act 11: Starry Eyed and Pessi-Mystic

But her hair is perverse
Upside down, she is reversed
Drinker of savior's blood,
Drunk off religion, her spirit stumbles;
She is the Queen of Clubs shaking her hypocrisy
At the rave
She plays chess with her environment
Manipulative – her medicine for ailment of anger, jealousy, and resentment
No apology with how she behaves
Narrow-minded corridor, focused on her gold chains – this slave
Newsmonger, she speaks liquid lies
Poured over her eyes, lathered lens – brain washed and cleansed
Rinse, repeat after pale shadow
Drink deep and become shallow

She is shy to her ancient light of lime
Her heart shrinks violets
Her face masks her fall from grace
Pride and ego hardened chemically
She speaks rough
"You cannot dance with me," she says.
"You remind me of another life too much.
I fell from grace. Leave me falling."
She dances. Volume high as she. Loud deafens already
She passes anger to her son. Lets her daughter inherit her Nothing
As mother
Soft memories. She stays forgetful. I walk away, scathed and burnt.

The sidewalk bends
I'm quiet. I wear an introvert's satchel
Keeping my thoughts close
Ponder wishes and hopes
And there she is, beautiful sable
Behind the wall
"Stand just there!" she shouts to me.
Out of sight, and in reach of queen

"My cup is out of touch
My chalice wants nothing more
Than to own your phallus

IN 13 PIECES

Act II: Starry Eyed and Pessi-Mystic

I can be you times two."

The world is tough enough
She restricts her feminine caress
Gives womanly attire to dress as a man
She wears manhood around her neck
She wears a king's crown
And hates what the mirror reflects
Believes her strength by taking a man's breath
"You cannot be what I already am.
I can be without you. My shadow is a man.
I am man as woman. Redundant and independent."
She wears the suit inherited from the father that abandoned her
She burns her mother's silk, and I move forward

A broom sweeps around me
"Keep clean. Clean. Clean."
Her beauty shines through dust
Sparkling. A diamond, rough.
Her children run wild as their fathers do
She's smothered, life is their life
Sons and daughters, all fathered by zero
"Cook. Clean. Nurture and care for," she repeats
And repeats. Rapid. Repeat.
She looks past me. Eight months, full sails – her belly
Her inner child borne physical
"I will eat and eat until I am full with responsibilities."
She still looks past me. Her age still climbs in the twenties.
"I will be this night's duty, and hand you child for a reward."
Father Zeroes haunt her
Cloak and scowl. Not protective. Competitive.
Lips drip savage. Sharp teeth licked. My image,
Wiry frame, satiates these Father Zeroes violent palate
I will remember her, as the dogs surround her

The next plausible I see
Believes in everything
She wears clouds as a crown
It rains smog in her eyes
Blurry head
Her heart paves her movement

IN 13 PIECES

<u>Act 11: Starry Eyed and Pessi-Mystic</u>

A walk down Honor Road that leads to a fiery place
She fits ancient robes
But she believes everything

Whispers and rumors about her
Pale shadows have saved her
She is a volunteer gravedigger
Burying her rites, ancient rituals of life
Covenant to Motherland, her reflection
Buried proper black definition
Her resentment is her skin
Light is not light enough
Pale shadow can help her birth self-hatred as love

The four I spy
Are multiplied
A house of mirrored
Horrors
I harden to cope
Speak with hope as I speak up to the water bearer and his maiden wife
"Your daughter down here resides
I will kiss her to open proper all the mansions in the sky, far and near."

Pale shadow property
Properly propagates propaganda
Our family tree – leaflets drop in the fall
Gentrification
Gene infiltration
Brain washed
And clean
Mother Nothings are everything they are not supposed to be
Winter comes early – they see blurry
And blizzards cover their hearts
Coldly they speak to tease and baptize me as Don Quixote
Because of how I see reality – see clearly my duty

I say, "Windmills are not giants
Neighbors are not squires
I am dissatisfied with pale shadow liars
And our walk reflects their talk
Am I an idealist

IN 13 PIECES

Act II: Starry Eyed and Pessi-Mystic

To want to strive to find
The ideal brother ally and a black queen at my side?
For neighborhoods to remove the hoods
And for the same to happen in the mind?
To shut the two physical eyes and see thru the centered glow of the trine?

Let the third eye become aligned
A favorable astrological aspect
Two celestial bodies degreed in lessons
One-twenty. Three-Sixty. Cipher our divine.
Should we not look past our enslaved past
Far back where we can find how we are truly defined?
Ye are gods, let me remind
Children of the Most High
You sit there high in a low state
We are that which is most high
We are the blackness of the sky
We are all the stars that inside reside
We are the spiral and the galactic wave
All that is creation, and all that creates
I will no longer be afraid of the heights I will obtain
Even in our imperfection,
We fit the perception of the ideal
Worship no idol, but your ideal.
That will keep
It
Real."

I sneak. Leave the city.
Only the black of night
And the moon's light
My trustworthy companions

From her side of the 'I'
Blinks beauty that has become blind
Moon, full and beaming
The stars, bright and twinkling
Kibaru sees she

That is [her] 'I' in his eye
Broken beauty wrapped in a tattered cloak

IN 13 PIECES

Act II: Starry Eyed and Pessi-Mystic

Hidden in hood, head made of smoke
A faint shadow, a glimmer
Black butterfly crowned in entangled web, silk cocoon
Smothers I, worn like pride
Shame of smoke-choked form, behind I hide
Time spent crying, as the Prince predicted and sang
Over seventeen mountains that stood so high

Clear, I now think – as a knight with sense of duty steps to me
My syntax intact. My voice speaks complete, "Do I spy
A knight here to bring me sunshine?
A perfect black here to deliver light?
O' handsome king
Wiry frame, a slender beam
I am for thee
The perfect queen
Like you, I am broken perfectly, as perfect as fragmented can be
Black as the cosmic sea
I hold my celestial parents in my belly, give birth to my creators
Star by star – I am physical, the water-bearer and the maiden's daughter
They are not as the stars would have you believe
My parents are pale shadow collaborators
My Mother Nothing? A maiden? No. A whore.
My Father Zero? Wisdom water bearer? A carrier of plague and poison.

Understand my truth: *I was shattered for pale shadow enjoyment*
My head, severed, held under black galaxy
Liquid universe, they make me drown within me, heir blocked from lungs,
I barely breathe
And I am barely a breath
So I whisper, voice like a slither, the way I wear my hair
Body plagued with tribulation, time heavy on my shoulders
This is my dis-ease
Legs and spine broken
Thrown to throne
My spine a decaying tree – broken oak – cracked like a parental oath
From base to throat, rotted curse
This lady's malady? Blistered words, syllabic cancers

My Mother Nothing and Father Zero
Play as dancers on a grave

IN 13 PIECES

Act 11: Starry Eyed and Pessi-Mystic

Filled with pieces of me
Thirteen makes me complete
Fixed to me, stars churn to make the moon dust
Split. Up. The compacted, solid celestial sickly satellite
False shine only by stealing the sun's light
Cracked open by Mawu's knife, and up into my sky
Three moons will rise and reside
Restore Motherland's covenant?
Smite my parents, and this action will bring balance
I am in thirteen pieces
Less than half a spirit lingers,
Much missing
From root to head
I would cry for my parents passing
If I had tears left to shed

Cold I sound as the space
Where heart once beat
Rhythmic
A drum in my chest
Dear knight, I task you
Put my parents out of my misery
Release them from my agony
Lay them to rest."

So much missing
Beauty radiates still
Like the hint of sunlight's rise
Behind closed eyes
Her words are alchemy
Trans-muting the sounds
That ground Kibaru in doubt
He. Hears. Her.
His wiry frame believes in its strength
Nimble. Lightsome.
In his words, "This is where
I lay my sword."
At. Her. Feet.
He bows

My ghostly, smoke-trail hand

IN 13 PIECES

Act 11: Starry Eyed and Pessi-Mystic

Commands him to stand
"Up. On two feet. Quickly, quickly!
Where I point,
You strike
And return my thirteen pieces to me.
My Mother Nothing
And my Father Zero
Dissolved of haloes
They don't reside in the sky
They prance in graveyards in the daytime
Behind the cage-city they hide
Bury them where they have buried me
Thirteen of me – my spirit taken physically."

He holds his heart up, heavy in his chest
With heavy task
Beat pumps cautious
His eyes serpentine my dismembered stars
Thirteen missing, black holes, wholly holy missing
Held by my Father Zero and Mother Nothing

I plead, "Restore to me
Thru violent alchemy, if need be,
My thirteen.
Father Zero and Mother Nothing to grave
Bed of roses
Lay my anger to rest
Return to me, my name."

Heart on the horizon, bright with what little light shines
Lithesome warrior
Heavy sword strapped to back
Pivots from this broken maiden
Forward to task

"I pledge, this is for the flesh of you
I will return, task fulfilled
You complete with the rest of you…"

And so, soft footprints light the wasteland

IN 13 PIECES

Act 11: Starry Eyed and Pessi-Mystic

Behind caged city
Lingers dust bowls, billowing sand
Scraps, graveyard grit
Of broken bits and tossed aside lives
Strewn out in crumpled mounds
Ash by the pound
A perfect place for Nothing and Zero to hide

One hand carries weapon for task
Dragging edge, sword tip kisses ground
Sketches scratched waves of snakes
I walk against the tide of walking dead
Who walk aimless and only fed conscious costumes
So cage city mouths can consume them, dubwana-burdened
They are nameless but numbered
Soft pale shadow voices sound like thunder to them
They are at command – their minds covered in forgetful snow
Memories melt
They are heavy wave, wind and flow
Determined to stop my go

I have memorized my stars
Jump
Up! Highest mound and look down
See where my stars hide and constellate
My Heru eye blurs reality blind
Static haze twists my gaze gray
While marks glitter yellow with intent

Poison-bearer and his madam wife,
Crippler of daughter's life
Down – I creep to kill, closer
Not deterred in deed
Determined in this need – strength heavy
As heavy sword dampens its weight
Two lives to take
This day, noted in memory
A day long remembered
A Mother Nothing and Father Zero
Will fall, accordingly

IN 13 PIECES

Act II: Starry Eyed and Pessi-Mystic

Damaged daughter
Inspired
I grip sword
Leap
Off beat
Madam wife hears my silent creep
Sickle, beaming blade
Swipes and shields my fatal strike
Sharpened ice, thrown like knives, cut air
My nimble frame – supreme, zig zags
Arm, leg, leg, arm, head
Sharpened ice misses
Sickle, beaming blade, makes raids on my person
Her Mother Nothing is something in a fight
Her Father Zero turns the rain into knives
Duck. Dodge. Weave.
Sickle, blade a beam
Swipe! And swish!
Each dodge, barely a miss
Move and twist, heavy sword rips air
Blades clink and clash, eyes locked in stare – mouths an arrogant sneer
Father Zero turns rain to ash
I inhale smoke
Cough – concentration broke
Mother Nothing, anger at her command
Cuts a snake on my arm
Bleed, drip – heavy sword knocked from grip
I, kicked back to the wasteland

Constellations stand above me
Physical mythology
Come to life, childhood stories that don't live up
To their view up close – Images broken

I yell to them, "You are lies!
Criminals! Breaking your daughter, your crime!
I am under her will to kill you.
Her candle, bright and broken,
You left her heart frozen, a void closed wide open
And love cannot fill it
You are harlot and buffoon. Water-bearer and maiden wife.

IN 13 PIECES

Act 11: Starry Eyed and Pessi-Mystic

You are poison and strife
Dead to me. Dead to rites. Kill me?
I'll resurrect, pursue you, and still end your life."

Eyes pregnant with perplexity
These black figures of mythology
Look back to me
Rain turns to ash, clouds my eyes, and
Lulls me to sleep…

…I awake, days gone in sleepy haze
I am still in defeat
Wrapped. Head to feet.
Mother Nothing next to me
Gentle hand rubs my brow
Father [now] Nothing stands over me

A room. A candle. Shadows dancing.
Father Nothing kneels and speaks,
"We are surrounded by lies at all times
The truth takes root in the ground 'round here
Our little shy fire has never burned so bright,
Signaling desperate knights
Our Sirene screamed to you a task to dispatch us
To her, this is justice."

Mother Nothing speaks through tears,
"We broke her, our daughter
Cruelty's kindness
Governor Tubal ordered
Death and slaughter
Of new children with old souls
Nu ancients
Mother Nothings and Father Zeroes
Obeyed, preyed on their own children
Mind pale like the shadows, perverted from lynched lessons
Black generation after generation, black did as told
Bold, we broke her to spare her
Removed her alchemy, performing mystic surgery
We hid her properties, buried

IN 13 PIECES

<u>Act II: Starry Eyed and Pessi-Mystic</u>

Her thirteen pieces were found
Cursed and bound to the walking titans
Governor Tubal, King of Golems,
Lord over the caged city
He manipulates all that is black
Through the thirteen pieces of our daughter's beauty."

Her Father Zero voices,
"You have allies
Young, but broken
Great spirits reside inside them
Your parents too did this to you
Wiry and weak
Words frail when you speak
All for a purpose
To hide you from the giants with a sky's view
To spot the children that will plot their crumble.
You misfits today will be messiahs tomorrow."

Wraps dissolve. Heavy sword
Falls against me
Father Nothing takes it from me
Placed in the fires of a forge
Hefty puff dissolves the heft of the sword
Carved from its dark matter, dipped in dark energy
An invisible influence and the unseen, on shadow movement of the cosmos
Shaken and stirred
Straight and sharp, there comes born from heavy sword, a black sun spear
Dear to any warrior's heart

Mother Nothing blesses me with the weapon
"You will restore her
Sirene, our daughter
The Shades be your allies – no one can conjure and cast shade against you
You were born from cosmic shadow, and rest in flesh made of dusk
Black galactic dust is your breath – add their shade to your house
As decoration – make black declaration
Align and fight against pale shadows' strife
Bring down the thirteen towers
That corrupt my daughter's power
Our ruse is no excuse on how we as mothers and fathers

IN 13 PIECES

Act II: Starry Eyed and Pessi-Mystic

Have treated you
Our spirits are solid
As Mother Wisdom
And Father Knowledge,
We are the last of the last of a failed generation
We, the last, give you task to restore the head
To the Great Mother, our daughter
Medu-Sa
Motherland covenant, give us redemption."

Her mother and father dissolve, but stay in thought
I stare at spear
Weapon as slender and nimble as I
I hold my soul
Out—into the world
Into caged city
I Heru eye view tattered buildings
I view my Mother Wisdom and Father Knowledge
Disguised in bondage

They are new to me
Complex in their villainous heroics
Stoic, wooden performance
Disserves applause
But there are still scars on the children
Can I forgive them?

Speaking aloud to the sun and stars behind the clouds,
"A generation failed because of passed down failure
Few spark new labors, disguised as despair
Parents wear masks to shadow their tasks
Open world curtain, trotted out on global stage
Whispered love, hidden under cloud of loud shouts
Lips sink in watered-down, mouthed curses
Mother Wisdom? Father Knowledge repent, cry verses behind closed doors
Re-verse-us—all of this
Sister's hand to brother's neck
Mother and father in distressed and unnamed
Ghettoes swallow themselves—Canaan-ballistics recovered at the scene
Self-inflicted gunshot wounds
Neighborhoods dressed in hoods, come burning crosses

IN 13 PIECES

<u>Act 11: Starry Eyed and Pessi-Mystic</u>

Orders taken from pale shadow bosses
We are now the hood wearers and cross bearers

I am disgusted with disguises
But now I seek alliances
To dissolve pale shadow systems
Hunt devil swine's pork barrel politics."

I flee city, and watch from afar, a ghostly black beauty
Her subtle fire
Barely burning
Ducking
Low
To escape the attention
Of her own light
A subtle fire that never burned so bright
Cloaked in smoke to hide her beautiful shade of the night
It only makes her glimmer shine
What marvelous beauty
Burns bright there once whole again?
This wondrous, black, feminine flame as she be – subtle and broken

IN 13 PIECES

Act III: Shadow Band

There tiptoes my knight
Clad in confidence
Heavy sword no more
He plays new instrument
Spear dipped in sun and the galactic core
Hands clean
Deed of judgment washed away
Ducking in shadow
He whispers to me when he says,

"Your Mother is nothing
Your Father, reduced to zero
That existence among the dead."

Carefully said
To hide what I don't spy
No thirteen pieces of me
Collected

Shy Fire Sirene:
"Where am I? The thirteen of me?
The pieces of my feminine degrees?
Anxious to kiss myself as grand conjure and wish
To be black whole
And absorb all light matter around me."

From shadow my knight parades, spear gripped
He holds his masculinity, flexing cocksureness – conviction
My knight, black warrior at my command
At the ready, at my attention
Stiff and still he makes my waters run
Auto-somatic – my nature does what's natural
Cloaked in smoke, but not muted
My eyes trace him as he traces our circumference, pointing
My ears open. His voice. Penetrates with bass.

"All around, strong and invisible – like winds and hurricanes
Stomp and step, not seventeen mountains, but thirteen towers
Your pieces of beauty power them
Possessing giants that possess them
Four stand at the four corners, split your air

IN 13 PIECES

<u>Act III: Shadow Band</u>

They breathe your breath and live by you
Nine more seduce, curse and scar
They keep the fog rolling, using nature to control our nature."

I beam a ghostly grin
"This is where
My whole body begins
Thirteen giants
You will slay them
Bring my pieces to me

Oh, but let us ponder this equation, matter-mathematical
The towers step quiet

They whirl invisible
You need proper lens to sight them
Proper speech
To cite them
I know of a woman with blessings
A great old one, wise woman with no eyes that can help you see
She comforted me. Made my separated, physical body unseen.
Mama Gran
We'll drink rum for her, cast cowrie shells – light a white candle."

I dance standing still
My inner electric lady snakes up my spine
Maîtresse Hounon'gon pupils my sight
I blink and light our campfire
Inner electric says we cannot chant without choir

My knight answers
"I will have thirteen allies by my side."

Smoke trails my words
"Mama Gran, great old one
Has and loves herself a great old man
Captain, conjuror of shades
Debas, he will recruit your army
Plucked from whatchu know no-goods and knaves
No problems, but 99 allies will number your shades."

IN 13 PIECES

Act III: Shadow Band

Dancing nude in the naked night
Pole star points
Gives my black warrior sight
Pole star sings
"This is where Mama Gran resides
Follow, follow
And when the sky turns bright and blue
You will still see me, pointing. Rest for the night.
I will meet you on the morrow."

I blow my smoke over him
A blanket and bed
To sleep
I lean back on cracked throne
A faint shade of fog

Soon whole with the thirteen pieces of me
A song from my body
Hums happy

Kibaru wakes and shakes of smoke's narration
The story through his eye, and at his attention

To my eye
Against the blue of the day's sky
There still shines
The light of the pole star
"Follow, follow," the star beckons bright
I track the point of light
Traipse through lands covered in sand
And snows
Fire, winds, and cold
To another forest lush and flushed with green
This is where pole star's light taps – atop quaint cottage – modest housing
Mama Gran in kitchen, stirring blessings
Her man, Captain Debas, outside
His imagination at his command to deliver him to battles passed
Glory days once had
He sees me
"A fool on an errand, a warrior at task
I am familiar with the math of you

IN 13 PIECES

Act III: Shadow Band

The sum of you
I recognize your attire, because I once wore those boots."

I spear the ground
Hand out, and declare peace
"Venerable spirit, Grand Captain, I am Zin Kibaru
I seek to see unnatural thunders
That step in silence, walking unseen
Golems, solid columns upholding
Chains scripted as laws
I come in the name of Motherland's broken covenant
Turned ghostly beauty
Her radiant thirteen pieces power mobile, invisible towers."

I see the glory days in his eyes
My task is a present of the past, a pleasant surprise
Captain Debas claps, his reactions put aside
"You serve mythologies, legends
Your golems, giants and towers are tall stories. We've all looked to decode
Ancient odes
To find prophecies and judgment days

Locked inside long-lived lessons – let them go
Governor Tubal's laws are the way
Bring your beautiful ghost here to stay
Live with a smile that you have escaped the city's cage."

Mama Gran steps outside, eyes in the lines of her hand
She reminds her man
That he too once wore and walked in the shoes
Of a younger man anxious for command
Anxious to dissolve the fog from the land
"You remember the chase you gave to mythology?
The search for the grand key to unlock the caged city?
How strong my man you did so believe
Recall that memory. Recall your fire to set the cosmic black free." To me she asks,
"What do you wish your eyes to see?"

"Thirteen giants," I plead. "In the distance,
Their unseen presence curses me
Constructed not of love, but blasphemy

IN 13 PIECES

Act III: Shadow Band

They move with the energy of a black queen's thirteen pieces
She sits broken on broken throne
Her tone resonates with skipped beats that pump the heart
Of femininity that misspeaks, walks of feminine nzambi – caged in caged city
Her true image is shattered, but there glows great beauty in this shade
A shy fire bright enough to cower the sun
She is Motherland's covenant given flesh
But she chokes on her own visitant smoke
I am tasked to restore proper heir to her
To give her life and breath."

Glory days haze Captain Debas
Possessed, he dances
"I'll prance, praise and sing, if I can raise and lead an army
You will have allies in great numbers and might
Mama Gran, give this boy sight
Let giants' blood run when we strike."

Mama Gran's grin closes my eyes
She breathes stardust on forehead
Taps blessed watered fingertip
Three times
Light shines
Open
No longer blind to giants roaming
All in my sight can see
Four stand still, cornered – possessed by the four breaths
Taken in from my shy fire's chest
A continent, Alcyrion, a land living off the keys
Of the caged chained in the city
The four, most massive of the thirteen
But their height shrinks as I blink

Captain Debas shouts, "An army! An army of shades!
We'll pull from the drunkards, those in a haze
The misfits will be our messiahs today."

We journey back to the cage
To gather
Sneaking through devil swine patrols
Governor Tubal's soldiers and troops

IN 13 PIECES

Act III: Shadow Band

There, sprawled in alley, are men and women drunk with fermented dreams
Age young to old
The life of nightmares
They rest their souls
Captain Debas culls the shadows of their brighter selves
Souls stand upright, we leave the bodies – shades and spirits in our army
I see three comrades stumbling
I pluck them like fruit, these recruits
Bwa, Phour, and Baron C
Allies to me
They now see clearly, Mama Gran clears their heads

We are a disturbance felt
Healed scars among the welts
First lady, Queen Malady
Governor Tubal's wife and wicked knife
She cuts through city streets
Devil swine flanked
She screams, "Shades have been pulled up,
And souls stand upright
Like windows, pristine and exposed, they beam bright with light."

Mama Gran has stitched ether
Making gossamer fabric
Knits cloaks
She covers the sleeping bodies recruited as shades
Fabric so unseen that all it covers becomes unseen
Mama Gran stays to keep safe unseen bodies
She on the streets a disguised hag in rags

Captain and I, with allies and shaded army – we leave the city
On waters rough, pale shadow pirate infested
We sink ships, recover provisions and weapons
Travel to Alcyrion
The land expands and expands and expands
Grand to giants
We are red ants, moving, and with claws wide open
But there are wulvz here, created creatures
Twisted and feral
Bristly bodies seep fog to creep, and howl as our army sweeps
Devil swine occupied, red areas restricted

IN 13 PIECES

Act III: Shadow Band

There are wild animals in this land – some come from the caged city

Phour points our path
Bwa carves weapons from earth and ash, discard pirated weapon stash
Baron C curses the air against our enemies' breath
We exhale revolution while they inhale death
The fog, like a mouth, opens
Wulvz and devil swine assail and beset
My spear whet for blood – wet with blood

Shades and Captain help wulvz and swine breathe Baron C's conjure
Choked

Fate teases me
Plays chess with me
Guides my spear toss
Taps on devil swine's foot, gives him rhythm
He sidesteps, dives into fog
Spear cuts and cuts and cuts and cuts air
Sliver, slice – tears into giant's flesh
Small as a pin
Sun and galaxy inner-g injected within

Thunder shivers when giant hollers
Single scream billows and rumbles
Mountains tumble
Earth quakes
Shakes the battleground
Tower bends knee to ground

Cry wounded! Giant summons brothers.
The corners of the land close in

I run, jump, pounce
Hand around spear
Dislodge – stab – climb by prick and pierce, up and up
Spear penetrated, sun and cosmic touched
Rough screams ripple the air
Ascend, giant's legs bend
Stab spine at root – pierce, wind up to crown
Atop head, I stab down

IN 13 PIECES

Act III: Shadow Band

Planted flag of victory
Screams cease
The breath of a queen escapes silently
Floats as pleasant wind, gentle and free
Breath swirls in place as one, waiting for three
Her siblings

Spear free. I, waiting.
A corner tower moves closer
Its brother falling
I run, pounce
I up as giant down
Dead tower turns to dust
Straight, dive – glide through the air
Stab eye and blind second giant's stare
Hold tight as thunders might escapes in wounded roar
Up on spear – perched, planted as plank
I look into blind eye, let the winds of his screaming cry
Die
Before final strike
Spear wrest from eye, as I pounce and glide over head
Slide down spine, turn and rest spear into giant's neck
      There escapes Sirene's second breath
Twirling around the first it goes, entangled – twist
Giant tumbles to death, bursts to dust, body thundered to the ground
I am grounded, spear in grip
Battle sounds of wulvz and devil swine, earth drenched in blood and grime

War stains
Purpose remains
Captain and shades control the rain of battle
Small army floods the field

Two giants infringe
Toss fire to singe the battlefield
Shades dive and sway
Move away from attacks
Bwa at my back
Phour gives a path
Devil swine and wulvz close in with pack
Baron C speaks death as incant

IN 13 PIECES

Act III: Shadow Band

Captain commands shades with battle plans and the warrior's way
Wulvz and devil swine rush with fangs, boomsticks and blades
Giants attempt to crush our numbers
I pounce, leave sound behind

At the foot of the giant
I stand tall
Look up and up
And underneath this mass of beast, I understand
It is nothing more than puffs of smoke, mirrors and tricks
Size enormous, this tower cowers
I stab, it kicks – swings hand to swat and hit
Miss, and I pierce its palm – read lifeline and know
Its time has come – with final strike, its oppression undone
Remove spear from where poked – jump, pivot and float
Airstrike, thrust to throat
This giant doesn't get to scream – no release, except
         For breath number three – somewhere a queen is no longer weeping
But waiting, anticipating breath trapped by these tall spires
Inhale. Inspired.

Giant falls forward – backflip
I retract with spear
Push
Off
Soar through air like the lark
Transpierce the fourth giant's heart
No scream coughed, expressive or resistant
Death is instant

Breath four adds to the core
Her cosmic winds are sovereign again
Gliding high
They first assist me
Gently down, to battle-worn ground
Captain and shades have chased away
Devil swine and wulvz
Land of giants and little light
Shines bright – stolen sun in land
As we have taken the day

IN 13 PIECES

Act III: Shadow Band

The cosmic winds, once trapped within giants,
Find their way to ghostly, smoky broken black queen

Shy Fire Sirene:
"Do. I. Dream?
This proper breath I breathe?
With this fresh heir
I can now speak whole,
Black complete, back to the days of when my covenant was complete
Ancient syllables tap like feet
The cosmic winds of me
I taste laughter and every word I speak
Honey and rose are the flavors I sing
My melodies in the ol' skool company
The hymns of my hers
The suns of my daughters
The black, cosmic community
Ear up! Hear me! Enemies, listen and be frightened.
Do not be fooled by my sweet verses
To you I growl and spit rough curses
The brightest darkness
Warriors made of promise have slain four of your most monstrous
The nine that remain? Disregard their height.
To my black men, and the shaded feminine warriors that walk with them
To the Captain, his shades and my knight – warriors made of Motherland covenant
Walk as giants over that distant continent."

Narration flips back to her
Someone hears her sound

Queen Malady stares me down
As I dream inside her dream
And she dreams inside my dream
She stares me down
We stare each other down
And she scowls, frowns
Images behind closed eyes, at rest
With renewed breath
When the sun goes down

IN 13 PIECES

Act III: Shadow Band

Queen Malady taunts me,
"All the shades of nature cannot hide you
I will find you
And cut the breath that fires you anew
I will use your breath to burn your natural retreat
You, child, will never be thirteen complete

We run on the weakness of warriors
And the heads of you Medusas – Medu Sa
Medicinal mothers of the sea, birthing glorious family trees
Whose leaves we've worked so hard to cut
Grown and sewn, woven – weaved, roped up
Hung from branches anointed and sacred
Used to scare the population of you
Hang you from your family tree
Bodies swung, kissed by the sun
Swinging dead, hating the roots they come from
You think we'll let you nick and prick
The trick we've planted, tilled, plucked and pulled?"

I open eyes
Ritual in my throat
Pitch perfect
Harmonize cosmic notes
I sing to the sky
The morning blue opens,
Just a little
Small circle of pitch perfect black of night

My four breaths
Up to heaven
And pole star listens to my song
"Call Mama Gran to me," I sing.
"Call her to me, again I must be unseen."

Pole star spins my voice
To caged city
Spin and spin on the wind
The breeze sings my warning for Mama Gran to hear
Voice of me dancing in her ear
Faint

IN 13 PIECES

Act III: Shadow Band

The garble of devil swine rhythms
Boots' drivel march – march – march
Onto city streets
At command of Governor Tubal
And Queen Malady
Searching for glimpses of me

My warning song
In Mama Gran's ear
Volume up, she hears me

"From the city streets!" Queen Malady screams.
"Beyond this caged city,
A ghost child – she possessed by the devil's covenant
From the untamed darkness of an abusive, abandoning
Motherland."

Mama Gran
Cloaked, unseen
Slips past devil swine march
Glides on gale
And leaves caged city
Knit and stich
Stich and knit
Unseen cloth, fabric fabricated
Conjured cloth
Made as cloak
Thrown over she and I
Masked unseen, we hide

And on the horizon
March devil swine
They come through the dense trees
Like a breeze
They flood the forest
Sweeping
They flow past Mama Gran and me
We are silent, tucked comfortable in our invisibility

Enter Queen Malady
Beautifully robed in disease and intention

IN 13 PIECES

Act III: Shadow Band

Determined to see what she cannot see
But she believes
I'm here
She creeps around our cloaked unseen
Grin bright as she begins speaking,

"I am a covenant too
My husband scripts laws on my back
And I uphold them
My smile regulates, and I seduce
I bring shaded men to forget you
I devise makeup dipped in your thirteen pieces
To walk as you
I was born to keep you broken
Shaded men frozen, stoned in gaze so that I
Might wear the crown of Medusa
Your writhing wisdom slithering atop my head."

She kneels – her back to me
But her imagination
Accords her a desired effect
I am there to her
Fashioned to be her reflection in a mirror

At the call of her husband
She leaves
The devil swine persist
To search for us, Mama Gran and me
Out in the open – unseen

Across an ocean of muddy waters and acrid mist
Shades warriors raise up their fists
The might of five fingers tight raise the murky veil
Continuing Zin Kibaru's view of this tale

Spear, swords and arrows
Point the way for determined eyes
Phour prongs position,
There, the horizon, our port of call
We believe giants cower behind mountains
Cover themselves with earth and snow

IN 13 PIECES

<u>Act III: Shadow Band</u>

But plots and tricks
Tickle their ears on purred wisps of speech

Confidence allows us to walk tall
But through this massive land
We creep
Crawl through fog
The night plays a haunting song
Wulvz snarl in the distance
And the wind accompanies the feral chorus
There spirals and stirs the sound of the gales' hulking bays
Trying to keep our courage at bay

Devil swine patrol
Boast boots
Marching
Over marsh and mud
Their rhythm and stomp
A gravelly choir of subjugation

But tyranny's song fades
Mutes
As we hear singing a beguiling beauty bouncing as voluptuous ballads
Prancing vocabulary ballet dances in our ears
Hymned and hummed
Honey-sweet voices lick us
Attentive
Bass moistens feminine shades
Vibrating drums on their thighs
While the masculine shades of our army
Hold smiles filled dreamy, eyes just as sleepy
But willing
Listening to the alluring swivels of trills
We men
Stand
Erect
Stiff and at attention
We walk with an aimless gaze

We see
The perfect

IN 13 PIECES

Act III: Shadow Band

Giants
Two voices intertwined
From single throat
Janus-gendered voice, rendered notes
Of man and woman
As the second dances like a pendulum
Back and forth
Feminine shades see a man chiseled from desire
We men see a woman, dripping with the ocean
Bewitched and bothered – enticed

Captain Debas wears the veil
Of Mama Gran on his eyes
Her voice in his ears
He is still – unmoved by dance and song
We go by, go by, go by, and go by him – 20 times 10
Shaded line, long

Sword to sky
Captain Debas yells high,
"Sorcery, tricks! Voice and sight
Negate growls that seethe through fog
And night
And we believe the giants sweet
Cover your eyes!
Listen close – hear that their rhythms are off beat, off key
Motherland's covenant, close to your heart and eyes, keep."

I blink
Exhale illusion
And rub the fool's deception and dream from my eyes
Three allies and I
Few shades see the giants' true

Synthetic solids, moldable
Grafted incant
They continue to prance closer
Spell cast
Huldra, the body
Sirin, the voice
They throw picture shows that stroke

IN 13 PIECES

<u>Act III: Shadow Band</u>

Black shades' egos

Lull to sleep with hallowed scandals
Bojangles, unchained conjured with rattled bangles
Untrue to fact, inexact love-crafted in this country
Entitled to tell Our Story
Fallacious covens fellating once conscious watch-men
Now entranced
As are the shaded women warriors
Cunning cunilingus from all of this – transfixed, spellbound
Some shades wave white flags, surrendering to sight and sound
Believing their enemies validate them proper
As Huldra and Sirin
Cast images of Legba and Samedi
For corporate cooperation
Some of our shades are fooled
Draw closer and closer – consciousness pushed away far
Some shades speak in happy dream, *They know who we are…*

Large eye smiles, beholder of shades
Titan Thunlibiri creeps from behind the fog
Flare, flash and streak – eye yells a beam
Many shades turn to ash as seduction reveals itself
A trap
Ensnared
Thunlibiri's single eye glares
Yells bright flash
Motherland covenant, these conscious shades failed to remember
Turned to cinder and embers
Bodies burned up, erased
Remaining shades shake awake!

Huldra and Sirin
Dance and chant
Swivel and sing
Frolic in front of smoke turned screen
To give the make of shade and shape
Their rhythms quicken, and they lull more true shades back to sleep
Flash to ash bursts Thunlibiri's beam
They give us speeding race cards to play
To charge a ploy, a gambit – and they react because we're conscious of this

IN 13 PIECES

Act III: Shadow Band

Chance to chants – a strategy laced with incant
Captain Debas commands
And we follow order
Baron C conjures fog, thick around the ears
Bwa blinds our eyes with leaves
Phour lights bright our third eyes' sights
We see clear, and we hear nothing sweet

Phour throws a cosmic cloud, washing Thunlibiri's eye
The titan screams, writhes
Dark matter water stings his sight
Time becomes our unreliable ally as the giant goes blind

By our will, we move closer and closer
Bwa sings nature into the air
        where Sirin breathes
Her mouth sprouts thistle, crabgrass, and pigweed
"Soon, she will too push up daisies!"
For now, silence becomes her song

Baron C binds Huldra's feet and wrists
With rope fabricated from cosmic mist
Huldra's fluid dance becomes stiff
Closer we drift
To giants high and tall, approximate feet of twenty-six
Crippled, these towers cannot signal a cry
        to devil swine or wulvz reinforcements

Captain Debas
Stabs the giant Huldra
Legs bleed as she screams
Falls to knees
Uncompromised shades helix-twist around her frame
Fighting and stabbing

Bwa's vegetation fills Sirin's mouth
And throat
Until she chokes
Now I pounce for fatal stab
Black sun spear through the back
Spring through fog, shove and press

IN 13 PIECES

Act III: Shadow Band

Spear through Huldra's chest
Lunge high
Pierce Thunlibiri's stolen third eye
And kill its physical form

Three giants. Pimp and prostitutes.
They explode. Silent.
Essence, three of thirteen
Abused body, voice, and eye
Arc across the sky
And find, unlike patrol of devil swine,
True Sirene
Her constellation reveals three more stars
All that surrounds her is her sky, her kingdom

She now speaks in seasons
Her body restored
Though missing head
And hands
But under unseen fabric, still unseen
She stands
Up from broken throne
With proper tone she wants to speak
But even a whisper would be a scream

Her voice, it is hard for her to swallow
When introduced to surprise
By the glow of her third eye
Her parents, and their true names
Come into sight
She even fights
Against anger for me, for what I did not keep
There stands evidence of my broken promise

Her thoughts think:
**I narrow third eye
But struggle with truth
Of what I see
Blending all I have known
And come to believe
My rotted family tree

IN 13 PIECES

Act III: Shadow Band

Dissected of heart
My Father Zero and Mother Nothing
Cruel images fade and shrink
But here stands benevolence

Knowing I'm unable to speak
They step to me
And confess their cruelty
A blessing of their affection

It will take time
Before they earn my smile
But lips quiver in reflex
When my Mother Wisdom
And Father Knowledge
Speak my proper name
"Ashaba," they say. "Ashaba-Sirene."
I flicker a smile, but hold stern emotion in place
I am whole
Without thirteen
All comes together better than I had dreamed
Six towers remain
My sentiments unchanged

To my black men, and the shaded feminine warriors that walk with them
To the Captain, his shades and my knight
Continue to disregard these towers' height
My warriors made of Motherland covenant
*Walk as giants over that distant continent***
We continue, to be
For her thirteen

Press pause
Press play
We press forward
All eyes opened
(we see more than fog)
Ears attentive
(we hear more than the taunts of devil swine and wulvz)
We hear the shackles worn by nature in this land
She, subjugated

IN 13 PIECES

Act III: Shadow Band

The fog leaves us in the open
Closed off from camouflage
We wish for a veil of shadows to blanket our army of shades

Mock! Mock! Laughter buzzes our ears.
A chorus of slithering sounds is near
Hiss. Rattle. – His babble of twisted knowledge cackles
And footsteps rumble earth
We file, deep in ranks – eyes everywhere see fog

Grand hands lift gossamer gauze
Wipes away the gray day
The sun cowers at the horizon
Where pours the snarl and charge of wulvz
And devil swine

We break line
Open like lotus
Blossom war and rage
On this familiar stage

A rampage of unalike in kind
Watch our eyes dine on battle
We dive into waves of uncaged ferocity
Giants dance away
A fleet of body and blood left in our wake

Grand hands that part the fog
Point to streams of blood from leg
To arm
And motion for our earth to open
And blood to flow, deep as the ocean
The power to heal wielded backwards

Shades bleed light
The giant Ache points
Joints quake
Shades breathe lighter
He points and scripts fate
Fills hands with lines of discord
And an off-key song, held in the palm

IN 13 PIECES

Act III: Shadow Band

Footsteps bellow, enter Sedua
A giant crowned with knowledge
He stands proud with crown atop the head
Thirteen points point straight like pitchforks and devil's horns
They dissolve to form the body of snakes
Writhing with hiss, fangs curved from their lips
They slither backwards – stop progressive thought
Writhe and writhe and writhe from the scalp
And around the heads of shades
Thought is squeezed and policed
Subdued to obey – this giant froths the venom of his snakes

Vubrawl, her spine an electric whip
From bottom, to top of tip
Lashes turn shades to ashes
Her screams gargle the air
Spinal whip tears through her allies, unaware
Wild, erratic attacks

Baron C opens earth
And speaks
"If graves you make
Of earth and lakes
Then drown and drip
Toes that tip, stumble and trip."

Earth sinks
A bowl to cup
Trip up,
The one to fall is Ache
We shades find relief from his point and quake
And the opening wider of our wounds
Captain Debas, shades and I
Continue battle through the rattle of our bones

Phour gives
And Phour gets
Wrapping the snakes
That are wrapped against heads
Into cosmic nets

IN 13 PIECES

Act III: Shadow Band

Tight! Tight! Tighter!
Cutting their breaths

I pounce
Slam spear down
Two snakes are cut to ground
An army more
Slithers from Sedua's head to the earth's
      Blood drenched floor
Entangled in the waltz of war, snakes
Overrun shades
And the day goes gray again with fog
My spear punctures, sprays red haze
Invigorates the shades
Captain Debas commands a raid
His words recruit allies three,
Bwa, Cimetiere, and Phour – a reiterated triad of soldiers
"Mud against wounds – and that giant cannot harm
Phour, confuse his eye to guide his hands against
      The electric whip and spine."

Soaked earth kisses our scars
And hugs tight
Deflects hexing point of finger
That would widen wounds
Phour moves in rush, tosses stardust into his hands
And crowns the eyes of Ache
The giant quakes – seeing stars
Fingers aimed, hexes scratch and scathe Vubrawl
Her spinal whip lashes strike back
Smack and crack against Ache

Captain Debas commands,
"Brother-C, bury deep and create pit
Let this giant's snakes sit there."

Ground opens deep
Snakes seep,
Their serpentine slither, slithers into the ground
Baron C's grip of earth
Drawn back like bow – let go

IN 13 PIECES

Act III: Shadow Band

Let loose a wave of snakes into the air
Earth follows them there, a wave of mud and rot
Drops Vubrawl's lightning vibration
And there my cue, my indication to strike

I pounce
Up into air
Plummet
Tumble underneath
Stab stomach
Ache bleeds his last breaths
His ashes drip
And the power in his hands
Is wrestled from his fingertips
The true healing touch for Motherland's covenant
Count. Down. One more of her thirteen restored.

Sedua's crown conjures snakes to the earth floor
He commands with roar
Wind kicks up the ground
Sedua makes fatal step on the burial
Of Vubrawl's mound
The lightning whip—wild lashes grip his neck

Swift move
I stab Vubrawl at her root
Retract – stab up into roof of mouth
Agony muted, no screams aloud
Retract – spear point crash through heart
Puff to ash – spinal energies returned to Sirene

Pounce – up
High above the wave of snakes
I strike down
Spear point through Sedua's crown
Eyes roll up
Body to dust
My feet slam against the earthen bed
Twisted, locked natural snakes
Return to their natural state

IN 13 PIECES

Act III: Shadow Band

Draped down, the lioness' mane and crown
Wisdom upon her head

We pause to breathe
At ease
This battle has reduced us
We are just us
An army of twenty, myself adds one
We hear wulvz whimper, humbled
They are tamed and domesticated dogs
As the winds growl through us
We carry the spirit of Anubis
Devil swine are the black pigs sacrificed to Marinette
We hear the fear pounding – a coward's heart in their chest
Assured, be rest – this army of black shades be conscious
We are the coming storm warned about

Scatter heat and cold, heavy rain and snow
– we are the climate
Our snarl mutes wulvz and the devil swine's finest
We shout to the last,
"Come out! – Let us battle, you remaining giants…"

IN 13 PIECES

Act IV: Whole, With All 13

I watch on wheeled throne
I am a garden of woman, watered and flowing
Alive, I as 1000 flowers stand at less than half broken
But there walks open the finality of me — the last three of my twisted 13
There. Walks. Fabrique. Composed of cosmic unseen
Shaped with femininity — caliginous timber,
Dark matter — haloed. On two feet. Dangerous giant.
She unmakes her adversaries, stomping with a nimbus mouth
Devouring flesh and spirit into nonexistence
She spatters warrior shades to starry matter, cosmic dust cloud disintegrates
Spirit through her is unmade — death through her
No soul in Heaven bathes

Only few warrior shades remain
And my handsome Kibaru, slender and strong
His captain
And three allies
Victory for them in reach, stretched long
Wulvz bear fangs, growl and help claim
Lives of warrior shades
Blood cloaked shields and blades
Devil swine pour from the mouths of caves
And a haze of red defines a once blanched soil

There beats and pumps
An emerald colossus that thumps
Four chambers of his person, defiled and ruined
When Yollj stomps, the sound of hate reverberates
Shades' discipline dwindles down
They long for system structure, dependent
Their spirit and love for freedom chained
Wulvz and devil swine cut them loose from life
Their screams like steam
Pump, pump through Yollj's four chamber person
He lives and breathes off the slaying of shades
And to us, the effect is monstrous

Allies and my handsome Kibaru, they fight each other
Their weapons and conjures smother — brother against allied brother
Captain Debas drowns in fright
Castrated — separated from courage

IN 13 PIECES

Act IV: Whole, With All 13

Behold a third behemoth
My mind trapped within it
Ill effect, grim scene rewarded atrophy
Chapeldamn
He is beyond reason, sick with demons – possessed
His breath fills the air
His demons seep into my warriors' hair and flesh
They are dressed in the cloth of devil swine
They mime the un-alike's hate

Wulvz and devil swine pause, take in
Giggle – laughing
The sight of my beloved, his shaded warriors, allies and captain
One another, fighting, not quite yet killing
But the red stained hands of shades and my Kibaru draws closer
Shades of ally blood
The last three of the thirteen have taken the day

And so cries my third eye
In the blink of the sky
It appears all the black-lighted stars that shine
Have been prophesized to die
Mama Gran and Mother Wisdom sing a new cosmic tune
Their voices glitter many colors, and they stitch
A spiritual
"Glory! Glory! Glory! Glory! Tell me how your
Story, story, story will conclude.
What will be the question of you?
How will you remember this moment
And what you did, and will do?"

The morning sun shines on me a smile
Through haze of a new day
I return her favor,
Inhaling spirit, I, inspired, count my treasured belongings
What do I have with me
What of the thirteen are now me?
My 4 cosmic winds bless my voice
My body, my spine, and the wisdom writhing as my hair
My hands, my body—fine—my third eye

IN 13 PIECES

Act IV: Whole, With All 13

I sing praises to me
In harmony with Mama Gran
And Mother Wisdom
And with them, what is there as me
Stands
Ten of my 13 at my command
The crescendo of song gleams
My body swirls into an air stream
Double-helix flight, swirling air covered in light
Arcing across the sky, over the conflict and strife
I land on the battlefield
Physical body wrapped in shield
Nine of me split into groups of three and distract the conflict
       And trick
Spoken silent from these giants' lips

My warriors exhale confusion
Handsome Kibaru blinks rapid
Thinking my presence
A rabid illusion
But I prove to him, with kiss and whisper
I am here

While my nine as three sets of 3
Penetrate the last of the colossal thirteen
Decoding weakness of structure
Pinpointing crucial spots to rupture
Pressure points to anoint with
Black sun spear tip

Wulvz and devil swine come back to life
Captain Debas commands remaining shades
Act as shield and blade against them
While allies three, on bended knee speak triangular symmetry
Combined conjure to keep at bay the giants' tricks
Nine attributes return to me, ten as whole as can be
With my body

Zin Kibaru:
I sing mathematically

IN 13 PIECES

Act IV: Whole, With All 13

Numbers supreme
Carved onto black sun spear point
My voice harmonizes strategy
Supreme alphabetically
Ancient script, scribbled from end to tip

I am light and rope
Wrapped around Chapeldamn
Force him to knees and bend
And my handsome, knighted, black Kibaru
Up and pounce
Down onto Chapeldamn's crown
Knowledge, wisdom, and understanding injected
Ignorance bled, actual facts and purpose resurrected
My light slips
Loose
Razor sharp,
Wrapped around neck like a noose
Head severed – Chapeldamn is ash

His death blesses me, my Medusa head story
Now restored
Onyx stone, I am crowned in glory
And the light of my spirit roars – a sound muted

The ground reverberates with hate
Yollj's stomp and gait bars my heart
I sing love
Standing before his mass, calmly
The wave of his abhorrence is hindered
"Come Bwa! Come Cimetiere! Come Phour!"
Their chants and conjures glow swords of cinder
Kibaru inspired
They pounce
Drive cindered swords to their mark
Three chambers of Yollj's heart
Up! Kibaru springs
Black sun spear – fourth chamber pierced
The emerald mass dwindles away in ash

Pump! Pump!

IN 13 PIECES

Act IV: Whole, With All 13

The green flows through me
Heightened courage
I stand determined
Third eye on Fabrique

Twelve of my 13
Reside in me
Motherland's covenant
Restored
Piece by peace
My disciples
At my command, disciplined
I can feel all that has been swallowed by Fabrique
Within – a faint existence
Twelve streams of light flow from me
Disappear into Fabrique, reaching and resurrecting
From inside
All consumed shades, those unmade – only preserved
Reborn, recreated
Her mass is inundated, overflowed with life
She bursts – broken, ashes
As remade shades escape her void and prison, risen

And there glows my halo
Dark matter
It swallows me to become me
And here I be
Whole, with all 13

I swing hand over land
All fallen shades once again stand
Our army, just as me, stands complete
Remaining devil swine and wulvz
Pulled into our gravity
Slain, no retreat
We will be the mouths that tell the tale

I, surrounded by shades
My handsome Kibaru
Captain and allies
This army that has fought for me

IN 13 PIECES

Act IV: Whole, With All 13

Restoring my thirteen
They give praise on bended knee

Gray land brightens with color, and
I turn to the sun in the sky
Smile, one hundred and twenty allies
At my side
My sight arcs to a crying city
I rise
High, stature strong
My beloved Kibaru looks up to me
Thirteen complete
In the distance, my third eye can see
Mama Gran visible
Her conjures twist and tangle
With Queen Malady's tricks – medicine dueling disease
Mother Wisdom and Father Knowledge engage devil swine
      In city streets
While they shout blessings to wake minds from sleep

"Let us join them!" say I
Stature colossal, head in the sky
The blue above, and sun and moon and stars, my crown
I am a tower of conjure
Shades, Captain, allies
And handsome Kibaru are blessed with flight
Forward we move
I am the force of nature – potential now blossomed in full bloom

I walk complete

Zin Kibaru:
She is the flesh of the cosmos – ancient, black and deep

Armies of wulvz and devil swine patrols
Look up in fear of me
I outstretch my hand, but not to greet
But to cleanse the land of their ailment
My blessings assail them
And their oppression and bodies
Blaze into fire at my command

IN 13 PIECES

Act IV: Whole, With All 13

***Her growth frightens even the Heavens*
*But they embrace her — long lost daughter fallen to the Earth***

I carry with me the waves of the sea
I flood the city, drowning Tubal's armies
I bring clouds to the sleeping souls
The refugees of urban slavery
My disguised Mother Wisdom
Masked Father Knowledge
Their blessings have blossomed
Supreme alpha-mathe-magically
Slaves once in dream
They are free with rapid third eye movement
From slaves to warrior-shades, broken chains
Spirit and soul is stirred through them
The ghetto, from their brow, drips away
Spinning, spiral swims beneath the skin — they awake to revolution

Zin Kibaru:
***Ashaba-Sirene — my mythology queen, cosmic royalty*
I grip black sun spear as weapon
Lead allies, captain and shades into rebellion
Phour lights path,
*Insurrection mounted in every direction***

I walk on city streets
Tear buildings down with claps and beats
Ally Bwa rebuilds naturally, earth, leaves and trees
Cimetiere dwindles the concrete
I see Queen Malady, and she sees me
I am a distraction
As Captain Debas and Mama Gran are
United, hand-in-hand against her

But her gown, composed of rot and disease,
Poisons the air as the bell of her gown sweeps
She smothers the breeze
Shaded allies, Debas and Gran
Forced to knees
Queen Malady grins

IN 13 PIECES

<u>Act IV: Whole, With All 13</u>

Staring up and up and up and up
At me

Zin Kibaru:
***I don't breathe—I chant my name, Kibaru*
Ingest knowledge and wisdom
Allied with parents now awakened, if ever they were asleep
They surround and safeguard me from Queen Malady's disease
This doesn't suffice as an apology
Their parental abuse, the emaciated emancipated
That failed our generation, their children
*The reflection of thought staggers my balance in battle***

Mother Wisdom weeps,
"Stand child. Wipe my sins away from your brow.
Sweat away my words that weakened you."

Father Knowledge insists,
"These wulvz and devil swine,
Slave laws and whores dressed in disease
You're stronger than them. You are all their giants
Multiplied by ten
You stood up and fought the God in me
Muted the anger of my words that lashed you
Worked against the expectations expected to trap you
Stand up, my sun."

The story's eye spies Kibaru's narrative
Warrior cloaked in heritage

I am under
Standing
An equipoise between
Wisdom and knowledge
Regain traction, black sun spear in hand
I pounce back to action

Enter Governor Tubal's laws and hexes
His tricked speech that resurrected
City ash to ragged wulvz
A new army of devil swine pulled from the air

IN 13 PIECES

Act IV: Whole, With All 13

Governor Tubal mounted, he rides the terrible
Hexum NightMare
Parents and shades that do not breathe
And allies three
Wade through air wracked with disease
Wulvz and devil swine drip with our blood
But I make them bleed

Through Ashaba-Sirene's eye
The story continues to glide

I see my shaded army of Khem Trails
Slowed by chem trails
I speak an incant and lace my lungs with a veil
I, colossal queen of the cosmos, inhale
Put the cloud of disease at ease
And exhale blessings on release

Kibaru resumes the poetic beats

Free of cloud
Allied shaded warriors take the weight
Of the fight
And I pounce
Black sun spear pierces Governor Tubal's mount
We topple to the ground

His head
Wigged and wild with blanched fire
Eyes bewitched with orange-yellow light
Mouth screaming exhaust, dark gray fog
His speech chokes me with legislation

My Mother Wisdom and Father Knowledge
Provide blessings, lessons
I align with cosmic ordinance and essence
Bypass Tubal's smoky bylaws, dubious regulations

Governor Tubal, this self-proclaimed giant,
Is not so tall – But he's calm, at peace
As his city falls and burns, crumbles to ash

IN 13 PIECES

<u>Act IV: Whole, With All 13</u>

Enslaved populace released
Free to rebel
Down to his last breath
Confident in the face of death
Or simply accepting of it

All he has as defense, an aegis of lies
His illusion of offense shaded into light
Color dampened
I thrust against hexed, domed buckler
Sparks and light express our stubborn vigor

But I think thoughts up to my grand queen: ****I don't fear defeat*
Because they have already killed me
U and I, majestic butterfly — we as family
Our death cannot be again, by any degree
We repossess this physical flesh, with spiritual depth
Inhale cosmic soul
*And spit dark matter and inner-g as weaponized breath***

She says down unto me,
As the narrative favors Ashaba-Sirene

**My dark hero and king, I see it all
Fights and brawls
Blessings and hexes
Focus centered, I enter I**

I see clear inside I — I am made of thirteen
So I take all of me
And release myself to destiny
Kingdoms erect everywhere I touch and speak
Everywhere my eyes gaze, new life rises
I am the body that holds everybody
All the heavenly bodies
I juggle healthy sun and waxen moon
Rearrange the sky
Parents, maiden and water bearer — starry, mythological characters
Shepard shimmering, heavenly critters into the Manjet-boat
Stay instead of sail through 12 provinces — this barque of millions of years
With this, I as Motherland covenant,

IN 13 PIECES

<u>Act IV: Whole, With All 13</u>

Rescript the heavens to prophesize our oppressor's end time
Set to now
Pull cosmic-cleansing moisture from the milky galaxy
Condensed into clouds,
I let Mayet reign down

Tubal's aegis evaporates
My handsome Kibaru, fixed earth sign
Black sun spear he thrusts
I move winds to push Tubal away
Leaving spear point left uncorrupt

Male shades and fathers' knowledge turn Tubal into a story
Flesh as syllables, broken vocabulary
Hexes exposed as illusions, imaginary
He is something we will speak about
In past tense

Feminine umbra and mothers' wisdom
Take the last warden of this prison
Queen Malady
She is stripped down to a memory
Faded into a reminder, talked up as warning
So that we may never be bound to her disease, her infectious hatred
Toxic thinking
Feminine umbra and mothers' wisdom think clean
Lively and lovely, seen – from the 16 shades of the dark flesh,
To the dark matter halo of our bodies
We beam
No longer lives Queen Malady
But all hail to the original Queens

The sun is up to shine bright
And the day
And the battle
Are won

I reduce in size

Zin Kibaru:
***Her steps put beats in my heart*

IN 13 PIECES

Act IV: Whole, With All 13

Her feminine sway, waves of dark matter beauty
*Walking complete to me***

My handsome Kibaru,
The warrior-shade – the dark brightness
My black sun spear-wielding knight

Zin Kibaru:
***We become light*
Black bodies swirling together
*Masculine and feminine forever***

Up to the sky we soar
Our light resting on black sun spear's tip
Double black helix

A crossroads beneath us
In the cardinal directions its four roads extend
As we soar up to the heavens

With all nature we commune
To animal, to the souls of shades,
To all that is natural, we speak, "Balance,
And the end of our tale comes soon."

Above the blue
Where beautiful
Original
Creative dark spirits bloom
Our divine, intertwined spirits
Penetrate the moon
The snowy heavenly body
Glows
Pregnant with its siblings
It births moon two and moon three
Its white fades to black, golden halo wrapped
And there on either side – red and green

Motherland's hant beams
"My covenant restored
My moons and their colors reborn

IN 13 PIECES

Act IV: Whole, With All 13

There, red black and green
Golden halos gleam – the world in balance
Consciousness uplifted – satisfied am I
Rejoice in all its glory
Thirteen complete – here ends our story."

Ink lighted script
Cobalt-blue and lilac
Fade to – and return all to original Black

End this final act

RONIN POETZ

Production dates: 1998 (concept created; first poem written); writing December 1999 to February 2000; 2005 revision.

TO ENLIGHTEN THE G.O.D.Z.

Production dates: 1999 (concept created); writing March 22, 2000 to December 2001.

THE SON DIAL TONE

Production dates: 1999 (concept created); writing 2003, 2004; 2011-2012.

IN 13 PIECES

Production dates: 1999 (concept created); writing 2013-2014

<u>RONIN</u>
so, let the sun rise high
as we all ra unite
for inner and outer collective
allies alike

<u>G.O.D.Z.</u>
free to love
inside our lips
our voices
our kiss
our skin

let us ponder angels
as we find eternal black love
and never lose sight again

<u>DIAL</u>
On the shore
Hand in hand
There is freedom for us
But we pray for more
It can't be just us; there must be justice
Our spirits remain as music
Playing
From existence fades the island
The sun, ready for bed, on the horizon
Our music will evolve

<u>13</u>
There, red black and green
Golden halos gleam – the world in balance
Consciousness uplifted – satisfied am I
Rejoice in all its glory
Thirteen complete – here ends our story
Ink lighted script
Cobalt-blue and lilac
Fade to – and return all to original Black

End this final act

</p>

MORE TITLES @

www.TwinGriffinBooks.com